PRAISE FOR RUTH RENDELL
AND HER
PSYCHOLOGICAL SUSPENSE THRILLERS

"Ruth Rendell's psychological novels are excellent."

Christian Science Monitor

"The books feature no heroic detective and no gathering of suspects for a summing up. Sometimes the precise nature of a crime remains known only to the perpetrator. The lure to the reader is not to see justice done but to understand the way a dangerous person apprehends the world."

Time

"The beauty of Rendell's psychological thrillers is that they always begin on that dramatic razor's edge between the commonplace and the macabre...subtle brilliance."

The Philadelphia Inquirer

"Rendell's tales of murder strike us as comedies of very, *very* bad manners...she gives the psychological thriller something different...a devilish delight in *plotting*."

The Village Voice

"The best mystery writer working today."

San Diego Union

TALKING TO STRANGE MEN

RUTH RENDELL

BALLANTINE BOOKS • NEW YORK

PART ONE

1

HE WAS CROSSING THE BRIDGE OVER THE RIVER FROM the western bank to the east. The bridge, for some forgotten reason to do with the Second World War, was called Rostock. It was a suspension bridge, painted a dull dark red, with walkways on either side. Up river three more bridges, Alexandra and St Stephen's and Randolph, gleamed with lights, both stationary and in motion, and the water beneath them looked black and glittering from the mass of lights reflected in its moving swelling surface. But when Mungo looked southwards all this illumination soon came to an end and there were no more bridges, only warehouses and cranes looming out of the dusk and the beginnings of a dark grey countryside. It was six-thirty in the evening, March, but already growing dark. A horizon of high hills could still be made out against a faintly paler sky. He was on the southern walkway of the bridge, alone, the lamp-lit wall between him and the deep water shoulder-high to deter suicides.

This evening the river gave off a strong smell. It was a smell of oil and fish and something sour and rotting. The dark grey mottled stones, granite perhaps, of which the embankment on the eastern side was composed had a greasy look. The water lapped against the stones, against the fringe of weed that was green by day. Mungo came off the bridge by the pedestrian stairs and began to walk along the embankment towards the Beckgate Steps.

There was no one about. Hardly anyone lived down here in the south-east. Sometimes a fisherman was to be seen sitting on the granite quayside but not at this hour. The squares of light that fell on to the broad shallow flight of steps were from the Beckgate pub, from the saloon where two people could be seen standing at the bar. That single lighted room, bright and snug, those companionable drinkers, served only to point out by contrast the sombre dreariness of the place, the absence of humanity, of any living creature, any green thing.

Years ago, before he was born, a girl had been murdered here. They had found her body on the steps, lying on the broad space or landing between the two flights. Mungo, at the age of eight, had been told of it by some older child, the spot pointed out, a search instituted for bloodstains. He had joined in, awed, aghast, not finding out till later that there would have been no blood, that she had been strangled. And much later a vague shame had afflicted him that he had played games here, made a mockery of that awful thing, playing murderers, none of them wanting to be her, but all vying for the role of manic slavering pursuer.

The real killer of the real girl had never been found. It was sometimes said that in a spot where some dreadful thing had taken place, a kind of unceasing vibration from these events caused a later haunting. As a small child Mungo had been afraid of that, brave when near this place in the company of Ian, say, or Angus, avoiding it fearfully when on his own. But he could have counted on his fingers the number of times he had mounted or descended these steps. They led nowhere he normally wished to go to and they ran down only to the river. His usual route to the flyover drop was by way of Albatross Street, and now, instead of taking Bread Lane, he made a prudent little detour, though there was no one to see him, he was nearly sure of that.

It was an ugly unfrequented district. There were a lot of buildings which he thought of vaguely as docks or wharves, and streets on which stood featureless, obviously non-residential blocks, a whole floor of windows lit and showing cardboard crates inside; strange old brick edifices between them, narrow whitewashed factories sandwiched, rows of ancient cottages, used by day as workshops. Here, on concrete stems like huge attenuated plants with hanging heads, greenish-white lamps shed a radiance that was curiously bright and dull at the same time. It lay on roadway and walls like a coat of phosphorescent liquid, still wet.

Above the main street, about five hundred metres from the end of Rostock Bridge, a flyover passed across, carrying a further line of traffic, this time that which was coming south from Alexandra, and bearing it towards the access road to the main north-south artery. This flyover had been built about twenty years before to relieve the pressure on the old city by-pass. They thought they had traffic in those days. They didn't know what traffic was. So they had built the flyover with one carriageway only and in the mornings the cars passed over it from south to north and in the evenings from north to south. There was no room for a two-way flow. Of course there were always plans to build a new three- or four-lane flyover but nothing had yet come of this.

The cars on the flyover made a sound like thunder above his head. Or perhaps like gunfire, he thought. He turned left into Albatross Street between a dark almost windowless block and a factory with Ahman-Suleiman in chrome capitals over its dirty front entrance. A man in a turban was replacing a pane of frosted glass in a window and a large yellowish ginger cat, having overturned and emptied a dustbin, was tearing apart a plastic bag full of rubbish. These two, the first living creatures apart from the two people in the pub he had seen since leaving the bridge, took absolutely no notice of each other.

He liked cats, he liked the colony of feral cats that lived down here, and he said hallo to this one, holding out his hand. It turned briefly to give him a look of cold dislike and the man in the turban, surprisingly, said:

'It will bite.'

'Thanks for telling me,' he said.

The man in the turban wiped his thumb along the strip of putty. 'It has bitten me twice and my wife once.' Gathering up his tools, he unlocked the right-hand door of the double doors. 'Devil!' he said to the cat and banged the door behind him.

The cat continued to behave as if no one had spoken, as if indeed no one was there. At the resounding slam the door made it did not even flinch. It was wrenching apart a chicken gizzard. Mungo was glad the man in the turban had gone in. There was no one to see him now, no one even to see which way he was going, except the cat which did not count.

Ahead of him the flyover appeared once more, making its downward curve towards the approach road. All along its length it was supported on uprights, steel pillars that were not cylindrical but rather, in section, cruciform, each with four grooves indenting it from top to base. These pillars grew, so to speak, out of the pavements and ends of roads turned into cul-de-sacs and the backyards of warehouses, but here, at this point, out of a triangle of grass that turned to wispy hay in summer but was now a cropped damp green, dotted about with small stunted bushes. The uprights did not exactly shake under the pressure of traffic but an illusion suggested they did. The roar overhead was like warfare in the sky.

Few cars came along down here, especially after the factory workforces had left for home. But he looked to the right and left before he crossed the street just the same. As much as anything he was looking for a possible watcher. The dull bluish light made midnight blue shadows, broad and deep and with invisible depths. He looked up and felt rain on his face, a thin spray of drizzle only. The night was so dark so early because of clouds hanging in a bulging canopy. But down here the lights glittered, few and far between though they were, their slab-shaped bulb cases vague in the mist the rain made.

There was no soul to be seen. And because it was constant, unvarying, the roar of the traffic was itself a kind of silence. He went across and stepped on to the grass which at once spotted the toes of his shoes with water drops. Under the shelter of the steel pillars he took the piece of paper out of his pocket. It was contained in an envelope he had made out of a small plastic bag, the kind you buy on a roll at a supermarket. Also in his pocket was a spool of transparent scotch tape.

He managed to tear off a fifteen-centimetre strip, impatient because the first time it tore diagonally and stuck itself back on to the spool. Carefully, at a level some way beneath his own head height, for he was exceptionally tall, he secured the paper in its plastic envelope to the inside of one of the grooves of an upright, the right-hand one of the two central pillars, choosing the groove that was of all forty-eight the least visible from any external point. He stuck it in there with two strips of scotch tape, pressing the tape against the smooth cold metal with the heel of his hand.

Turning round once more to check if it was possible the 'drop' had been observed, he thought he saw a movement on the far side of the road he had crossed to reach the green, at the opening to a narrow passage between the red-brick side of a deserted, no longer used, boarded-up church, and the stucco wall of a squat unidentifiable building with a flat roof and metal-framed windows. These buildings lay in semi-darkness between two widely spaced lamp stilts. He crossed the empty street, leaving behind and above him the steady roar, feeling the hair on the back of his neck prickle.

Keeping in shadow, he crept past the great sandstone arch in which the double doors were battened up, past a Victorian flying buttress, its bricks chipped where a truck had hit it, flattening himself against the shadowed stone, emerging suddenly into the alley. And seeing what the movement had been, had probably been: a sheet of black plastic, originally a rubbish sack, that someone had nailed up to cover a broken pane in a window on the stucco wall, a corner of which had worked free and flapped in the wind. He was aware then of the wind that had got up, blowing the rain into his face in spurts, sending to trundle and clatter along the street with appalling noise, with a ringing hollow cacophony, an empty cuboid oilcan.

He must have imagined that he had seen the man in a black oilskin jacket who for one split second had emerged from the dark of the passage to eye him and the copse of metal trees. Yet for a moment he considered returning to the sacred tree and removing the message from the long fissure in its trunk. If he did that it would mean he was saying it could never be used again, its life as a drop was over. And what of Basilisk coming for it, at some danger to himself, Basilisk whom he could think of no way of warning? Mungo knew himself to be a visionary, he did see things that weren't there, or that other people said weren't there.

On the other hand, he couldn't ever remember seeing visions in this sort of situation before. But he would leave it. He would trust to common sense and experience, not to visions. One last look down the passage and then back past Ahman-Suleiman. The cat had gone, leaving grains from a bird's crop and bones spread about the pavement. It was growing cold and the wind gusted round corners. Mungo knew he was not followed, he was positive there was no one to follow him, but he pursued a tortuous route homewards just the same, plunging into a network of little winding streets. If there had been anyone he had shaken him off. Mungo was adept at losing a 'tail'. Time was, soon after he became Director General, that Moscow Centre had put a tail on him steadily for weeks, months maybe. But he had always known, had known from the beginning. He turned down a street that would bring him out at the Shot Tower. Before he reached the end of it he could see the thick-set concrete shape of Alexandra, the bridge lying low on the water (for no vessels of any size came up higher than Rostock), the incised lines and parabolas on its sides painted in a red and green which the lights bleached of colour. If someone were following him— and it would have to be a very clever, almost invisible, someone—this person would hardly dare cross the bridge. He would know where Mungo was bound for.

In the middle of the bridge he was very vulnerable, very alone. There were cars but only one other pedestrian, someone he didn't recognise but young and of the male sex. This person was walking towards him on the pavement, on the parapet side. He wasn't wearing black oilskin and he was coming from a wrong direction anyway. Even one of Stern's Stars—a Moscow Centre pun from the Utting German Department—couldn't be in two places at once.

They passed one another with studied indifference. At least, Mungo's was studied. He lifted his eyes from an apparent scrutiny of the river's rippling surface and looked across to the western bank and the tower on the CitWest insurance building. Green digits on its crest told him the time was six-fifty-nine, the temperature six degrees Celsius. And then the cathedral clock, the clock that from here was invisible, hidden on the north face of the apse, began striking the hour. It was always fractionally fast. The mist which the rain had become gave to the grave and majestic cathedral an otherworldly look as if it floated the way a palace might do in a dream, its twin spires and saint-laden east front no longer anchored to the earth but soaring to heaven.

The road came off the bridge under the cathedral wall. Mungo felt the vibration from the clock's notes thrill through his whole body. Up above him gargoyle faces in decaying stone grinned or grimaced or made rictus mouths of agony. They seemed to emerge from the mist, these faces, as if attached to bodies, as if belonging to medieval people who moved to peer at passers-by over a high stone wall. Mungo shook himself.

Stop seeing visions, he said, there's nothing there, there never was anything, and coming out into the square with its trees, thought, I'll run the last bit, I could do with a good run.

ƒƒƒƒƒƒƒƒƒƒƒƒƒƒƒƒƒƒ **2** *ƒƒƒƒƒ*

THE SUDDEN COLD CAUSED JOHN CREEVEY TO PULL up the zip on his jacket. It was not of black plastic, this jacket, but very dark blue leather and a light skin of rain on it made it glisten. It had belonged to his wife and would once have been too small for John, but lately he had lost a lot of weight and his shoulders were in any case narrow. He wore the jacket because she had worn it, because it was one of the few really personal things of hers he still had.

Without thinking, he had come out of the passage into that exposed place, into the light. His mind had been occupied with the green and the messages, wondering why for instance there had been nothing there for a month, but actually to catch sight of someone in the act of depositing one, that had hardly crossed his mind as a possibility. Immediately, of course, he retreated. He did not think he had been seen by the very tall, very thin man on the green, whom he had himself seen only briefly. Back down the passage he concealed himself in a doorway just round the end of it. Here he would stand for a full ten minutes, he thought, until he could be sure the bearer of the message would be gone. After all, he had all the time in the world, he had the whole empty evening before him, and his sole purpose in using this route had been to keep that pillar under observation, to feed his curiosity, to try and find some clue as to what it was all about. Three months it had been going on now, he calculated. Well, it had probably been going on longer than that but it was in December that he had found them out.

The hands of his watch crawled. At exactly seven he left the shelter of the doorway and made his way back along the passage. For one moment he had a nasty feeling that he would be punished for his nosiness if the tall thin man were to be waiting round the corner for him. With a cosh perhaps—or a gun. But he made himself go on, cautious, prepared. And there was no one.

The stream of metal flowed on over the flyover. The pillars that supported it seemed faintly to vibrate. Where the roadway dipped right down and the pair of pillars were shorter than a man, a cat crouched in the scrubby grass. John could see its bright, piercingly green eyes. He was allergic to cats, their fur gave him a sort of asthma, but it was usually all right out of doors, they didn't bother him so much there. He went across the street and on to the grass and up to the pillar where the message must be. It was funny what a thrill of excitement he felt each time he saw one of those little packages up there. He reached up and took down the plastic envelope, not tearing it but unpeeling the scotch tape with care. As he had known it would be, the message was in code. He wrote the words down in a small notebook he had bought for the purpose, going back across the street and standing under a light to do this. Then he folded up the paper again, replaced it in its envelope, and returning to the green, taped it back inside the groove of the pillar once more, reaching up to find the spot where the tall man had put it.

The first time he had come here he was on his way back from Nunhouse where he had been standing opposite the cottage in Fen Street which Jennifer lived in, just watching the place, watching the windows and the front door. That time—it was just before Christmas—there had been no one at home. But he had returned, in spite of himself, a few days afterwards and was rewarded by the sight of her, a dim figure moving behind the clouded glass of the living-room window. Going home by bus, looking out of the bus window in a kind of stunned misery, he had caught sight of something stuck inside one of the flyover uprights. But he had been too wretched then to think much of it, still less follow it up.

Going to Nunhouse was unwise. It was worse than that, humiliating and somehow perverted, voyeur's behaviour, Peeping Tom's. But he couldn't help himself. He went back, and waiting on the opposite side of the road, at last caught a glimpse of her at an upstairs window. There he had stood, watching her hungrily until she revealed more of herself, lifting up the curtain and smiling, then waving. Unable to believe his eyes, trembling with relief, he had been on the point of stepping out from under the hawthorn tree, crossing the road. But then he saw who was coming from the other direction, who it was she was smiling and waving at, who she had been waiting for, and he turned and walked quickly away.

The village of Nunhouse had been half-swallowed by the expanding city. The dilapidated cottage was the best he could do for her, John thought, the best he could offer a woman for all his university degree and his posh voice. The bus ran only every two hours and John had walked all the way back, though it was a long way and he didn't enjoy walking. But she had made him ashamed of the motorbike, the Honda. If she saw him there he didn't want her to see the Honda too. Perhaps it was true, as she had once gently said, that motorbikes were best for people under thirty. What then if you were over thirty but couldn't afford to run a car?

Walking back this way, along what had not so long before been a country lane, then on to a main road which was almost disused since the coming of the motorway, he had somehow missed the turning that would bring him to the eastern suburb where he lived and had come up under the flyover. Immediately he realised where he was when he had started to retrace his steps.

Another two or three minutes walking in that direction, nearer and nearer to the East Bank, and he would have come to the place he had avoided for going on twenty years.

He crossed the street in the direction he had come from and began taking a short cut across the green, making his way between the uprights that supported the overhead road. Why had he looked back? It must have been because he remembered what he had seen from the bus. Misery has to be very deep, has to be at suicide point, before it can quench curiosity. That thought actually came to him when he saw the little package. It had been about six feet up. He unpeeled the tape and took the folded sheet and on it was the first of the coded messages.

He had waited until he got home before studying it. John knew very little about codes and what little he did know he remembered from schoolboy books he had read when he was very young, twenty-five or thirty years ago. But he was so intrigued by this unlikely message found in this unlikely place that he had shown it to Colin Goodman, though without telling Colin the circumstances in which he had discovered it. Not that he had known then that Colin was interested in codes, though he was aware that he did crossword puzzles, and no mean ones at that, *The Times*, no less, and sometimes the *Guardian*. Codes, however, it turned out were something Colin also dabbled in. He looked at the groups of letters and quickly came up with what seemed a sound idea of the kind of code that had been used, though that was a long way from being able to decipher the message. No more appeared for a while after early January, then there were two in mid-February, this one now, all equally indecipherable, equally mysterious.

Twenty-five Geneva Road was a small semidetached house in a street of small semi-detached houses, but what distinguished his was its garden. Even from the end of the street, two hundred yards away, you could make out his garden and see what set it apart from the rest. An early-flowering prunus was in full bloom in the tiny front garden, a pale shimmer in the gathering dark. The lamplight took away its rosy colour but not the gauzy delicacy of its flowers. And as he approached he could see the clusters of blue star-shaped scillas at the foot of the tree, a drift of aconites, iris stylosa, its unfolding lilac petals half hidden by its long fragile leaves, while his neighbours' gardens, though neat and trim, were barren, all in their phase of pre-daffodil sterility.

It was still impossible for him to understand why Jennifer hadn't appreciated the garden. He had said that to Colin in the days when he had had to open his heart to someone and Colin had been there and willing to listen.

'I don't suppose,' Colin had said gently, 'that having a nice garden would keep a woman from leaving her husband.'

John let himself into the house. It was shabby inside and not very clean. When he came in like this after being out for some time he was aware of the smell. It was the smell of somewhere that hasn't been properly cleaned for a long time, where all the curtains need washing and the carpets shampooing and the windows opening. But after he had been indoors a little while the smell faded. There was nothing to remind him particularly of Jennifer. He switched lights on, took the blue leather jacket off and laid it over the arm of a chair. Jennifer had added scarcely anything of her own to the furnishings of the house, nothing at all down here, she had been content to live with his parents' things—because she had never intended to make this her permanent home? He sat down, opened the notebook and looked at the latest message. This was the sixth. He had told Colin they came from a friend of his up North with whom he had been corresponding for years. As schoolboys they had been keen on codes and lately the friend had taken to sending these cipher messages. He didn't know whether Colin believed him. It wasn't a very convincing story.

'The code is probably based on a line from a book,' Colin said. 'Let's take a sentence, any sentence. For instance: now is the time for all good men to come to the aid of the party. The first letter N would represent A, the second letter O would represent B, W would be C, I would be D, S E and so on.'

John had objected, 'It seems very simple.'

'It is very simple. But if you don't know what the sentence is it's virtually indecipherable.'

'Could it be deciphered without knowing the sentence?'

'I expect there are some people who could do it but I couldn't. It's most likely to be the first sentence or the last and a first is more probable than a last.'

'Why is that?'

'Because you could reach the end of the book before you came to the end of the alphabet,' said Colin patiently.

After he had gone John had tried testing out the coded messages against the first sentences of a selection of books. His father had been a great reader of detective stories and there were a lot of these in the house as well as nineteenth century novels which he enjoyed because they offered him a more absolute escape from day-to-day life in this city in the eighties than any modern fiction could do. He tried the Bible and he tried Shakespeare, Dickens's novels and the Brontës. In spite of what Colin said, he tried final sentences. He moved on and tried the first and last lines of Kipling, Trollope, Hardy and Conrad. He tried John Creasey and Agatha Christie. Sometimes he found himself devoting whole evenings, and once practically a whole Sunday, to trying to discover the book that the code maker had used.

It was rather cold in the living room. There was no central heating. He would have had it put in for Jennifer but she had been indifferent when he suggested it. He reached out with his toe and switched on both bars of the electric fire. Then he began setting the letters of the alphabet against the first lines of Rider Haggard's *She* which he had borrowed from the library that afternoon. 'In giving to the world the record of what, considered as an adventure only, is, I suppose one of the most wonderful and mysterious experiences ever undergone by mortal men...'

ͲͲͲͲͲͲͲͲͲͲͲͲͲͲͲͲͲͲͲͲ **3** ͲͲͲͲͲ

IT WAS THE HEART OF THE CITY THAT MUNGO WAS bound for, specifically a tall narrow early Victorian house on the corner where Hill Street met Church Bar. From its upper windows, especially from the windows of his headquarters on the top floor, you could see everything, Fonthill Heights and the hills beyond, a segment of the gardens, a gleam of the river, a buttress of the cathedral, all but the tower whose green digits blinked. You could see the green dome of the city hall, or part of it, and a corner of the polytechnic's shabby black brickwork, and the opening in the old wall they called the Fallowgate.

The front door was approached by a flight of steep steps and it had long sash windows in which the glass seemed particularly clear and glowing. But Mungo let himself into its garden by a gate in the wall. It was a green door rather than a gate and with a curved top which fitted the arched opening in the wall of white bricks that in the summer would be thickly overgrown with a round-leaved climbing weed. On the left hand side of the door was a brass plate on which was engraved: *Dr Fergus J. Cameron MB, FRCP* and under it, *Dr Lucy Cameron MB, MRCP.*

Mungo closed the gate behind him and entered the house by a stained-glass door in the side wall, a door which was kept locked only at night. Inside it was quite silent. Then, from high up in the house, he heard music playing very softly, the peculiarly civilised, lilting Baroque music Angus liked even when he was working. Mungo began to climb the stairs. There were fifty-two to the top of the house but it was seldom that anyone but he ever went beyond the second floor. The door to Angus's room was open and Angus could be seen sitting at the table at work on his computer. He had had the computer only a few days and was teaching himself to use it. Boccherini tinkled out of the record player.

Mungo went up behind him and read on the VDT screen: *Well done, Angus, that wasn't so bad, was it?*

'Isn't it a bit uncanny the way it talks back at you?' Mungo said.

'Christ, you made me jump.'

'Sorry. But isn't it?'

'It's only while I'm doing the lessons. Shall I get it to say something to you?'

'No, thanks,' Mungo said, as Angus called up on to it a column of figures. 'Could it do codes?'

Angus took his hands from the keyboard and started to laugh.

'What are you laughing at?' Mungo said, though he knew.

'Was I ever as keen as you?'

'I don't know. I think you were.'

'You've been up to something now, haven't you? Some cloak-and-dagger stuff. You've got that furtive look.'

Mungo didn't say anything.

'Mum's taking Dr Marsh's surgery on account of he's got flu and Dad's been called out to a private patient.'

17

'I'm starving.'

'Yes, well, Mum's bringing takeaway in with her. She won't be long. Sometimes I think what I like most about the holidays is being able to eat junk food.'

'It's because they're doctors,' said Mungo. 'Doctors always approve of junk food. It's the amateurs want you to be eating brown rice. Can I have one of your truffles?'

Angus always kept a bag of chocolate truffles in his desk drawer. They were rum-flavoured, rolled in chocolate vermicelli.

'You can have one. They're expensive.'

'Oh God, I could eat fifty of these.'

'Why don't you buy yourself Mars bars?'

'I've got gourmet tastes in chocolate.'

Angus made everything on the screen vanish but for a small dancing green arrow. He switched the computer off at the plug. Red-haired, ruddy-faced, the shortest of them though not short, he looked up at Mungo's great height.

'How old are you now, Bean?'

'Fourteen. I'll be fifteen in July. You're my brother, you ought to know how old I am.'

'I scarcely know how old I am myself.'

'You're seventeen,' said Mungo. 'You had that thing for your seventeenth birthday. Right? Why did you ask how old I am, anyway?'

Angus didn't answer him directly. 'You must be about six feet four.'

'Six feet three but I don't think I've grown since Christmas. I worry about it sometimes, Ang. I think, suppose I've got acromegaly.'

'What the hell is acromegaly.'

'It's when your pituitary goes wrong and you grow and grow and they have to take it away and it makes you sterile.'

'For Christ's sake, you've got both parents doctors and you think they wouldn't know about a thing like that? The whole family are giants. Ian's taller than you. Dad's taller than you.'

'Yes, but Ian's twenty and God knows how old Dad is, about fifty.'

'I didn't ask you how old you were because I thought you were too tall. I asked because I was wondering how you felt about Spookside.'

'We don't call it that any more,' Mungo said rather loftily. 'What do you mean, how do I feel?'

Angus had an air of choosing his words carefully. 'I mean are you still keen?'

'Sure I am. Of course. Why?'

'Well . . . Nothing. You're only fourteen. OK, forget it. There's Mum. I heard the car.'

Mungo went up to his own room, a crow's nest at the top of the house, the ceiling sloping, following the lines of the roof. It was so big because a hundred years before it was shared by the four maids who kept the house clean. The two windows were round, set under eyelid dormers, and from them you could see over the tops of leafless trees across old slate roofs and new tiled roofs to that wonderful view.

Unease troubled Mungo, slightly marring what had been a happy and busy day. It's because of what Ang said, he thought. What did he mean? Why had he said that? After all, it was he who began it, he and Guy Parker, he who handed it on, a finished and beautiful thing, to his heirs. Mungo liked that phrase and he repeated it to himself. A finished and beautiful thing to his heirs. He might become a writer. There was too much of this medicine thing in their family. Could it only be that Angus regretted giving up the directorship himself?

Mungo dropped his jacket absentmindedly onto the floor. He picked up a book, turned the pages, considering. Then he pulled the blinds down over the round windows that were a bit like ship's portholes. His stomach reminded him that his mother was home. There reached him, as he started down the third flight, the scent of Indonesian takeaway, his first favourite.

TROWBRIDGE'S GARDEN CENTRE WAS ON THE OLD BY-pass. John Creevey first went to work there as a school leaver aged seventeen. In those days he had been the boy who swept up, graduating to become the boy who put the compost in the seed trays, the 'nurseryman', the assistant manager. He was nurseryman when Cherry died and by the time Jennifer came in to buy something suitable for window boxes, he was the boss. He had recommended fuchsias to Jennifer, plus a couple of ivy-leaved geraniums, trailing lobelia, white alyssum, the usual stuff, and a canary creeper which was a bit more out of the ordinary.

'Why is it called that?'

'Canary creeper?' he had said. 'You wait and see. Its flowers look like yellow birds.'

Those had been the first words they had ever said to each other, apart from the requisite good morning and hallo and can I help you? And they had been here in the main greenhouse where he was now checking on the fuchsia cuttings, all in their individual fibre pots. Alice Hoffman, Jennifer had had, and Thalia. And later she had invited him to the flat to see how the plants were doing.

'My mother died a year ago,' she had said, 'and I came in for her house, so I sold it and bought this flat. I moved in two weeks ago and there were these empty window boxes.'

'My mother died a year ago too—well, a year and two months.'

20

She smiled at him, rather sadly. She was a quiet-looking girl. Modest was the word that came into his mind. He could remember exactly what she had been wearing on that first occasion: a pleated skirt in a check pattern, two shades of brown, a camel-coloured sweater over a white shirt, brown shoes, very well-polished, with low heels, but not flat shoes. Not a scrap of make-up, she never wore make-up. Her hair was a bright sparkling yellow-brown that hung to her shoulders. No, not 'hung', flew out and curled in its abundance like a chrysanthemum. He had never seen a face so soft as hers and so expressive. The skin was soft and the lips, the rather full cheeks, the thick furry eyebrows and the liquid eyes. Of course it was Cherry she looked like, though he hadn't realized that then, not aware at that time that one woman can resemble another though one is ugly and the other beautiful.

In the fuchsia house John had a look at the thermometer. Fifteen degrees—which he was getting used to saying instead of sixty—not bad for the end of March with the heat only on low. Easter was coming. Tomorrow would be Good Friday. John didn't enjoy holidays these days. Marriage had taught him loneliness. But perhaps Colin would come over and there was always his aunt to whose house on the other side of the city he had a standing invitation. Don't go over to Jennifer's, don't hang about outside Jennifer's, he found himself muttering as he returned to the shop. Sharon at the check-out eyed him.

'Just reminding myself to take a look at the fish before we close up, Sharon.'

He said good night to her and to Les and told Gavin to lock up after him. Gavin was the new assistant manager, only twenty-three, a graduate of the local horticultural college. Latin names tripped off his tongue. He was the only person John had ever known who didn't pronounce aubrietia 'orbreeshia'. The mynah bird, which he seemed fond of, he had given the name of Grackle, from its designation of *Gracula religiosa*, he explained.

'Ciao, chief,' said Gavin in the multi-national lingo he used when he wasn't talking Latin.

John called in at the library on his way home to return *She* and *Wisdom's Daughter*. They hadn't got *King Solomon's Mines* in. But John Le Carré didn't let him down and both *Smiley's People* and *The Honourable Schoolboy* were on the shelf. John liked espionage fiction but he hadn't read much of it. He asked the girl what else she could recommend.

'Do you like it all made up or factual? I mean something like *The Riddle of the Sands* would be founded on fact while Ian Fleming wouldn't be.'

'I like a bit of realism,' said John and immediately wondered why he had said that because surely it was escape he was seeking.

'This one's non-fiction. *My Silent War* by Kim Philby. I expect you remember about him going over to Russia.'

It was ancient history to her, something the grown-ups talked about when she was a child. John took the book and said he would try it.

She was smiling at him in a friendly way. He thought, I could ask her to come out with me. I know how it's done. I didn't once, I hadn't a clue, but I do now. You chat for a while and find out what she likes doing, walking, for instance, or seeing films, or going to fairs or botanical gardens (that would be a piece of luck) and you say, We might go for a walk sometime or we might take in that film together at the Astoria and if she looks keen you just say, How about tomorrow evening then? I'll call for you, shall I?

Her expression was a little puzzled because he was staring at her. Quickly he looked away, turned back to the shelves. He didn't want to go out with her, it would be boring and embarrassing. And he would end up telling her about Jennifer. My wife's former fiancé turned up out of the blue and she went off with him. Poor you, how awful for you. But she would be embarrassed too, not knowing what to say. He sometimes thought he would never be alone with another woman for as long as he lived. The books were heavy but he made a detour to cats' green just the same. A thin kitten, white with tabby patches, was sitting in the grass at the foot of the central pillar. It retreated a little, mewing, when John came up. He didn't dare touch it in case it started him off coughing and sneezing. The message had gone from inside the upright but a strip of scotch tape remained, one end still stuck to the metal.

A blue sky showed between the flocks of cloud and from the end of the alley next to the disused church, he saw the glint of water. He had walked down here almost without knowing it. A young woman was pushing a child in a pram in the direction of Albatross Street but otherwise there was no one. She was going John's way and it would have been natural for him to follow her but then he thought, it might scare her to have a man walking behind her. It's a bit rough down here and not another soul about. He turned in the opposite direction, heading straight for the Embankment and river walk, and found himself suddenly, almost before he knew it, at the head of the Beckgate Steps where Cherry's body had been found.

The place had changed unrecognisably, only the broad flight of ancient steps remaining as they had always been. The red brick chapel had gone and the ruined maltings been rebuilt, the huddle of Victorian cottages transformed into a wholesale clothes place and the pub refurbished and renamed. But the steps were the same, and the remoteness and the quiet, for the wholesaler's was closed for the evening and the pub not yet open. At the foot of the steps, beyond the stone-flagged embankment, the river glittered with innumerable wavelets. A segment of it only could be seen with the further bank beyond, trees on that side and blocks of expensive flats with protuberant balconies on every floor. The sun was shining but no sunlight penetrated to the double flight of shallow dark steps. They were made of some kind of black and grey mottled stone, those steps, and with an iron railing on each side, polished to silver by the hands of those who mounted and descended. He felt a nervous clutching sensation in the region of his heart. It was sixteen years since he had been here. All that time he had lived no more than a mile away but he had never returned to this spot.

John found that he was squatting down, staring at the blackish stones as if he expected still to find there some signs of Cherry's murder. There had been no signs even then. And in two of the intervening winters, before they built the weir, the river rose and water came up the Beckgate Steps as far as the half-way mark. He jumped up and ran down the steps to the river walk, swinging his bag full of books.

A letter for him was a rarity. He picked it up from the doormat, noticing that the name and address on the envelope were typewritten. At first he thought it was an estimate from the builder he had asked to renew the guttering on the rear of the house and he did not open it until he had made himself a cup of tea and opened a can of ravioli for his supper. The letter was typewritten too. It started, 'Dear John'. He knew what a 'Dear John' letter was but there hadn't been one waiting for him when she left. Face to face she had told him, she had been honest and brave. She had talked to him and told him everything. He began to read: 'Dear John...' and realised that this was the first letter she had ever written to him. They had been married for two years but she had never had occasion to write to him. That came only—ironically—when they were apart and their marriage apparently over. It hurt him that she had typed it, though he remembered her handwriting was nearly as indecipherable as the codes.

Dear John,
I don't know if you will be surprised to get a letter from me. We saw you outside this house back in February and we did discuss inviting you in but by the

time I came to the front door you had gone.

John, I think we ought to meet and have a talk. I expect you hate me and think I treated you badly. You would feel more kindly towards me perhaps if you knew how terribly guilty I have felt all these months. It's no use saying that I did warn you, I did say that if Peter ever came back and wanted me I would go to him. Obviously this isn't the sort of thing one should say when one is married. And I'll admit now that it was a stupid and unkind thing to say. I also seem to remember saying that when you get married in a Registrar's Office as we did you don't actually have to make any vows. I'd like to apologize here and now if I made you unhappy saying those things.

So can we meet? Emotions surely won't run so high as they did when we talked last time. I am no longer on the crest of a wave and I expect—I'm afraid, oddly enough—you no longer feel about me the way you once did. There are many kinds of love and I would like to think we can still be fond of one another, that we can pick up the pieces and each of us start again.

I'd rather you didn't phone me. I'll tell you what I'd like us to do. Not for you to come here or me to go to you but for us to meet in Hartlands Gardens, have tea there perhaps and maybe go for a walk. You took me there in April once and I remember you said it was a good time when the narcissi are out.

So if you agree, what about next Saturday, ie April 2nd? Peter will be out that afternoon. I will be at Hartlands Gardens in the tea place, the cafeteria, at three. Will that be all right?

I don't know how to sign this really.

Yours affectionately,

Jennifer

He read it several times, his heart behaving oddly at first, beating hard and irregularly, it seemed, then as he took deep breaths, he gradually accustomed himself to what was in front of him, a letter from Jennifer, a letter from his wife. She had been going to invite him in, she wanted to see him. If he hadn't been such a fool and rushed away he would have talked to her, sat with her ... Of course Peter Moran would have been there too. His eye once more followed the lines of typing down the page.

She wanted to see him alone. She made a point of saying she wanted to see him when Peter Moran was out. Did that mean she wanted to meet him without Peter knowing? It must. Surely she was saying that after what had happened they could never feel quite the same about each other, the starry-eyedness would be gone, but there were many kinds of love, the quiet mature sort which might be as good as passion. He stood by the window, looking out into the street he had looked on to since he was a small child. It was hard for him to imagine any other outlook from a window where one lived, anything but the pairs of houses opposite, the monkey puzzle pine in front of the fourth house on the left that he had seen planted when he was eight and which was now a large, ugly, ridiculous but somehow endearing tree. The pink prunus was shedding its petals and they lay like rosy snow, half-covering the scillas. She remembered about the narcissi in Hartlands Gardens and remembered he had first taken her there in April. She must mean this projected meeting as a reunion ... Stop thinking about it, he said fiercely and aloud. On the seat of the armchair in the bay he had dropped the string bag full of books as, letter in hand, he had walked first of all into this room. The two Le Carrés, the Philby book, a novel by Disraeli he didn't think he would get round to reading, Rider Haggard's *Allan's Wife* as a substitute for the *King Solomon's Mines* that wasn't in.

I'll try the first lines and the last lines, he said to himself. I'll do that. I won't think about Jennifer, I won't let myself dare to hope ...

Mungo sat up in his room under the eaves looking at a document headed FTELO—For the Eyes of Leviathan Only. Between the end of last year's spring term and the beginning of this one they had secured advance information on three planning applications and four instances of quite amazing police leaks, recovered fifteen 'borrowed' books, abstracted any number of architects' plans, rearranged restaurant bookings, secured invitations to a number of official functions, and more or less reorganized to suit their own purposes the plans for the city's annual festival of arts. Not to mention all kinds of rather more frivolous exercises. Since then, though, during the past term, things had proceeded less satisfactorily. Undisputed success was a thing of the past.

He was eating dry-roasted peanuts, having an idea they were better for him than chocolate. Nothing gave him spots or did anything to change his extreme gauntness but he sometimes wondered if it was all this eating between meals that helped him grow so tall. He had some yogurt-coated hazelnuts as well but these he was saving until after he came back.

From his window he could make out the roof of his father's surgery building. His mother was an anaesthesiologist at Hartland Mount Hospital, not a GP, though she sometimes helped out when one of the partners was sick or on holiday. There were three doctors in the practice besides Fergus Cameron. They worked from a listed building, one of the oldest in the city, that Mungo's father had bought nearly twenty years before and now wanted to extend. He wanted to build a new waiting room and consulting rooms on to the back. A group from the city planning committee had already been to view the premises. If they agreed to building, listed building consent would almost certainly be given. Their decision depended almost exclusively on the advice given them by the city planning officer, a man called Blake, who was in some way related to Ivan Stern.

'They don't know the meaning of speed,' Fergus Cameron had said. The family were all at lunch, Fergus and Lucy, Angus, Mungo, and Ian just home from medical school for the Easter break. 'Those representatives of the planning committee came to see the place two days after the monthly meeting. Which means we have twenty-four days to wait for a decision. And in the meantime I could lose that other property.'

The other property was a much more modern building at the western end of Ruxeter Road. Fergus could get it comparatively cheaply if he bought it now but would very likely lose it if he waited three weeks. And suppose the planning committee's decision went against him?

'There's absolutely nothing to be done, darling,' said Lucy, eating salad with a fork and reading the *Lancet*. She was a large placid woman of perfectly even temper who had sat—and passed—her examination for membership of the Royal College of Physicians when nine months pregnant, answered the final question, laid down her pen and gone into labour. Ian was born five hours later. She turned the page. 'It's all in the lap of the gods.'

Mungo wasn't too sure of this. It might be in his lap. That was why he had gone straight upstairs really, apart from taking comfort from the 'most secret' document. March 25th today was. Only six more days' use to be got out of the current code, after which he'd have to start a new one. Might use Stern's *Childers* which would be rather amusing.

But now for his father's planning application. The difficulty wouldn't so much be in acquiring the advance information as in convincing his father that the advance information he had was accurate. Deal with that when the time comes, thought Mungo. He'd use the drop under the flyover. Instructions alone wouldn't be sufficient, there would have to be a meeting. In the safe house possibly and it shouldn't be postponed. Monday at the latest. He looked about him but couldn't see the book anywhere.

That Ian, he thought. The minute he's home he's on the nick. Nothing's sacred. The first thing he heard when he opened the door was a girl laughing. Ian's girlfriend Gail that would be. Mungo went downstairs and saw them all in Angus's room, Angus showing off the computer, Gail pressing one of the keys and making a picture of an explosion come up with *ka-boom* printed in the middle of it.

'You've got my Albeury,' Mungo said.

Ian grinned at him. 'Have a heart. I've nothing to read.'

'You can't have that. Not till next Thursday anyway. You can have the latest Yugall if you like.'

'That's very handsome of you, Bean.'

Mungo wondered why Angus was looking at him like that, half-smiling and yet as if he were somehow sorry for him. He didn't like it much and it made him feel a certain regret he was too old to go and trip his brother up and stick out his tongue at him.

bich, though no harm had yet been done.
sy result in disaster.
in one of the north-eastern suburbs, three

6

FERGUS CAMERON WAS AS NERVOUS AS HIS WIFE
was placid. He worried about everything. He worried
about his wife and his sons and his home and about
money, though as he very well knew none of these
people or these matters afforded genuine cause for
anxiety. Not of the stuff of which general practitioners
are ideally made, he was nevertheless enormously popular with his patients. There was nothing godlike
about him. When they told him they were worried or
depressed he said he understood and he commiserated
with them. They could tell he was sincere. When they
came to him worried they might have cancer or mus-
cular dystrophy or heart disease he said that he worried about those things too, even though he had no
more cause than they. Because he did not know he
had anything to feel superior about, he chatted to
them as might their next-door neighbours and as often
as not told them of his own worries. As a physician he
was no better and no worse than the other doctors in
the practice and less well-qualified than his own wife,
but he was much better liked than any of them.

It was on account of his pleasing personality and reputation for being easy to get on with that the City Board
of General Practitioners had appointed him their repre-
sentative on a particularly awkward mission. This was to
call on an 82-year-old woman who still had a medical
practice and still saw patients and explain to her in the
gentlest and most tactful way that it was time she retired. Old Dr Palmer had been making mistakes in pre-

scriptions which, though no harm had yet been done, might one day result in disaster.

She lived in one of the north-eastern suburbs, three or four miles away. Fergus had been worrying about this visit and what he would say to her not just for the whole of Saturday but Thursday and Friday as well. In the event—as was so often the case in the event—things turned out perfectly satisfactorily and with the minimum of pain. Almost the first thing Dr Palmer said was that she was glad to have an opportunity to talk to him alone because she was thinking of retiring and would like to hear his views. Driving home again, one anxiety removed, instead of relaxing, Fergus perforce allowed the worry which the Dr Palmer business had temporarily displaced, to return.

What was he going to do about the surgery extension?

If the city council's planning committee allowed the extension there was no problem but there was no way he could know for the next three weeks whether permission would be granted. In the meantime a building that had been specifically constructed as a private clinic had come on to the market. In a moment or two he would pass it, it was up here on Ruxeter Road. The asking price was seventy thousand pounds, rather less than the extensions were going to cost. He would have to take out a mortgage anyway, there was no question of anything else. His boys were at present costing him and Lucy the maximum with Ian at university and Angus and Mungo both at their public school. And he would prefer to keep the beautiful old building in which the practice was currently housed. The top floor, for instance, would one day make an excellent flat if any of the boys should want it.

While he waited for planning permission it was most likely that the clinic building would be sold to someone else. The estate agent had told him as much. He was passing it now and, stopping at a red light, turned to look at it. That stark sixties architecture, that box construction and plate glass windows weren't to his taste but how much did his taste matter? It might so easily happen that planning permission was refused and this building simultaneously lost to him.

The lights changed. It was as Fergus was moving off that he caught sight of his son Mungo walking along the opposite pavement in the direction of a row of derelict houses, condemned to demolition and boarded up, and a public house called The Gander. Since Mungo could scarcely have any business at the condemned houses he must be going to the pub. Because of his great height he could easily pass for four years older than he was. Fergus very much disliked the thought of his youngest going into pubs at the age of fourteen but he didn't know what he could do about it. He drove on with a fresh worry in reserve.

On one side of the wide road were row upon row of little poky shops, opposite them a bingo hall and the old Fontaine Cinema. All those houses awaiting demolition didn't improve matters. But when they were demolished and new blocks erected, what then? He could offer for that clinic building and proceed with negotiations while he was waiting to hear if planning permission had been granted. And then, if he got his permission, withdraw from the purchase. It would be dishonourable and underhand and Fergus knew he couldn't do it.

But suppose he lost both? What would happen then was that he would have to look around for other premises and whatever they were, they would cost him a hundred thousand pounds, not seventy. He put the car away in the garage at the bottom of the garden, a converted coachhouse. The Cameron garden was a pleasing wilderness of old pear trees and lilac bushes growing out of shaggy grass. Or Lucy said it was pleasing and the boys used to play in it when they were young. Fergus would have liked a pretty garden with flowerbeds and rose bushes like his grandmother had had in Oban, but he wouldn't have liked to do the gardening, as Lucy pointed out.

She was lying in an armchair with her feet up. Ian and Gail sat on the sofa, holding hands and yelling with laughter at *Some Like It Hot* on television.

'How did it go, darling?' said Lucy in her sleepy, smiling way.

'OK. Fine. Much better than I thought.'

'Things are always much better than you think.'

Fergus smiled rather sadly. 'If life has taught me anything it's that while most of the things you've worried about have never happened, it's a different story with the things you haven't worried about. They are the ones that happen.'

If Gail hadn't been there he would have said something about Mungo. He went downstairs to get himself a drink. Fergus usually made himself a cup of cocoa in the evenings and in the mornings too sometimes. He made it with whole, full-cream milk and real cocoa—not drinking chocolate—and white granulated sugar, first mixing cocoa, sugar and a little of the milk to a paste in the mug, then pouring on the milk at the zenith of its boiling. His wife and children laughed at this and always refused offers of his cocoa which Fergus had never understood, why it should be funny, why there was apparently something intrinsically funny in the very idea of cocoa when in fact it was the most delicious drink he had ever tasted.

He found his son Angus in the kitchen, with a slice of cold pizza in one hand and a blue cardboard box, something to do with the computer, in the other. Since he and Lucy had given Angus that computer for his birthday he had been obsessed by it.

'I was looking for somewhere to keep the floppy disks.'

'Why can't you keep them in your room?' said Fergus, opening a new tin of cocoa.

'When I've saved a file to archives I don't want the floppy discs in the same area as the hard discs, do I? I mean, suppose there was a fire in my room?'

Fergus didn't know what he was talking about. For form's sake, he offered cocoa. Angus shook his head abstractedly, climbed up on to a stool and put the box on the top shelf of a cupboard, up among the wine-making equipment no one had used for ten years.

'Angus, do you think Mungo goes to pubs?'

'Mungo? What would he do that for? He wouldn't even have a glass of wine at my party.'

'I thought I saw him going into a pub.'

'Unless maybe he's a secret drinker.' Fergus's children were never much comfort to him. They seldom allayed his fears. 'Where was this pub then?'

'Ruxeter Road, near where all those houses are going to be pulled down. I shouldn't talk to you about him. It's not fair on you or him. I daresay he was just walking home, only it was a funny way for him to be going.'

'I wouldn't worry if I were you, Dad,' said Angus. This was a sort of thing people always said to Fergus. He knew they wouldn't worry, that wasn't the problem.

He took his mug of cocoa back upstairs. Angus stood eating his pizza. It was quite clear to him where Mungo had been going, to the safe house which was one of the middle ones in the condemned row between The Gander and Collingbourne Road. He would have been meeting someone there or even hiding someone there from Stern, would most probably be there now.

And Angus realised that he too worried about Mungo, not like his father did, not jumping to crazy conclusions about Mungo's slinking off for illicit pints or gin and tonics, but about Mungo's being so—well, fixated on Spookside. Did he ever think of anything else? Didn't his school work suffer? He was probably a bit young to be thinking about girls, Angus could understand that, but did he have ordinary friends? Did he have any other interests at all? This mantle that had fallen upon Mungo's shoulders was his own. And 'fallen' was the wrong word anyway, for he had taken it off himself and placed it over Mungo. He had taught Mungo everything he knew, had inculcated in Mungo a passion for espionage which he himself no longer shared. At fifteen he had grown out of Spookside. Surely the same would happen to Mungo, surely there would soon be signs of weariness...

ANGUS COULD REMEMBER IT ALL VERY WELL. SOME-times, now he had the computer, he thought of putting it on that and keeping a record, though he didn't know for what purpose. For his own children, if he ever had any? For some sort of future social study?

The beginning of it all. Its inception. 'Out of the strong came forth sweetness'—Angus had read that under the picture on the Lyle's Golden Syrup tin but apparently it came from the Bible. He thought it expressed what had happened with him and Guy Parker and Spookside, as someone had christened it. As Guy had christened it. And now it was a world away, down there in his childhood when he had had other priorities and other needs.

He had been thirteen and Guy Parker had been thirteen too, a month or two older. They had known each other all their lives, been friends since, according to their mothers, those mothers met at the baby clinic. And Mrs Parker used to mind him and Ian while his own mother was working at the hospital. Guy and he went to prep school together, Hintall's, where Ian had been and Mungo was then in second form.

Candidates usually sit the Public Schools Entrance in June. The examination is the same for all schools within the Headmasters' Conference but papers are marked and results judged at the particular school of the candidate's, or more probably his parents', choice. There was no question but that Angus would go on to Rossingham. His father had gone there and Ian was there. And Guy Parker was also going to Rossingham, it was an understood thing that they would be attending the same public school, and no one, as far as

Angus knew, had ever disputed this. Later, in all fairness though, he couldn't have categorically stated that Guy had actually told him so.

The results came and Angus was in, which was no great surprise to anyone. It was holiday time and the Camerons were all off to their annual fortnight in Corfu, so he had no opportunity of seeing Guy Parker until after they got back. Besides, he hadn't felt any pressing need to see Guy. He knew they would both be going to Rossingham in a month's time and they'd be bound to meet a couple of times before that.

He went round to the Parkers' because Mrs Parker phoned up and asked him and Mungo to lunch on one of the days both his parents were working at the same time. Mungo was only a little kid of ten then and it was always a bit of a problem getting him looked after in the holidays. When he got there Angus realised he had never actually asked Guy if he had passed that exam, though he was bound to have done. It was a well-known fact that you had to be quite dim not to pass and Guy was very bright. They were alone together in the place the Parkers called the playroom, having exiled poor old Bean to the kitchen with Mrs Parker and Guy's little sister.

'Have you got all your gear yet?' Angus asked. 'I reckon those hats are the end, the pits. We had to go to London to get mine. Tuckers don't stock them any more.'

Had Guy looked embarrassed or ashamed? If he had, Angus hadn't noticed, but perhaps he hadn't. For a moment or two he didn't say anything, then:

'I don't have to have a hat.'

'Yes, you do. It's on the list.'

'They don't wear hats at Utting.'

Angus didn't have to ask him to elucidate. He knew at once. Guy had the grace to look abashed. They were silent. It was a long awkward unpleasant silence. And in those minutes, while Guy took from his bookshelves the paperback novel of espionage he was going to lend Angus, while they descended the stairs together in response to Mrs Parker's shout of 'Lunch!', Angus felt the first real pain of his life. Or he thought of it that way, perhaps it wasn't. But no one had ever done anything like that to him before, no one had ever deceived him.

Going to schools like Hintall's was supposed to start you off on the stiff upper lip thing. He could remember his Scottish grandfather calling it that. He hadn't had much faith in it himself but perhaps it was true. At any rate he was able to conceal his feelings and eat Mrs Parker's lunch—he even remembered what it was, a very good lunch too, steak and kidney pie, scalloped potatoes, fresh garden peas, black-currant shortcake and cream—and to keep his cool. After lunch Guy explained. He didn't want to go to Rossingham. It was conventional, reactionary and old-fashioned.

'I mean, look at that hat thing.'

'What hat thing?'

'Well, having to wear a bloody straw boater. Who needs it?'

Utting was progressive. They took girls in at all levels. They did a Russian course. They had an amazing new technology department. You could play polo if you wanted or learn to fly a helicopter.

'Are you kidding?' said Angus.

'Well, they've definitely got a helicopter. And an ice rink. And it's all first names and everyone gets to have a bedroom of their own.'

Angus took his pain home with him. He thought it was only being deceived that he minded but he found he also minded the loss of Guy. He would not see Guy again until half-term and probably not then, for the half-term holidays of Rossingham and Utting would not necessarily coincide. Three months, which was the length of a term, is a very long time when you are thirteen years old. Guy ought to have told him, at least when they sat the exam if not before, that he planned on going to a different school. But this dislike of being deceived was as nothing compared to their separation.

People said of their family that Ian and Mungo were like their father, tall and skinny and fidgety, while he was like their mother, not only in physical appearance but in temperament too. He was supposed to be placid. Angus did not think anyone was ever very much like anyone else. He wasn't placid but he was good at not showing his feelings. No one suspected at home that he was unhappy, that he carried Guy's betrayal around with him as the boy in the fable carried the fox that gnawed at his insides.

His dismay turned to anger. He had borrowed the Yugall paperback from Guy—it was *Mole Run*—but when he had finished it, instead of taking it round to the Parkers' house he got Mungo to put it through the letterbox when he was passing on his way to his fencing class. A couple of days after that the Rossingham autumn term started.

Angus missed Guy very much. New school was strange anyway, and although the old fagging system had been abolished and things were quite civilised compared to in his father's day, although bullying had virtually gone, there was still bewilderment to contend with and mystifying rules. He told himself he hated Guy and was glad to see the back of him. Soon he made a couple of friends, one of them being Bruce Reynolds who he supposed he could say was now his closest friend. Half-term passed without occasion to go near the Parkers but when the Christmas holidays came, a few days after Rossingham broke up, Guy phoned.

His mother took the call. He heard her speak Guy's name and then he went and hid in the top floor lavatory, not answering when she called him. He knew she would tell Guy he would call him back, which in fact she had done. Angus thought he and his brothers were lucky to have a mother who never fussed, who wouldn't dream of asking such searching questions as where had he got to and what was he up to and why hadn't he answered when she called him. On the other hand he knew better than to ask her to tell lies for him over the phone or anywhere else. She would never have stood for that.

He didn't call Guy back. The Parkers always went away for Christmas, to Mrs Parker's sister in Devon or Mr Parker's sister in France, and by the time they got back the new term would have started. By Christmas Eve he was rather regretting he hadn't called Guy back. He was missing him again. Among his Christmas presents was the new Yugall novel. Guy and he were crazy about espionage fiction and they loved all the great masters of the genre but their current favourite was Yves Yugall, whom for a while they preferred even over Len Deighton, though it was a close-run thing.

Yves Yugall had written about twenty books by that time and he and Guy had read them all, *Mole Run* being the latest. The latest in paperback, that is, for they couldn't afford to buy hardcovers. Of course the books always came out in hardcover about a year before the paperback appeared but they just had to wait unless they could get them out of the library. The new one, *Cat Walk*—Yugall always had the name of an animal in his titles—was from his mother and father along with the track suit he had asked for and the really good ballpoint pen they thought he ought to have. It was a brand new hardcover, seven pounds ninety-five and with an artist's impression of the Brandenburger Tor on the jacket.

Angus read it at a sitting, or a lying really. He read it in bed on Christmas night, staying awake till three to do so. When he had finished it he thought, I've read it and he hasn't. Too bad. If we were still friends I'd have passed it on to him the moment I finished it. Probably what he would have done was to send Guy a coded message—a note by hand of Mungo or some little pal of his—letting him know he had the book and to come and get it. Guy would have had to break the code and decipher the message. But they were good at that. It had really started because their parents all made a fuss about the amount they used the phone and what it cost.

Cat Walk went back to school with Angus. Bruce wasn't interested, he didn't want to read it. Angus started thinking a lot about Guy and one night he dreamed about him. He was at Utting, visiting Guy, and it was an amazing place with bedrooms like in an hotel with *en suite* bathrooms and an ice rink and saunas and one helicopter to every ten boys, flying lessons being a weekly event. Guy had his own built-in cupboards in his room and a chest of drawers and two bedside cabinets instead of the drawer under his bunk and narrow hanging cupboard which was the lot of boarders at Rossingham. When Angus woke up he thought that if the dream had gone on he would have secretly put *Cat Walk* into the top drawer of the chest in Guy's room for Guy to find when next he opened it to take out a pair of socks.

It was funny how the idea of doing this obsessed him. If he wanted to make things up with Guy there was no reason why he shouldn't have sent him the book in a parcel or, if that was rather costly, given him the book at half-term. This term their breaks coincided, being the middle week of February.

Angus didn't really want to wait that long. He wanted to get the book to Guy and somehow to get it to him in a mysterious way. Bruce had a cousin in the preparatory department at Utting, the junior school. When Bruce's relations came up one Sunday to take him out to tea Angus had the book ready wrapped up with a note to the eleven-year-old inside plus a fifty-pence piece. Would they please pass this on to their son when he came home next weekend? The juniors went home most weekends though seniors never did unless, for instance, one's grandfather had a ninetieth birthday or one's sister got married or something.

The note said to get the book secretly into the drawer

under Guy Parker's bunk in the study Guy shared with nine others—for this was the reality even at Utting. Bruce's cousin had told him all about it. Weeks went by and Angus heard nothing. For all he knew the cousin might have kept the fifty pee and dropped *Cat Walk* into his study wastepaper basket, if little ones like that had studies. On the other hand, things were much freer and easier at Utting than at Rossingham and the senior houses were very likely not out of bounds to juniors. It might be that the cousin had to do no more than walk openly from Andrade House where he lived into Fleming House which was Guy's house and up the stairs. He could do it during prep, for Angus had found out that the Lower Fourth at Utting did their prep in the library, not in their studies.

The Camerons took the local daily paper as well as *The Times*. It had a circulation not only in the city but across the whole county. February the 14th fell on a Monday, the first day of Angus's and Ian's half-term holiday. They had come home the evening before, having been fetched by their mother. Ian got up early on the Monday and rushed downstairs to get the *Free Press*. Angus found him sitting at the kitchen table reading page seven which, on 14 February, was devoted entirely to St Valentine's Day messages.

Looking over his shoulder, Angus read: 'Cameron, I. M., Violets are blue, My Valentine is you. Lorna.' He didn't think much of that. Ian looked up at him.

'There's one for you.'

'There can't be.'

'No kidding. You're Cameron, Angus H., aren't you?'

'There must be lots,' said Angus.

'I doubt it.' Ian pointed out the piece he had himself inserted. 'Markham, Lorna: I am, you are, love is. I.M.C.' He seemed proud of it. Angus looked back at the left-hand column where his own name was. 'Someone must fancy you,' said Ian. 'D'you know who it is?'

'Haven't the foggiest.'

41

'Cameron, Angus H.,' Angus read, 'ASKLTRV BNDFRT UYVGHTWS PNGHT YF REDCR TFV. NJULJK FDEBJU.'

It wasn't signed, or if it was the signature was incorporated in the code. Angus knew who it was, of course. He felt happy. Last year he remembered telling Guy that Ian's girl-friend Lorna had put a Valentine's message in the paper and the two of them had teased Ian who at first had tried to pretend the message wasn't for him. Guy must have thought of that when he was wondering how to thank him, Angus, for the loan of the book in suitably mystifying fashion.

Mystifying it was, though. No doubt Guy had used a line from a book to base his code on. That was what they had always done. Angus spent most of the day trying the code on the first lines of all the works he possessed by their favourite authors. It would be a novel of espionage, he was sure of that, and very possibly a novel by Yves Yugall. Angus tried the code on the first lines of *Scorpion Road*, *Tiger Toll*, *Monkey Wrench*, *Tarantula Town* and *Wasp Sting*. Surely Guy wouldn't have used a line from the middle of the book, would he? After all, he would want his code to be deciphered. He would want to give Angus a hard time of it but he would want his code deciphered in the end.

Another thing to be taken into consideration was that Guy would only have a limited number of books—that is, works of fiction—with him at Utting. And he must have composed the message at Utting, even though he would be at home now. Angus didn't know about Utting, but at Rossingham, what with sports and clubs and flexi-prep and the Combined Cadet Force, there wasn't much time for reading apart from required prep reading and one's housemaster didn't like one to stuff one's drawer with books. What books would Guy have with him? Maybe a school set book? Angus, rather dubiously, tried the code on the first lines of *Julius Caesar*, *To Kill a Mockingbird*, and though it seemed a bit way out, Daudet's *Lettres de Mon Moulin*. Nothing worked. He pored over the code, going through books all day Tuesday and most of Wednesday, and on Wednesday evening they all went over to some friends of his parents for supper. The friend had two Siamese cats one of which had injured its leg falling out of a tree.

'Look at the way that cat walks,' she said. 'I'll have to take her to the vet. I thought she'd be OK but she's going to have to have that leg seen to.'

Cat Walk, thought Angus. Why didn't I think of that before? That was one book I knew for certain he had at Utting. That's the book he used. The ridiculous thing was that Angus himself no longer had a copy of it, for he had sent his copy to Guy. He couldn't buy another, it wouldn't appear in paperback for nearly a year, and there would be a long waiting list at the library for the hardcover, he knew that from past experience. Next morning he went down to Hatchard's, a branch of which had just opened in Edge Street. *Cat Walk* was still on the best seller list and copies of it were prominently displayed. Angus picked one up and opened it. As soon as he had tried the first few letters of the coded message against the first line, he knew he had found the right book.

Shop assistants looked suspiciously at Angus. He was afraid that one of them, a thin cross-looking girl was going to come up to him and tell him he wasn't supposed to read the books without buying them first. But nothing happened. He deciphered the message without having to write it down. He kept it all in his head.

Guy had written: 'Great stuff. Why don't we keep this up? Moscow Centre.'

That was the signature, Moscow Centre. And somehow, standing there in the Edge Street Hatchard's, Angus had known exactly what Guy had meant. He wanted to start a spy network. They had talked about doing that in the past. They had wondered if they could set up a sort of MI5 or SIS (or CIA) and somehow use it. But they had never quite been able to decide what they would use it for. And then of course they had nothing to use it against. They were together, they were at the same school. But now they found themselves on opposing sides. Literally so, for like the West and the Soviets they were divided by a barrier which in fact separated east from west, in their case the river that split the city. Utting was on its eastern outskirts in what had once been the village of Utting. Rossingham, on the other hand, lay some twenty miles to the west in (according to the school prospectus) some of the most beautiful arable land in England. They were apart in a not dissimilar way from that in which the western and eastern blocs on an international level were apart.

Angus wanted very much to reply to Guy but he knew he mustn't. Contact had been made and now there must be no more. In falling in with Guy's suggestion, Angus realised something else: that in gaining Spookside (the name was invented two days afterwards) he would lose Guy. Oh, they would have the game, the network, the intrigue, the codes, the trappings of the game, but they would never again meet as they had once done. They would meet only as the heads of the SIS and the KGB, say, might meet, at some diplomatic party in Vienna. Their friendship as such would be over.

The attractions of Spookside were such, though, as to make Angus discount this. And if he now regretted it it was too late, for the game was over for him and he had gone his way and Guy his and they never saw each other except by chance. If they met in the street they would acknowledge each other with a raised arm and a shout of hi. But at the time this prospect, if prospect it was, seemed unimportant. Spookside was all.

His answer to Guy was to recruit two field agents from his own house at Rossingham, one of whom had a cousin at Utting. The cousin admitted that Guy had already tried to enrol him but he fancied working for western intelligence. The first thing Angus got him to do was get the book *Cat Walk* back from Guy. That

44

was the signal really that things had started. Guy changed the code from the day he lost the book. And he started using a drop actually inside the grounds at Utting.

For a while they only did joke things, to test themselves, to see if they could do them. Things like abstracting each other's possessions. Guy's second-in-command had an electric toothbrush which he kept with him in Oppenheimer House. He was known as the Controller of the Chamney Desk, Chamney being the next village to Utting, so that it was something of a triumph when one of his best officers managed to get hold of it and bring it over without detection. Soon after that the officer turned out to be a double agent. But by then they had moved on to higher, more involved and serious things.

There were the defectors, for instance, and the excitement of the debriefing sessions. But the first really important thing they did was to get hold of the plans for the block of flats it was proposed to build next door to Bruce Reynolds's parents' house. The architect happened to be Ivan Stern's mother's best friend's husband. They used the best officer for that and somehow he infiltrated the architect's studio on a visit to the house with Stern and Stern's parents. While the others were in the garden eating food barbecued by the architect he took the top sheet of the plans, the one with the general outlay and the building heights and so on, round the corner to the late-night instant print place and photocopied it. This was a daring coup. But the agent was a sort of genius, Angus (or Chimera) sometimes thought, and it was a bitter blow to him when he found out he was working for Guy at the same time. Guy learnt all about the plans coup before the photo-copy was on Bruce Reynolds's father's breakfast table, placed there by Bruce in a blank envelope with no covering letter. Mr Reynolds had actually believed in the validity of those plans and had acted accordingly. He thought the envelope had come from a town councillor known to be crooked. Instead of selling his house as he had planned to do should the block of flats have turned out to be as large and tall as he had feared, he withdrew it from the market and set about building the extension which would provide an indoor swimming pool and double-size bedroom for Bruce.

That was the kind of thing they did. Better things and worse. Pointless things and absurd things too, and sometimes dangerous things. Until one day, in the summer holidays just before he was sixteen, when he was in the fifth and O Levels were coming up the following year, Angus woke up in the morning, remembered what he had to do first thing, go down to the safe house and begin the debriefing of the latest defector, and thought, Oh God, what a drag, do I have to...?

ffffffffffffffffffffff **7** ffffff

'THEY ARE JUST LIKE SCHOOLBOYS,' FERGUS SAID, turning off the television. 'Like so many schoolchildren playing games.'

The main item on the early evening news had been an account of the latest spy trial currently taking place in the United States.

Mungo grinned to himself. It was not the first time he had heard this comment from his father and it never failed to afford him private amusement. Not quite private, in fact, for once or twice he had caught Angus's eye.

Now his father said, 'It must be the game element that keeps it all going. No rational person can see any sense in it. It's of no positive benefit to the world.

Rather the reverse. I sometimes think it's actively dangerous. I mean, without this insanity would we even have the high level of tension that exists between East and West?'

'Probably not, darling,' said Lucy.

Mungo excused himself. They had been eating one of Lucy's junk-food, what she called her scratch-as-scratch-can teas, baps and mustard pickles and German sausage out of packets, all sitting in armchairs up in the den. Only Lucy had the sofa. A woman of her size needed exclusive possession of the sofa, she said. There had been pineapple juice to drink and a bottle of white wine. Mungo couldn't understand why his father offered him a glass of wine and gave him such a searching look when he refused it. He always did refuse it, after all.

In the next hour or so he had to get down to the flyover drop and see if there was anything for him. He was expecting to hear from his agent Nicholas Ralston (or Basilisk) that he had solved the problem, that he had found a way of eliciting from Blake his decision over the surgery planning permission. And if Basilisk's efforts failed, he was keeping Charles Mabledene (or Dragon) in reserve. Dragon, Mungo thought, was by far his best agent, the best agent he had ever had, better than any of Stern's Stars.

Charles Mabledene had been his first defector, come over to him before he had assumed the headship of London Central, when he was still Angus's right-hand man. It was in the summer term, when Angus was thinking of giving up, was schooling Mungo to take his place, only no one knew that, it was still a dead secret between them. Mungo had been up in his study, doing flexi-prep, and Angus was still in town, according to his entry in the house book. It was policy at Rossingham to put brothers in the same house unless they specifically asked for this not to be done or their parents asked. The O'Neills, for instance, had requested that Keith and Graham be kept apart on account of Graham being so much brighter. But when Mungo started at Rossingham he was put into Pitt with Angus. Ian had left by then but he too had been in Pitt, though Fergus all those years before had for some reason been in Gladstone.

There was a phone in the house common room. There was a television set too which you were at liberty to watch once your prep was done. But use of the phone was very much restricted. Once you were in the sixth form you could do practically anything you wanted anyway, or things were a whole lot less constrained, but even then you weren't supposed to receive calls on that phone. It was strictly for making essential outgoing calls, such as if one of your parents was ill or you had to cancel their weekend visit to you, something like that. And it was a pay phone too which made it unlikely it would be used unnecessarily.

To the outside world the number of that phone was unknown. It appeared in no directory. Even parents didn't know it. If they needed to phone up and enquire about something they were supposed to call the headmaster or one's housemaster on a private phone in his flat. Angus told Mungo afterwards that in all his three years at Rossingham in Pitt House he had never heard that phone ring or been told that it had rung. And there was Mungo, on that evening in June last year, sitting up in his study doing his biology with his best friend and second-in-command Graham O'Neill (or Medusa) sitting beside him doing his history, when he heard a bell ring downstairs. They didn't know what it was, they thought it must have been Mr Lindsay's phone ringing in the flat, that maybe he or Mrs Lindsay had left the door open.

It was someone he didn't know all that well, not one of his agents, who came up to tell him the call was for him. Mungo thought someone must be ill, even dying, for his people actually to phone him at school. He got up quickly, starting in the direction of the housemaster's flat.

A shrill whisper: 'The phone in the common room!'

'I don't believe it.'

The whisperer shrugged.

'Who is it, for God's sake?' Mungo said.

'They wouldn't say. They sounded scared shitless.'

Half a dozen men were sitting round the TV but they weren't looking at it. They were all looking at the receiver of the phone, lying there resting on the pay box. When it rang it must have shaken them more than the fire bell would have, Mungo thought. He'd never forget picking up that receiver, quite mystified, and a squeaky kid's voice that hadn't even started breaking said:

'I'm called Charles Mabledene. I want to come over.'

'You what?' Mungo wasn't as on the ball then as he had become later.

'I want to defect. I could bring you something good. I could bring you Guy Parker's code book.'

Remembering it nine months later, Mungo smiled to himself. He was passing Mabledene's now, the big garage that had the Volvo concession on the western side of Rostock, though the family lived ten miles out in one of the villages. This was only the second light evening. At midnight on Saturday the clocks had gone forward. It wasn't cold but mild and damp, visibility poor, giving to this deserted place an air of mystery. Moisture lay on the flight of stone steps that ran down to the embankment and yellow light from the pub windows made it gleam. Mungo went up the steps from the river, crossing the place where that girl had been strangled, up Bread Lane this time, the steepish hill that wound between high brick walls with broken glass on top. Easter Monday and the flyover shook under the weight of traffic, cars going northwards tonight, returning from holiday resorts. But underneath all was still, shadowed, undisturbed. Mungo saw the king cat's eyes, points of green fire, before his fur was visible. He crossed the road and put out his hand but the animal twisted away and slid under one of the stunted bushes.

A folded piece of paper in a plastic envelope was

taped inside the central upright, fixed there at the level of Mungo's chin which would just about be head height for Basilisk. It came away very easily, Mungo thought, almost too easily. The tape peeled off as if it had already been unstuck once since Basilisk put it there.

I wonder if I am imagining things, Mungo said to himself, as he put the message into his pocket.

ƒƒƒƒƒƒƒƒƒƒƒƒƒƒƒƒƒƒƒƒ **8** ƒƒƒƒƒ

JOHN CREEVEY WAS SIXTEEN WHEN HE FIRST NO-ticed his sister was ugly. She came into the living room to tell him something about a cake. A birthday cake, that was it, so it must have been her eleventh birthday. She came to tell him tea was ready in the dining room and her cake was on the table with its eleven candles. He looked up and seemed for some reason to see her face for the first time. Perhaps it was because she surprised him, he hadn't heard her come in. He saw her bulging forehead that seemed to over-hang her eyebrows, her cheeks as round as apples, her snub nose and sickle mouth. She was ugly and he had never noticed it before.

He began to wonder what would become of her. Would any man ever want her? Would anyone ever want to marry her? When she was older he noticed that she had developed a good figure, large breasts and shapely legs, and she had beautiful hair, thick and of a rich light chestnut colour, but that did nothing in his eyes to redeem those coarse ill-fashioned features. One day he saw a reproduction of a picture by Velasquez and the court dwarf in it had a face just like his sister Cherry.

He wondered how she came to look like that. He knew he wasn't bad-looking, ordinary but passable, and his father was much the same while their mother was positively pretty. Then when he was looking through an album of old photographs he saw a family group with his father's father and his father's aunt in it and then he knew. Genes behaved like that. He started watching her as if she were an invalid, someone with a dormant disease whose terrible symptoms would one day show themselves. She wasn't even clever. She couldn't be a teacher or a secretary. The job she got when she left school was sending out the invoices for a builder who had an office in a wooden hut down on the west side of Rostock. Sixteen she was then and with a host of friends, all pretty girls, it seemed to John. It made him sad to see her with those girls and her not even aware of the contrast. Maitland the builder had the reputation of being a womaniser, in spite of being married and with children and grandchildren, but that never worried John. A man like that wouldn't give Cherry a second glance.

And then she met Mark Simms, handsome, tall, with fine straight features and good teeth and dark eyes, broad shouldered, slim. And he had a nice personality and a good job. John couldn't believe it when she told him they were engaged. He thought she must have made a mistake, she was so innocent she'd mistaken some remark of his for a proposal. But he met Mark and knew at once it was all genuine, it was all as Cherry said, and the amazing thing was it wasn't one-sided, it wasn't a case of Mark being sorry for her or indifferent, he was crazy about her. You only had to see the way he looked at her to know that.

It was in this very room in the house in Geneva Road that Cherry had introduced him to Mark. Seventeen years ago it must have been, nearer eighteen. And here was Mark back again, still slim and handsome, still with those nice white teeth, his hair going a bit grey but that was all. A failed marriage behind him and seemingly half if not entirely forgotten. John didn't think he had forgotten Cherry though. He might have found someone else eventually and got married but the place in his heart was for Cherry.

He and Colin Goodman were watching snooker on John's television. They had all been to a pub and thence to an Italian restaurant, and now here they were, all three of them, sitting here drinking Carlsberg, Mark smoking his pipe, both bars of the electric fire switched on. He hadn't seen Mark for years, ten years probably. They had talked throughout the Italian meal but it had been small talk, not real. And now John wondered if the truth was that he had only asked Colin to join them to make any heart-to-heart unburdenings impossible, to rule out the possibility of confidences. Yet it seemed to him there hung in the very air a yearning for confession, for openness.

The snooker came to an end and no one wanted to see the play which followed it. John switched off the set. Kim Philby's *My Silent War* lay on the low table which stood between the settee where Colin and Mark sat and the television, and Mark leaned forward and picked it up. He looked inside, turned a few pages. John remembered that Mark had always been a great reader, though it was almost unknown for Cherry to open a book.

'Still racking your brains, are you, over that code?' Colin said.

John nodded.

'John's got this pal sends him letters in code, only he can't read them.'

Mark didn't seem much interested. John wouldn't have said this to anyone else but it was all right thinking it. Mark wasn't interested in others and their affairs. His favourite word was 'I', John's father had once said, with 'me' a close second. John had thought this a bit unfair at the time but now he wasn't so sure.

'Nineteen sixty-eight, this was published, the year I

met Cherry. I always think of it as the year I met Cherry.'

'Was it really that long ago?' Colin looked embarrassed, sounded gruff.

'We were engaged for nearly two years,' Mark said.

His eyes met John's and it seemed to John that they were full of sorrow—no, more than that, full of grief. He was sure then that Mark was going to say something more, that in spite of Colin's presence, he was going to speak of his love for Cherry that still endured. And John felt mean for thinking him such an egotist. But instead Mark put the book back on the table and said in quite a different tone from that he had used when talking of her, 'There's rather a good novel I read about him, about Philby I mean. Well, a thriller. By Ted Albeury. I can't remember what it's called. They'd know at your library, I should think.'

They left soon after that, Mark shaking hands with him rather formally. He hadn't mentioned Jennifer all evening which made John think Colin must have said something before he got to the restaurant. John imagined them in the car, Mark asking what exactly did happen about his wife, and Colin saying, she left him, went off with some chap she used to be engaged to. Colin would add that the marriage was over. But now John was refusing to think of it in those terms.

He had replied to Jennifer and posted his letter on the way to the restaurant. Well, not on the way really, for he had made a detour to take in cats' green. There he had unpeeled the plastic envelope from the inside of the pillar and copied down the coded message into his notebook. Emptying Mark's ashtray, putting their glasses into the sink, he came back to the living room, sat down in front of the electric fire once more and picked up the Philby book. Philby had been a spy, these were spy memoirs. Why shouldn't the sender of the messages have used the first lines of this book for his code? It seemed as likely as any other. John got out his notebook and tried the coded messages against the first lines of *My Silent War*. Wrong again. No again. Why do I bother? John asked himself. And he was aware that since the arrival of Jennifer's letter and his replying to it the messages had meant less to him, they had been less of a diversion. They had not served to distract his mind as efficiently as he expected. He would look at the coded words and speculate and then gradually feel speculation being displaced by images of Jennifer and by memories of when they were together. Above all he would have this very vivid recollection of the second time they went out together and he had told her about Cherry and she told him about Peter Moran.

'I suppose we were really very dull ordinary sort of people in our family,' he had said to her. 'Not interesting, nothing special, any of us. My dad worked for the Post Office. I don't think Mother had ever had any sort of job, it wouldn't have crossed her mind. We were such a happy family, we honestly never had a cross word, I suppose we just didn't disagree about anything. We—my sister and I—didn't want to rebel and our parents didn't try to stop us enjoying ourselves. We were always doing things for each other. I mean when someone wanted something one of us would jump up and say I'll get it or I'll do that. We all liked each other, you see. And we liked to see the others happy. We were always laughing. Does that sound crazy? I mean we had little family jokes and catchwords and we'd tell each other funny things that happened at work. It was a regular thing every evening and Mum would say, "Don't you do any work, you lot? It's all play by the sound of it."'

She was looking at him dubiously. Her expression was kindly but puzzled too. 'It doesn't sound like you—well, what I know of you.'

'I was different. I changed. We all changed. A death like that, it blows a world apart.'

'Your sister was going to be married?'

'In two months' time. Her fiancé used to be with us most days. I mean he and Cherry would go out together, of course they would, but we weren't the sort of people to keep a friend to ourselves. Cherry and I brought our friends home. It was natural for her to bring Mark home to eat his meals with us and stay the night sometimes.'

She was looking at him enquiringly. He felt the colour come up into his face.

'We only had the three bedrooms but Mother would make up the couch downstairs for him.'

'What happened?' she asked.

'One evening she just didn't come home from work. It was winter and the evenings were dark. Mark called round at the place she worked, down at Beckgate. He had been going to pick her up and they were going out somewhere, but she had already left and the place was locked up. They found her body lying on those steps that go down to the embankment below Rostock. She'd been strangled. They never found the person who did it. There were no witnesses, nothing.'

'And that changed you all?' she said. 'That broke your family up?'

'It was like,' he said, 'you imagine being struck by lightning. We were—blasted. The next year my father had a stroke. Oh, they said it had nothing to do with Cherry's death, it would have happened anyway. Perhaps it would. He was more or less bedridden for years. My mother looked after him. It sounds melodramatic, it sounds exaggerated, but I don't think she ever laughed any more. I never heard her laugh. We clung to each other for support, the three of us, but we couldn't support each other. Can you understand? There was no comfort to give.'

'You stayed with them? You lived at home?'

He had never considered an alternative. Jennifer seemed astonished, as if he had made a sacrifice. He told her about his father's death and his mother's but said nothing about his own loneliness. She looked at him. She had a way of looking intensely into one's eyes. Her face was wide at the temples, full-cheeked, the pale skin freckled, deep charming dimples at the corners of her pretty mouth. And everything about her was soft, it was in this that her uniqueness lay, her voice, her gaze, her touch. Oh, beyond all, her touch! Of course he had known nothing of that then. Those were early days. But even then he had recognised her apartness from all other women, her quality of hushed velvety sweetness. He enjoyed looking at art books, the kind that have reproductions in them of famous paintings. And he would identify the looks of people he knew with the subjects of portraits. If Cherry was the Velasquez dwarf, Mark Simms looked like El Greco's picture of the poet-scholar Paravicino and Jennifer—well, Jennifer was Rembrandt's Juno.

'I like the sound of your family,' she said. 'I'd have liked to know them. If you'd known me then would you have taken me home to meals?'

It was so unexpected he blushed again. He stammered, 'You're too young. You'd have been a child.'

'If I was as I am now, would you have?'

'Of course I would, of course.'

She looked away. 'My family weren't like that. My father was ill for years too, in and out of hospital, and he made us all suffer for that. It sounds unkind but it's true. My mother had learnt to repress her emotions. Not committing herself, not talking of anything but the weather and the shops and what the neighbours said—that made her feel safe. Do you know what I mean?'

He nodded. 'I think so.'

Looking down, her eyebrows drawn close together, she said in that voice he had never heard raised, then or later, 'I'll tell you what happened to me and the man I was going to marry. It was awful. It was the most terrible thing. Can I tell you?'

Don't hurt me, he wanted to say. You can hurt me, already you can. But he only nodded again and her eyes on his, into his, she began...

THE FIRST DAY BACK AFTER A HOLIDAY WAS ALWAYS busy. People had all the long weekend in which to look at their gardens and decide that only a new shrub here or a row of perennials there would be enough to transform them into Sissinghurst or Kew. There was a run on dahlia tubers and gladioli bulbs, showy things that John didn't much like. He overheard Gavin persuading a woman to buy *Eucalyptus salicifolia* for planting in an exposed north-facing garden where of course only *gunii* was likely to survive. Gavin didn't like to be told, though John did it discreetly enough and out of anyone else's earshot. There had been a willow-leaved eucalyptus in Hartland Gardens but the severe frosts of two winters before had killed it. John and Jennifer had gone for a walk there and seen the poor gum tree, its trunk like stripped bone, its leaves dried and curled and rattling in the wind.

On his way home he called in at the library. The book Mark had talked about was in. It was called *The Other Side of Silence*. They had *King Solomon's Mines* too. John thought, knowing it was the way a lonely, nearly friendless man thinks, I'll have two good books to read over the holiday. Of course he wouldn't start on either until it got dark. He had the fallen prunus petals to sweep up and the wallflowers to plant out. They were in a seed tray in the lean-to greenhouse attached to the back of the kitchen, where for want of a garage he also had to keep the Honda. John imagined the orange flowers they would bear in May and June and their rich yet delicate scent.

The tiny plants were delicate and fragile. He watered them in, went back into the house and washed his hands at the kitchen sink. Scrambled eggs would be the easiest dish to make, scrambled eggs on toast with half a tin of fruit to follow and Longlife cream. Out of politeness he had never read at table while Jennifer was with him, though at home they had all read books or magazines at mealtimes if they had wanted to and it hadn't seemed anti-social or rude. At home—John realized the phrase he had used. Wasn't this home then? Wasn't this the very same house? Home is where the people you love are, he thought, the people who love you.

He opened *The Other Side of Silence* and read the opening lines. 'The snow lay thick on the steps and the snowflakes driven by the wind looked black in the headlights of the cars.' Almost mechanically, because he did it with every book he started, he began placing the alphabet against the letters. Not in the book itself, of course, but in his notebook, using a pencil. He took a mouthful of egg on toast. A would be T, B would be H, C would be E, D S, E N, F O, G W, H L . . . It was going to work out—or was it?

The first word in the latest coded message was HCRKTABTE. If you used the first lines of *The Other Side of Silence*, that came out as LEVIATHAN. Well, 'Leviathan' was a word or at any rate a name. 'To Basilisk', it continued. There followed 'Take Sterns Childers'. John had a vague idea 'childers' might be old-fashioned or dialect English for children. 'Take Sterns Childers' didn't seem to mean anything.

Never mind. He had more coded messages in the notebook. Feeling disproportionately excited, he began matching letters in the second message against letters in those first lines. The results were slightly more comprehensible. The second message when deciphered read: 'Leviathan to Basilisk and Unicorn. Fifty-three Ruxeter Road is safe house', and the third: 'Dragon to Leviathan. Commencing Blakeprox Tuesday'. At least they seemed to be real words in English. But what did they mean? On the theory that two heads were better than one, perhaps he ought to ring Colin. Colin might be able to help. Also John had that feeling common to all humanity in his sort of situation. He had made a discovery, triumphed really, and he wanted to tell someone about it. The person he would really have liked to tell was Jennifer. He got as far as the phone and the dialling of the first three digits of Colin's number, and then he put the receiver back, asking himself if he wanted to share this with anyone. A more satisfactory thing might be to go to 53 Ruxeter Road and see what these people meant by a 'safe house'.

As he turned the Honda into Berne Road he felt the sting of a raindrop on his face. He would regret this adventure if the rain came on like it had last night, he thought. Adventure it was, though. He wondered what he was getting himself into. Nothing presumably that he couldn't pull out of again. There had been a lot in the papers and on television lately about drugs and it sometimes seemed to John as if everybody except himself had taken drugs at some time or other. To hear them and read about them you'd think the whole nation was permanently stupefied by dope and crack. What if these people he had got on to were involved with drugs? What if that was what they were up to and why they needed this code and these messages?

The wind had dropped and the river lay calm and flat with a dark oily surface. At the other end of the bridge the street narrowed, passing under the cathedral walls, then between tall office blocks, widening into Nevin Square where behind green lawns and a fountain that never played after 6 P.M. stood the city hall. The clock on St. Stephen's Cathedral struck an uncounted number of strokes. There were few people about, few cars. On the pedestal of the statue of Lysander Douglas, philanthropist, explorer and former mayor of this city, sat two punk people with bright coloured hair, dressed in leather far more bizarre than his own and eating fish and chips from paper bags.

John went round the square, leaving by the third exit of the roundabout which was Nevin Street. Neon digits on top of the CitWest insurance tower told him it was nine-O-two and the temperature nine degrees. The whole left-hand side of this street was dominated by the buildings of the polytechnic. The swing doors on the main entrance opened and John saw Peter Moran come out and start to walk down the steps. He had only seen him once before but he would have known him anywhere. We no more forget the faces of our enemies than of those we love.

This was the man his wife was living with. John told himself this in so many words as he slowed and turned his head and looked at Peter Moran. Fairhaired, nothing special to look at, a lantern jaw and glasses so thick that he must be very short-sighted. Of course John couldn't see the thickness of his glasses at this moment but he had noticed them before on the single occasion they had met, an occasion he remembered with pain but could no more forget than he could forget Peter's face. Peter, of course, didn't see him. A man on a motorbike is the most anonymous, the most invisible, of people. He is scarcely a man, more an adjunct of the bike, furnished in black and chrome and upholstered in leather like itself.

Two days before her wedding day, she had told him, that man had said to her he couldn't marry her after all. They had been living together, sharing a bedsit, but she had gone home to her mother for a week before the wedding. To please her mother who had cancer, who was shortly to die, they had arranged a big wedding. Invitations had gone out to two hundred people.

'He didn't really give a reason, just said he couldn't go through with it. I didn't believe what I was hearing. I thought it was some sort of joke. We were at my place—

well, my mother's. My aunt was staying with us, she'd come from Ireland for the wedding.'

'You knew it wasn't a joke though,' John had said.

'After a while I did. I said was it all the fuss, I mean a white wedding and all those people coming, I said was it that which was upsetting him. I said it didn't matter, we could get married in a register office, we didn't have to do what Mother wanted. He said no, it wasn't that. It was just the idea of being married, of marriage itself he couldn't face, he wasn't the kind of person who could ever be married. And suddenly there wasn't any more to say. Can you understand that, John? There was nothing to say. We just stared at each other and then he said, well, good-bye then, and he walked out of the house and closed the front door behind him. My mother came in and said Peter hadn't gone, had he, without being introduced to Auntie Katie. I said he'd gone and there wouldn't be any wedding and she started laughing and crying and screaming. Those repressed people, they're the worst when they break out. I didn't cry, not then. I was stunned, I wasn't even angry.'

'I can't imagine you angry,' he had said to her.

John parked the bike down a side street called Collingbourne Road. A pub called The Gander was advertising something called a 'Neez-up Nite' for the coming Saturday but for all that it had a gloomy look, its lights dim. Between it and the road where he had parked stood a terrace of Victorian houses, tall, bleak, the rough grey plaster with which they were faced cracked or broken away, their windows, rectangular and of uniform size, sealed with boards. Sheets of corrugated metal covered where the front doors should have been. Number 53 was on the middle house of this row of five. It was the only one with a gable and in the centre of this gable, on a circular plaque of smoother stone, were engraved the name Pentecost Villas and the date, 1885.

For a moment or two John doubted if he had come to

the right place. But this was Ruxeter Road and Pentecost Villas were not separately numbered from the rest of the houses in this long street. Carrying his crash helmet and visor, he walked back along Collingbourne Road to see if there might be a way in at the back but the long gardens of those grey houses were separated from the pavement by a high wall of yellow bricks unbroken by any gateway. When the wall came to an end he turned left along Fontaine Avenue. The gardens ended in a fence here and in the fence were five solid-looking gates. He could see this by the light from a series of street lamps on the opposite pavement, behind which instead of more houses was the green space, called Fontaine Park. John couldn't recall having been down here since he was about ten. He was alone in the street. As usual there was no one about, the only sign that people were in the vicinity, those inevitable parked cars.

He tried the first gate in the fence but it was bolted as he had feared and probably locked too. So was the next one. They all would be and that would be that. But because he had come all this way and must when he started out surely have intended to find out what this 'safe house' business was all about, he tried the third door. The latch yielded and it opened.

John looked round. He looked to the right and the left and behind him but there was no one. He went into the garden and closed the gate behind him. A wilderness met his eyes, a waste land of rough grass and sprawling shrubs, tree stumps and trees overgrown with rampant ivy. The back of the house seemed boarded-up too where it wasn't festooned with a cobweb-like creeper. As he approached it the shadow of the fence loomed up behind him, rising up the house, quelling the light, until by the time he reached it he and it were in darkness. He shouldn't have come at night, or he should have brought a torch. But he had hardly expected something like this. What had he expected? He didn't know.

As he went down the shallow flight of steps he thought, suppose the door is unlocked and I open it and go in and the whole place is a blaze of light and there are twelve men sitting at a round table and one of them gets up with a gun in his hand...? By the time he had thought that he had tried the door and it yielded and he was inside. There was no light though and when he fumbled on the wall for a switch and found it and pressed it, nothing happened. It was deathly dark in there, as dark as a mine or a tomb, and dampness touched the skin of his face like cold rubber. He moved warily across a floor which had a slippery feel, realising before he reached the doorway that it was hopeless. In the absence of light or access to any source of light, he could go no further.

Anyway, there was no one here. More accustomed now to the darkness, he peered about him, searching for what he thought those sort of people would leave behind them, empty bottles, cigarette stubs, half-smoked joints perhaps, though he doubted if he would recognize these. Pinned to one wall, to peeling wall-paper and squashed rotted plaster, was a sheet of paper that seemed to have writing on it. Impossible to read the writing here. He pulled it down, folded it and put it into his pocket and tugged the door open, relieved to be out in Fontaine Avenue once more, the neat little park opposite, its hedges and trim trees lit by splashes of yellow light. What a fool I am, he thought, coming all the way out here. Like a school-boy. Like a kid. And for what? What did I hope to find? He retrieved the Honda, put on his visor and crash helmet, and started back.

WHEN HE WAS GOING TO GET MARRIED JOHN HAD bought only one new piece of furniture and that was a bed. All his life, up till then, he had slept in the three-foot-wide single bed in the smallest of the three bed-rooms. His parents had slept in the large bedroom at the front and Cherry in the large bedroom at the back. When she died, or at any rate after she had been dead a few months, he might have taken over her room but he never had. No one ever again slept in that room, and it began to be kept as a sort of shrine. John suspected his mother sometimes went up and sat there. Colin had once suggested he ought to find a tenant for it, people were always on the look-out for rooms, but to John the idea was sacrilegious.

Jennifer and he would of course use his parents' room but to sleep in his parents' bed seemed gro-tesque. He and Cherry had been born in that bed and no doubt conceived there too. His bride and he couldn't sleep there. Without consulting Jennifer, he went out and bought a big double bed, a bed the shop assistant called queen-sized. Now when he lay alone in this bed it seemed enormous.

John had told himself he respected Jennifer too much to attempt to make love to her before they were married. But wherever else he failed he tried to be honest and he knew in his heart it was not respect, whatever that might really mean, which stood in the way, but fear. He was thirty-seven years old and he had never made love to any woman, he was a virgin.

It was not all that unusual, he suspected. He wouldn't have been surprised to learn that Colin was too, and still was. Somehow, if you didn't get to go with a girl when you were sixteen or seventeen you sort of missed the boat and unless you got engaged and married that was it. There were no opportunities, especially in a place like this and if you lived with your parents. Suppose, he asked himself, he had met a girl and they had wanted to sleep together and she was living at home too, what would they have done? He had no car, he couldn't have afforded an hotel room and would have baulked at the open air. Anyway he never seemed to meet any girls.

He admitted quite freely to himself that he was afraid to try making love to a woman. How did you go about it? How did you begin? How would you know you were doing right? He couldn't imagine the first move. Well, the kiss he could imagine. By then he had kissed Jennifer many times. But how to take the next step? And what would the next step be? Her breasts, the books said. He shrank with diffidence and shyness at the thought. It seemed an assault. How could you get hold of a girl's breasts and feel them? By what right? She was not a virgin, he knew that. She had lived with Peter Moran. Therefore she would know what was due to her, she would know what men who were real lovers did...

When the new bed came he put the old one, his parents' bed, into Cherry's room beside her single divan. Cherry had been innocent, a modest, chaste girl. He had thought her plainness kept her that way until he had seen her with Mark Simms and seen the way Mark looked at her, with passion, with devotion. Then he knew she was naturally pure or pure by conscious choice. One day she said to their mother that she and Mark planned to save their money, they wouldn't have a honeymoon. Holidays abroad could wait till later on, till they had their home together. And their mother said maybe that would be too late, maybe she would have other commitments, and though he had known what she meant, that Cherry might have children, Cherry herself hadn't. There had been explanations and Cherry had seemed quite put out, offended even, which was almost unheard of for her, and their mother had said that children would come unless Cherry took precautions to see they didn't. He had made some excuse and left the room after that. It was strange though that all the time he had sensed Cherry's underlying anger and something impatient or even derisive in her manner.

Perhaps there was something about their family, something in the individual members of it that shied away from sex. Jennifer had been so kind to him, so good. Once she understood what the problem was, the lack, she had been patient and caring and together they had... He put the memory of it along a shelf in his mind until it crashed off the end. No more of that! He turned over in the empty queen-sized bed, seeking elusive sleep, not unhappy though, full of hope.

Those terrors were gone now. Thanks to her, with her, he could be tender and assured. As he thought of it his penis uncurled itself inside his pyjama leg, stiffened. After she left him it had not so much been desire he felt as simple longing for her company. He had missed sex less than companionship. But this was desire. He laid his hand upon his stiff penis and, contrary to what should have happened, it shrank under his touch. He turned his face into the pillow, his arms crossed now, a hand on each shoulder, and felt like a child waiting for his mother to come in and say good night.

11

FERGUS ALWAYS DROVE A VOLVO, KEPT IT FIVE YEARS and then turned it in for a new one. The latest came from Mabledene's which had opened its city branch about two years before.

'Extraordinary name,' said Fergus.

'Is it?' said Mungo. 'There's a Charles Mabledene in my house at school.'

'It must be the same family. Poor chap. I daresay he gets teased.'

'Teased? Why should he?'

Fergus gave him a look indicative of sorrow that his youngest son was simple-minded. 'Well, Mabel. I suppose he gets called Mabel, doesn't he? He would have been in my day.'

Mungo didn't know what his father meant. He had never heard of Mabel as a girl's name.

'Things have changed since your day,' said Lucy.

Girls in the sixth form, she meant. People called by their Christian names. They had girls in at all levels at Utting and Stern's new second-in-command was a girl. Mungo thought what a funny thing it was his father and he didn't seem to speak the same language. It was rather as if, while both speaking English, they had each learned it in parts of the world separated by thousands of miles, in countries where the customs and traditions were totally disparate. He sat at breakfast after his father had gone off to his morning surgery, trying to fathom what he had meant about someone deserving pity because they might be called by a girl's name no one had ever heard of. But after a while he gave up. You couldn't, anyway, imagine feeling sorry for Charles Mabledene, he wasn't that sort of person.

Charles Mabledene had defected and Stern had been furious. No wonder. Agents of Charles's brilliance didn't grow on trees. He had been in the junior school at Utting, in Andrade House with Stern's brother Michael, and it was just after they had both taken the Common Entrance that he phoned Mungo. The situation, Angus said when told about it later, rather paralleled his own experience with Guy Parker. For the nub of Charles's conversation with Mungo that evening was that, without saying a word to Ivan or Michael Stern, or indeed anyone but his own parents and the powers-that-were at Rossingham, he had elected to come to Rossingham not Utting when term started in September.

He meant, of course, more than this. He meant he wanted to defect to the West and be enrolled by Mungo.

'Recruited,' Mungo corrected him kindly. 'It's enemy security officers who are enrolled.'

Then Charles said what he would bring with him as evidence of good faith. For a long time Mungo had dreamt of getting his hands on Guy Parker's code book. Guy was still nominally head of Moscow Centre at that time, though he was to hand everything over to Stern during the summer holidays. The codes he used were not based on the first lines of books, or any lines from books, but on secret sentences in this code book which Angus had long suspected was entirely in foreign languages, and probably obscure foreign languages such as Serbo-Croatian and Friesian. On countless occasions he had sent people in to attempt the theft of this book, or better still make a copy of it. The double agent Hydra, who was in the Lower Fourth at Utting with Stern, had tried to get hold of it. But Guy Parker, alerted to what was going on by a clumsy attempt, took to carrying the book around on his person, opened and pressed flat against his chest between his shirt and his vest.

Mungo didn't believe Charles Mabledene could get hold of it, and it was to be months before he learned how this had been effected. July and August went by and he heard not a word. Term began on 8 September, Mungo moved into the Upper Fourth and into a study in Pitt that he shared with only three others instead of the former nine. Angus, in the Lower Sixth now and a prefect, went along to the new ones' studies at lights out to give them his pep talk. He reported back to Mungo the presence of Charles Mabledene. But by that time a photocopy of the code book was in the drawer under his bunk. He found it there when he went to get out his pyjamas.

The safe house they were using then was one of the rooms in the old physics lab. New labs had been completed in the previous year but the original Edwardian buildings still stood, their fate being undecided. A proposal to convert them into two gardeners' flats was later rejected on grounds of expense and demolition was begun. But back last September the rooms still stood, and stood empty and locked up. Charles Mabledene, of course, got the keys and had copies cut. He could get any keys, could Charles, make his way in and out of anything, come to that. Before he was ten he had been no mean conjurer—a 'tregetour' was what he called himself—and he was studying escapology.

Mungo debriefed him in the old physics lab. Charles told him everything Parker and Stern had been doing and everything they planned to do. He found out from Charles how Parker had discovered their code system and the drops they were currently using. For weeks he had been wondering how it was that his efforts to secure four invitations to the Mayor's garden party had been continually frustrated, had ultimately failed. It was Charles who told him that Hydra was a double agent and that the Mayor had two sons at Utting. And Charles told him how he had got the code book. It was on Sports Day when Guy Parker was swimming in the 100 metres. He thought he was safe because all the changing rooms had lockers with keys. But opening a locker was nothing to Charles Mabledene. He used credit cards and not even old ones but Mabledene's personal cards they issued to their customers. Charles took the code book over to Technology about a hundred yards away, photo-copied it and had it back in Parker's locker by the time he was emerging from the water.

Then began a period of triumph. The other side continued to use the code book all that term and Mungo was privy to all their secrets. Months of work were undone by the loss of the code book, Stern's Deputy Controller Rosie Whittaker was reputed to have said. It was Christmas before they found out about the code book and then they thought an agent of their own was the traitor. Mungo would have welcomed this agent, he would have liked him to come over, but he wasn't all that bright and Rossingham didn't want him. Charles Mabledene, on the other hand, was one of those rare people who had been awarded a scholarship on his Common Entrance results. He didn't even have to apply for it. His parents must have got a pleasant surprise when the letter came saying he had not only passed but they would be getting five hundred pounds off their annual fees bill.

Those were the days when Mungo had led Michael Stern a dance all over the city at Christmas time and locked him up in the warehouse; when he had been shown all Stern's drops and substituted all Stern's messages with those of his own. But triumph had not been long-lived. Since then, during this past spring term in spite of what had been accomplished, they had known few real successes. For one thing, Moscow Centre had formulated its new code, a marvellous code that began with a number and ended with a longer number and defied all attempts to decipher it. And then there was the dawning possibility Stern had a mole in the very heart of the department. But if he could pull off this Blake business much would be paid for, much made equal.

Mungo climbed the stairs up to his room and closed the door. It was 31 March and he had two things in mind: one, to play an April Fool's trick of some sort on the other side and two, to formulate a new code. For the code, he had more or less decided to use Erskine Childers's *The Riddle of the Sands*. This was the book he had, at half-term, got Basilisk to abstract from Stern because he was pretty sure Stern was using it as an arbitrary source for code-making. But it occurred to him that Stern would quickly guess that the Childers was being used, had probably guessed already and was anticipating this. Mungo looked round his own bookshelves and took down a thick volume, turned the pages and read: 'In the third week of November, in the year 1895, a dense yellow fog settled upon London. From the Monday to the Thursday I doubt whether it was ever possible from our windows in Baker Street to see the loom of the opposite houses.' That would do. What was the loom of a house anyway? Mungo didn't think it mattered.

12

GETTING INTO HIS LEATHERS TO GO HOME FOR HIS half-day off—early closing was on Thursdays—John felt in his jacket pocket and pulled out the piece of paper he had taken from the wall at 53 Ruxeter Road. 'Chimera, Leviathan, Dragon, Basilisk, Medusa, Scylla, Unicorn, Charybdis, Empusa, Hydra, Minotaur', were printed on it in two columns. A dictionary in the library told him the words on the list were all names of fabulous animals or mythological monsters. John had no doubt however that they related in some way to the gang that was sending the coded messages. He made a detour and went home via cats' green where, inside the central pillar, he found a fresh message.

'Leviathan to Dragon and Basilisk,' he read. 'Ignore all Tosos commands. Bruce Partington commences Friday.'

That told him at any rate what the list of fabulous beasts implied. Leviathan was some kind of boss and Dragon some kind of servant or agent. But what was Tosos? Another imaginary animal? He tried his own pocket dictionary but it wasn't there. Bruce Partington, presumably, was some new man they had taken on. He had been out in the garden for half an hour, a trug full of weeds beside him, when he heard the phone ringing. He had half a mind to let it ring—but suppose it was Jennifer? Suppose it was Jennifer changing the time on Saturday or even the day, or even saying she wanted to come here to the house instead? His hands were earthy and there was dirt in his nails. You couldn't garden properly with gloves on. He ran indoors, not pausing to rinse his hands. The prospect of hearing her voice hung a weight on his chest, constricting his breathing. She had a soft, quiet, unhurried voice that never became impatient, but when excited was infinitely sweetened and enriched...He lifted the receiver in his earthy hand.

It wasn't Jennifer. It was Mark Simms. John had difficulty in suppressing an actual cry of disappointment.

13

MUNGO PATROLLED THE SAFE HOUSE WHILE HE waited for Graham O'Neill. It wasn't very light in there but it was light enough to see by. The house was a warren of small, high-ceilinged, badly proportioned rooms in which the last owners had left behind a certain amount of furniture. Mungo walked about in those rooms sometimes when waiting for one of his agents, liking the solitude and the decay, the ruined evidence of a lost life, an ancient pink silk chaise longue propped up on bricks where it had lost a leg, a chest of drawers from which all but one of the drawers had gone, the curtains that were rags held together by dust, scored by the depredations of moths, windows across which a blind of cobwebs stretched. You scraped away the cobwebs and held nothing in your hand but a shred of dry greyness. Through the clouded glass you could see the river like a metal strip undulating slightly, treetops that were still bare but reddish with buds, the cathedral spires and the tower with the digital clock on it, green, winding, eternal: six-forty-two and eleven degrees.

A narrow, very steep, flight of stairs led up to the top, the third floor, where there were two or three attic bedrooms under the sloping roof. It was a bit like his own room at home up there, but empty and forlorn. You could get out on to that roof by means of a trap door and a pair of steps strung up to the ceiling on ropes. Several times he had unwound the rope from the cleat and lowered the steps and climbed out on to the roof, parts of which were flat with broken metal railings, but one day someone had seen him and pointed up and for a while after that he had been afraid the owners of the house would find out people were using it and seal it off impenetrably.

It wouldn't start getting dark for two hours. Mungo, sitting on a table in the kitchen, on the greasy oilcloth that covered it, wondered why Medusa or Dragon had taken away the list of agents' aliases. He had wanted to add to it Cockatrice and Gryps, names for two new Lower Fourth recruits. Perhaps it was wiser to hold these things in one's head.

He wouldn't hear Graham come. To make audible movements, footfalls that could be heard, would have been a cause of shame to any of the names on the list. The door would simply edge open. Like all the other basement doors in this block of houses, that of number 53 had been locked and further secured by two wooden crosspieces, only here one of the battens had started to come away. It was this which had made them fix on 53. They had removed both pieces of wood and Charles Mabledene had picked the lock, got it open with one of his credit card implements. Waiting, watching the door, Mungo asked himself why it was he didn't much like Charles. Generally speaking, he wouldn't have admitted to a dislike of people younger than himself but excused the propensities in them he objected to on the grounds that they were just kids still. Not that he could have said what it was, if anything, in Charles that he objected to. On the other hand, you wouldn't ever think of describing Charles as 'just a kid still'. He somehow gave the impression of never having been a kid, indeed of being about thirty now and having been born that way. There was something cold and remote about him, something not exactly condescending—Mungo sought for a word—calculating, perhaps. Graham O'Neill felt the same about him. He and Graham usually did have similar feelings about people and things, which was why they got on so well, had become friends. His father was still friends with men he had been at school with, and Mungo liked the idea of that, in which there was something secure and enduring.

The O'Neills didn't live in the city but somewhere in Norfolk. Graham and Keith were only here until tomorrow when they were off to join their parents newly home from Saud. They had been staying with an aunt up at Hartlands. Graham might have difficulty in getting away, Mungo thought, he had no idea what the set-up was at this aunt's.

Silence prevailed. Distantly, sitting there in the dimness, he could hear the wail of a police car's siren. The door opened and Graham came in, closed the door behind him. Graham was tall—not so tall as he, but who was?—with dead black hair and a pale shiny face, long rather hooky nose and chin, gooseberry-coloured eyes like a cat's. Both O'Neills looked like that, though there was no problem telling them apart. Graham had jeans on that looked new and stiff because he seldom got the chance to wear them. In the middle of the front of his tee-shirt was printed an octopus with red and black writhing tentacles.

'The nearest I could get to a jellyfish,' Graham said. His alias was Medusa.

Mungo grinned. 'Are you going to be back here before term starts?'

'No way. We've got to go to Guernsey for a week.' Graham cast up his eyes. 'No way will I be back.'

'I'll see you in Pitt on the tenth then.'

'I've got something for you.' Graham handed him a small piece of paper, a page torn off a lined notebook.

'Minotaur to Medusa. Dragon advises planning permission granted. Definite repeat definite,' it said. Minotaur's family lived out in the country near Dragon's family, which accounted for the roundabout route the message had followed.

Mungo looked up from the paper, shaking his head

the way one does when wondering in an admiring sort of way. 'How did he do it?'

'Search me,' Graham produced from the pocket of his jeans a crushed dirty pack of cigarettes, offered them to Mungo.

Mungo shook his head. 'Do you have to smoke in the safe house?'

'That's all bullshit about passive smoking, you know. You wouldn't get cancer from my cigarettes if we sat here with me smoking for the rest of our lives. You ought to smoke anyway. It might stop you growing. You're always saying you wish you could stop growing.'

'How d'you reckon Charles Mabledene did it?'

'I told you I don't know. No way can I guess. Why do we always call that guy Charles Mabledene instead of just Charles? Have you ever thought of that? Why do we?'

'I don't know but I know what you mean.'

Graham snorted smoke out of his nostrils. 'Have you got any money?'

'Not what you'd call real money,' said Mungo.

'I don't mean real money. I mean enough for fish and chips. I fancy fish and chips.'

'OK. Anything to get away from your fags. You know what day it is, don't you? It's the thirty-first. New code starts tomorrow. The Bruce-Partington Plans.' Graham's face registered incomprehension. 'Why are all my officers illiterate? I bet Stern doesn't have this sort of thing to contend with.'

They were young enough still to lash out at each other in play but too old to keep it up. A year ago they would have grappled and rolled on the ground. Graham took a final sideswipe at Mungo who ducked and pulled the door open.

'Did you take the list off the wall?'

'Not me. No way.'

'It must have been Charles Mabledene then,' said

Mungo and realising he had done it again, they both laughed.

The fish and chip shop they went to was on the eastern side and was in a side street in a block of shops between Randolph Bridge and the Shot Tower. Claims were made that it was the best in town. Another distinction of this shop was that you could eat there too if there was room. There were four small marble tables only, each with only two chairs. All the tables were full. At the one nearest to the door sat Guy Parker with a girl. They were eating scampi.

'Good evening,' said Mungo in a breezy tone.

Guy Parker said hallo and gave one of his small grins, showing no teeth. The girl with him was rather plump and dark, olive-skinned and with black hair, the front of which was streaked with orange. At the counter Mungo gave their order, two portions of chips and two of skate, two pickled gherkins.

'Who's that with him?' he said to Graham.

'Don't you know?'

'I wouldn't ask if I did.'

'It's Rosie Whittaker. I heard he was giving her a whirl.'

'Hm,' said Mungo.

He thought he only liked beautiful women. Or he would only like them when he came to start thinking about going out with women. A tall thin blonde with a long neck and hair down to her waist and big green eyes, thought Mungo. Rosie Whittaker wasn't his cup of tea. He and Graham took their parcels of fish and chips. A table at the farther end from Guy Parker and Rosie Whittaker became free as the couple sitting at it got up to leave.

As they were sitting down Graham said quietly, 'Dragon never speaks to them, you know.'

'What do you mean?'

'Well, if he saw them like we did he wouldn't have said anything, he'd have just walked by.'

'Uncivilised,' said Mungo. He wanted to add something that he had felt about Charles Mabledene for some time, that he seemed to be without ordinary human feeling, but he did not care to say this to Graham. Not how —illogically and quite unfairly, he knew—it got up his nose rather the way Charles Mabledene had betrayed Stern. No more deeply dyed traitor could be found. Kim Philby had nothing on Charles Mabledene, for Philby presumably had done what he did for an ideal of Communism while Charles Mabledene had betrayed Stern for nothing more than power and glory. Of course he, Mungo, had taken absolute advantage of Charles Mabledene's betrayal and the West had profited by it. He was in no position to condemn the conduct of the agent who had taken the name of Dragon. 'Best bit of skate they've had here for a long time,' he said to Graham and Graham nodded his agreement.

14

COMING HERE AT ALL HAD BEEN UNEXPECTED. MARK, on the phone, had talked of meeting for a drink, had named his own new flat for the rendezvous. It was an invitation John would have refused if he could have thought of an excuse. But he had said a reluctant yes to Mark, with the proviso that he mustn't be late back. I sound like an old woman, he said to himself as he put the receiver down, and immediately he remembered how Jennifer had hated that expression, how she had said it was sexist.

'Why not an old man? Why are old women supposed to be stupider than old men?'

At the last moment he put Jennifer's jacket on. The evening was mild for the time of the year so he still needed his leathers, but the blue jacket was smart and comfortable and he reminded himself that he had felt shabby on Monday by contrast to Mark's neat dressing and good taste. Now in the flat in Fonthill Court they were seated by the window, looking down on to the trees and terraces and shrubberies of Hartlands Gardens and the lights coming on in the city and a huge expanse of darkening sky, still reddish at the horizon from the setting sun. Under observation John felt, exposed there, though there was no one to see him except possible aircraft crews. Mark had produced beer in cans, so cold that John had feared it must actually be frozen solid. It was becoming clear to him why Mark had wanted to meet him again and what he wanted to talk about.

'Have you ever done any encounter groups?' he had begun.

'Me? No, I haven't. I only just about know what they are. Why would I have done them?'

'Business people do. It's supposed to enhance social interaction.'

'Not my kind of business,' said John.

'I asked because they work on the same principle that it's good for you to talk about your feelings and hear other people's frank views on you and that sort of thing.'

At this stage John was mystified. The beer was headache cold. It brought on a niggling pain in one temple.

'It's just that I thought it might be good for us to talk about our feelings, it might help us. You and me, I mean. I've been thinking about this for a long time. Well, for years actually. Having—well, quite a lot in common really. I mean I thought it would do us both good to express our feelings about the other and our feelings in general really. It might bring a lot to the surface.'

The lights on the by-pass were a double string of yellow, the motorway white, the through road that became Ruxeter Road an old-fashioned soft amber. The CitWest clock could just be seen winking away, a lime green star too far off for John to read the time or the temperature. He turned to look at Mark. What things did they want to bring to the surface, what buried pain?

'Wouldn't you like to talk to me about Cherry?' said Mark. 'Haven't you got things you'd like to get off your chest? I'm sure you must have. You mustn't be inhibited about this, John. You can say anything to me.' How was it he realised then that Mark didn't really mean him at all? Mark meant himself, he meant that he wanted to talk to John. 'We've never talked about her, John. We buried it and then we pretended it hadn't happened.'

John wanted to say, speak for yourself, but he only nodded. He knew intuitively that little as he wanted to, he now only had to listen. In an hour or so he could make his escape. Mercifully, Mark seemed to have forgotten to replenish their glasses with more frozen beer. Not looking at John, leaning forward, his hands resting on the windowsill and staring out as if trying to identify some particular light down there, he began talking about Cherry. He talked about the first time he had taken Cherry out, the funny things she had said, about how six months later they had gone to buy the engagement ring and how she had wanted an opal. Opals were unlucky, even the shop assistant in the jewellers had been discouraging, but Cherry had asked how could a stone bring misfortune?

Mark paused. Then he said, 'Say something.'

'You're quite young still. You'll find someone else.'

'What do you know about it? How can you know? I hate that sort of specious advice. Bloody counselling.'

I've been married too, John wanted to say. But Mark

seemed to have forgotten this, to have forgotten that John was any more than a receiver or recording device. He talked on. He seemed to remember every word that Cherry had ever said to him, her clothes and what she had worn on particular days. It made John uneasy, for it seemed obsessive. It was all seventeen or eighteen years ago. He looked surreptitiously at his watch, but not surreptitiously enough.

'You want to go. I'm boring you. You're a very conventional person, aren't you, John? You'd sacrifice real living to a principle of going to bed at the right time and getting up at the right time. Life will always pass you by because your petty rituals are more important to you than your own or other people's pain or happiness. I'm being very frank. We agreed, didn't we, that we were going to be quite open about our feelings for the other one?'

John didn't think they had quite agreed to that. On his way home he told himself not to be offended, that Mark said things he didn't mean. St. Stephen's clock was striking midnight, it was April the first now. Intuitively, he felt sure there would be a new message at cats' green but he didn't go there until the following day and when he copied down the words on the paper he had no doubt he would be able to decipher them.

The first word of the message was nine characters long, the second two characters, the third six. John started placing them against the code alphabet. JKIFTVGHC OV WSZLKN. That was as unlike real words as the coded message itself. If, as seemed likely, the message began, 'Leviathan to Dragon', the TH of Leviathan should be AB in the code, not VG, and the T of 'to' would be A. John couldn't understand it. What had happened? More slowly this time, concentrating, he tried again. JKIFTV...And then he realised, he saw plainly what had happened. A new month had begun and they had changed the code.

They had made an April Fool of him.

ANGUS WASN'T KEEN ON MORNING SUNSHINE. HE had his bedlamp on. Mungo knocked politely, though the door was as usual wide open. Everyone in the house had to put up with Purcell or Gluck or whoever it might be until Lucy lost patience and told him to turn it off or shut the door. When Angus saw who it was he said, 'I don't suppose you happen to know who said, "Beware of all enterprises that require new clothes," do you?'

'Me? No, I don't know. Why would I? I came to ask if I could use the computer. As a great favour.'

'It would be easier if I just did it for you.' Angus looked penetratingly at him. 'You don't want me to know what it is, do you?'

'I don't mind. Not really. Only we ought to do it before lunch and catch the afternoon post. I want him to get it tomorrow.'

'Get what?' Angus got up and sat on the bed but he didn't turn Dido off.

Mungo closed the door. His father was out but he wasn't sure about his mother. She was usually at the hospital on Fridays. He explained about the planning permission and Blake and Charles Mabledene. Angus started to laugh.

'You're never going to write to Dad and tell him permission's been granted!'

'Why not?' Mungo said cautiously. 'I thought it would look official done on a computer. I've got a bit of the right paper. Well, it's not quite right but Dad won't know. It's City Council paper, not City Planning. I've had it ever since Hydra got ten sheets for me when he did the rates thing. I want to say there's been a supplementary meeting held in camera at which it was resolved to grant permission...'

'You mustn't sign it with Blake's name. You'd better make up someone. And I won't put that "in camera" bit, it's crazy. I suppose you're absolutely sure about this?'

'About it being true? Charles Mabledene is completely reliable. I'd trust him with my life.' As soon as he had said this Mungo knew he didn't really mean it. He wouldn't trust Dragon an inch but he knew he would get his facts right.

Angus switched on the computer and sat in front of it, commanding it to edit a new file. 'Suppose Dad rings up the planning people?'

'Why would he?'

'I don't know.' *Dear Dr Cameron*...Angus pattered away at the keyboard. 'What's your next project, Bean?'

'I'm getting all my officers working on finding out who it was dented in the wing of Unicorn's brother's car. And then I want two invitations for Graham and me to the Conservative Association's cocktail party. I've never been to a cocktail party. I reckon we ought to get that all wrapped up before term starts.'

ffffffffffffffffff **16** *fffff*

PETER MORAN HAD COME TO PICK JENNIFER UP ON the day she left John. She had wanted them to meet, she thought it might help John to understand. But it insulted John that Jennifer preferred this man to him.

He spoke in an effete public school drawl, spare of words, supercilious, seemingly indifferent to what anyone's opinion of him might be. And there was more to it than that. Later John thought he must have imagined this, it must be that just anything bad he could think of he had applied to this man, but in fact he had thought at once: there is something nasty about him, something awful. Of sexual deviation he knew little but he could sense its monsters lurking. Such a monster sat behind Peter Moran's eyes, he had thought, crouching behind those eyes that were dull as stones, screened by the windows of his glasses.

'Is this all the stuff you're taking, Jen? I thought you were coming for good, not the weekend.'

Since Peter Moran made no move to pick up her suitcases, John carried them down the path. He had a stupid hope the neighbours would think Jennifer was going off on holiday somewhere and this man was just her driver to the station. Peter Moran, watching him do this, said, 'Shades of Sacher-Masoch.'

Next time he was at the library John looked Sacher-Masoch up in an encyclopaedia and found out that he was a man who derived sexual enjoyment from suffering. He had accompanied his wife and her lover on a tour as their servant in order to witness their most intimate moments together. This, then, was how Peter Moran saw him. And his first thought was of that phrase when he awoke on Saturday morning. A dawn dream had developed out of it in which Jennifer and her lover disported themselves and he was in the humiliating position of waiting on them. After that he couldn't go back to sleep again.

The bedroom didn't look exactly dirty but frowsty and it smelled stale. He got up and dressed, opened the windows and began putting clean linen on the bed, sheets fresh from the laundry, white and crisp. When he bought this bed he had been afraid of lovemaking. His virginity, which had been nothing before he met Jennifer, which had seemed to him the normal condition of a single person, became a burden no longer willingly carried, a dragging weight and an absurd embarrassment. He would have felt it less if she had been a virgin too, only he knew she wasn't. There had been Peter Moran, and others for all he knew. More than once she had hinted to him that they ought to live together—his expression, a euphemism—before marriage but he had said not exactly that he respected her too much but that he wanted to save love-making for when they were married, for their wedding night. Smiling, she had accepted. Perhaps he should have minded that she showed no disappointment.

It was all right on the night. Strange what an application that common phrase could have. It was just all right. An exercise he had never performed before, as using some unfamiliar machine might be, but possible if one followed the directions. The earth didn't move, nor did he soar to heaven, and he was sure she didn't. It was enough for him in those early days that he had acquitted himself respectably. He knew how to do it, apparently, and he had certainly done it. The burden had been dropped and left behind in the middle of the road.

Two days before they were married she said she thought she ought to tell him that if Peter Moran ever came back and wanted her she would go to him. She wouldn't be able to help herself. Jennifer was tired and a bit weepy and he put this down to pre-wedding nerves. He didn't really believe her. Peter Moran was in America, she said, teaching at a college in the Middle West, though how she knew that when she never had letters from him John didn't know. John had laughed and said he would have something to say about his wife running off with an old flame. But in the Registrar's Office she had remarked on the fact that they were obliged to make no vows.

Between these sheets she was kind and polite to him, but after a while, after the time of indulgence was over, he didn't dare ask her for love more than once a week, and then not more than once a fortnight ...But he knew himself, he knew he would never speak to her about it. Frank talking, openness, wasn't in his line, the kind of thing Mark Simms seemed to advocate wasn't for him. To his astonishment it was she who approached the subject, who said with a sort of admirable simplicity that it was awful, their love-making, boring at best, painful at worst. She couldn't stand it, it would make her ill. She spoke so softly and gently but she was firm. Couldn't she, wouldn't he let her—she baulked a little here, but she came to him and put her arms round him—suppose she were to try to teach him? Suppose they were to try together?

And there began his happiness, the learning of love with a woman who loved him, or who he thought loved him. That which had been a novelty, a source of satisfaction of various kinds, became a glory and a sensuous triumph. 'Going to bed' took on quite a different meaning for him. She would draw back the curtains and fill the room with light, slip back into his arms and nuzzle him and whisper. Sometimes in the day she would embrace him downstairs and quickly lead him up to bed. She promised him she would never pretend to a pleasure she didn't feel, so he knew that first orgasm she had and all the subsequent ones were real and he had given them to her. Feverishly she talked while he moved and strove, 'yes, yes, yes' and his name repeated, and 'my darling!' and a cry of such evident bliss—from Jennifer who otherwise never made so loud a sound. Into the midst of this, at the peak of it, it seemed to him, when they had found each other and the heights of mutual sensuousness, Peter Moran came back and she left and went to him. Peter Moran came in his little Citroën Diane and sneered at John, comparing him to Sacher-Masoch, and then he took her away.

To distract his mind, or to attempt to, from the afternoon ahead, he got out his code notebook and studied it.

Already, because he knew the first word must be 'Leviathan' and the third 'Dragon' he had made a little headway. Then he had got stuck. But now, immediately, as if his subconscious had silently, during the night, been working on the problem, he saw what 'Tosos' meant. 'Ignore all Tosos commands' was now clear. It meant to disregard any messages that might be received in the *The Other Side of Silence* code. But did the bit that preceded it therefore mean that now April was here, a new month, the Bruce Partington code must be adopted? Who, anyway, was Bruce Partington?

Not some participant in this mini-Mafia, John thought. They all had those fabulous beast aliases. He might be an author of espionage fiction. He was rather disappointed when the librarian said they had no books by Bruce Partington. She looked through the author files they kept on a computer and showed John that there was no writer on record between Robert B. Parker and Harry Paterson.

'The name does ring a bell, though. I don't think it's actually a writer. More a name of something. Like a firm or a make of something.'

It didn't much matter. Next week, anyway, he might not have the time or inclination for breaking codes.

It was twenty-five past two when John walked through the main gates into Hartlands Gardens. He had had lunch, a very sparse lunch, and bathed and put clean clothes on, washed the dishes, dried them, put everything away and it was still only one-thirty. And then it was simply that he couldn't stay in the house any longer. He had to be out in the air and walking about.

A summer's day it had become, a freak hot day, the leafless trees having a strange look against that blue unclouded sky. The broad central walk which led from the gates of Hartlands Gardens up to the Douglas mansion were bordered with masses of golden-eyed white narcissi, thousands upon thousands of flowers, and their rich heady scent had been brought out by the heat. John left the main path and took a right-hand turning, heading for that part of the grounds that was always known as Lady Arabella's Garden, after the wife of Lysander Douglas who had designed it. It was a white garden that somehow managed to have flowers blooming in it at three seasons of the year. Yew hedges enclosed it and it was not until you had walked down one of the passages between them and under an arch that you could see the flowers at all. John was astonished to see so much in bloom, such a variety of narcissi, white tulips coming into flower, snowy arabis, ivory crocus just touched with mauve, honesty and some type of early iris he didn't know the name of. The branches of a cherry tree were clustered with fat buds, not yet open, but a clematis that overhung the wall of the small pavilion was covered with star-shaped delicate papery blossoms.

He found himself quite alone in the garden. The beauty of it, with the scents and the warm sun, affected him strangely so that he felt tremulous and weak. He could have gasped aloud. He sat down on one of the stone seats and thought, suppose she were to come in here now, come in from the other end behind the pavilion, and walk up to me? It was possible, it was even likely, for she couldn't be far away. He looked at his watch. Two-forty-five. Perhaps he would bring her back here after they had had tea. There were white violas growing everywhere between the stones, on the edges of the symmetrical flowerbeds, among the other flowers, as if the gardener had opened and scattered packet after packet of seeds. John thought, I shall will her to come in here now, and he closed his eyes, concentrating, praying really. But when he opened them he was still alone. Only a butterfly had arrived, a winter survivor, fluttering above the arabis and as appropriately white as its petals.

He left the garden and walked back towards the house along one of the high terraces. From these it was possible to look down on to the circular stone-paved courtyard where in summertime tables and chairs were set out and the doors to the restaurant thrown open. Normally, so early in the year, it would have been too cold for this but as John came along the narrow path and leaned over the railing, he saw that the tables were out and even one or two sunshades up. At a table in the full sun, sitting upright in her chair and apparently reading a newspaper or magazine spread out in front of her, was Jennifer.

She was dressed as he best liked to see her, simply enough in skirt, shirt and pullover, but the skirt must have been a very long very full one, for it spread out in thick folds nearly to the ground, showing only her fine slender ankles, her feet in pointed flat pumps. The sun shining on her hair had turned it to the tawny gold Rembrandt used for Juno's crown, John thought, admiring her, wondering if he could bear the pleasure that would come to him if she turned and saw him and waved, or if it would be too much for him, for his heart, and he would die of it.

His heart wasn't put to the test. She continued to read. She turned a page. He walked to the next set of steps, experiencing now that sensation we have when tremendous anticipation is over, when the end is achieved and the consummation come—an absence of thought and blankness of mind. Like an automaton he approached her table and she, hearing his footfalls, turned and got up, standing there and gradually managing to smile.

He understood very quickly that of course he couldn't kiss her or shake hands with her or even touch her hand. She said, 'Hallo.'

He said, 'Hallo, Jennifer.'

The long tweed skirt hung like a bell. She held her hands clasped up against her chest. Her fingers were bare, the wedding ring gone.

'It's good to see you.'

She nodded. It might mean anything.

'Would you like a cup of tea? Shall we have tea and cakes?'

'I don't want anything,' she said. 'You have cakes if you like. You've lost a lot of weight, haven't you?'

'I expect it's better for me.' He watched her pick up her magazine, fold it, start to put it into the big carrier of woven straw she had with her. 'If we're not going to eat,' he said, 'we could go for a walk. We could walk to the white garden. I've just come from there, it's beautiful, you'd like it.'

'I'd rather sit here. We may as well stay here.'

He knew then. He knew from her tone and the look on her face, a bored, rather miserable expression, anticipating an unpleasant task ahead, that she wouldn't be coming back with him. She sat down and he sat opposite her. The sun hadn't gone in but he had a feeling that it had. She put her left hand on the table and made nervous finger movements like someone testing the tone of a piano. And suddenly it seemed to him that sheepishness, passivity, would no longer do. What had he to lose from speaking? What to gain from this devoted humble patience? He had already lost everything.

'Why did you ask me to come here, Jennifer?' He surprised himself with the sharpness of his voice. 'What is it you want?'

'A divorce,' she said, looking him straight in the eye. 'I want a divorce.'

The clean sheets on the bed, he thought. He had made a fool of himself, if only to himself.

'Are you going to marry him?'

She nodded.

'And what guarantee will you have this time that he won't turn tail and leave you two days before the wedding?'

'That's my problem,' she said. The blood came up into her face and he exulted because he could still upset her. 'He won't, though. It's different this time.' She said quickly, in a rush, 'I don't want to wait two years. I want you to divorce me for adultery with Peter.'

'Why should I?'

'Because I ask you, John.' He winced at her use of his name. 'It was a mistake our marrying in the first place. We made a mistake.'

'I didn't make a mistake.' He found out of his misery a wonderful articulateness. He was able to express himself as he never had before, with perfect heartfelt lucidity. 'I fell in love and I married the woman I loved and as far as I was concerned I hoped and meant to stay married until I died or she did. I'm still in love and I still want that.'

'It's impossible!'

John burst out, 'What is there about him? He's not good-looking or good company as far as I can see.'

'He's clever and he's cool, he's an intellectual. He's funny. He makes me laugh. We speak the same language.'

That was bitter to hear. 'He hasn't a job, he can't even provide for you properly.'

'You don't love people because they're good breadwinners.'

'He deserted you once, he left you more or less at the altar. Did you ever find out why?'

'It doesn't matter,' she said. Her face looked as soft and vulnerable as one of those paper-petalled flowers that bloom for a day, that bruise at a touch.

'I'll never divorce you,' he said. 'You'll have to wait five years. But he'll have left you by then.'

He jumped up and walked rapidly away. He was determined not to look back and he didn't, keeping his eyes fixed on the green lawns ahead, the blue sky, the white shimmering mass of narcissi. Very nearly colliding with a woman walking towards him, he was surprised that there were other people in the world. He looked about him, saw children, a man with a dog on a lead, and felt dazed, stunned. For half an hour he and she had been the only man and woman on earth—and now there was only himself.

TWO DAYS AFTERWARDS THERE WAS A PIECE ON THE local television news about Lady Arabella's Garden. Even the white butterfly—perhaps the same white butterfly—appeared in the film, fluttering about. But the main item was concerned with the missing schoolboy. A boy of twelve, a pupil at Hintall's, the prep school, had disappeared on Saturday afternoon while out on a supervised nature walk. The last anyone had seen of him was by the river on the other side of Nunhouse where a group of boys, keeping very quiet and still, had been observing the behaviour of herons. During this silence and stillness James Harvill had vanished.

Any mention of Nunhouse caught John's attention. But it was to be quite a long time before he connected the disappearance of the boy with something in Jennifer's letter.

PART TWO

1

HE WAS ONE OF THOSE SMALL NEAT PEOPLE, THE kind that never look ungainly or, come to that, anything but spruce and spotless. Beside Mungo he seemed very small indeed. He had elfin ears, the tops of them not pointed but not rounded either, ever so slightly peaked. His pale hair was always sleek and well-cut. The squeaky voice that, nearly a year before, had told Mungo on the phone that its owner wanted to defect, was still unbroken. Trimly dressed in the clothes ordained for Rossingham casual wear, grey flannel trousers, dark green pullover, without a tie because it was after six, he accepted Mungo's offer and sat down at the study counter in the chair that was normally used by Graham O'Neill. There he cast the eye of one who is insatiably inquisitive over the books Mungo had been using for his French prep.

Mungo reached across and slid his attempt at a translation out of that eye's range and as he did so an arm came out and produced first an egg from his pullover sleeve and then a couple of dozen yards of paper streamers from his trouser pocket.

'Don't do that,' said Mungo. 'You make me nervous.'

Charles Mabledene smiled with his lips closed. That

was a habit with the Moscow Centre lot, they picked it up from Guy Parker, and it served to remind Mungo of Dragon's antecedents, as if he could ever forget them. His trousers fitted him snugly and his pullover was even rather small on him, far too tight to conceal an egg and all those streamers, yet egg and paper had unaccountably appeared and as unaccountably vanished.

'Why are you called Mungo?'

'After Mungo Park, the explorer. He was Scottish too and a doctor and we're all doctors in our family.'

'I've heard your brother call you Bean. Is that because of mung beans?'

Mungo felt irritated. 'I think so. I've forgotten.' He added, 'No one but my brothers calls me Bean, absolutely no one.'

The smile reappeared.

'I got you down here to ask you how you got that piece of information out of Mr Blake.'

'My mother asked him.'

'Your mother? All right, go on.'

'My mother wants to open a new salon...'

'A what?'

'A salon. A hairdresser's. I got her to ask the Blakes to dinner. She didn't know them but she does Mrs Blake's hair or one of her stylists does. And Mrs Blake kept on saying she wanted to see my mother's sauna. I'd told my mother I'd heard the doctors' place was coming up for sale, that a friend of mine had told me, and that was all I needed to say. Mr and Mrs Blake came to dinner and I knew she'd tell them, I knew that was why she'd invited them. Blake said he was surprised to hear that as he understood the doctors would be extending their premises.'

Simple. Mungo looked at diminutive Charles Mabledene, a child in looks if not in mind and guile. Still, no doubt he was reckoned sufficiently adult to be present at his parents' dinner parties...

'I wasn't there,' Dragon said. 'I taped it.'

'You what?'

The door opened and Graham came in, wearing tennis whites and carrying his racquet. Charles Mabledene got up courteously to give up his chair but Graham waved him away.

'It's OK. I'm going to have a shower.'

Coming out of the adjoining room where their two bunks were he slung the towel he had gone to fetch over his shoulder and six tennis balls all dyed different colours bounced out of it. Charles Mabledene's eyebrows went up and he smiled, without modesty.

'I was just saying,' he said, 'that I taped the conversation. Of course it's a bit muzzy and parts of it you can't hear at all on account of my having to conceal the recording device behind some dead grass. I mean, my mother goes in for these dried flower arrangements and I stuck it behind that.'

'Do you often do that?' asked Graham.

'If I think something useful might be said, yes.'

'Useful?'

'Something I could put to use,' said Charles Mabledene, and he began juggling with his coloured tennis balls.

After he had gone Mungo pondered for a while before returning to the passage from de Maupassant he was rendering into English. His father had believed in the letter and acted accordingly, or rather, not acted. By now, presumably, it being the last week of April, he would have had a real letter about the decision of a real meeting but Mungo wasn't going to worry about that. Fergus might find it odd but everyone was always saying how unaccountable councils and bodies like that were in their behaviour, apparently you came to expect anomalies. Dragon had done very well. Mungo asked himself why he found his methods distasteful. Or was it Dragon himself he found—well, not so much distasteful as somehow cold and repellent? After all, there wasn't anything strictly wrong about recording a conversation when the end you were going to use it for was good, was there? Mungo thought he had heard some saying or principle or whatever about the means being justified by the end or was it the end by the means? He would have to find out.

Half-term would be coming up in three weeks' time. Sports Day on the Saturday and then home on the Sunday until the following Monday week. So far no one had been able to discover the perpetrator of the damage to Unicorn's brother's car, though Mungo had had Basilisk, Empusa, Charybdis and Minotaur all working on it. Charybdis, whose real name was Nigel Hobhouse and who went to a day school in the city, might be getting somewhere by now. The great advantage he had over other agents, at any rate in Rossingham term time, was that his parents had a weekend cottage at Rossingham St Mary which meant that Charybdis could use the school grounds drop.

Mungo wrote the last two sentences, closed his dictionary and put it back on the bookshelf. He still had maths to do but that could wait. Out in the corridor he met Graham coming back from the showers and then Mr Lindsay. The Pitt housemaster was a zealous man, frequently on the prowl, his aim to keep every man in his house usefully occupied from morning till night. 'You look as if you might be at a loose end, Cameron' (or O'Neill or Mabledene or Ralston) was a favourite phrase of his.

This time, it being out of school hours, he addressed Mungo by his Christian name.

'I left my biology essay in the New Library, sir,' said Mungo.

This was true, as a matter of expediency as much as ethics. Mungo had taken care to leave his half-completed explanation of the working of a rabbit's alimentary canal on the desk where he had begun flexi-prep at six.

'That was careless of you.'

Mr Lindsay's speech was as spare and ascetic as his physical self. He seldom used adverbs; adjectives, sparsely indulged in, were never qualified. He had been a classical scholar, was reputed to have taken a Double First at Oxford but had few calls on his knowledge at Rossingham where Greek was no longer taught and Latin only as a special subject. This was a source of permanent frustration to him. By way perhaps of compensation, he laced his speech with Latin words and phrases.

'Our *biblioteca* will be locked up by eight-thirty, so you had better hurry. Oh, and Mungo...'

'Yes, sir?'

'If you are going to prowl about the grounds at dusk, may I suggest you slip into tracksuit and trainers? Running is one of the best forms of exercise, I'm told. *Currite, noctis equi*, or in this case *noctis pueri*.'

That meant Mr Lindsay must have spotted him going out to the drop. He didn't miss much but Mungo realised he must have been careless. Mr Lindsay now turned his attention to a member of the Lower Fourth heading for the Common Room and known for his addiction to commercial television.

'Finished your flexi-prep, Stephen?'

The New Library stood on its own, a rotunda, or at any rate an octagon, built only the year before Mungo came to Rossingham. In the same style of architecture as the physics and technology wing, nineteen-eighties Victorian, it was constructed of fashionably dark materials, dark red brick, black woodwork, dark grey polished slates. The trees for which Rossingham was famous, mostly limes and chestnuts, made a high screen behind these buildings, a screen on which the new young leaves looked livid at this hour. The fine weather of early spring had given place to a chilly greyness with sharp spurts of rain.

Mungo went into the library. Those who preferred to do their flexi-prep in here were sitting about at desks or the long pine tables that occupied the central aisle of the reference section. The supervising prefect, by a piece of luck, was Angus.

'I confiscated your essay, Bean,' Angus whispered, 'plus the obscene illustrations.'

'They're only a rabbit's innards,' Mungo protested.

Angus gave him the two sheets of paper. 'What are you up to?'

'Counter-intelligence, of course.'

Angus announced that it was eight-twenty-five. Five minutes to clear up in and he'd be closing and locking the doors. Mungo slipped out before he could get asked any more awkward questions. The drop was at the back of the cricket pavilion, on the other side of the pitch that was said to be the finest piece of grass in the West of England. Mungo had to skirt round it, keeping close to the hedge. The essay he had folded up and stuck inside his pullover, for the rain had begun again. A loose brick to the left of the foundation stone when removed revealed a deep cavity. Mungo eased it out and withdrew from inside a paper in a plastic bag. It was still just light enough to see the paper. 'Charybdis to Leviathan,' he read, but for the rest of it he would need the Bruce-Partington key...

ⲅⲅⲅⲅⲅⲅⲅⲅⲅⲅⲅⲅⲅⲅⲅⲅⲅⲅⲅⲅⲅ **2** ⲅⲅⲅⲅⲅⲅ

MARK SIMMS AND JOHN SAT IN JOHN'S LIVING ROOM, sharing a bottle of wine. The television was on and they were watching a programme of no interest to John and of little, he suspected, to Mark. But he was sick and tired of Mark and of his conversation, his criticism of John and defence of himself, his curious obsession with

Cherry and his memories of Cherry. Having this quiz programme on was a way of preventing or perhaps only postponing talk.

John knew that he had brought all this on himself. On that Saturday four weeks ago when Jennifer had told him she wanted a divorce and in his rage and misery he had walked away from her and out of Hartlands Gardens, he had been visited by a desire to get drunk. This was something he hardly ever did. He drank very little. The idea of getting drunk as even a temporary solution to his problems astonished him at the time. But it was what he needed, or thought he needed, as much because he dreaded being alone that evening as for the solace of alcohol. Hardly thinking, not permitting himself to reflect or reason, he had gone home and first phoned Colin Goodman, then when Colin said his mother wasn't well, Mark Simms.

They had gone to several pubs, then bought wine and taken it back to Mark's flat. John had not meant to say a word about Jennifer to Mark but the drink in its well-known way had overcome his inhibitions and later that night he had come out with it, all of it. Mark hadn't been very sympathetic. He was a tremendous egotist, too self-centred to care much about the suffering of others and his comments had been of the 'Forget her' and 'Make a clean break' kind. In a way this had been more acceptable to John, for he was pretty sure that by now Mark had forgotten all that had been said to him.

Without actually disgracing himself, John had succumbed to the unaccustomed amounts of wine and fallen asleep. He was obliged to stay the night on Mark's settee. Since then—and he realised he had only himself to blame—there had been no possibility of putting Mark off. Indeed, Mark rather took it for granted that they should spend the greater part of their free time together. Yet John didn't think Mark particularly liked him or preferred his company over that of others. He was just a listener, a presence instead of a void.

He hadn't mentioned Jennifer again, though he had come to believe that it was only while he was with Mark, and perhaps to a lesser extent while he was dealing with customers at work, that he was not thinking of her. She had written to him during the intervening time, the first letter was cold, the second pleading. John had replied to the second one, refusing to meet her and Peter Moran as had been suggested and reaffirming his intention to remain married to her. Curiously, since writing that letter, his heart had ached less. Decisiveness made him feel stronger, convincing him he might prevail. This morning, though she had not asked for it, he had wrapped the blue leather jacket up in a parcel and sent it off to her with a covering letter saying he knew she would return to him, it was only a matter of time. And then he had cleaned up the living room, taking curtains and chair covers to the dry cleaners, and on the way back made a detour to cats' green to look inside the flyover upright.

There was nothing there. There had been nothing there since he had found the second message in the new code. That had been on 9 April, the day he had made up his mind not to consider a divorce. Feeling if not more cheerful at least more positive, he had gone to the flyover and found the message. Of course he had been unable to decipher it. A search of the city's Hatchards and its six other bookshops, new books and secondhand, had failed to discover a Bruce Partington among the authors. But the searching had been good for his morale. Now, though, the messages had ceased to appear. Did that mean they were no longer using the cats' green location or something more sinister?

Another thing that had changed was his level of drinking. Under Mark's influence he was drinking a lot—for him. Not spirits but beer and wine, a lot of wine, at least a bottle every time they met. It had the effect of making him sleep heavily and not think about

Jennifer during those vulnerable night hours, and for some reason not even dream about her. He reached across and re-filled Mark's glass, laughing because it seemed expected of him at some outrageous reply made by a contestant in the quiz game. Because the windows were uncurtained all the headlights from all the cars that passed made bands of light that rushed across the ceiling and down the walls. The programme came to an end and football started. Mark reached for his glass and John picked up the *Free Press*. He had lately got into the habit of going through it story by story to see if there was ever anything that might give him a clue to the group he called the mini-Mafia. Mark watched the football for no more than ten minutes. He switched the television off without asking John.

'The way those lights keep flickering across the ceiling is very irritating,' he said. 'It makes it impossible to relax. Why don't you have curtains or blinds or something.'

'I told you, they're at the cleaners.'

'You should have had them done express,' said Mark. He began on one of his favourite criticisms of John, his condemnation of what he called John's 'cheeseparingness'. John caused himself absurd inconvenience by penny-pinching. The absent curtains were a case in point. And why did they have to bring wine and beer in by the bottle and can when anyone else would have beer in the fridge and a rack full of wine? His face, though handsome, had a peevish look, John noticed not for the first time, a sour down-turning of the mouth, a pinching of the nostrils. But the wine had so thoroughly quelled his own social inhibitions that he even picked up the paper again and searched idly for some reference to a gang or disreputable syndicate.

'The least you could do is give me your attention while I'm telling you these things. You must be the only living soul I've opened my heart to in this way. It's rather galling, to say the least, that you prefer the columns of the local rag.'

John said he was sorry. Another part of his mind was wondering if the two men charged the day before at the Crown Court with possessing heroin could have anything to do with these messages. One of them was called Bruce, though his surname was Chambers. Mark suddenly asked him what he was thinking about. He could tell he had something on his mind. John didn't make it up or say it because he thought it would please Mark. It came, unsummoned, into his head.

'I was just remembering something about Cherry.'

'What? What were you remembering?'

'How she used to spend a lot of time with an old neighbour of ours, a more or less bedridden woman, a Mrs Chambers. She used to go shopping for her and sit with her, just drop in and sit with her. She was a very kind, thoughtful girl, wasn't she? But of course you know that.'

'You know nothing at all about women, John,' Mark said. 'You've had three women in your life, your mother and Cherry and that wife of yours and you don't know a thing about any of them. You don't know a thing about women.'

'You talk about women as if they were a different species,' John protested.

'That's just what they are.' Mark began driving the corkscrew into the cork of the long-necked hock bottle. 'The way you talk about Cherry proves you didn't know her. You saw what you wanted to see, not what was really there.'

'Are you saying she went to old Mrs Chambers for some ulterior motive or something?'

'Oh, forget old Mrs Chambers. I'm not talking about that.' He pulled the cork out with a long whoosh and John saw how red his face had become. The wine was poured—slopped, rather. John took his wet slippery glass. 'I knew Cherry, I knew her too bloody well.' And then Mark started to laugh. He lay back against the settee cushions, bare and crumpled without their covers, and laughed in drunken whoops. He reached for the bottle and drank from it, the wine slurping down his throat. John turned his back on him, picked up the glasses and took them to the kitchen. Returning after a few minutes, he found Mark fast asleep. The wine bottle had fallen over and wine poured out over the bookcase with his father's books in it.

John heaved Mark's legs up on to the settee, went upstairs and fetched a blanket to cover him. He got a cloth from the kitchen and set about wiping the books, his father's favourite classic detective stories. He had to wring out the cloth in the sink and this time he fetched a bucket back with him. The Conan Doyle books were in the worst state and one of them would have its pages permanently corrugated. John started on the Sherlock Holmes collections, the *Memoirs, His Last Bow*. Opening this volume, he began to wipe the pages and his eye was caught by the title at the beginning of one of the stories, 'The Bruce-Partington Plans'.

I've found it, he thought. Not a man, not an author, but the name of a story. And a story about spies. I shouldn't wonder. And then he understood that it was too late anyway. Half an hour past midnight, his watch told him. It was May the first. A new month had begun.

ƒƒƒƒƒƒƒƒƒƒƒƒƒƒƒƒƒƒƒƒ **3** ƒƒƒƒƒƒ

LIGHTS-OUT FOR THE LOWER FOURTH WAS NINE-FIF-teen. When Fiona Ralston heard that flexi-prep didn't end till nine but her Nicholas was still expected to be in bed and composing himself for sleep by a quarter past, she said it sounded like Tom Brown's Schooldays. Mr Lindsay had done his best to explain that a boy was not obliged to be still doing prep at nine, he could get it all done by seven if he chose, this was why it was flexi, but Mrs Ralston was unconvinced. She didn't care for the names of the houses either. If there was a Churchill why wasn't there a Lloyd George? If a Gladstone, why not a Disraeli? She had to be content with her Nicholas being put into Pitt, a statesman who had lived so long ago as hardly to have been, in today's terms at any rate, of any particular political persuasion.

Her elder son, nearly ten years his brother's senior, had been at a comprehensive school. That was in the days before the Ralstons made money. Ralston the elder had come to fetch Nicholas on the last day of the spring term, taken him into the city for tea, and while they had been eating cream pastries in the Fevergate Café, someone had backed his or her car into Ralston's parked car, smashing the headlamp, breaking off the wing mirror and denting the wing. The cost of repairing the damage was estimated at six hundred pounds. Witnesses there had certainly been but no witness came forward. The police weren't interested, for no injury to anyone had occurred. Ralston would either pay up himself or, if his insurance company paid, lose his no-claim bonus. Autoprox was what Mungo called the investigation. A significant fact was that a flat in the building overlooking the car park was said to be occupied by the sister of Mrs Whittaker, Rosie Whittaker's mother.

Of all this Angus Cameron knew very little. Spookside interested him now only insofar as it affected his brother Mungo. He very much wanted Mungo kept out of trouble until he grew out of this obsession of his. Passing along the second-floor corridor on his way upstairs—as you ascended the ladder of seniority at Rossingham so you descended the stairs for your study accommodation—Angus glanced through the glass panel in Mungo's door. Graham O'Neill was there, drawing some sort of diagram on a sheet of file paper, but Mungo was not. There was no reason why Mungo should be there at nine in the evening, Angus reassured himself. His prep was very likely done. He could be at the drama society of which he was a member or the chess club or even in the common room watching television. Lights-out for the Upper Fourth wasn't till nine-forty-five. I get all these guilt feelings, Angus told himself, because I started it all. I and Guy Parker were responsible for it.

He went up the last flight. All but ten members of the Lower Fourth had by now received their first summer term pep talk from a prefect and only those in the study at the far end remained. Angus made a noise on purpose as he approached, walking more than usually heavily and clearing his throat. There were scuffling sounds from behind the door. They were all in bed, sitting up breathless and rumpled, when he entered the room. Or all but Charles Mabledene whose bunk, for some reason, always looked cleaner than anyone else's, the top sheet as if it had just been ironed, the pillow plump and uncreased. Charles's bunk had no poster over it, no mobile hanging from the bunk above, no snowstorm paperweight or china pigs or polythene monster on the bedside shelf. It was odd, reflected Angus, how when you thought about Charles Mabledene you somehow pictured him as looking Chinese. In fact he didn't look in the least Chinese, for he was fair of hair and light of eye, and his cheekbones were not high nor his face broad. Was this illusion perhaps founded on the smooth blankness of his features and the inscrutability of his expression?

Nicholas Ralston was in the bunk above, a photograph of himself and his golden retriever puppy on the shelf beside him. He was big for his age and unfortunately spotty. The Harper twins, younger brothers of that Harper who was Hydra, the double agent, were in the next pair of bunks, then Robert Cook, then Patrick Crashaw...Angus was a conscientious prefect and knew the names of everyone in Pitt. He frowned mildly at the disorder, an overturned wastepaper bin, a drift of pencil sharpenings, dirty tee-shirts, shorts and socks dropped where they had been taken off.

'The linen lady's going to have something to say to you lot,' he said.

'Crashaw,' said Charles Mabledene who always called everyone by his surname, 'will clear it up in the morning.'

'You'll all clear it up in the morning,' Angus said, severely for him. 'You know very well nobody's to be turned into the study servant. Right?' He sat down straddling a chair, his arms along the back of it. They sat waiting for him to begin, knowing what to expect, wanting only to defer the moment of lights-out. 'Well, you're coming up to the end of your first year at Rossingham,' Angus began, 'and I think you've all settled in pretty well, don't you, and found your feet? I'd like to think you were enjoying the place too and that's what I...'

Downstairs, in his study on the second floor, Mungo stood looking down at Graham who still sat with a felt-tipped pen in his hand.

'Are you saying we've got a leak in the department?' Graham said.

'What other explanation is there? I smelt a rat first when Rosie Whittaker never took up that dead letter at the Mabledene garage drop. I sent her there but she never went. And no one knew I'd sent her outside the firm. Even Angus didn't know.'

'We've got a mole in London Central, is that what you're saying?'

'This is what every departmental head dreads, Graham,' said Mungo. 'You know what I'm afraid of, don't you?'

'That when you get home at half-term you'll find planning permission for that extension was refused, not granted.'

'Absolutely,' Mungo said.

4

THE KING CAT HAD A CARCASE OF SOMETHING HALF-hidden under the bushes. It was meat or fish and it emitted a pungent reek. As John approached, the king cat began a threatening sing-song noise. There were half-grown kittens everywhere in the long grass, thin and leggy, with pointed faces and hungry eyes. It was all too much for John who began to sneeze. The king cat picked up his carcase and fled across the road with it. John came to the central pillar and looked up inside it but there was nothing there. There had been no message, either in the Bruce-Partington code or whatever might have succeeded Bruce-Partington, for five weeks.

He would have to resign himself to the likelihood that it was all over. It might very well be that the moving spirit behind it had been the man Chambers who had been charged with possessing heroin. And certainly the last message, which with the help of the short story in *His Last Bow*, John had been able to decipher, seemed to point to some drugs connection. 'Dragon to Leviathan: No news on bang. Awaiting developments.' John had a vague idea 'bang' might be a slang term for heroin. When he went to the library in Lucerne Road and looked it up in the appropriate dictionary he found the word defined as meaning narcotics in general or an injection of a narcotic or a marijuana cigarette.

He was on his way to work. They were coming up to one of the busiest times of the year. In the garden centre Gavin was trying to teach the mynah bird to talk.

'I'm a basket case,' he said. 'I'm a basket case.'

John hadn't the least idea what he meant. The mynah said, 'Ha ha ha, damn!' which was all it ever did say. It was a handsome bird, about ten inches long, with glossy black feathers and white wing patches. Its beak and legs were yellow and its wattles the orange of marigolds.

'I'm a basket case,' said Gavin, his face up to the bars of the cage. 'I'm an empty nester.'

John told the boy called Les to open the front doors and hook them back. A woman came in and went straight to Sharon's counter asking for plant-food spikes. In the houseplant house there was a subtle fresh scent that arose from the damp foliage of begonias and ivy-leaved geraniums. John walked along the central aisle, plucking out from the fibre pots an occasional tiny weed. It was Thursday and his half-day. He and Mark Simms were supposed to be going out into the country in Mark's car to a village where there was quite a famous pottery. There Mark meant to buy two large ceramic pots to stand in his large window and which he would fill with an oleander and a *Ficus benjamina* from the garden centre.

'I hope you don't mind my saying so,' Colin Goodman had said when they encountered each other by chance at lunchtime the day before, 'but it's a bit peculiar, isn't it, spending all your time together, the way you and Mark do? I mean I don't want to imply anything, but it seems a bit strange, you both being men if you see what I mean.'

John saw what he meant. He also thought it absurd coming from Colin whose remarks suggested he himself took women about when in fact he led a celibate existence, living in his mother's bungalow.

'You know me better than that,' was all John said.

It wasn't as if he wanted to spend all this time with Mark. But he had begun to be afraid to say no, afraid, that is, about Mark's mental state if he said no. He thought Mark might be on the verge of a nervous breakdown. Besides, though he had felt angry on the previous Saturday night, his feelings had been much softened by Mark's subsequent behaviour. He reminded himself too that it was Mark who, though unwittingly, had twice provided him with clues to the mini-Mafia codes. In the morning the apologies had been unexpectedly profuse. Mark said he didn't know what had come over him, what was the matter with him these days. Or, rather, he did know but John was the last man he could confide in.

'Though, frankly, you've been my lifeline these past few weeks, John. I don't actually know how I'd have gotten by without your support.' He added rather pathetically, 'I'm all right when I'm not drinking, aren't I?'

He was even more carping and critical when he wasn't drinking, John thought, but he didn't say so. And on the Monday evening Mark had made restitution by coming round to Geneva Road with a magnificent leather-bound copy of the complete Sherlock Holmes stories and all the volumes of Father Brown in paperback. After that John couldn't very well refuse the invitation to go out to Rossingham St. Clare and the pottery place even though this would entail a meal out afterwards and the inevitable bottles of wine taken home. Mark's hands had started shaking again after he had handed over the books and sometimes John saw an awful expression on his face. He would be staring at the wall or the window with his eyes very wide and that frown very deep as if he could see something abominable, but of course there was nothing there to see.

A stout white-haired man with his elderly wife and an infant who was probably a grandchild was asking Gavin about the mynah. How old was it? Would it bite? How much was it? Gavin looked alarmed.

'You wouldn't want him around kids. There's a disease you can get from mynahs. Newcastle's Disease, it's called. How about a budgie?'

Later he told John with an air of guile that this was an illness to which only birds were subject. He led them off to look at budgerigars. John put his hand into the pocket of his jacket under the canvas work coat and felt the letter he had put there after he had read it that morning. Jennifer was trying again for a meeting between him and her and Peter Moran. They should all talk about this divorce like reasonable people. John thought that a funny way of putting it, as if they weren't reasonable people but should try to behave as if they were. Perhaps there was no such thing as a reasonable person.

Could he bear to see her in the company of Peter Moran? Suppose they touched each other in his presence? If he saw Peter Moran even touch her hand or look at her in a certain way he could not answer for what he might do. Why then was he even considering the possibility of seeing them? There was no question of his divorcing Jennifer, for he knew that if he waited Peter Moran would eventually behave as he had done before and leave her. Or go back to whatever it was he really preferred doing to making love to Jennifer. John asked himself if he was contemplating agreeing to meet them because in this way, and only in this way, he would have a chance of seeing Jennifer again. If this were true it was pathetic and humiliating.

A customer was standing meekly beside him holding up a handful of seed packets. John apologized and hastened to answer the stream of questions put to him about seeds which the packet said would grow into a banana passion flower.

'Ha ha ha, damn!' shouted the mynah bird.

In the pottery shop, which was dim and cavernous inside and smelt of clay, Mark bought two large earthenware jars ornamented with flowers and swags and silenus faces, and John, though he had not meant to, found himself buying a lamp with a heavy bulbous base glazed in grey and coffee brown. In the back of his mind was a half-formed idea of arranging that meeting in his house and of making the place look more attractive before this happened. The chair covers had come back from the cleaner's and the curtains were up. Why not splash out a bit and buy those two jugs to match the lamp and a couple of flower pots too that he could put geraniums in . . . ?

'You were the one who didn't care about coming,' said Mark, 'and you've bought more than I have.'

He seemed particularly nervous today. John hadn't been able to relax in the car. Mark had overtaken a truck as they were coming out of Ruxeter and for a terrible few seconds John hadn't thought they were going to make it. Sweating, his mouth stretched into a gargoyle grimace, Mark had pulled in just in time to avoid an oncoming removal van. But he drove back to the city in an apparently calmer frame of mind, talking to John in a very ordinary rational sort of way about what plants to put in the new pots and even asking his advice. Only when John explained to him that Trowbridge's would be closed now, that this was the one afternoon of the week that they closed, did he begin grumbling again, asking what the country was coming to, how could Britain expect economic stability when shops still kept to that ridiculous old-fashioned early closing system?

A newly opened Indian restaurant called the Hill Station in Alexandra Road was suggested as a desirable place to eat. Mark wanted to go into a pub first and parked the car on a meter in Collingbourne Road. Fontaine Park was a mass of greenery, its lawns scarcely visible between the beeches and sycamores. Since John had penetrated the condemned house all the trees had come into leaf and it was scarcely possible any longer to see its rear windows from here. He looked curiously at the front of the house as they passed it but its boarded-up ground-floor windows and metal-sealed front door gave nothing away. Suppose, when he looked up, he had seen a face at a first- or second-floor window? The face perhaps of the very tall young man who had come that evening to the cats' green drop? John was not at all sure he would know that face again. Perhaps it had been the man called Chambers.

Mark pushed open the saloon-bar door of the Gander. It was the kind of pub John most disliked, an inner-city pub of Edwardian origin with a lot of stained glass, ornate but dirty ceilings, marble tables, apathetic barmaids and strident clientele. A strong smell of beer met him on a hot wave.

Mark said, 'Oh God, we forgot to buy any wine for later.'

John would have been happy to go on forgetting, though he knew that when the wine was there he would drink it. It wasn't yet five-thirty with half an hour to go before the wineshop in Ruxeter Road would close. John was given a half-pint of lager and settled at a corner table while Mark went off in quest of cheap Riesling. All the time they had been out Mark hadn't once mentioned Cherry and John was glad of it. He felt that Mark had a very different picture of Cherry in his memory from the one that he personally cherished and he was made to feel uneasy when they came into conflict. Mark seemed to remember her as some sort of beautiful goddess, a fatal woman, while to him she was the little sister he had first realized was ugly when she was eleven years old.

But without Cherry, or Mark's marriage, which was another favourite subject he hadn't touched on, what on earth would they have to talk about? The empty evening seemed to yawn before him. It would end perhaps in silent moody drunkenness. An idea came suddenly to him. Why not ring up Colin and get him to join them? If only, between the three of them, they knew some women! But John didn't really want to know any women except Jennifer. He had a notion that a married man shouldn't really know other women, except as casual acquaintances.

Mark took the suggestion about Colin with his old belligerence.

'I'm boring, I suppose?'

He drank nothing but beer during the meal. Wine, John had often reflected, doesn't seem to go with spices and curries. It had been somehow taken for granted that they would end the evening at Mark's flat, though this would mean John's taking a taxi home unless Mark were still sober enough to drive him. Silence prevailed while they were eating and John was able to relax a little. It was still broad daylight and the evening had become much warmer with one of those unheralded rises in temperature that sometimes occurred at about this time of day in late spring. Mark said as he started the car:

'Do you know what day tomorrow is?'

'It's May the twenty-second.'

'It's Cherry's birthday,' Mark said. 'She would have been thirty-five.'

John felt a sinking of the heart. Not because he had forgotten Cherry's birthday, he would have remembered it next day, and it wasn't important anyway, remembering her birthday. But he sensed that Mark had used this ploy to bring the conversation back to her or, rather, to resume where they had left off last Monday.

'She might have had teenage children by now,' Mark said.

He was driving up the steep road that skirted Hartlands Gardens, the terraces of which, hung with blossoming trees and others in full fresh leaf, fell away to the house in its parkland and to the city below, its spires and towers and grey slate roofs, the curling river, the green everywhere among the brick and stone. The sky, now the sun had gone, was melon-coloured, a very pale red-gold.

Suddenly Mark began speaking rapidly, a high-voiced gabble. 'The first time I ever came to your home, to your parents' house, I thought it was wonderful, I'd never known anywhere like it. Everybody was so nice to everyone else, polite and kind and sort of praising everyone. I'd had a rotten childhood. My parents never spoke to each other unless they had to.

I never heard them say anything pleasant to each other, not ever. My father was always telling me horrible things about my mother behind her back, how hopeless she was and stupid and how he had married her when he was too young to know any better. And my mother used to tell me he'd ruined her life and hint at appalling sorts of sexual mistreatment. I went away to college and never went back, I just lived in furnished rooms after that. I'd never known what a real home was till I met Cherry and she took me to Geneva Road. Do you know one of the first things that happened when I got there? Your father came home from work. He put his arm round your mother and said, "How's my sweetheart?" I've never forgotten that. I never will. I thought, one day I'll marry Cherry and we'll be like that. We'll still be like that when we're old.'

'We were an exceptionally happy family. All that changed, of course.'

Mark took no notice. 'Your father asked Cherry's opinion of something. He asked her what she thought. It was some international thing, something out of the paper, not women's stuff. I couldn't believe it. And she answered him very intelligently but it was the way she answered I'll never forget. He was sitting down and she laid her hand on his shoulder and her cheek against his hair. She called him Daddy. She was eighteen but she still said Daddy. I thought she was lovely. I was breathless and sort of frightened because I thought she was too good for the likes of me and I might so easily lose her.'

Mark threw back his head and broke into a horrible kind of staccato laughter, cold and humourless and self-mocking. He banged his foot on the accelerator and the car shot into the Fonthill Court car park, juddering and squeaking to a halt.

Mark opened the first bottle before he had even sat down. He went straight into the kitchen with it. John sat in the window looking at the clear sky whose colour was now a greenish gold, already punctured by a few bright winking stars. It gave him a strange feeling sitting there, so exposed, so out on a perch, as if he might suddenly be precipitated off the edge. In the gardens below, the thickening foliage was a deep, dense and mysterious green. The flickering tower pointed up to the stars, to the transparent slice of moon.

John didn't know why, he was sure there was no cause for it, but he had a sense of panic, as of something awful being about to happen. In that moment—for there was a precise moment at which he became aware of this feeling—he knew that he ought to get up and go. He ought to go out and find Mark, tell him he felt ill or had remembered some appointment, run out into the street and find a taxi or walk down and get the bus. Mark would be offended and might never speak to him again but what would that really matter? John knew his being there wouldn't really save Mark from having a breakdown if such a thing was imminent. And he desperately wanted to go. If that window had opened on to a lawn, would he have stepped out quietly and vanished without a word to Mark?

Convention held him back. Mark had said he was ruled by convention and it was true. Abruptly to leave someone who was opening a bottle of wine for the two of you to share was something he couldn't do. It must be surely that he would prefer to face whatever was coming to him than provoke a scene with Mark or have to stand up to him. But nothing was coming to him, it was all nonsense, all imagination...

Mark walked in with the bottle on a tray and two glasses already filled. The dishes of nuts and crisps John served were never provided here. John put out his hand for the glass with a sense that it was too late now. Whatever was going to happen would happen.

Mark said, 'D'you want a light on?'

The sky was so glowing still, the city such a bright galaxy of lights, that John had scarcely noticed how dim it had grown indoors. He looked into the shadows of the room, then up at Mark. It was a distorted face that he saw, its expression that same staring look of horror.

'I suppose so,' John said. 'It will be dark soon.'

Mark drank his glass of wine at what seemed to be one swallow. He immediately refilled the glass, his hand trembling, slopping the wine.

'I don't want lights,' he said in a fierce belligerent way. 'I want the dark. You'll have to sit in the dark whether you like it or not.'

John shrugged. 'OK.' The wine was sharp. He was aware of its cold passage down through his chest and of a tremor of nausea. 'Look at that sky,' he said. He had to say something. 'Look at that wonderful clear colour. It's going to be a fine day tomorrow.'

'It's going to be a fine day tomorrow,' Mark mocked him. He was still standing. He was standing over John. 'It's enough to make anyone puke the way you go on. Clichés and small talk. You're programmed, did you know that? You're a floppy disk the Great Computer Programmer has put a file of words and phrases on. Two hundred for average daily use. That's a good name for you, floppy disk. I think I'll call you that. It implies feebleness and learned responses in the right proportions. Christ, no wonder that wife of yours left you. What did you say to her every night before you went to bed, floppy? "It's going to be a fine day tomorrow. Me for Bedford. Up the wooden hill"?'

John knew that he hadn't blushed but had turned very pale. Mark was still standing there, shaking all over now. And suddenly, to John's horror, he fell on his knees. He fell on his knees at John's feet and lifting up his face holding up his hands, muttered at first incoherently, then all too articulately, that he was sorry, that he didn't know what had come over him, that he was a bastard.

'I don't know why I say these things. I take it all out on you. I can't go on like this, behaving like this. I'll crack if I don't tell you. It's been weeks since I've known I've got to tell you, that's why I got in touch in the first place, but I'm a coward, I couldn't do it. So I insult you instead. Say you forgive me.'

An inkling of his own value, that he too had his rights, that he shouldn't be Mark's punching bag, held John back. He wouldn't say it. Why should he, after the things Mark had said? Mark had attacked him without provocation in his most vulnerable part. Instead he said:

'What is this you've got to tell me?'

'Please forgive me, John. Later on you won't be able to forgive me.'

'Get up,' John said. 'Don't kneel there.'

Mark slid back across the floor. He sat on the floor with his back to a chair and his face in shadow. The second glass of wine was swigged down like the first and looking with open eyes at John, he said:

'I killed her.'

'What? You did what?'

'I killed her,' Mark said. 'I killed Cherry.'

ƒƒƒƒƒƒƒƒƒƒƒƒƒƒƒƒƒƒƒ **5** ƒƒƒƒƒ

FERGUS CAMERON WAS GLAD IT WAS ALL OVER. HE could never attend a Sports Day at Rossingham without remembering that terrible Sports Day in 1953, a week after the Coronation, when he had been beaten in the putting the shot event by a rank outsider from Churchill. Everyone knew he would win, he had no rivals, yet here quite suddenly was this newcomer from a new house—Churchill was then only four years old—and as soon as the shot flew from his hand Fergus knew it was all up with him. Strange how it still rankled after more than thirty years. Hobhouse,

the Churchill man's name had been, but his boys
didn't come here, he wouldn't be here.

Fergus remembered how he had congratulated Hobhouse and, with his heart full of bitterness and rage,
held out his hand and grinned while an inner voice
whispered to him that it was winning and losing which
mattered and to hell with playing the game. A lot of
water had flowed under Rostock, Alexandra, St. Stephen's and Randolph since then.

'I pity that one's son,' he whispered to Lucy, indicating an amazing woman who looked like a magazine
cover with purposely tangled stripy hair and a dress that
was a knitted tube of emerald green with an armour-
plated belt round the middle.

'I've a notion boys don't mind as much as they used
to,' said Lucy.

'Human nature doesn't change.'

'You know who it is anyway, darling. It's Mrs Mabledene who's married to the garage man. She's a hairdresser. Well, she's got a hairdressing shop.'

She began a conversation with the O'Neills' aunt.
Their parents were back in Saud. The tent had been
decorated with hanging baskets, white flowers and
green foliage, the Pitt colours, by Mrs Lindsay. Angus
appeared with a tray of teacups and tuckshop cake. He
had rather distinguished himself by coming third in the
long jump while Mungo, hardly famous for his sports
prowess, had at least been among the first five in the
mile. Mungo, whom Fergus hadn't yet spoken to, now
joined them rather breathlessly. He was still wearing his
green and white striped tee-shirt and shorts, though
Angus had changed into grey flannels and blazer as be-
fitted a prefect.

'That lady in the green dress is Mrs Mabledene,'
said Angus, starting on madeira cake. 'Don't you think
she's very beautiful? She is my idea of an English
beauty.'

'What an extraordinary thing to say!' exclaimed
Fergus.

'Why? You mean you don't think she's beautiful?'

'I certainly do not but that isn't what I meant. Please don't take this amiss, Angus, but I do think it is a most peculiar and unnatural comment for a male person of your age to make.'

'Hardly unnatural, darling. Anyway, I'm always telling you times change. Your sons aren't carbon copies of you.'

Mungo had been sitting in a kind of bursting silence as if unless a lid were quickly removed he would explode. Now he said on rather a high monotone:

'Did you get planning permission, Dad?'

'What?' Fergus seemed confused. He looked from the younger to the elder of his sons with an almost distressed bewilderment, and then back again at Mungo's intense staring face.

'Did you get planning permission? For the surgery extension? Did they say you could do it?'

'Yes. Oh, yes. Of course they did. Weeks ago now. I told you I'd had a letter before you went back to school.'

Mungo said warily, 'And that was all right, was it?'

'What do you mean all right? Of course it was. Why shouldn't it be?'

'I just wondered.' Mungo wondered whether he dared, then decided he must. 'You didn't ever hear any more?'

Angus flicked him a look. With a face as blank as Charles Mabledene's Mungo gazed innocently at his father.

'It's funny you should say that,' Fergus said, 'I had a second letter, not exactly confirming the first but saying what amounted to the same thing. These departments, you know, the right hand doesn't know what the left hand is doing. But I thought it was rather strange. Still, the main thing is we can go ahead. Why are you interested? I can't imagine why it should interest you.'

Angus said quickly, 'Mrs Mabledene won't be able to have her salon there after all.'

Fergus forgot the suspicious circumstances of Mungo's inquiry in his anxiety to know how Angus could be aware of events in the life of a woman twenty years his senior, a woman whom he appeared to admire and had just called beautiful. Was it possible that his seventeen-year-old son...? Could he possibly have...? Worry dug lines all over Fergus's face.

'I have my spies,' said Angus.

TRADITIONALLY, AFTER THE SPORTS, ON THE SATUR-day evening, the long Summer Half began. Rossingham would be down until the following Monday week. Before joining his parents and Angus in the car, Mungo picked up the message Charles Mabledene had left him in the cricket pavilion drop. It was in the June code, based on the first lines of William Crisp's *Spytrap*. 'Dragon to Leviathan. Agree safe house Sunday 7 p.m.'

The flood of relief, which had come when his father told him of the arrival of a second letter of permission, settled now into a steady feeling of satisfaction. Very likely Dragon was all right. Most probably Autoprox had come to a dead end simply because there were no witnesses of the car park incident and not for the more sinister reason that Moscow Centre had been secretly forewarned. Walking back from the cricket field, Mungo found himself remembering the time of Charles Mabledene's defection, those glorious weeks with Guy Parker's code book in his possession, Stern's rage, Stern had been beside himself with anger... Mungo stopped in his tracks and stood still for a moment on the steps of Pitt.

How did he know Stern had been so angry? Because Charles Mabledene had told him so. There had been no other source. Dragon had told him that when Stern had heard that one of his best men, whom he had thought a mere sleeper in enemy territory, had defected, he had 'gone mad'. But he had had nothing more than that to go on. For all he knew Dragon might have made it all up.

He might have made it all up because in fact he had not come over at all, he was not even a double agent, but still working entirely for Eastern Intelligence. And who was to say that Guy Parker's code book was not simply a plant? True, the codes from it had continued to be used for a week or two but possibly only for the passing of information Stern wanted him to have. It could all be a colossal con...

'You look as if you're at a loose end, Mungo,' said the voice of Mr Lindsay.

Mungo looked up at the window behind which was the Lindsays' living room. 'Just going home, sir.'

'A *negotiis publicis feriatus*, eh? Have a good holiday.'

'You too, sir.'

There was a rumour that the Lindsays went to a health farm every holiday. No doubt they needed it. Mungo went upstairs, collected one small suitcase, and made his way towards the car park.

ƒƒƒƒƒƒƒƒƒƒƒƒƒƒƒƒƒƒƒ **6** ƒƒƒƒƒ

REVELATIONS THAT OVERTURN A WORLD CAN ALSO change a man. John felt himself radically changed by Mark Simms's confession and by Mark's reasons for doing what he had done. He realized that all his life up till now—and this in spite of Cherry's death—he had acted as if the world were a quiet ordinary place in which people followed a routine of work and duty, lived by rules, loved and made marriages which endured, in which at best a cheerful acceptance and at worst a stoical resignation prevailed. Now he felt that he saw things differently. He saw the world as a dangerous place, the seemingly ordinary men who lived in it as dangerous, and himself as potentially so. The events of that evening in Mark's flat he had many times relived. He had gone over and over in his mind the things Mark had said. At first, though, he had tried to forget, had tried to close his mind and give himself up to innocent things, to his own flowers at this most beautiful season of the gardener's year. But the real events, the real words, bored through, like worms, like termites.

Also there was the impulse to take his knowledge to the police, though this was gradually receding. He was almost sure now that he wouldn't go to the police, for he couldn't see what good that would do to anyone. There was only himself left of the people who had been close to Cherry—unless you counted Mark. For his own part, he couldn't imagine deriving any satisfaction from knowing Mark had been arrested and brought to trial. At the time of the confession his feelings, though, had been very different. There had been a moment when he had wanted to kill him.

Facing John, crouched on the floor with his back against the legs of a chair, Mark had made that incredible confession. His face was in shadow but his eyes gleamed. A trickle of wine ran from the corner of his mouth.

'I killed her. I killed Cherry.'

'You mean,' John said, staring, breathing shallowly, 'you physically murdered her? You killed her with your own hands?'

'What other way is there of killing someone?' Then Mark seemed to understand what John implied, that he might only figuratively have killed her. With unkindness, for instance, or by neglect. 'No, I mean I murdered her, I strangled her.'

'But why?' John cried out. He didn't wait for an answer. 'Oh, I don't believe you. You're making it up.'

'I tell you, I killed Cherry. I strangled her on the Beckgate Steps.'

'Were you mad or something? Had you gone mad?'

Mark was quiet and still. It was almost dark in the room by then. He wiped the trickle of wine off his chin. John said:

'Are you really telling me you killed my sister?'

'How many times do I have to say it?'

'It was you all the time and no one knew it.' John felt as if his eyes were starting from his head. He stared at Mark with strained bared eyeballs. It was as if he were seeing him for the first time. He said in a hoarse whisper, 'Do you understand what you did? It wasn't just Cherry you killed, it was my parents too. And you made us all desperately unhappy. You said how wonderful our family life was and what it meant to you, yet you destroyed all that...'

'I wasn't exactly happy about it myself, you know.'

All Mark's shaking had stopped and his face, or what John could see of it, seemed to have relaxed. He got to his feet, stood at the window, stretched. John felt the shock of what he had been told fully reaching him, effecting a buzzing in his head, a palpitating of the heart. He said it again, his voice breaking:

'Was it a temporary madness, a fit of madness?'

Mark sat in the chair, on the edge of it, leaning forward. 'It must have been, when I actually physically did it. There wasn't anything mad about my reasons for doing it.'

'Why did you do it?'

'Jealousy. Rage. Hurt.'

'But you hadn't any reason to be jealous of Cherry. She loved you. She never looked at any man but you and I'm sure no man ever looked at her.'

Mark gave that brittle laugh of his. 'Are you kidding?' He said in a very artificial way, like an actor in a bad film, 'She was the biggest whore in town.'

For the first time that he could remember John knew what it was to be totally out of control. His body acted without his apparent volition. A redness of the kind you usually only see when looking at the light through closed lids appeared before his eyes. He jumped up and lashed out with both fists at Mark. But Mark dodged and was struck only a light blow on the neck. He sidestepped and when John lunged again he found himself pummelling the upholstery of the chair. Mark reached for the table lamp and a switch by the door and the whole room was flooded with brilliant blinding light. John fell head foremost into the chair and crouched there in silent misery.

'YOU AND YOUR PARENTS,' MARK SAID. 'YOU MUST have been living with your heads buried in sand. From the time she was fifteen, long before she left school, she was going with anyone. And it wasn't some sort of insecurity, mark you, it wasn't because she needed her ego bolstered or anything like that. It was because she loved it. She was mad for sex, it was the mainspring of her life. I suppose that was what made her so attractive.'

'Attractive?' John said. 'Cherry attractive?' He felt dreadful saying it, wicked and abominably disloyal, but at the same time that it didn't matter what he said, nothing like that mattered or ever would again. 'She was one of the plainest girls I ever saw.'

That hateful laugh of Mark's made him wince. 'Those eyes,' he said. 'That hair. She had the most beautiful body. She had a breathtaking body.'

John faltered. 'You mean you'd seen...?'

'Of course I'd seen. Do you think she'd go to bed with all those others and not with me? She was going to marry *me*. At least she did want me—only she wanted all the others as well. Anybody, old, young. I suppose she couldn't help it. I really do suppose that. It was a pity I couldn't take it, wasn't it? It was a pity I couldn't say to myself, this is the most wonderful woman I will ever know and the best sex I will ever get, surely I can put up with her promiscuity if she's discreet about it, if she doesn't broadcast it. I was right thinking it was the best. My marriage was a travesty compared to that. But I couldn't put up with it, John. I couldn't take it. Not when she'd promised me to change and then I found she was sleeping with old Maitland.'

'I don't believe it!'

'I know. That's what I said. A sixty-year-old bricklayer with a bricklayer's hands. He stank of Guinness. He had white stubble on his face.'

'But when was all this? When could she have . . . ?'

'Half those visits to Mrs Chambers were never made, for instance. Nearly all the times she was supposed to be staying with your aunt she wasn't there. It was very convenient for Cherry, your parents not having the phone. And as for old Maitland, at work of course. I walked in there unexpectedly one evening—I was half an hour early fetching her—and I found her sitting on his knee.'

'Perhaps she was sick,' John said. 'She was ill.'

'Nymphomania? Don't give me that. We don't say a man's ill if he's crazy about sex, if he can't get enough sex. Why should a woman be different? You're the one that says women are the same as us. There was nothing wrong with Cherry. It was me that was wrong, that was inadequate if you like. I killed her because she admitted going with other men and said she couldn't stop, it was no good her pretending she could stop.'

'You could have left her. You could have broken the engagement and left her.'

'I know, but I didn't. I'm going to tell you what happened. I called for her that night. Well, about five. It was already dark. We walked along the embankment quarrelling. She told me quite frankly that old Maitland had been screwing her every day, or as often as he could make it. She said she didn't see any point in lying to me, nor would she have lied to her parents if they'd asked her, or you, only none of you ever asked. We came up Beckgate Steps. I got hold of her. I put my hands round her throat and once they were round her, John, I couldn't let go. It was as if my hands were fused there. I squeezed and squeezed and I heard something snap and as soon as that happened the life went. She went limp and slipped down, she fell through my hands and lay on the stones...'

He stopped and was silent. He closed his mouth and bowed his head. John felt hollow and worn out as if he had not eaten or slept for a long time. It was then too that he was aware of the world having changed.

'Why have you told me?' he said in a strange voice that sounded unlike his own.

'I had to tell someone. Do you know what it's like going about with something like that on your conscience? It's like a weight that pulls you down...'

John got up. The city lay below him, embroidered with light and lit by the moon. He thought, irrelevantly, how many times, a couple of hundred times by now, that moon had waxed and waned since Cherry had died, and all that time Mark had held on to his stupid cruel secret. He gasped out, still in shock:

'I'm going. I don't want to see you again.'

'I'd better drive you home.'

'No, thanks. You're drunk.'

'I drive better when I'm drunk,' said Mark, and John thought he looked better than he had done for weeks, he looked happier.

He left the flat quickly without saying any more. It must have been very late. For some reason his watch had stopped. Sometimes it was possible to pick up a taxi here that was returning to the city after dropping a fare at Fonthill. But there were no taxis that night. He began the long walk down, confused, shocked, his head still swimming from it, but resolving as he walked to go to the police. A kind of angry horror took hold of him when he remembered that relieved happy look on Mark's face as he was leaving.

The road brought him down among the big houses of Hartlands. A few last lights gleamed between the trees in gardens that were like woodland clearings. He saw no one, passed no one. The lights of an occasional car swept the road ahead, the grass plots in the pavement. There was a police station at Feverton, down near Randolph Bridge. They would think he was mad, going in there with a thing like this at that time of night. For suddenly, now, the CitWest tower clock reared up ahead of him, still a mile away but plainly visible. The time was twelve-forty-two and the temperature eleven degrees. It would be better to go to the police in the morning...

That Friday was the first day John had ever stayed away from work for less than sound reason, for real illness or, for instance, a funeral. He had taken a morning off for his mother's funeral and an afternoon for his father's. But before he went to bed he knew he would take the day off. And the Saturday morning when he was supposed to be working he would take off too. After lying awake for an hour in the dark, he understood that he had only gone to bed because that was what one did in the night time. It was a rule, a convention, and he lived by those. But the world had changed.

So he got up and dressed again and sat downstairs and after a while he went out into his garden. He buried his face in the cold blossoms of a pink rose. He sat on the little stone seat and closed his eyes and he was surprised at the blankness of his mind, his inability to think. But he didn't sleep there either and at four the birds started. I will never rest again, what will happen to me? an inner voice asked, and as the dawn came he wandered indoors and out again, waiting for the time when he could reasonably phone Gavin...

That had been three weeks ago. He hadn't gone to the police and on the Monday he had returned to work. Being born again, he thought, generally seemed to imply being reborn for the better, but why shouldn't it also mean being born anew into a grimmer world and with the knowledge that life was hard and terrible? He also had some curious feelings about what pain can do

to you. Perhaps it could cut into and damage that part of
your brain we call the mind. Perhaps in this way it could
alter you and make you a different, less scrupulous, less
timid person. The old John, he felt, would not have said
harshly to Gavin:

'Leave off talking to that damned bird, will you?
There's a queue of customers at the goldfish pond.'

The old John wouldn't have let Jennifer's letter lie
about for a week before answering it, nor when he did
answer agree in clipped cold terms to the proposed
meeting, stipulating only that it should be in his
house. Certainly, the old John, when Mark phoned to
suggest talking it over more fully, would not have replied:

'I've nothing to talk about with you,' and replaced the
receiver.

⌐⌐⌐⌐⌐⌐⌐⌐⌐⌐⌐⌐⌐⌐⌐⌐⌐⌐⌐⌐ **7** ⌐⌐⌐⌐⌐⌐

A RECURRING DREAM FOR ANGUS CAMERON LED HIM
through a series of large shabby high rooms where the
wallpaper, of faded roses, hung in strips from beneath a
crumbling cornice, broken chandeliers were suspended
precariously from the ceilings by a single chain of
prisms, and split or missing floorboards revealed
through fissures sooty depths where beetles crept.
Sometimes, along his fearful route through this dream
house, Angus would see ahead of him, through a floor-
board hole, a bony hand rise up. And then he yelled out.
When he was a little boy Lucy would come, calm and
comforting. Now it was different and he groaned softly

in an empty room. It was just as well perhaps that he had only once entered the safe house at 53 Ruxeter Road and never been higher than the ground floor. To walk up that staircase as Mungo did and wander from decaying room to decaying room would have brought up goose pimples on his flesh and one of those dreams that night...

They never opened the windows. They hardly knew whether it was possible to open them. Eventually it would have been noticed and their presence detected. On a warm June night, still daylight at nine and after, the drawing room on the first floor was airless and smelling of dust and moth, a dry powdery smell that made you sneeze. Moths had scored the dirty pink silk curtains with furry runnels. A great cobweb, a multi-layered structure of rigging and galleries, hammocks and swinging ropes, stretched from vine-leaf cornice to dust-clotted pelmet and held a hecatomb of dead flies. Graham O'Neill, wearing his octopus tee-shirt, sat on the ragged chaise longue, Mungo on the garden seat of metal loops and curlicues. The slanting rays of the setting sun came in here through dirty panes and made squares on the floor the colour of fire.

'He's late,' Graham said.

'Your watch is fast. I'll be surprised if he's late. Whatever he may have been up to, he won't be late. He's not a late person.'

Mungo went to the window, not to look down into the street, but up at the sky and the tower.

'Eight-fifty-six,' he said, 'and nineteen degrees.' He stood with his back to the window, his eyes on the door which was shut. It was a panelled door with fingerplate and knob of heavy blackened brass. 'I've got something to tell you before he comes. Stern has got our June code.'

'What do you mean, got it?'

'There are two possibilities, aren't there? One is that he or one of his field agents happened on it by chance. It could be done with a lot of guesswork and a lot of work. He would have to have found out it's espionage fiction we use. OK, that was always possible, but *Spytrap*? It's quite an obscure book. It's a spy-novel buff's book. I mean it's not in the *Smiley's People* class, is it? The other possibility is that someone gave it to him.'

Graham said nothing but he made his mouth into a whistling shape. Reflected in his cat's eyes, the window panes could be seen and the red sun. Mungo waited for him to ask how he knew and when he didn't ask, said:

'Basilisk got a command in *Spytrap* to abandon Autoprox.'

Mungo stopped talking abruptly. He listened. One of the stairs creaked, the fifth from the top. No matter how you trod on it and at which point, it would creak. Not when it was he mounting the staircase, of course, for he would jump it. He thought he had heard something, not a creak, more a tremor in the depths of the house. Silently he moved back to the metal seat and sat in the middle of it. The door opened and Charles Mabledene came in, but the stairs hadn't creaked. He, too, had learned to miss it.

He looked very small, a little boy with a child's face. With his soft fair wavy hair and his swimmy blue eyes, his expressionless rather flat face, he looked stupid. He was the only brilliant person Mungo had ever known who looked stupid.

'I suppose you know why we've asked you to come here.' I sound like Mr Lindsay, Mungo thought, I sound like the headmaster. But what other way was there? 'You can sit down if you want.' A shifting of the blue eyes reminded him. 'Don't do any conjuring tricks, please.' Mungo asked the question sharply: 'How does Stern know about Autoprox?'

'You're asking me?'

Mungo nodded. It was Graham who said:

'Basilisk was given a fake command. In the June

code. The real command was removed and a fake one substituted in *Spytrap*.'

Charles Mabledene's small feet in immaculate white trainers only just reached the floor. One of the squares of red light bathed them, they were set in the centre of it as if in deliberate quest of symmetry. But the sun was setting, had almost set, and quite quickly the colour receded, faded, was gone. Dragon, who could scarcely have been less aptly named, looked down at his feet, at the vanishing light, the dying fire, then lifted his eyes and looked at Mungo.

'Are you saying I'm a traitor?'

Instead of replying directly, Mungo said, 'You defected. I know it's hard. It's a hard doctrine that the defector is always set apart from one's own, but there it is. In a way it's a paradox, because the defector in order to want to come over has to have powerful feelings of allegiance to the firm he's going to, and yet...'

'What he means is,' said Graham harshly, his gooseberry cat's eyes gleaming, 'once a traitor always a traitor. If you could betray Stern you can betray us.'

'But surely the argument is that I never betrayed Stern, that I'm still Stern's man?'

Charles Mabledene was cleverer than Graham, Mungo thought, and he didn't want to think that way. The voice that hadn't yet broken, the choirboy's treble, said:

'What do you want me to do?'

Mungo hadn't thought that far. He was aware of dusk coming, of more than dusk. Dark clouds had come up to cover the sunset's afterglow. The room was filling with shadows and the smell of dust and rotten wood was a sour cold smell. He didn't want to lose Charles Mabledene but his skin grew cold and crept when he thought of every secret, every new exercise, passing stealthily to Stern.

'You must prove you're ours,' he said.

JOHN KNEW SHE DIDN'T MUCH CARE ABOUT HOUSES and furniture, that sort of thing, but she must surely notice the improved look of the place, the clean covers, the new lamp. And the garden, even she who had been indifferent couldn't fail to admire the garden. The wisteria that covered the front bay was out, long mauve tassels draping the window panes, the patch of lawn was cut to the precise length of one inch and the edges trimmed, and among the last of the Siberian wallflowers the first pansies were coming out. On an impulse he brought a big plaster tub back from Trowbridge's and, though this was the kind of cheating he had formerly despised, filled it with geraniums and begonias that were already in bloom. It seemed to him that he kept on doing things he would not have done in the past, that his whole nature was changing.

The old John would have waited at the window for them, staring at the street, at his opposite neighbour's monkey puzzle tree, or paced the front bedroom, on every count of a hundred peering to right and left round the edges of curtains. Instead he went into the greenhouse to nip the side shoots off his tomato plants and pot up capsicum seedlings. He didn't even worry about getting dirty, for he hadn't dressed up, he hadn't done what he once would have and changed out of the clothes he had worked in all day. She is my wife, he had said to himself, and you don't dress up for your wife, that is the point of marriage, that you can be your natural self, you can behave as if you were alone. And he regretted a little the lawn and the tub but it was too late to do anything about them now.

Every year for years and years he had grown green peppers, yet he had never liked the taste of them, growing them rather for their appearance and the fun of it. When they were ripe he picked them and gave them away, to Colin or Sharon or his aunt, though she didn't like them either. The only one in their family who had was Cherry. He shied away from naming her, he didn't want to think about her ever again, yet she kept returning to his mind. A thousand small associations called her up. He wanted to forget her because she was not what he had thought her, he couldn't forgive her for having been what she was. And the strange thing was that he recoiled almost more from her, the memory of her, Mark's victim, than he did from Mark who had killed her.

Yet two days before, he had gone back to the place where she died, had made a kind of pilgrimage to those scenes of her dying and her death and the time preceding her death, to the building where Maitland's office had been. The builder's premises had been no more than a room at the back of a great white decaying Victorian house with a trailer clamped on the side of it to give more space. It had stood in a wilderness of nettles and brambles, bisected by a railway line that was disused even then. He had gone there a few times to meet Cherry after work. Flinching from the thought of it, he imagined her on her best behaviour for this prudish brother, putting a reluctant stop to Maitland's gropings and kisses, or those of any other man presumably, who might drop in about a roof repair or bricklaying job. It made him shiver. That broad face, bunched cheeks, snub nose, dwarf woman's distorted face, that fibrous glittering hair, came before his eyes now as a portrait of malevolence as well as lechery.

The house was still there but utterly changed. He only recognized it by the tree which grew in front of it, a rather rare tree for England, a lyriodendron, much bigger and taller after sixteen years and hung with a web of yellowish-green lyre-shaped leaves. Some company that sported an etched steel doorplate had bought the house and refurbished it. The facade glistened shining ivory, the roof with dark silver-coloured slates. Its grounds had disappeared under a windowless hangar-like shopping mall. And this whole area of the embankment the city council had converted into one of its river walks, with paved paths, decorative railings, raised flowerbeds, suitable shrubs.

The Beckgate was open on this summer evening, spilling patrons out on to the steps. The hanging basket of ivy-leaved geraniums that hung above the saloon-bar door he had sold the licensee himself, wincing when the man gave his address. John went up the double flight and straight on ahead, trying to imagine Mark's feelings after the deed was done, after he knew Cherry lay dead behind him. But it was impossible. He could only think of his mother at home growing more and more anxious, of having to go next door and use the phone because they hadn't got one, of Mark at last coming to Geneva Road and seeming so *normal* . . .

He had walked a long way without much noticing the route he took and now he found himself on the pavement opposite cats' green. It was feeding time and though there was no cat to be seen, the pans of milk and plates of tinned food were being set out among grass that had by now grown as high as the woman's waist. A faded, middle-aged woman with a gentle face—but what was she really? Another such as Cherry, as lascivious and insatiable, as uncaring of loyalty and faithfulness, of common decency?

She saw him watching her. It made her hurry to pick up her milk cartons, the empty cans, yesterday's empty plates. She takes me for some sort of would-be molester, John thought, and the idea, though fantastic, didn't altogether displease him. Why not he as much as any other man? In a world full of terrible things, why should he be set apart, islanded? Men were dangerous and women, in their way, dangerous too. He started to cross the road and felt a very real pleasure, a pleasure that was almost sexual, in seeing her hasten away, walk far more quickly than was natural across the road, look back once, plunge into one of the narrow alleys.

Shame quickly succeeded that pleasure. Wickedness is contagious, he thought, I am catching it from others. Somewhere, once, he had heard or read the phrase: Evil communications corrupt good manners. The Bible or something Victorian? It didn't sound like the Bible. He looked up at the rumbling bouncing flyover and saw, there inside the central upright, five or six feet up, a plastic package secured with tape.

They were back. They had survived whatever had kept them away, arrest or even imprisonment, and started up again.

ƒƒƒƒƒƒƒƒƒƒƒƒƒƒƒƒƒƒ **9** ƒƒƒƒƒ

THE LAST OF THE CAPSICUM PLANTED AND WATERED in, John turned his attention to the tomatoes. None of the fruit had yet begun to redden. He would stop the stems after four trusses, but next week would do for that. He began mixing plant feed into a can of water and could not prevent himself catching sight of his watch which told him it was five past eight. They were due at eight. He watered the tomato plants, flooding the pots, forcing his thoughts back to the message he had found at cats' green. He had copied it into his notebook—strange how he had gone on carrying that notebook even when he thought his mini-

Mafia disbanded—and as soon as he got home had applied to it the first lines of 'The Bruce-Partington Plans'. But as he feared, they had changed the code. They were logical. Court appearances, imprisonment, whatever it had been, they stuck to their monthly routine. It was June now, so the code had changed.

Twelve minutes past eight. He had better, at any rate, wash his hands. How could she be late for something so important? But perhaps it was Peter Moran who made her late. John washed at the kitchen sink. He had begun to feel sick. There was just time to run upstairs and change his clothes. Up he went two at a time, flung off baggy trousers, check shirt, put on white shirt, new tie, grey flannels, his heart racing. A car was stopping outside. Wait, he told himself, don't have the door standing open before they get up the path. Holding his fists clenched, he looked at them through the bedroom window. Both doors of the car opened simultaneously and they both got out. John's heart squeezed and seemed to move a little at the sight of Jennifer in her cotton dress, her sandals, the long bright hair tied back with white ribbon. He transferred his gaze to Peter Moran and then he turned quickly away and ran downstairs.

Inside the door he made himself pause before opening it. Waiting those few seconds was like waiting through a lifetime. If they don't ring that bell, I will throw myself at that door, he thought, I will beat it down with my fists. Yet when the bell did ring he jumped. And still he waited, counting. When he had counted thirty, it was impossible to do more, it was beyond his strength, he had to open the door.

Jennifer said, 'Hallo, John.'

She looked neither sad nor happy. Her face was composed as it always was. Not for her the careless untidiness of a frown, a puckering of the lips or a half-smile. Peter Moran didn't say anything, but John didn't think this was through embarrassment. Again he was aware of that indifference to the opinions of others.

'The garden looks nice,' said Jennifer.

He was happy because she didn't say 'your garden'. They walked into the living room and he saw her look at the lamp, the jugs, the two new books that lay on the coffee table. He found it hard to keep his eyes off her and he had to compel himself to stop looking. He had forgotten all about making plans to give them food or drink. There was no coffee in the house, not even instant. Wine he had. Two bottles of wine were in the kitchen somewhere, last remnants of those sessions with Mark Simms.

'Would you like a drink?'

She looked surprised when he offered wine. It made him hope, it made him think she might like the new John better.

'Thanks. Wine would be nice.'

Peter Moran still hadn't spoken. Without appearing to look at him, John had taken in every detail of his appearance, the thick glasses, the floppy fair hair, the rather pasty face. His skin had a greyish look, his hair was greasy, his ill-fitting loose jeans stained. For this important visit, this meeting which was to decide his fate, he hadn't even been bothered to have a bath and put on clean clothes. He looked bored; he looked— 'laid-back' was the expression, John thought, casual, relaxed, not so much in control as uncaring as to who might be. Cool, Jennifer had called him. John fetched the wine, uncomfortably aware that it should have been chilled, not brought straight out of the cupboard that was next to the immersion heater. Jennifer said:

'Muscadet—that's my favourite.'

Why hadn't he known that? It suddenly seemed terrible not to know what was your wife's favourite wine. He found it actually physically difficult to pour wine for Peter Moran and hand it to him. Peter Moran still hadn't sat down or spoken, he was still moving idly about the room. But now he took the glass out of John's hand, not looking at it or him or saying thanks. John might have been a waiter.

It went against the grain to start drinking without raising one's glass in some sort of a toast but John couldn't think what to say, he couldn't bring himself to say Cheers! It was Jennifer who settled it by lifting her glass, looking hard at Peter Moran, and saying in a deliberate, almost ritualistic way:

'To our futures—all our futures.'

That sent a chill down John's spine. It sounded so final and so somehow loaded against himself.

'Right,' Peter Moran said, and he took a long sucking draught from his glass, emptying it at one go. He pushed the glass across the table towards John and John was so surprised he found himself re-filling it. Jennifer began speaking in a nervous monotone, very quickly for her.

'John, you know why we've come and we have to start talking about it. It's very nice of you to—well, sort of entertain us and all that but we mustn't lose sight of why we're here. I do want a divorce and I want it as soon as possible. You know that, I've explained about that. We made a mistake, you and I, and it's no good, I'll never come back, even if you won't divorce me I won't come back. Don't you understand that?'

'I think that in time, if I don't divorce you, you may come to see you're better off with me.' John spoke coolly, surprising himself.

She shook her head vehemently. 'I love Peter and he loves me. We want to get married. We want to make a public statement of our commitment to each other and marriage is the way to do that.'

'You've made one of those already—to me.'

'I've told you, that was a mistake. And what use is all this? You can't keep us apart. We'll still live together. All that will happen is that instead of getting married in six months' time we won't for five years—well, four and a half years now. Only'—Jennifer essayed a smile at him, a rueful inquiring smile it was, and his heart moved—'only we'd sooner it was in six months.'

'We?' he said, and he was aware of a breathlessness. 'We? I don't hear his views in all this.'

She looked at her lover. The midsummer evening light fell on the lenses of his glasses in such a way as to seem to change them into planes of opaque metal. He had pushed his empty glass across the table a second time but John ignored it. At last he spoke. His voice was beautiful, John had to admit that, it was the sort of voice you associated with Oxford and the diplomatic service and aristocrats. It was Received English Pronunciation and more than that. The words he used seemed to have an intellectual cast and to John at any rate they were incomprehensible. It was Sacher-Masoch all over again.

'He thinks he has the lodestone,' he said.

'What does that mean?'

'Never mind,' Jennifer said, sweet-voiced, like a teacher to a class of little boys. 'Never mind, what does it matter? What does any of it matter? We just have to make John understand we're serious, we're committed to each other and we aren't going to have a change of heart just because...'

It was at this moment, before she had finished her sentence, that the front door bell rang.

For no particular reason John was certain it must be Mark Simms. It would be just like him, after getting the receiver put down on him and no answer at all to his further calls, to come round. Probably he hadn't done with his confession and there was more he wanted to say, more details to fill in. The bell rang a second time.

'Aren't you going to see who it is?' Jennifer said.

He left them and went to the door. The caller was Colin Goodman. His car was at the gate and his mother was sitting in the passenger seat. Something in John's face made him say:

'It's all right, we're not coming in, not if you're busy. It's just that I was giving Mother a run out and as we were passing this way...'

John never learned what his intention was in calling

—to invite him to join them perhaps?—for at that point the sitting-room door opened, Peter Moran came out and said in his polished newscaster's voice:

'Where's the loo?'

John was affronted. 'Upstairs,' he said coldly. 'Upstairs and to your left.' In order to reach the foot of the stairs Peter Moran had to come nearly up to the front door, so John had no choice but to introduce him to Colin. Would Colin remember who this man was, that he was Jennifer's lover? John couldn't remember if he had previously told him the name.

'Colin Goodman, Peter Moran,' he said.

There was nothing in Colin's face to show that it meant anything to him. He had that rather weary resigned look he usually wore when he was taking his mother anywhere. In these circumstances it wasn't unusual for him to call on friends or acquaintances for half an hour or so of their society. He retreated down the two steps, though slowly.

'I won't stop, seeing you've got company.'

And as John glanced again at the car—an aged Triumph Dolomite but far smarter than Moran's dirty Citroën—old Mrs Goodman looked up and rapped on the window. Having summoned her son, she waved cordially to John. Peter Moran had disappeared upstairs.

'Look, sorry, I'll ring you,' John said. He forced himself to wait until Colin reached the gate before closing the door.

Jennifer was alone in the living room. Husband and wife looked at each other in silence and then John said very simply.

'Please come back to me, darling. I do love you very much.'

'I can't,' she said, her voice very low and gruff.

'No one could love you as I love you, don't you know that?'

'But I love him like that,' she said.

It was a blow that made him close his eyes as if he feared a fist in his face. Peter Moran came back. In pain, with a pain that was physical, John forced himself to look at him, pondering the mystery of love. What was there about the man? True, he was four or five years John's junior and an inch taller—but all this was nonsense. Somewhere in the man's make-up must be some secret ingredient. His mouth was full and slack, his eyes lazy, bored. Looking at Jennifer now, he gave the ghost of a wink—or John thought he did, he couldn't be sure. And Jennifer's face remained grave and unhappy. The awful silence endured. She broke in, her tone anxious, tentative. John thought in a kind of bitter triumph, I've moved her, I've upset her by what I said.

'John, will you think about it, please? Would you say, take a week and give it some thought? I mean, about how we're going to settle all this? If you won't divorce me for adultery, will you divorce me on grounds of incompatibility after two years? That is, next November twelve months?'

'I'll think about it,' he said. 'I think about it most of the time anyway. But I won't change.'

Peter Moran poured the last of the wine into his glass, drank it down. 'We're wasting our time here,' he said. 'I don't know why we came.'

The old John would have accepted that meekly. The new John said:

'For free-loading, by the look of things.'

Jennifer looked from one to the other, pleading, 'Please, don't quarrel!'

'I won't divorce you. And one reason is you'll be better off with me than him,' John said. 'I'm better for you. He'll only make you unhappy.'

'For God's sake,' said Peter Moran, 'let's go.'

He watched their departure from the front door and then he ran upstairs and watched the car till it disappeared. After that came a feeling of let-down and of emptiness, a sensation of being alone in the world and with nothing to do. It was still light, it was still only nine o'clock. Making an effort to expel Jennifer and

Peter Moran from his mind—an effort that could only be partly successful—he returned to the living room and cleared away the glasses, put the empty wine bottle into the waste bin. It was nearly a month since the estimate from the builder about the guttering had come. He sat down and answered it. He got out his notebook and tried the latest cats' green message against the first lines of all the fiction in the bookcase that was even remotely associated with spies, including Conan Doyle's *The Naval Treaty* and a couple of Father Brown stories. Yves Yugall had published a collection of short stories since *Cat Walk* and he had managed to get a copy from the central library. The collection was called *The Armadillo Army* and comprised eight stories. Labouriously, he tried the message against the first lines of each story, but the June code wasn't based on any of them.

It was after eleven when he stopped, lay back in the armchair and closed his eyes. On the dark red retina, print appeared in paler letters and as it faded he seemed to see there the face of Jennifer, her soft full cheeks and her unhappy eyes.

ffffffffffffffffff **10** ffffff

IT HAD BEEN A BUSY SATURDAY MORNING AT TROW-bridge's. Sunshine always brought the crowds out at weekends, though no true gardener would plant anything out in full sunshine, the worst killathon of all, as he had heard Gavin tell a customer. Gavin wanted to know if he might take the mynah bird home with him for the weekend and John hadn't been able to see any reason why not.

'When I'm not here he suffers from benign neglect.'

John wasn't sure what that was. He hadn't much hope of anyone ever buying the mynah. The black shiny head with its bright yellow beak poked out between the bars as Gavin carried off its cage.

'I'm a turnaround, I'm a super slurper,' sang Gavin, but the mynah said nothing, only looking apprehensively at the great outdoors.

It wasn't until after they had gone that John thought he might have asked Gavin what a lodestone was. He seemed to be a mine of curious information. The dictionary John consulted at the central library told him loadstone or lodestone meant a magnet. Why then had Peter Moran suggested he was in possession of a magnet? Was it some sort of insult? In that context it seemed to have no more meaning than 'turnaround' or 'super slurper'. As he entered the house the phone was ringing. Mark Simms, he thought, and he braced himself to deliver another sharp rejection.

Jumping to conclusions, he had made the same mistake as he had on Thursday evening.

'It's Colin. I've been trying to get you all the morning.'

'It's my Saturday morning at work.'

'I tried yesterday too.'

People who resented the fact that one wasn't permanently sitting by the phone waiting for their calls exasperated John.

'Well, I'm here now.'

'That chap I met at your house on Thursday, is he a mate of yours? I mean, is he a close friend?'

John said slowly, 'Do you mean Peter Moran?'

'That's him, yes. The guy who came out and asked where the loo was.'

Colin spoke as if John had had a whole houseful of people with him that night, a party. But of course he might have thought he had, he might even resent not having been asked. John said, choosing his words:

145

'He isn't a friend of mine. He's the man Jennifer is living with. She was here too. It was all very awkward, that's why I couldn't ask you in. I don't really want to talk about this on the phone, Colin.'

Colin's voice sounded very strange. He said, 'Are you sure Jennifer is living with him? I mean, like that?'

'I don't want to talk about it, Colin. I said I didn't.'

'Look, you couldn't come over, could you? Or I could come to you? Mother would like to see you. Come and have a cup of tea.'

John said decisively, 'Not to talk about Jennifer, I don't want to do that. Really, Colin, that's not on. I have to sort all that out on my own.' He relented a little. Colin, after all, was his oldest friend. Colin had listened to his confidences far more readily than he had when hearing the confessions of Mark Simms. 'I hope Jennifer will come back to me, I'm hoping it's only a matter of time. You do see, don't you, that it's really not on to discuss it with any outsider. Even you,' he added.

'I don't want to talk about Jennifer,' Colin said. 'I wouldn't dream of it. All I want to do is give you some information about Peter Moran I think you might find useful. I want to tell you where I last saw him.' Colin paused to give his statement the fullest dramatic impact. 'It was in court.'

GOING HOME FOR THE WEEKEND WAS ALMOST UN-
heard of at Rossingham but most people got taken out
on Sundays. Parents came or godparents or uncles and
aunts. On the whole, going off for lunch and tea with
those vaguely designated 'friends' wasn't encouraged.

'It's remarkable,' Mr Lindsay had been heard to say,
'how many of the senior men in Pitt have beautiful
aunts no more than eighteen years old.'

He might have been including Angus Cameron who
one Sunday in late June was called for by a pretty blond
girl who arrived in a Mini. Mungo, on the other hand,
was taken out to lunch at the Mill Hotel in Rossingham
St Clare by his parents with Ian and Gail. It was Charles
Mabledene's sister's fifteenth birthday and after the
whole family had been out to lunch and tea they would
take her back to Utting.

'Isn't it rather peculiar,' Mungo said to Graham
O'Neill, 'that we never knew till now he had a sister at
Utting?'

'We never knew he had a sister, full stop. He's very
secretive.'

'I suppose we shall all be on top of each other for
lunch,' said Mungo gloomily and he was right, the Mabledenes, Camerons and Graham's uncle and aunt being
given contiguous tables. Angus and his girlfriend had
disappeared in a blast of black exhaust from the Mini
which needed a new silencer.

Charles Mabledene was well aware of the implica-
tions of his sister's school. He and she had been in the

junior school at Utting together and she had continued there after the Common Entrance, while he, on that historic and never to be forgotten occasion, had 'come over'. But he wouldn't stoop to explain all this to the Director of London Central. Early in his life Charles had adopted the enigmatic dictum, 'never apologize, never explain'. Indeed, he had had no personal contact with Leviathan, Medusa, or any other agent of Western Intelligence since the interview in the safe house at 53 Ruxeter Road. On that occasion Leviathan had told him he must 'prove you're ours' but so far no test had been set him. Apart, that is, from the normal run of his duties. And even these had not been pressing—a small photocopying job, the setting up of a new drop—leaving him plenty of time for experimenting with Banham locks and, of course, for his flexi-prep.

The new drop was under a loose stone beneath the horse trough in Rossingham St Mary market place, the one in the cricket pavilion having ceased its function when the brickwork in the wall was unexpectedly repaired. On the pretext of buying a birthday card for his sister, he had been given Mr Lindsay's permission to go to the village on Friday afternoon, and there he had taken from under the horse trough the latest command in *Spytrap*: 'Repossess Reynolds' books.'

Charles knew what this referred to, a work on chess and two on yachting which Angus's friend Bruce Reynolds had two years before lent to an Utting man called Simon Perch, who was one of Stern's Stars. Though repeatedly asked, Perch had never returned them and this was the only way to get them back. It would be quite easy, Charles thought, seeing that he was actually going to Utting later that day, though Leviathan had not known that when the command was issued, assuming only that Dragon had another kind of special 'in' at Parker's and Stern's school. Was this then the test? Would it almost be better for Dragon not to secure the borrowed books?

Nicholas Ralston, or Unicorn, whom he could see

with a huge family party at the opposite end of the dining room, might just as well have been asked. It was more his mark really. In a way it was rather a feeble task to set someone of Dragon's undoubted acumen and brilliance. If he was being tested, would it be to his credit to fail? On the other hand, he would be very surprised if by now Leviathan and Medusa didn't know very well that he had a sister at Utting. On balance, the test should be passed.

It was Charles Mabledene's overriding ambition that when Mungo Cameron retired, as next year he surely would, the mantle should fall upon his own shoulders and the directorship of London Central become his.

While they were having coffee he did his new trick and produced a bunch of carnations from the sleeve of his mother's rather strange new white satin jacket. She shrieked with delight. Charles had picked the carnations in Mrs Lindsay's private garden very early that morning before anyone was up. The locked front and back doors of Pitt presented no problem to him. His parents and his sister seemed to assume that some occult agency was at work and even to suspect that the flowers weren't real. Charles smiled indulgently at them.

There were areas of his mind which sometimes troubled him, but not the area that did the magic. That was a mere matter of the quickness of the hand deceiving the eye and of a rather gruelling discipline. His gift for discerning what others thought and, more than that, of divining what might happen in some future anticipated situation—this was what gave him pause and made him wonder. The thought processes of others interested him, he was one of those rare people who, though selfish and unscrupulous, are more interested in others than in themselves.

Now, for instance, he was wondering where they would go that afternoon. It was his sister's choice, for it was her birthday, and there were many options open. Several great houses in the neighbourhood as well as

Rossingham Castle; the wildlife park at Songflete; the otter sanctuary on the Orr at Orrington; the Life in Tudor England exhibition at Togham Hoo; a boat on the river from Orrington up to Rostock Bridge. Her face told him nothing. She was fond of clothes and the Tudor exhibition had plenty of dresses in it. And she liked boating, she was cox of the Utting junior boat.

Otters, he said to himself and he didn't know why. It was this not knowing why that sometimes made him uneasy. When his prediction was as unlikely as this one he would have liked to be wrong. They had profiteroles for pudding. Profiteroles were her favourite. Charles watched the Camerons leave the dining room, marvelling at those men's height. They were like another race. Mungo was probably a whole foot taller than he. His father looked across the table.

'Have you decided where you want to go, Sarah?'

'Otter sanctuary,' she said. 'I'm torn between that and Togham but I really do think the otters.'

Charles sighed to himself.

There were European otters and Asian otters, pairs of them each in their own section of the river. At feeding time which was at three-thirty they dived and swam for the fish the keepers threw in out of reeking buckets. Charles was a better photographer than his sister, so to oblige her he took pictures of otter cubs. On the way back, after tea in Orrington, they got in a traffic jam on the motorway caused by weekend roadworks and the car threatened to overheat.

'I'll ruin this car if I drive her any further,' said his father. 'I'm going to drop her at the works and pick up another one.'

'The works' was what all the Mabledenes called the garage at Rostock. Charles's father drove the BMW on to the forecourt and let himself into the office to find the keys for one of the secondhand Volvos which were lined up for sale outside. Charles hadn't been down at the works for ages. He didn't know what it was that made him get out and wander about among the cars, through the big shed with the turntables and out to the back where vehicles awaited repairs or service. That flair he had, he supposed later, that ESP or second sight or whatever you called it. The red car, a Datsun, had its offside rear wing quite badly dented and the light unit smashed. There was a very obvious smear of green on the bodywork where the red paint had flaked away. Charles was glad now that he had taken those otter pictures for his sister, for the camera was still slung round his neck. With a quick glance round to see that no one was looking he took two shots of the red car, carefully ensuring the inclusion of the number plate.

He returned by way of the office, having composed his face into that expression of innocence and naïvety which seemed so much to please his mother. It was becoming second nature to him now and he no longer needed to practise it in front of a mirror. Through the big plate-glass window he could see his father still rummaging around in the office. Charles pushed open the door and felt it stick as it seemed to be obstructed by something in its passage across the doormat. He bent down and picked up the envelope which he could feel contained a bunch of car keys on a ring with a fob. On the envelope was printed the number of the car he had photographed and the name Whittaker...

By now his father had found the Volvo keys. Feeling pleased with himself but revealing nothing of this, Charles handed the envelope to his father, they all got into the Volvo and set off for Utting in the outer eastern suburbs.

'Shall I get this film developed for you?' Charles said to his sister and added untruthfully, 'Someone I know in the camera club at school will do it for free.'

Naturally, she agreed. Charles decided to finish up the film in taking some useful pictures of Utting. You never knew when that sort of thing might come in handy. His sister was in Curie House, but in the general mêlée of boys and girls returning from Sunday outings and the in any case far freer atmosphere than ever prevailed at Rossingham, he had no difficulty in penetrating Huxley and inquiring of someone who looked like a prefect where Simon Perch's room was. The prefect seemed to know Perch quite well, might even have been a friend of his, and helpfully told Charles he wasn't back yet and wasn't expected before eight. The worst part for Charles was picking the lock of Perch's door. Not because it was difficult—those simple locks on interior doors never were—but because of the risk of being seen, the process necessarily taking two or three minutes.

He found two of the books on the shelf above the counter top Utting people used as desks. The chess book wasn't there though and a search of the room failed to find it. Perch had probably taken it home and left it there or never brought it to school. The only thing of real interest in the room was a telescope mounted on the windowsill with its sights turned to the city. Charles had a squint through it. It was amazing how much was to be seen and how clearly. He could even see the clock on the CitWest tower and read that the time was six-twenty-two and the temperature seventeen degrees. In the absence of a flash bulb he wasn't able to take much of a photograph of the room but he did his best. As far as he knew, this would be the first picture anyone at London Central had of the interior of Utting. He left the building without mishap, carrying the two books in a green and white Marks and Spencer's plastic carrier he had found in Perch's wastepaper basket.

Re-entering Curie where his parents were still closeted with Sarah's housemistress, Charles passed Rosie Whittaker in the hall. She knew Sarah and looked as if about to speak, but he froze her with a cold uncomprehending stare.

12

CONSTANCE GOODMAN BELONGED TO THAT CATE-
gory of women who are nice to their children's friends
but not very nice to their children. This had been
evinced in the friendly wave she gave John from the
car after rapping crossly on the window to summon
Colin. In her seventies now, she was known to three
generations whom she had taught at primary school.
John—and Cherry—had been among her pupils,
though her own son never had. Those former pupils,
when she met them, she tended to call 'pet'; her son,
though the term was often less than affectionately be-
stowed, was 'chickie'. And Colin did have something of
a chicken-like look with his pink beaky face, small
dark eyes and curly hair. He had seemed quite excited
when he let John into the house, rather resembling
Harpo Marx when suppressing glee.

'Nice to see you, pet,' Mrs Goodman said, creaking
about on arthritic joints, laying the table for a tea John
hadn't felt he could possibly eat. 'I'll make myself
scarce for ten minutes and you and Colin can have
your chat.'

She had made it very plain that she knew what it was
Colin had to impart but was being discreet.

John waited until she closed the door and said, 'What
on earth is it?'

That was three weeks ago now and he had done
nothing with his information. He had been torn, in
perhaps the worst dilemma of his life. It was as if he

needed something to happen, something that would either trigger off a disclosure or show him that he must bury what Colin had told him. Present always in his mind was a desire not to behave badly, yet perhaps disclosing this would not be bad, would be a duty as well as his own salvation. Scarcely a vestige of triumph remained that without guessing precisely, he had been right about the thing that lurked behind Peter Moran's dull eyes.

Making his way out to Colin's on the Honda that Saturday afternoon, his feelings had been very different. He had been curiously buoyant and hopeful, though with nothing then on which to base this optimism. Colin and his mother lived a long way out of the city, on the outskirts of Orrington really, and it took him nearly half an hour to get there. The bungalow, which he hadn't visited since Jennifer left him, had such a stark and barren look about it that you might have thought it brand-new but for the unmistakable building features—you couldn't call it architecture—of the early sixties. The garden consisted merely of closely mown grass, flowerless and treeless, while the house was a low-roofed L-shape of light pink brickwork with square metal-framed windows. Once John had tried giving Colin rooted shrub cuttings and boxes of seedlings but what became of these he never knew, certainly they never appeared in that garden.

When he and Colin were alone together and two more doors had been heard to close on Mrs Goodman, a woman of ostentatious tact, Colin again asked him if it were really true Peter Moran was living with Jennifer.

'I've told you so,' John said. He was beginning to learn that people don't necessarily listen attentively when one confides in them, but still he said, 'Surely I told you so when Jennifer first left me.'

'You may have done. The name didn't ring a bell—then.'

'I wish you wouldn't be so mysterious.'

'How much do you know about—this chap, this Moran?'

'He's about thirty-five. He comes from around here—or I think he does. He's got a degree, economics or philosophy or something. I believe he was once a teacher, I'm not sure. He hasn't got a job now, that's for sure. He's renting a tumble-down sort of cottage out at Nunhouse that I suppose the dole pays for.' John knew he sounded contemptuous but he didn't care. 'Oh, and he's got one of those little French cars that aren't really cars, if you know what I mean.'

Colin started to laugh. 'You really love him, don't you?'

'What do you expect?'

'How did Jennifer meet him?'

John didn't much care for the question. 'I don't know how she first met him. It was a long time ago.' He hesitated. He said with difficulty, 'They were engaged but he broke it off just before—the wedding. That would have been about four years ago.'

'Four years ago,' said Colin, 'I served on that jury at the Crown Court at Orrington. Do you remember that?'

John remembered. Colin had made a fuss about taking time off work and the inadequacy of a juryman's pay.

'When I saw Moran at your house on Thursday I recognized him at once and when I got home I looked him up.'

'What do you mean, looked him up?'

'You know me, making notes of everything. I noted down everyone who came up in court and made a few comments of my own. It was helpful at arriving at verdicts. Your Peter Moran was one of the people before that court. Do you want to know what he was charged with?'

'Of course I do.'

'Assault on a child under the age of thirteen,' said Colin. He moistened his lips, evidently embarrassed. 'I mean indecent assault.'

Mrs Goodman put her head round the door.

'Finished, chickie?'

'You know what I've been telling him, so I doubt if it matters much.'

'Don't be sarcastic with me, chickie. I can't spend all night in the kitchen.' She dumped on the table a tray of tea things, including a huge brown teapot and an equally dark and heavy-looking fruit cake.

'Please, Mrs Goodman,' John said. 'I honestly don't mind.' He looked at Colin. 'I can't believe it.' But he could. It explained so much, Peter Moran's abrupt leaving of Jennifer, Jennifer's belief that she was the only woman there had ever been in his life, his failure to get work in his own field, above all that suspicion of horror John had always felt about him. 'What happened to him?' he asked. 'I mean what was the'—he couldn't find the right word—'punishment?'

'It was a first offence. Or the first time they'd caught him, more like. He got three years' probation on condition he spent six months in a psychiatric clinic.'

Mrs Goodman was pouring out half-pint-size cups of dark brown tea. Colin reached for his and slopped from the overful cup into the saucer.

'You did that, chickie, mind, not me.'

'All right, Mother, I'm not complaining.'

'Did he spend six months in a psychiatric clinic?'

'I suppose so. He must have.'

John didn't like having to ask this question in front of Mrs Goodman. He could never be in her presence without recalling her as she had been in class, biggish, gaunt, beaky-faced, writing sums in long division on the blackboard or walking down the aisle between the desks and pausing to look over one's shoulder. Not looking in her direction, eyeing his plate on which reposed a thick slice of Dundee cake, he said: 'Was it a girl or a boy?'

Mercifully, Colin needed no further elucidation. 'Oh, a boy.'

'I wonder why it wasn't in the papers.'

'It was in the Orrington paper, pet. Perhaps it wasn't big enough for the *Free Press*.'

'He pleaded guilty, you see,' said Colin. 'It wasn't much of a case. It was all over in half an hour.'

John knew what they were thinking. And he too repeated her name with a silent inner voice. Jennifer, Jennifer... He said abruptly to Mrs Goodman:

'Do you know what a lodestone is?'

'A magnet, isn't it?'

'That's what the dictionary said.'

'Wait a minute, pet. Wasn't it supposed to be a kind of magic magnet which—well, if a husband possessed it, he could use it to get back a runaway wife?'

'Charming,' said Colin. 'So much for your well-known tact.'

Mother and son had begun quarrelling after that in a kind of gruff controlled way. They never quite lost their tempers, though Mrs Goodman would sometimes laugh unpleasantly and Colin's eyes flash. It ended with Mrs Goodman remarking that John would hardly now want to spend the rest of the evening in such a disagreeable house whose occupants sparred all the time and made their guests uncomfortable. How do you respond to that one? Of course John hadn't wanted to stay and didn't, taking his departure with all sorts of fabricated excuses while Mrs Goodman shook her head sadly and said it was just what she had foreseen, Colin had driven his friend away by his rudeness.

John could see a parallel between his present behaviour and the way he had reacted to Mark Simms's confession. Returning home on the Honda, he had been full of plans for how to use his new knowledge just as, on that previous occasion, he had intended to go to the police. That evening he had spent in restless speculation and by the next day he had decided he must know more facts. Consulting the newspaper files in the library of the *Orrington Onlooker* was a far simpler process than he expected, but the account of the court proceedings was brief, for the child's name could not be given or any personal details about him included. The boy hadn't been injured in any way. Peter Moran had not attempted to deny what he had done. In fact, there was little more to be gathered from the paper than Colin had already told him.

If he was like that, though, why did he want Jennifer? To persuade himself, presumably, that he wasn't like that? To be saved from himself and protected? Because there was something very motherly and caring about Jennifer? Or simply because Jennifer wanted him and with her love provided a cloak for his activities? Speculating, John realized how little he understood of abnormal psychology. And he shied away from the thought that Jennifer might want her lover more than he wanted her. Perhaps Peter Moran had been cured in the clinic he had attended—if he had attended it.

But there was a memory which kept returning to John and a question he continually asked himself. That Saturday when he and Jennifer had met in Hartlands Gardens, 2 April, that was the afternoon on which Peter Moran had 'gone out' and the afternoon also on which twelve-year-old James Harvill had disappeared. Was it fantastic to connect the two, knowing what he now knew? The question John kept asking himself and receiving, of course, no answer to, was: Does Jennifer know?

The information seemed to lie heavily in his keeping like a ponderous inert mass or like the lodestone that was a magnet with supernatural powers. He had only to lift it up and show it to the light of day to draw his wife back to him...

ƒƒƒƒƒƒƒƒƒƒƒƒƒƒƒƒƒ 13 ƒƒƒƒƒ

'**H**AVE YOU EVER THOUGHT,' ANGUS SAID, 'THAT IT might all end in tears?'

They had encountered each other after prep in the New Library.

'Why would it?' Mungo looked seriously puzzled. 'We never do anything illegal.'

'You sail near the wind sometimes. And things go wrong, even things that start innocently. You could get yourselves expelled, you could get into some disaster.'

'You sound like Dad.'

That was on 29 June, the day Mungo sent out a directive to his agents to ignore all further *Spytrap* commands and adopt *Armadillo Army* Three. It went out in *Spytrap* and the direction for the new code referred to the third story in the Yves Yugall collection, a sharp little thriller called 'Gila Haunt'. He preserved the Utting photograph Charles Mabledene had taken in a file marked 'Most Secret'. The two books on yachting were restored to Bruce Reynolds and the photograph of the Whittakers' damaged car conveyed, via his brother, to the elder Ralston.

No efforts on the part of Mungo or any of his experts had been able to break Stern's code, nor was there any clue as to what that preliminary number and those ultimate numbers signified.

During the first week of July Unicorn received a letter from his father which seemed to indicate the possible imminent loss of 53 Ruxeter Road. Unicorn's father wrote to his son of the possibility of buying a flat in Pentecost Villas when the block had been converted. Demolition, it seemed, was no longer envisaged. Mungo, in *Armadillo Army* Three, instructed Basilisk and Empusa to find out more. The blow fell when Unicorn, paying a routine call to the horse trough drop, picked up a message to abandon Pentecost Villas research. He had given up all work on the elaborate plan to have his father secure building dates and plans and on his own initiative called off Basilisk, before the discovery was made by Mungo that the directive was a false one and came from Stern or Stern's mole. Moscow Centre had broken the July code.

This didn't necessarily mean that Stern knew the location of the safe house. In all commands, since the primary reference to it when its precise address had been given, it was referred to as PV for Pentecost Villas. Stern very likely didn't know. But he had broken the code within days of its formulation.

Mungo, three days before the end of the summer term, changed the code from *Armadillo Army* Three to *Armadillo Army* Seven, reasoning that such a daring choice wouldn't be suspected. The change, initially, was known only to Unicorn, Basilisk, Medusa and Charybdis. On the last day it was also imparted to Dragon, who was Charles Mabledene.

ffffffffffffffffff **14** ffffff

JENNIFER'S LETTER CAME ON THE FIRST DAY OF John's holiday. Of course he wouldn't be going away. He would have a go at the garden, maybe redecorate a room, spend a day with Colin and his mother, visit his aunt. How dull it sounds, he thought. In spite of the world-changing pieces of knowledge he held in his mind, he felt himself lapsing back into the old John. Outwardly, there had been no alteration in the way he lived. But he knew he was waiting for a sign and perhaps that sign was contained in the letter. He opened it slowly, not at all in a feverish anxious way.

Dear John,
You said you would think about what we asked you when Peter and I came to see you. That is over a month ago now and we haven't heard from you. You said you would think about a divorce, if you wouldn't divorce me for adultery that you might at any rate let us have a mutual consent divorce after two years apart. We have been talking to a solicitor and he has told me that I would have a right to a share in the house, even possibly as much as a third of its value. This may sound a bit outrageous seeing that the house is basically yours and I didn't pay for it or anything. But the law works like that and of course I have nothing of my own, as you know, except what I got from selling my flat which had a big mortgage on it anyway. Peter has nothing, absolutely no assets at all. It wouldn't be an exaggeration to say we are on the breadline.
But what I want to say is this, that if you will let me have a divorce so that we can get married I won't ask for anything from you. I mean that I promise I won't ask for any alimony and I won't demand any share in the house. I think that is quite a fair bargain to make.
Please do think about this. I am not going to threaten you, John, but you must understand that if I have to wait five years I would have to have some support during that time and some sort of capital sum at the end of it.
Yours ever,
Jennifer

Peter Moran had put her up to that, John thought. So that he wouldn't have to get a job, or rather, so as to reconcile himself to being unable to get a job. Could a woman who had only lived with her husband for two years, a childless woman, claim a share in his house? John didn't know and he didn't want to ask a solicitor. He would never do that, he wouldn't need to. It was only just nine in the morning. They might not be up, but he didn't want to think about that. He gave Peter Moran's address to directory inquiries and they found the number for him. Thought, consideration, might have given him pause but he didn't think. He lifted the receiver and dialled the number.

The spare economical voice with the beautiful accent answered. John nearly put the receiver back. He said hesitantly:

'This is John Creevey.'

As if he had never been to his house, drunk his wine, stolen his wife, 'Yes?'

'I'd like to speak to Jennifer.'

No request for him to wait, hold the line. Silence and then the sound of footsteps going away. It seemed a long time before Jennifer came.

'Hallo, John.'

'I had your letter,' he said. 'It's just come.'

'Don't say no just like that, John. Think about it. You don't have to give me an answer now.'

'I wasn't giving you an answer. I want to see you. I've got something to tell you.'

'Can't you tell me now?'

What did she think it was? That he was moving? Changing his job? Had even found another woman?

'I can't tell you on the phone. When can we meet?' He added quickly, 'Just the two of us, mind. I don't want him there.'

He heard her sigh, a sad troubled sound. 'I've got a job,' she said. 'Only part-time but it's better than nothing. It's secretarial, with a firm in Feverton. How about Thursday afternoon? I stop at lunchtime on Thursdays and you do too, don't you?'

'I'm on holiday,' he said.

She told him where she worked and agreed to meet him on Thursday at one o'clock. After he put the phone down, the enormity of it hit him. It wasn't long enough for the thinking he needed to do, four days wasn't long enough. Then he reflected on how readily she had said she would meet him. She had even seemed to want to meet him. Was the boorishness of Peter Moran proving too much even for her? He looked again at the letter, convinced anew that Jennifer hadn't written that unaided.

Newspapers had never been delivered to the house in Geneva Road after Cherry's death. When John wanted a paper he went out and bought one—the *Free Press* usually. Paying for his paper and taking a copy from the top of the pile, he wondered if perhaps the story of Peter Moran's conviction and sentence had in fact appeared in the *Free Press*. How would he have known whether it had or not? If it had, Jennifer might already know. She might always have known...

A heatwave had begun. Funny that you could always tell, that you always knew when a fine day was going to be isolated, a flash in the pan, and when it was the start of a hot spell. He walked along the embankment and over Randolph Bridge into Feverton. Jennifer had told him she was working for Albright-Craven in the Feverton square complex. They were a building firm about fifty times larger in scale than Maitland had been, yet the analogy with Cherry couldn't be ignored. His life seemed full of parallels and omens.

She would be there now. Mondays, Tuesday mornings, Wednesdays and Thursday mornings, she had told him, and he looked up at the windows, wondering which was her office, as in days gone by he had stood opposite Peter Moran's cottage, watching for her. The sky was a strong dark blue, the sun on all that glass and silver metal making a blaze that seared the eyes. He thought of walking, or more likely taking a bus, over Rostock to cats' green but he had been there several times in the past weeks and there had been nothing inside the central upright. It seemed that his mini-Mafia had once more gone into retreat.

Nevin Square was full of people. Like a piazza in some foreign city, he thought, milling with tourists. The sun had brought them out. The council had done the flowerbeds with coleus in brilliant variegated oranges, browns and sharp green, alternating with cockscombs, red and gold silken plumes, and *Amaranthus caudatus* that was called love-lies-bleeding. John sat on the low wall that surrounded the statue of Lysander Douglas, looking at the trailing crimson tails of blossom, and beyond them to the fountains in whose vaporous spray the sun made rainbows. Once, one hot day, when he was a big child and she a small one, Cherry had dared him to jump into the basin under the fountain, but he hadn't been adventurous and he hadn't dared. Now he opened the paper for something else to look at and his eye fell at once on a story about the court appearance of members of a protection racket.

Two of them had been charged with demanding money with menaces. It was an old story, though more familiar to John from the pages of thrillers than from his experience of life. The gang, if gang it was, had promised various shopkeepers and publicans freedom from vandalism in return for a weekly tariff. One of the witnesses was the licensee of the Beckgate and there was a photograph of the Beckgate in the text, showing that very hanging basket over the saloon-bar doorway which had come from Trowbridge's and which John had himself chosen and recommended.

The licensee said in evidence that when, after paying for week after week the rather paltry sum which had been demanded, he finally refused, the telephone in the passage at the back of the building was smashed and the chair seats in the small lounge bar ripped open. Half a dozen more witnesses were lined up and the case was expected to continue for several days. John turned back to the front page and saw that the missing schoolboy James Harvill's drowned body had been found in a lake somewhere in the Midlands. It was more than two months since he disappeared. John shivered a little in the heat.

ＦＦＦＦＦＦＦＦＦＦＦＦＦＦＦＦＦＦＦＦ **15** ＦＦＦＦＦＦ

'LORD, DISMISS US WITH THY BLESSING,' MUNGO sang, 'Fill our hearts with joy and peace; Let us each, Thy love possessing, triumph in redeeming grace...'

When the whole school was assembled in the chapel at Rossingham it was so crowded you had to keep your elbows tucked in not to prod the next man. Most days they had to hold staggered services, third and fourth forms first, fifth and sixth second, but it was different on the last day of term, the last of the school year. There was talk of extending the chapel, the Rossingham intake had increased so much. It was rather hard to see how this could be done without ruining what his father said was a monument to Pre-Raphaelitism. Mungo glanced round at the blue and crimson windows, moneychangers and bird-sellers, lilies of the field, fowls of the air, loaves and fishes, and back along the neighbouring pews.

'O refresh us, Travelling through this wilderness.'

It was extremely hot, the shafts of sunlight stained

azure and vermilion holding a suspension of dust motes. Graham O'Neill stood next to him, mouthing the words only because he was tone-deaf and forbidden to sing, while his twin, three men down the pew, sought refreshment in the wilderness in a fine true baritone. The Lower Fourth were in front, Patrick Crashaw and Charles Mabledene piping in yet unbroken voices, Robert Cook braying in a near-tenor, Nicholas Ralston a little bit flat as always.

'Let us pray.'

Not for the first time Mungo thought it a bit odd asking to depart in peace, as if they were all going to die. But there probably wasn't a suitable bit in the Bible about a school breaking up. Graham was coming home with him for part of the holidays and accompanying the Camerons to Corfu while Keith went with his aunt and uncle camping in Sweden. And when they came back next term they would be in the Fifth, O Levels ahead, private studies, greater freedom. But first I'll break Stern's code, said Mungo to himself.

He had got permission on the previous afternoon to go down into Rossingham St. Mary but there was nothing from Charybdis under the horse trough. Next year he wouldn't need permission. Signing the book would be sufficient. Strange really that Angus had given up the directorship just at the point when he attained the freedom essential to the head of London Central. As they filed out Mungo could see Angus ahead of him and for a moment he was aware of something he seldom felt even when Angus was mildly admonishing him, the gulf in ages between his brother and himself. It was an abyss that he too must leap one day, the girlfriend and the applications to medical schools waiting on the other side.

But now no more school for eight weeks, the formal good-byes to Mr and Mrs Lindsay, the obligatory word of thanks to the linen lady, the final survey and clean-up of the study one was quitting for next year's larger room and lower floor. He seemed to have more baggage than anyone else. The London Central 'most secret' files, and various books associated with what Angus persisted in calling Spookside, took up a whole case.

'Have you seen my *Armadillo Army*? I need it for the code.'

'It's already in with the files.' Graham said. 'I thought you'd changed when Stern got wise to it.'

'Only from Three to Eight. I reckoned that was rather subtle.'

They got Robert Cook to help them down with the cases. In Fergus's day he would have been obliged to do it and had a beating with a hairbrush if he had refused. In the present liberal climate with fagging the dirtiest word, they had to pay him.

'Those were the days,' said Mungo.

Mr Lindsay shook hands all round. He looked as if he couldn't wait to get to his health farm.

'Send me a postcard from Corcyra,' he said.

Angus sat in the front seat, Mungo and Graham behind. Fergus, remarking on the discovery of James Harvill's body, said to Mungo that he hoped he was aware of the dangers to people of his age from unknown men who might make overtures.

'Dad,' said Mungo patiently, 'I'm taller than you.' And he was—just. 'They'd be scared of me.'

The so-called climate control on the car failed to work and circulated hot air. They opened the windows instead. Fergus said worriedly that Mabledene's had promised to fix the air conditioning but had let him down.

'I'm not surprised,' said Mungo and he and Graham exchanged glances.

LATER THAT DAY, FROM THE AUDACIOUS DROP STERN used in the very heart of Mungo's empire, the narrow space between the bronze hand of Lysander Douglas and the book he held open, Mungo extracted a piece of cardboard six centimetres by ten with a message on it in the indecipherable code. As always, he copied it and replaced the card between hand and book.

It was still extremely hot. Indeed, looking up at the CitWest tower, Mungo couldn't remember ever seeing this particular combination of figures before: eight-thirty-one and twenty-six degrees. He remarked on it to Graham who sat waiting for him in the Laughing Burger where they had eaten their evening meal. They walked up Nevin Street into Ruxeter Road. It was at the point where the street widened and the shops began that Mungo realized they were being followed. He slowed down and dawdled at a window full of fishing gear.

He said to Graham, 'Don't look but Stern's put a tail on us. I think I recognize him. His name's Philip Perch.'

'Carrot-haired kid with a prosthesis?'

'That's one way of putting it. I'd call it a brace.'

They separated, Mungo to take Howland Road, Graham to continue northwards along Ruxeter but on the left-hand pavement. How Graham could possibly have seen from that distance and without even looking back that Philip Perch wore a brace on his teeth, Mungo couldn't fathom. He must have amazing eyesight. It was he, Mungo, whom Perch had decided to follow. Presumably he thought Western Intelligence's goal more likely to be in a back street than on a main road. Through the dusty streets Mungo led him and round the back of Fontaine Park, an area he was sure he knew a lot better than Perch would. The gates to the park were locked and on this side a high wall surrounded the green lawns and shady avenues. Mungo walked alongside the wall, knowing Perch wouldn't dare follow until he had reached the end where trees grew out of the pavement and big houses began, and at this evening time there were areas of deep shadow.

The air was hot and windless, full of flying insects. Where the wall ended and before the first garden, a narrow alley went down. Mungo stepped over the low railing into the garden instead, an extensive shrubbery of laurels and hollies and bushes he didn't know the name of. There he lay down on the ground, on leaf mould creeping with insect life, feeling against his skin the prickle of dried holly leaves.

A minute or two and Perch came trotting up. Without hesitation he turned down the alley and Mungo heard him start to run, his trainers making a soft thumping on the tarmac. Mungo didn't waste time. He got up, brushed off his jeans, and ran the last bit down into Fontaine Road. A chained bicycle fastened to one of the meters told him that Charybdis was already there. He needed to be more discreet, Mungo thought, making a mental note to tell him so. At this time of the year the long garden of the central house in Pentecost Villas was like a piece of savannah. You wouldn't have been surprised to see some wild beast stalking through the long grass, pushing aside metre-tall thistles, man-high grass. Not Mungo-high though, not quite. Like some old-time explorer—like, perhaps, Mungo Park himself—he strode through the wilderness, his head just above the stinging nettle tops, the thistle sword blades, while bramble tendrils caught at his legs.

They were all there, on the top floor. It was lightest up there, the electricity in the house having long ago been cut off. It was also hottest. Reasoning that it would be quite safe, Mungo pushed up the sashes on a couple of windows but it didn't make much difference. The temperature on the digital clock still stood at twenty-four. It winked away up in the jewel-blue sky. Charles Mabledene sat cross-legged on the floor up against the far wall, his pretty infant's face a little flushed from the heat, his fair silky hair longish the way his mother liked it. Spotty Patrick Crashaw who was called Basilisk was the first to deliver his report. There was a battle of wills going on at Moscow Centre, a vying for supremacy between Ivan Stern and Rosie Whittaker, and Rosie had Guy Parker, that *éminence grise*, on her side.

'Stern's not thinking of resigning, is he?' Mungo asked.

'Not yet. He may not. But there's a split coming.'

Nigel Hobhouse, or Charybdis, reported entry by way of a family chain to the Conservative Association Headquarters at Chamney where his sister's boyfriend's sister, temping secretary to the Secretary, an Utting teacher, had added the names of Mr Mungo Cameron and Mr Graham O'Neill to the wine and cheese party guest list. Their invitations should arrive in course of time. Mungo, anticipating cocktails, was disappointed. Nicholas Ralston reported the successful outcome of Autoprox. His brother had written to the Whittakers, visited the Whittakers and produced Dragon's photograph, and they had finally agreed to meet the first four hundred pounds of the repair bill. Mungo congratulated Dragon in the rather austere way he had, receiving in response a modest inclination of the fair head. Almost immediately a dozen balloons which no one had noticed before, though they must have been there, floated down from the ceiling to brush the floor and bounce lightly. Mungo felt annoyed. He tried to ignore the balloons and talked about the new projects, finding out when building was to start on this house, reviewing the new Rossingham intake—would anyone, for instance, be coming from Utting Junior as Charles Mabledene once had?—and the breaking of Stern's code, the task that was always with them, the unalterable goal, their *delenda est Carthago*, as Mr Lindsay might have said.

Mungo talked on, his eyes resting longer on the impassive face of Charles Mabledene than on any other. Was he Stern's mole? Mungo's conviction that he was had been a little shaken by the photographs. The yachting books meant nothing, the merest sop they were, but those photographs, especially the shot of Philip Perch's brother's room, gloomy and obscure though it was, with all the books about and the posters on the wall and the poised telescope on the windowsill—would Stern's mole have taken that? Of course the argument was that Stern's mole with access to almost any corner of Utting would be the most likely to have taken it...

Basilisk, Unicorn, Charybdis, their attentive faces watching him—it might be any of them. It might be Empusa who lived down in Cornwall but wasn't out of the running in term time. It might—unpleasant thought—even be Keith O'Neill, called Scylla, who was at this moment probably crossing the North Sea, bound for Gothenburg. He would subject Charles Mabledene to a test, think up a task for him which no mole of Stern's could creditably carry out, only at the moment he had no idea what such a thing could be. He could merely set Dragon, along with Basilisk, the job of inquiring into building plans for 53 Ruxeter Road. And while using the flyover drop for fairly innocuous messages, see how quickly Stern learned the current code was based on another story from *Armadillo Army*.

The light was fading. If they stayed much longer they would need to get out the candles that were kept in a drawer in the basement. Mungo closed the windows and they began to leave, going separately, remembering Philip Perch the tail who would not have disappeared, who would be about somewhere, hoping for something, fearing Stern's wrath. Only Graham and Mungo left together. They left last, Graham remarking that the rope which held up the stepladder to the roof was badly frayed at the point where it first wound round the cleat.

'That would make a hell of a crash if it came down,' said Graham.

'We'll see if the builders are coming. If they're not for six months, say, we'll renew the rope.'

They made their way down the staircase which at the top here was very steep. It had grown suddenly quite dark.

Twenty-two steep stairs led down to the landing where the shallower flight began. Mungo counted them. Light from the street lamps outside Fontaine Park, shed through a long window in the stairwell, made orange-coloured geometric patterns on the dusty broken floor. And above the light which lay like a bright mist, the sky was a dark mysterious blue, full of stars.

ʃʃʃʃʃʃʃʃʃʃʃʃʃʃʃʃʃ **16** ʃʃʃʃʃ

THE CASE AGAINST THE MEN RUNNING THE PROTEC-tion racket ended on Wednesday, both were found guilty and given prison sentences. Among the witnesses was a shopkeeper who claimed to have been beaten up and another who said he had been in fear of his life. John read all this in the copies of the *Free Press* he went out specially to buy. What surprised him was that the messages had begun again. The gang had apparently been undeterred by retribution striking two of its members.

He copied down the message he found inside the cats' green pillar, though its meaning, of course, eluded him. A yellow kitten, its sire's double, came rubbing it-self against his trouser leg. John didn't dare bend down to stroke it. He thought ruefully of how he had discovered the source of the Bruce-Partington code at the very hour at which its usefulness was over. He must try again with this one but it was already the nineteenth of the month...

The meeting with Jennifer loomed ahead of him. After collecting her from Albright-Craven, he must of course take her out to lunch. That would be fine in one way, but to impart such a piece of news in a restaurant, across a table? In the newspaper library he had asked if he might make a copy of the page with the story about Peter Moran on it. They hadn't allowed this but said that they would do it for him and ten minutes afterwards a Xerox had been handed to him. This sheet of paper, his lodestone, he would almost certainly have to produce to confirm his story. Passing it across the tablecloth seemed grotesque. But perhaps she wouldn't want to eat. John was sure that once he had told her, if he did this immediately after they met, she wouldn't want to eat at all. If he had had a car they might have sat in it. All the city centre pubs were very crowded at lunchtime. She wouldn't come home here alone with him. It was necessary to be realistic, to face facts, and he was grimly sure of that fact.

The phone rang in the middle of the afternoon as he was coming in from cutting the lawn. He had a premonition it was Jennifer phoning to cancel their meeting, but he was wrong. It was Gavin. The mynah was off its food, had eaten nothing since the previous morning, and its feathers looked dull and ruffled. Should Gavin take it to the vet? John had never really thought of vets as being bird doctors, but why not? He told Gavin to wait another day and then if the mynah was no better to take it to the vet after Trowbridge's closed at lunchtime. How coincidences happened, he thought as he picked up *Armadillo Army* which he had left face-downwards on the settee and saw it was open at the story called 'Mynah Magnum'. He remembered how he had tried the June code against the first lines of some of the stories in this book and tried them in vain. That had been before he started to read it. Now he saw the book was nearly a week overdue.

The espionage genre was perhaps not well suited to the short story. At any rate he hadn't enjoyed the three stories he had read in this collection nearly as much as Yves Yugall's novels and had no inclination to finish it. The library was closed all day Wednesdays. He would take *Armadillo Army* and the other two books back in the morning, but first why not try the coded message in his notebook against the first lines of these short stories?

The first lines of the stories yielded only a jumble of nonsense. He tried 'Armadillo Army', 'Mynah Magnum', 'Gila Haunt', 'Rodent', 'Strontium Strain'. The seventh story was called 'Brontosaur'. John wrote the letters of the alphabet under the letters in its first lines and tried it against the message. Immediately he knew that once more he had broken the code.

It was extraordinary the feeling of triumph he had. Nothing in his personal life had changed, his two tragedies were still with him, the momentous events that were to take place on the following day still hung over him, but he felt suddenly euphoric, bubbling with excitement almost. He felt on top of the world. For not only had he done it, had he broken the July code, but he now had the key to every future coded message, since instructions as to the source of the next one must of necessity appear in the current one at the end of each month.

John read the message he had deciphered: 'Leviathan to Dragon and Basilisk: Thursday p.m. find Whittakers' fisherman. Remove and eliminate.'

It was mysterious, not quite meaningless, but you had to be in the know, you had to be privy to the gang's secret knowledge. For the first time he was aware of an element of menace, even of violence, in one of the messages. Of course he had long known that the gang itself indulged in violence but this was the first message with anything sinister in it. The tiny sensation of alarm he had was like a splash of water from a fountain on to warm skin. What did that last bit mean? What did 're-move and eliminate' mean?

PART THREE

ƒƒƒƒƒƒƒƒƒƒƒƒƒƒƒƒƒƒƒƒ 1 ƒƒƒƒƒƒ

THE WHITTAKERS LIVED HALF-WAY BETWEEN UTTING
and Chamney in a red-brick house of such size, proportions and general appearance as can be found in the
wealthier suburbs all over England. Its front garden was
an extensive rockery through which a stream trickled
over slabs of limestone. The stream, Charles Mabledene
remarked to Patrick Crashaw, must be pumped electri-
cally. It wouldn't be a natural spring. They had been
keeping the house under observation for most of the
morning. A cricket field opposite was divided from the
road by a fence of wide wire mesh along which trees and
lengths of hawthorn hedge grew. Charles and Patrick
were in the field, walking up and down, sometimes sitting on a bench.

'What do you reckon he wants it done for?' Patrick
said.

'Ours is not to reason why.'

'OK, but don't you want to know? I mean it's only an
old gnome. What's he want it smashed for?'

'For a start he never said he wanted it smashed. He
says "eliminate". If he wanted it smashed I'd think it
was like the heads of Napoleon in the Sherlock Holmes
story.'

Patrick gave him a puzzled stare.

'One of them had diamonds inside,' Charles said.

'Do you reckon Rosie Whittaker's old gnome's got diamonds inside?'

'No,' said Charles coldly. 'No, Crashaw, I don't.'

He turned his head to look once more across the road. The object of his attention was a plaster figure in red cap and green jerkin which, seated on a stone that jutted out above one of the small waterfalls, trailed a fishing line in the water.

'How do you eliminate a gnome except by smashing it?' Patrick asked.

Charles ignored him. He was watching the rising and folding of a door on the garage opposite. The car he had photographed at the 'works', now repaired and resprayed, began slowly to emerge. From the other side of that garage he had long ago seen Rosie's father's Mercedes come out. That had been just before nine, Charles having been brought into town by his mother and dropped off on her way to the salon. Rosie and her mother were still inside. Or had been. He saw Rosie get out of the passenger side of the car, close the garage door and return to sit beside her mother. She had all the gear on, he observed, black footless tights, black tee-shirt, black jacket and her black hair standing up in spikes and streaked with green.

Then something curious happened: The car stopped in the middle of the drive, Mrs Whittaker jumped out and ran back into the house. Within seconds the stream, which had been quite a rushing torrent, slowed up, became a trickle and ceased. Charles started laughing, he couldn't help himself. For reasons of economy, no doubt, the Whittakers switched the pump off while they were out.

Literal-minded, very logical, Charles took Leviathan's command precisely to the letter. If he said p.m. he meant after twelve and it was still only ten to according to his watch, which, admittedly, had been losing lately. He was getting a new watch for his fourteenth birthday, along with a tregetour's special outfit made with twelve secret pockets. You couldn't see the CitWest tower from here, or not from the ground. You probably could from upstairs in the Whittakers' house.

Mrs Whittaker came back and she and Rosie drove off. The fisherman looked rather ridiculous now, trailing his line on a drying river bed. Was he going to smash it? The alternative way of eliminating would presumably be to drown it, drop it off Alexandra, say. Moving off towards the gate in the cricket field fence with Basilisk by his side, Charles came to a decision. He would very slightly disobey the command he had been given.

2

TELEMANN'S *SUITE IN A MINOR*, THE ANDANTE, poured out of Angus's room, reaching the ears of Mungo on the top floor and of Lucy who had just come from the hospital and was standing in the hall. In the outside cupboard, where deliveries were put, laundry and cumbersome mail and things of that sort, she had found a large awkwardly shaped parcel marked 'fragile' and addressed to Mungo. Lucy put it on the hall table. It felt like some kind of statuette and she hoped they weren't going to have it standing about down here. She would tell Mungo to keep it in his own room.

All the afternoon Mungo had been working on Stern's code, principally with the aid of the latest messages which he had copied down at the Nevin Square drop. Stern was very confident. He must be well aware London Central knew about that drop. For one thing, Philip Perch had probably been following him for some time before he, Mungo, saw him in Ruxeter Road. Perch must also have seen him take the message out of the hand of Lysander Douglas. Since then there had been another. They were still using the drop. It was obvious they didn't care how often Mungo read their messages, so confident were they in the impenetrability of the code.

Each of the messages, like each one he had ever read of Stern's commands, began with a number and ended with a number or row of numbers. You couldn't tell whether the end one was supposed to be one large number or a series of single figures. First came a single number of one or two digits, as it might be 6 or 17, then letters all run into one another without a break, then a series of digits: 22 NDITBHGTYIBSWONMWPSCSWX-APNUGN 931, it might be, and the second message, 24 WQBHTSOPMHPSTRITVCXWTYRN 1003. The second ultimate number was higher than the first by eight but that didn't seem to get anywhere. He tried adding the figures together, nine plus three plus one equals thirteen and trying a code based on an alphabet starting at the thirteenth letter, which is M. Then he tried adding one to three and a code based on an alphabet starting wtih the letter D. Neither worked. And what about the 22 and 24, anyway?

The window was wide open because it was very hot. He worked by the window, since the air was too still and heavy to blow his papers about. Angus's music drifted in through his open door. Maybe there was some way he could get Angus to put the code on his computer but even a computer couldn't tell him what those numbers were, could it? Graham with Ian and Gail came into view walking up Hill Street. They had all been swimming at the municipal pool in Fevergate. A green van with Mogul Palace printed on its side drew up down below in Church Bar. The driver got out and unloaded a stack of circular aluminum containers. Next to Indonesian, Mogul cuisine was

Mungo's favourite, and he leant out of the window hoping for a sniff of it but the containers were too tightly sealed to give anything away.

He made his way downstairs as the Mogul van man disappeared round the back way. The numbers might be pages in a book, he thought, only it would have to be a pretty long book. The Bible? A whiff of tandoori chicken which now greeted him, coming up the stairs from the kitchen, suggested it might even be the Koran. Were there a thousand and three pages in the Koran?

The parcel on the hall table was addressed to him. Mungo knew what it was by the feel of it through the paper. He was somewhat appalled and his hunger, which up to that moment had been raging, slightly abated. He began picking off the sticky tape. The last thing he had expected was that Dragon and Basilisk would actually do it—well, Dragon you might as well say, for he had no doubt whose had been the directing force. He had been sure Moscow Centre would have been alerted well in advance and the fisherman moved before Charles Mabledene got there. Of course there was a possibility Rosie had tried to move it but had been prevented by her parents to whom the truth could not be told. But somehow Mungo didn't believe this.

Angus ran down the stairs and on down to the kitchen, turning briefly to look at Mungo, frowning. The fisherman now unwrapped, Mungo stood it on the crumpled brown paper and stared at it. Charles Mabledene had been instructed to eliminate it but presumably had had misgivings about that. He was getting too big for his boots. Mungo sighed. He had been so certain the fisherman wouldn't be there that he had given no thought to the result if it was there. There was no doubt that this was stealing and he had always drawn the line at actual stealing. He couldn't help thinking of what Angus had said about things ending in tears or even disaster. Still, disaster wasn't going to come by way of this fishing gnome if he could avoid it.

And as to Charles Mabledene being the traitor, nothing was proved except his deviousness, his subtlety.

'Mungo!'

'Coming,' called Mungo, but his father had already appeared at the head of the stairs.

At the sight of his youngest contemplating a large plaster figurine fresh from its wrappings, Fergus said worriedly:

'Now, Mungo, what on earth possessed you to buy that? It must have cost a fortune. You haven't got that kind of money. We don't want that kind of thing here anyway. It'll have to go back.'

'Yes, Dad, I know,' said Mungo. 'Don't you worry, it's going back tomorrow.'

ƒƒƒƒƒƒƒƒƒƒƒƒƒƒƒƒƒƒƒƒ **3** ƒƒƒƒƒ

JENNIFER CAME DOWN THE STEPS OF THE ALBRIGHT-Craven building at a few minutes past one. She was wearing a light summery dress of white cotton with grey spots and flat white sandals and she had sunglasses on with very wide frames and dark lenses which concealed a good deal of her face, hardening it and robbing it of character.

She came up to John unsmiling, so much hidden behind those black glasses.

'It's terribly hot. I can't stand this kind of heat, it's so humid.'

He had never known her to complain about heat

before. She had seemed to long for the sun and revel in it when it came. He thought she looked tired and strained. On his way he had gone into a wine bar in Fevergate and seeing that they had tables out on the pavement with striped sunshades over them, had booked one. The table they had given him was in the deep shade cast by the largest remaining fragment of city wall, a bastion of narrow Roman and medieval brickwork hung with wallflowers and virginia creeper. Jennifer, who had hardly spoken, sank down into the cane chair, laid her arms on the table and said in a rather breathless pleading tone:

'Have you thought about what I asked you? Are you going to do it?'

She seemed to have forgotten the purpose of their meeting.

'Would you like a drink, Jennifer? We could have a bottle of wine or a soft drink, something cold.'

'I don't mind. Wine, if you like.' She looked up and said rather miserably, 'I expect you think I was threatening you, it did look like that. I'm sorry. I didn't mean to. I wouldn't take any money from you, you know, I wouldn't dream of taking a share of your house.'

He felt as if a hand had wrenched at his heart. He thought, I know why people, those old writers and poets, talk about the heart, about the heart breaking, it's because that's where you feel it, in your chest, in the middle of you.

'I want us to share the house,' he said. 'Do you know how much I want that?'

She was shaking her head. A waitress came and he ordered the wine and some ice in case it wasn't cold which it probably wouldn't be. Jennifer said:

'I wish I smoked. There are times when it would be wonderful to have a cigarette, only I don't smoke. I never could take to it.'

'Nor me.'

We have so much in common, John thought, we feel

the same about such a lot of things. He was sure now that like him she wouldn't want to eat though there was a menu there written up on a blackboard.

'I don't want anything to eat,' she said. 'It's too hot.'

He wasn't wearing a jacket, just a thin cotton shirt with the sleeves rolled up. In his trouser pocket he could feel the sheet of paper, folded in four, on to which the newspaper library had photocopied the Peter Moran story for him. The slippery surface of the paper felt cool against his fingertips.

'We should never have got married,' Jennifer said suddenly and rapidly. 'It was an awful mistake. I married you because I couldn't have Peter, you must know that. I was fond of you but I wasn't in love with you. I ought to have known he'd come back one day.'

'Has he ever told you why he went away?'

She seemed surprised by the question. Before she could answer the wine came. After the fashion he had learned from Mark Simms but never would have followed in the old days, John drank a glassful down. Jennifer's answer wasn't really a reply. She said, looking into the golden, faintly sparkling wine in her glass:

'I have to be with someone who needs me. I've found out I have to be with someone who needs me to look after them. Most of my life I've looked after people, my father was ill all those years, and then my mother. Well, you know all that. There's something wonderful about feeling you hold someone in the hollow of your hand, their fate, their life. They're absolutely in your keeping. I thought you wanted looking after, John, but you don't, you're strong. You were going to look after me. Peter depends on me, he leans on me, he'd be lost without me.'

John's voice shook. 'I am lost without you.'

'No, that's not true. You're a survivor. He's not. He clings on to me as if I were—well, some kind of life-support machine. I have to ask you again, I have to keep on asking you, will you give me a divorce? Please, John.'

John poured himself a second glass of wine. He thought, now or never. It's right to tell her anyway. It's right for her to know. I am her husband and any means I can use to get her back are right for me to use, any lodestone that will draw her to its pole. Why then did he feel he was about to do something wicked and wrong? She had bowed her head and sat there patiently. The black glasses still covered her eyes but now she put up her hand and took them off. John's hand slowly withdrew the folded paper from his pocket and as he looked up he saw over Jennifer's shoulder that Mark Simms was sitting at one of the tables near the wine bar's entrance. He was alone, a carafe of red wine in front of him and a plate of some sort of salad which he seemed to have left untouched. John turned his head sharply away. He said:

'I said to you on the phone I'd got something to tell you.'

'I'd forgotten,' she said. 'What is it?'

He was certain then that she already knew. That was what she meant by all that life-support stuff. It was a damp squib after all, this revelation of his. Perhaps it was better that way. He began to talk in a rapid neutral voice, setting out the facts, telling her what he had learned, giving a précis of the newspaper story. When he got to the part about Peter Moran pleading guilty to molesting the child, he saw that all the colour had drained out of her face. She was quite white, with a purplish bruise-like mark on the bridge of her nose where the sunglasses had pressed.

'I don't believe you,' she said when he had finished.

'You didn't know, then? I thought you might already know.'

'You've made it up.'

Feeling sick now, he pushed the paper across the table to her. A drop of spilt wine made a grey stain in the middle of it. He drank some more, pouring and spilling some more. She read the account, one hand up to her forehead. There was sweat in beads on her upper lip, on that livid whiteness. He looked away. He looked at Mark Simms and then wished he hadn't, for Mark saw him and raised one hand in a tentative wave. To his horror, Jennifer began to cry. At first she sobbed soundlessly, dry-eyed, sitting stiffly upright, then she lowered her head to the table, on to her folded arms, and wept bitterly, her whole upper body shaking.

People going by looked curiously at her. John felt nothing but a kind of emptiness, a deadness. He remembered a phrase that came from he didn't know where about being cruel only to be kind. He had been that, he had had her welfare at heart, or he thought he had. Had it only been his own?

'Jennifer,' he said. 'Jennifer, I'm sorry.'

She made no answer. He touched the shaking shoulder and had the dreadful experience of feeling the flesh shrink away under his hand. His eyes briefly squeezed shut, he asked himself what he was going to do, what was the next step? He opened his eyes to find Mark Simms bending over him.

'Is there anything I can do?'

'No,' John said. 'Thanks, but no.'

'I thought perhaps I could help.'

'How can you help? Just leave us alone. You've done enough damage.'

Jennifer suddenly flung up her head. She looked terrible, white and feverish and distraught, her face swollen and actually wet with tears.

'I'm going,' she said. 'I must go. I must go back.'

She didn't say she must go home. John noticed and exulted in the midst of his fear. Mark Simms stood there, looking at them, waiting for an introduction. Moving like an old woman, Jennifer struggled to her feet. She rubbed at her eyes with the back of her hand. John took a handkerchief, which was clean though not ironed, out of the pocket where the newspaper photocopy had been and offered it to her. It was absurd how his heart leapt when she didn't refuse it, but took it, covering her face, spreading hand and handkerchief across her face.

'I'll go and get a bus,' she mumbled through her fingers.

'You're not fit to go on your own.'

John had to find the waitress and pay. He looked round rather wildly but she had disappeared inside the wine bar. Jennifer had sagged against the table, leaning there, supporting her body on her arms. The whole thing was suddenly taken out of John's hands by Mark Simms—whose presence, whose existence, he had forgotten—saying:

'You're Jennifer, aren't you? My name's Mark, I'm an old friend of John's. Let me help, let me take you home.'

The taxi seemed to materialize before them, it was as if Mark summoned it out of the air. John's eyes met Jennifer's and they held each other's eyes for a long moment. Then she was gone and the taxi gone before he had even paid for the wine.

WHAT HAD HE EXPECTED? THAT SHE WOULD promptly repudiate Peter Moran and throw herself into his, John's arms? Or that she would defy him and declare herself loyal to Peter Moran whatever he had done? One or other of these he had expected while knowing things are never as you anticipate them. At home, pottering about the garden after an almost sleepless night, John tried to tell himself things were good, the outcome of their interview had been the best possible. He must allow for the effects of shock and simply wait for it to wear off.

Nothing that could happen now would surprise him, he felt. If Peter Moran himself arrived raving or Mark Simms turned up as a self-appointed intermediary, if Colin rang to say it was a different Peter Moran, he had made a mistake, if Jennifer phoned asking for time to make up her mind, she was no longer anxious for a divorce—if any of those things happened he would be prepared. For half the day, though, he felt he shouldn't go far from the phone. But when it didn't ring and no one came, as the hot sultry day shambled on towards afternoon, he took his books back to the Lucerne Road library and on an impulse walked the further half-mile down to the flyover and cats' green.

There was a message inside the upright. John opened the plastic package, copied down the message and deciphered it there and then. 'Leviathan to Charybdis,' he read, 'Martin Hillman, Trevor Allan, investigate and report.' Who were these people? Shopkeepers, proprietors of small businesses the gang wished to intimidate? And why did he care? Surely he had more pressing personal matters to concern him. He replaced the message in the upright.

There were no cats about today—or was that a gleam of yellow fur under the last stunted bush where the curve of the road dipped to meet the ground? John hardly knew why he went closer. Perhaps because of the stillness of it, the absence of glinting eyes. He pushed through the dusty coarse grass, the litter of picked bones.

The king cat lay stretched out dead, its eyes open and glazed, in this heat the flies already busy. Yet there seemed no mark on the body, no blood. The stiff muzzle had a white frosting, he had been an old cat, perhaps old enough to die a natural death. John didn't even like cats and this one had been no purring pet but a savage near-wild animal, yet he felt absurdly moved, distressed even by this death in the heat, this untended corpse left a prey to scavengers. If it had been possible to bury the cat he would have done so but all he could do, in a futile gesture, was pull up handfuls of grass and cover the body with it. By the time he had finished he was choking and gasping for breath. Whatever it was in feline biology that promoted asthma, it survived death.

It was a slow homeward journey he made, his chest full of phlegm and his eyes weeping. He might actually have been crying, he thought, for the king cat and for his own loneliness and Jennifer's pain and for Cherry. But no one he passed looked at him. In stupefying heat people didn't look at each other, they lost their alertness, their desire to observe. The phone was ringing as he entered the house. He thought it must be one of them, any of them, Jennifer, Mark Simms, Colin, even Peter Moran. But it was only Gavin.

'I thought you'd like to know Grackle is OK again.'

For a moment John couldn't remember who Grackle was. Then, when he did realize, he thought aggrievedly that it was only because he was alone, a kind of widower who never went away or did anything exciting, that Gavin thought he could call him up like this and talk nonsense. Gavin was going on and on in his barely comprehensible slang about the mynah's illness, some kind of bird virus, and its B-cells, whatever they might be. He had taken it to the vet three times.

'I suppose the firm is expected to foot the bill,' John said and immediately wished he hadn't, for after all the mynah belonged to Trowbridge's and was worth a lot of money.

'I'll pick up the tab for that,' said Gavin.

The phone didn't ring again. This was his holiday, John thought when it got to seven, and he hadn't been anywhere, he hadn't even been to see his aunt. Constance Goodman answered when he phoned Colin's home and seemed to take it for granted that the invitation to go out somewhere for a drink would include herself, so John found himself in the snug of an unpopular country pub where the tables were dirty and the licensee indifferent, apparently committed to an evening of conversation with Mrs Goodman on the subject of the decline in standards of British primary school education. No one mentioned their last meeting or Peter Moran but after a while Mrs Goodman began to talk in a very dogmatic way about modern marriage, how glad she was Colin had never married, for he and his wife would surely have split up by this time. Mrs Goodman scarcely knew of any marriage in which the parties were under fifty which had lasted. She enumerated the many she knew of that had come to grief. Colin yawned.

'I'm sorry if I'm boring you, Colin. If that's the way you feel I'm sorry I gave in when you insisted I should come.'

'I insisted? That's rich, that is. That's very funny. John rang up and you'd rushed in where angels fear to tread before I even got into the room.'

'Are you calling me a fool, Colin?'

They went on sparring like that until John got up and said he had to get back. He and the Honda returned to the city via the village of Ruxeter and down Ruxeter Road. A glance at 53 told him nothing, for the house was in darkness and the windows of the lower storeys still boarded up. The clock on the CitWest tower registered nine-fifty-three and twenty-one degrees. A bright star, a smaller, more brilliant winking light, passed behind the green digits and reappeared on the other side, a meteorite or a satellite perhaps or just an aircraft very high up. John went over Alexandra, over the glassy still river, reflecting lights like a mirror, down into the hinterland of the east, into Berne Avenue, Geneva Road. It wasn't until afterwards that he noticed the car, the Diane. There were so many cars parked on both sides of the street at night. He was humping the Honda up over the pavement to shove it through the gate and down the side way, when she came to him out of the shadows like a ghost, she seemed to glide from under the branches of his flowering tree, to stretch out her hand and lay it on his arm.

'Jennifer!'

'I've been waiting for you for two hours,' she said and her eyes were glittering in a wild white face.

THE ADMIRING CIRCLE ROUND THE MYNAH'S CAGE broke up when John came in, Sharon drifting back to her check-out, Les resuming his sweeping of the floor, and only Gavin and the two customers, a young couple, remaining to hear the mynah utter once more and incredibly:

'I'm an empty nester!'

John was late.

'Thought you'd forgotten it was back to work today,' Sharon said.

He tried to smile. The young couple went off towards the fertilizers and seed packets with their wire basket. Gavin turned to John.

'Did you hear that? Did you hear what he said? I taught him.'

'Congratulations.'

'What's with you, then? A right Tafubar, by the looks.'

'A what?' said John.

'Things are fucked up beyond all recognition.'

'I'm an empty nester,' said the mynah bird.

'*Gracula religiosa*,' said Gavin, 'is the world's best talker, better even than your grey parrot.'

It was Monday morning. John put on his canvas coat and walked through into the greenhouse where the chrysanthemums were, their bitter scent which he rather disliked making a tingle in his nostrils as he opened the door. Rain drummed on the roof and ran down the glass walls so that all you could see of outside was a blur of various greens. The heatwave had broken on the previous night in a spectacular thunderstorm which kept John awake, though he probably wouldn't have slept anyway.

A deep depression, a trough of low pressure, the meteorological people said. This change in the weather had a similar effect on him, casting him into his own deep depression. For up until yesterday evening, though unhappy, devastated, almost distraught, he had still been full of rage, a need to fight, a desire for revenge. It was in that mood that he had gone back to cats' green and taken that curious step, an action he couldn't explain to himself at the time or later, of taping his own coded message into the central upright of the flyover. Someone had taken away the cat's body. He had approached the place shrinking a little, expecting a swarm of flies, a foetid smell, but when he looked towards the pile of grass he had made, when he forced himself to look, there was nothing. Even his grass was gone. Had there ever been anything, a death, the covering of a corpse? Was the cat dead or had he imagined it?

In the heat of the day, the sun that made sizzling mirages on the deserted roadways down here, the melting tarmac, in the absence of the cat's body, John had a sense of unreality, a feeling of being in an uncomfortable dream. Without thinking, or thinking only of his hatred of Peter Moran, whom nothing could expel, whom nothing apparently could dislodge from Jennifer's consciousness, he had removed the message from its plastic envelope and substituted another of his own devising...

He passed along the central aisle of the greenhouse and on into the next one where the seedling alpines were and the begonia leaf cuttings. Gavin had taken care of everything efficiently in his absence. The plantlets were damp but not wet, green and healthy-looking, the place swept clean. But John could feel no enthusiasm for it, only aware of a dreary sensation that he might as well be here as anywhere else, he might as well be here as at home.

For a while he had believed that his interview with Jennifer marked the last occasion on which they would ever meet and this certitude returned to him now. Yet when she had come up to him, white-faced, out of the shadows, he had thought with a leap of the heart that she was returning to him. And she had said nothing, only preceded him into the house when he unlocked the front door, gone straight into the living room ahead of him as if it were still her home, as if he and she would sit down in there together, have a nightcap perhaps, turn out the lights and go upstairs to bed.

What had actually happened was that she turned to face him as soon as they were together in that room. He switched on the new table lamp. The atmosphere was warm and rather stuffy. Her face was grim, almost tragic. He had never seen her look like that before, a changed woman.

'I decided to come and tell you what you've done,' she said.

He said nothing, he just looked at her.

'I've been waiting for you for hours but I'd have waited all night.'

To repeat that he had made that revelation to her for her own sake suddenly seemed the rankest hypocrisy. He stood facing her. Oddly, the settee was between them, she holding on to the back of it as if to a barricade.

'I'll be honest,' he said. 'I told you to put you against him. I was in possession of a piece of information that I thought would turn you against him. I saw it as being to my own advantage and I used it—as a weapon.'

She nodded, as if he had confirmed what she already knew. 'The police came—after that little boy went missing, the one who was found drowned. Drowned,' she said, her voice hoarse, 'after being—abused. The police came to question Peter. I didn't know why. How could I?

195

They talked to him alone, I wasn't there. Did you send them?'

'Of course I didn't. They go to people like him as a matter of course when something like that happens.'

'I hate you, John.' Her voice was still sweet, she couldn't change that. 'As if Peter would hurt a child... Whatever he may have done he wouldn't do that.'

'I don't know.' John was still wincing from what she had said. 'I don't know what he would do.'

'You thought telling me would get me back. I want you to know it was the worst thing you could have done. Do you think that makes you love a person, telling them a thing like that? You hate any bearer of bad news, it's well known. And when it's that sort of news—John, I was angry with you before, I was bored with you, I was sick of it all but I didn't hate you. This has made me hate you.'

He shivered under the onslaught. His body shook. Instead of defending himself, he said:

'You can't still love someone who has done what he's done. You can't love a man who molests little boys.'

'I hate you for telling me,' she said, her tone growing calmer, colder. 'You didn't have to tell me. If you love someone the way you say you love me, you ought to want their happiness, you ought to want to protect them from suffering.'

That one didn't work, he knew that, though he couldn't have said why.

'What good did it do, telling me? What did you think, that I'd jump into your arms and say it had all been a dreadful mistake?'

Some curious intuition, some reading of her mind that was in itself an agony because it bore witness to their mutual knowledge, made him say with slow realization:

'It's made you feel differently about him though, hasn't it? It has changed you. You don't care for him so much.'

A wave of pain passed across her face, or rather it was

as if something under the skin, inside the features, dragged briefly at the muscles. She wouldn't lie to him, he thought, she never would, even though now it would have been easy, it would almost have been expected of her. She said remotely, in the tone of one who has been dealt a blow:

'It has made a difference, yes. I don't feel the same about Peter. How could I? You did that, you're responsible for that.'

'I'm not sorry.'

'No, you wouldn't be. But I'll tell you something. It's made me understand he needs me to look after him more than ever, he needs me to protect him—from himself as well as other people. While he wants me I'll stick to him whether you divorce me or not. And there's another thing, John. Maybe you never considered this. I know why he left me the way he did before our wedding. It wasn't for another woman or because he didn't love me, I know that now. It was because he thought what he'd done would come out and he might go to prison.'

'And suppose he goes to prison in the future? What then?'

She made no answer. She turned and walked out of the room, looking over her shoulder and saying as she reached the front door:

'I'll never willingly see you again, John. I'll never speak to you again.'

Regrets first for playing it the way he had and saying the things he had said, then anger, then a desire for revenge. Wriggling in among it a worm of hope, the only vital thing in that carcase of negative emotions. If her passion for Peter Moran, her starry-eyed love, was over, killed by what she now knew, there was hope for him, wasn't there? Yet she had said she would never see him again.

At cats' green on the Sunday he took the message from the inside of the pillar and added Peter Moran's name to the two names already printed there in the

'Brontosaur' code. The message now read: 'Leviathan to Dragon: Martin Hillman, Trevor Allan, Peter Moran: observe and tail.' What was the good of it John hardly knew. He had some vague idea of thus harassing Peter Moran, of causing him anxiety or even fear, and he derived great satisfaction from what he had done for quite a long while. He felt better, he felt that at last he had made an attack on Peter Moran instead of waiting passively and effecting no retaliation. Besides, what was the use of being in possession of the key to the codes if he never took advantage of it?

But during the early hours of the morning, this morning, while the storm rumbled in the surrounding hills and the rain pounded on his bedroom window, he awoke out of an uneasy doze to a kind of shocked realization. What had he done? What absurd game was he playing? Was he really setting a bunch of gangsters on to his wife's lover? Dismay soon gave place to reason. They wouldn't know who Peter Moran was. He didn't have a phone, they wouldn't be able to find him. It was then that, inexplicably, depression descended and enclosed him, remaining with him now, dulling all his perceptions, as he walked through the greenhouses and out into the covered way that led to the gardens and the tree and shrub grounds. The rain was falling in straight rods with a perfect steady evenness. He turned back into the shop and was immediately appealed to by a woman wanting to know how to get her last Christmas's poinsettia to bloom again this year.

THE RAIN WENT ON ALL MONDAY EVENING AND through most of the night. They probably didn't pick up those messages at cats' green every day, John thought, and heavy rain like this was as likely to stop their activities as other people's. If he went there before going to work in the morning he might be in time to change the message back again, to remove Peter Moran's name. When he inserted it into the message he must have been a bit mad. Well, not mad exactly but off balance, unhinged as his mother used to put it, as if the mind were a room with a door to it that somehow got slewed off its hinges. And it was true that he had felt like that in the heat and humidity and in his misery.

The temperature had fallen dramatically. A fresh breeze ruffled the water that reflected a sky of clouds and rare patches of blue. The rain had laid the dust of summer and everywhere had a washed look as of a huge clean-up operation that extended even to the leaves on the trees and the annuals in the flowerbeds. Pools of water still lay in the hollows on Beckgate Steps, a lake of it on the landing of stone slabs. John shied away from thoughts of Cherry as he had done ever since Mark Simm's confession and his revelations as to her true nature. He gave his attention instead to the Beckgate pub, closed of course at this hour, a slow drip-drip of water falling from the hanging basket over the saloon-bar door. The gang he was involving himself with had damaged furniture and a phone in there and threatened worse violence. John climbed the Beckgate Steps rapidly and broke into a run up the lane, impelled now by an urgent need to get to cats' green as soon as he could.

A steady rumble came from the flyover, carrying its morning load of traffic southwards. A thin young tomcat with wet orange fur was licking itself dry, sitting on an upturned wooden box which hadn't been there on Sunday. Was this the new king? John didn't want a repetition of Friday's asthma attack and he kept well clear of the cat. Because of this he didn't see the interior of the upright until he was close up to it. For the first time, there were two messages inside, two plastic envelopes taped to the metal. But even before he took them down John could see that the one to which he had added Peter Moran's name was gone.

He had a curious unaccountable feeling of excitement. And as he unfolded the papers he remembered how he had used to think of his investigations into these messages as a kind of therapy. His interest in them and his curiosity about them had saved him from falling into total despondency. He ought now to be aghast at his action in giving the gang Peter Moran's name, that he was too late to remedy the mischief, but he felt no remorse. He had an inexplicable desire to laugh but of course he couldn't start laughing there, out in the open street. He read the two messages with the aid of the key in his notebook. The first said: 'Unicorn to Leviathan: Stern resignation confirmed effective 1 August.' The second meant more to him personally. Reading it, he had a momentary sensation of dizziness. 'Dragon to Leviathan: Peter Moran not known. Address required soonest.'

John replaced the message about Stern in its envelope and attached it once more to the upright, using a fresh length of tape from the roll he had brought with him. The other he put into his pocket. As he walked away and up to the bus stop the excitement seemed to ebb away and depression to return. Without knowing why such an idea should have come to him as he walked along a street where there was nothing to evoke her, not a name or a picture or an object to remind him, he realized suddenly and clearly that Jennifer would never leave Peter Moran. Somehow he had never quite accepted this before, he had always had hope, always believed that marriage itself, the solid fact of it, would draw her back. Now he didn't. While Peter Moran remained she would stay with him, and the lodestone, instead of exerting a magic pull over her, seemed to have further toughened the bond between them.

They—or he whose code name was Dragon—had actually asked for Peter Moran's address. John kept on thinking about this and in a kind of wonderment, perhaps at the fact that his own message had been taken seriously. But why not? How could it have been otherwise? Dragon believed the message to have come from

Leviathan and he was obviously accustomed to obeying Leviathan's commands. The code would change at the end of the week, John thought, and he might easily miss the announcement of what the new code was to be. Therefore, if he wanted to pass any information to them he ought to act in the next few days.

A sense of reality returned to expel these ideas. He was a law-abiding citizen, middle-aged and respectable, too dully respectable perhaps. If he had been a lawbreaker with criminal tendencies his wife might have loved him, have stayed with him. The ideas came back again when he returned home to his lonely empty house in the evening. Most people in his position wouldn't hesitate, he thought, people who found themselves by sheer chance with access to the services of hit men. What did they call it? Putting a contract out on someone? Gavin would know but of course he couldn't ask Gavin.

On the Wednesday evening he did what he had been promising himself to do for some time, he phoned his aunt, and as a result found himself spending the following afternoon and evening with her and his uncle. They didn't know about Jennifer and he didn't tell them, just said she was at work. Returning home on the Honda, taking a route via cats' green was one of the possible options, so of course he went that way. The message inside the upright read: 'Leviathan to Dragon: October men to take over from Sunday.' John got out his notebook and added to the foot of it in 'Brontosaur': 'Twenty-two Fen Street Nunhouse.' He replaced the message, telling himself that by not inserting Peter Moran's name he had not really taken any significant step, he hadn't done anything wrong.

But on the next evening when he saw the police car draw up outside the house and the man and woman—plainly CID people—get out of it, he thought they had come to arrest him.

THEY AGREED THAT GRAHAM SHOULD SET THE TEST for Charles Mabledene. It was neither more nor less than that Dragon should get Stern's code—or Rosie Whittaker's code, as they must now call it. If he had the 'in' at Utting which he claimed to have this should be possible, only loyalty to Moscow Centre would prevent it. If he got the key to the code he would prove his loyalty to to London Central beyond a doubt. Graham wasn't going to use the flyover drop—indeed, Mungo didn't think he even knew of the location of the drop, using for his particular agents (Scylla, Wyvern and Minotaur) another near the Shot Tower—but intended to meet Dragon at the safe house.

Mungo usually looked forward to Corfu but this year his expectations were tempered with doubt. Could he afford to be so long as a fortnight away from the centre of operations? The situation was especially touchy now that Rosie Whittaker had taken over. Mungo suspected Rosie of a special brand of dynamism. And he wondered who would be coming into Utting among the autumn term's intake, more effective recruits for Moscow than Martin Hillman and Trevor Allan, he thought, whom Basilisk had reported as being scared by the prospect before them both academically and (as Basilisk put it) spy-wise.

Graham had packed his case before he went off to Ruxeter Road but not put his digital travelling clock in, Mungo noticed. They could do with that, he would remind him when he got back. Strains of Monteverdi filled the house, mixing oddly with the smell of dim sum and black bean sauce hanging on from their supper. Angus was sulking—or going about looking grim and stoical which was his way of sulking—because they couldn't take his girlfriend Diana with them. He understood of course that this was only because the request to take her hadn't been made till after their flight and hotel were booked but it was still hard to take when Gail was coming. Gail, in fact, would be staying the night because they were making such an early start in the morning.

The Chinese takeaway meal having been eaten an hour and a half ago, Mungo went downstairs to find something in the fridge. His mother was making coffee and reading the *Lancet* while she waited for the kettle to boil. His father paced up and down.

'If anyone had ever told me when I was a young man,' Fergus was saying more in sorrow it sounded like than in anger, 'that a request would be made to me for my son's girlfriend to share a bed with him under my own roof, I would have laughed in derision.'

'Not laughed, darling. Sneered in derision.'

'Well, sneered then. What does it matter? Is this going to go on while we're in Corfu? Are they to go in the same room? I find it bewildering, I find the assumption bewildering.'

'Times have changed since you were young. I'm always telling you. Anyway, you're not going to refuse, are you? If you do they'll only creep about in the middle of the night and you'll think it's burglars, you know what you are.'

'I find it so terribly worrying, Lucy. I mean, the assumptions and the possible consequences, the whole concept.'

'Oh, darling, there won't be a concept, I promise you.'

Fergus made an impatient gesture. He realized for the first time that his youngest son was in the room. 'Mungo, I didn't know you were there. Have you heard what we've been saying?'

'Yes,' said Mungo, eating the last slice of a mushroom quiche.

'Well, you must try to put it out of your mind.' Another awful revelation struck Fergus. 'You booked, Lucy. You must have booked them a double room.'

Lucy poured boiling water on to the coffee. 'If Mungo's to put it out of his mind you'd better not say any more till he's gone.'

Previously uninterested, Mungo began to find the issue intriguing. But the anxious misery on his father's face swayed the balance. He reached for his mug of coffee. 'I'm on my way.'

Angus sat hunched over the computer, a bag of chocolate truffles beside him for comfort.

'There's coffee for you if you want it,' Mungo said, adding, 'Make a bit of noise before you go in though, fall down the stairs or something.'

Up in his room he studied the latest of Stern's codes. As always it began and ended with numbers, 9 followed by a row of letters, 1132 to end. The previous two he had read began with a 5 and a 17 respectively and ended with 931 and 1003; the first he had ever seen, the one which appeared after Moscow Centre realized the West was in possession of Guy Parker's codebook, had begun with a 4 and ended with 817. What did they have in common, those numbers? Nothing much, as far as he could see. The initial numbers were all quite low, the ultimate numbers all quite high. He had never seen an ultimate number below 700, for instance, or come to that anything higher than 1258.

Could those final digits be house numbers? Only in North America did house numbers come that high. Or phone numbers? That was more likely. But the difficulty with that was that here in the city after the four-digit code you always got a six-digit number, or a completely arbitrary three-digit number following a more or less fixed three-digit number. Well, 931 and 817 might be the last digits of a number with ten in total... Mungo went to shut the round window under the eaves. Nights had been cold this past week but they wouldn't be cold in Corfu. There wouldn't be clouds there either, there wouldn't be mountain ranges of vapour, scored with darkness and topped with gold, white foaming glaciers splitting them, green sky like marble appearing between... On the other side of the river scaffolding had gone up round the Shot Tower. Was there time for a quick message to Unicorn to find out why and how long for? Probably not. He hadn't packed yet.

Round the corner from Hill street came Graham in the octopus tee-shirt, wearing his crazy sunglasses even at this hour, black hair falling down over his forehead. Mungo raised his hand in a salute and Graham waved back. He dropped his cigarette and trod it out.

6

NEVER IN HIS LIFE HAD HE FELT FEAR OF THE POLICE. There had always been the feeling they were on his side and this had specially been true since Cherry's death. Perhaps the only comfort his parents and he had had was the support of the police, the knowledge that they and the police were united against the man who had broken in and destroyed their happiness. Mark Simms, if only they had known it.

A middle-aged ordinary-looking man and a young pretty woman. How had he known they were police? For he did know it from the moment they stepped out of that anonymous lamp-less unmarked car. Perhaps it was because the driver remained behind, impassive at the wheel, reminding John of police drivers from that time sixteen years before. But it was of his own intervention in the gang's activities that he thought as he saw the man open the gate and come up the short path toward the front door. That also told him they were police. Almost anyone else would have opened the gate for the woman with him and let her go first.

The doorbell rang. Though he knew it must ring, the sound of it still made him jump. He thought, what a fool I have been. They have come to me because of all the men in this city I am the one to have the biggest grudge against Peter Moran, I am his chief enemy. Somehow they have found the message and somehow discovered Peter Moran is unknown to the gang. Things will be worse for me if I tell lies...

Almost the first thing the man said to him, after he had said good evening and that he was Detective Inspector Fordwych, was that there was nothing for him to worry about. His face must have looked worried. They probably said that to you just before they arrested you, it meant nothing. He said to come in and led them into the living room. It was then that he recognized the inspector, or had a vague sense of recognition which only crystallized into certainty when Fordwych said:

'I've been in this house before. It was sixteen years ago. I was a DC then. I don't suppose you remember.'

'I think I do,' John said.

Probably he had changed as much as this man had. They were both forty now and if time hadn't made them fat, it had thickened their muscles and their bones, put grey into their hair, blurred their features and dulled their eyes. By contrast, the girl who had been introduced as Detective Constable Aubrey looked wonderfully young, fair-haired, fresh-faced, buoyant with energy. John looked helplessly from one to the other. He could think of nothing to say and he was already convinced Fordwych would play with him, keeping him in suspense, for minutes before coming to the point.

'May we sit down?'

John nodded. He was remembering more about Fordwych now. He had been keen and lively in those days, probing whenever he got the chance into every detail of their domestic life, inquiring, intuiting, ambitious seemingly. His ambition had got him promotion but it had not advanced him very high and it hadn't lifted him out of this backwater.

'I don't know if you have any idea why we've come, Mr Creevey?'

'Should I have?' It was the cautious reply of the guilty that the police often hear.

'Not if I've calculated correctly and there's been nothing yet in the media.'

John felt himself close his eyes briefly. He thought, Peter Moran, something has happened to him. For the first time the girl spoke. She had a voice like her face, fresh, earnest, rather intense.

'I expect it's still painful even after so long.'

So long? What did she mean? Even to someone of her age two days wasn't very long.

'I'll explain why we've come, Mr Creevey. A man has been arrested in Bristol and charged with the murder of a young woman. The likelihood is that later on he will also be charged with the murder of a second girl and of your sister Cherry.'

ᚠᚠᚠᚠᚠᚠᚠᚠᚠᚠᚠᚠᚠᚠᚠᚠᚠᚠ **7** ᚠᚠᚠᚠᚠ

MARK SIMMS, THEY HAD ARRESTED MARK SIMMS. John stared at them. He tried to say something but all that happened was a trembling of his lips.

'It's a shock for you,' the policewoman said.

Fordwych was less tender with him. He said in the tone which had once been eager but had become characterless and automatic:

'He's a man who was living here up until about sixteen years ago. He'd no record, he'd even got a steady job in one of the factories up at Ruxeter. When he left here he spent several years as a voluntary patient in a mental hospital.'

John said hoarsely, 'What's he called?'

'I think I can tell you that. It'll be in the papers tomorrow. He appeared in court this afternoon. His name is Maitland, Rodney George Maitland. He's the son of the man who employed your sister.'

They had charged the wrong man. Out of some reserves of strength John had managed to summon enough voice to ask for the name, but now it was lost again. If he spoke he knew it would come out as a croak. Fordwych was explaining the reason for their visit. To inform him, as Cherry's only surviving relative, in advance. To warn him he might be asked for further information. To warn him also that he might have to appear as a witness at the Crown Court. John was aware that the girl was looking at him compassionately. Of course she must think he was so bowled over because the business of his sister's murder was being revived. And he was, he was. But the chief reason for his feeling of total shock was his private knowledge that this Rodney Maitland—a man he thought he had once met, had at any rate seen—must be innocent, at least of Cherry's murder, for Mark Simms was guilty. He managed to stammer out a question.

'When did you say—when—he's appearing in court today?'

'In the magistrates' court, yes. But as I said, it's likely he'll go back again to be charged with your sister's murder.'

'And someone will want to come and—talk to me?'

'Just routine, Mr Creevey. Of course we have your original statement and your parents' on file. I expect you'll merely be asked to confirm one or two things.'

How much did they know of Cherry's true character? All of it, no doubt. This stolid unimaginative man must know all about her, and this sweet-faced girl would know too. I must tell them the truth, John thought, I have no choice. But not yet perhaps, I can wait a day or two, I can think about what I know, weigh it all up. The man they have charged is, after all, probably guilty of the other murders, and he won't be kept in a remand prison on account of a murder he didn't commit.

'I'm sorry we've given you such a shock, Mr Creevey,' Fordwych was saying as he got up to go. The words were sympathetic but the expression on his face sardonic. He evidently felt John was a poor thing, not much of a man. These sentiments came out in his exit line. 'You'll come to see things differently, I expect, when you've pulled yourself together a bit and seen this as a matter of justice being done at last.'

But Detective Aubrey gave him a sweet smile, wrinkling up her nose a bit as if to say, take no notice, or even, it'll come all right, really it will.

8

THE DIMINUTIVE SIZE AND BABYISH FACE OF HER SON Charles were a source of pleasure to Gloria Mabledene who was less happy being seen about with her daughter Sarah, a tall well-developed girl. Charles was often taken for no more than eleven and the mother of an eleven-year-old might easily be under thirty. It was a pity he insisted on having his hair cut so short, though. The tips of golden locks, showing incipient curl, tumbled to the floor as Donna snipped away. Charles, seated between a blue-headed seventy-year-old having a perm and a middle-aged redhead undergoing lowlights, demanded coldly in the voice that only this week had disconcertingly begun to lose its treble note:

'Shorter!'

'Darling,' Gloria wailed, 'you're not having a crew cut!'

She put out one hand, the nails lacquered violet, to stay Donna's scissors. Charles reached behind and drew from her flowing sleeve string after string of coloured beads, red, blue and yellow plastic, not at all Gloria's style. She let out a nervous shriek.

'I nearly nicked your ear,' said Donna. 'Now you keep still and I'll be done in two ticks.'

Charles got down from the chair, well-satisfied with his cropped head. He had come into town with his mother and would either return home with her at five or with his father at six-thirty. It was still quite early. He came out of the salon into Hillbury Place and looked up at the tower which told him the time was nine-twenty-two and the temperature eighteen degrees.

Three buses an hour went out to Nunhouse. The next one was due at nine-thirty. Charles walked up to the bus stop in Hill Street and the bus, a few minutes early, arrived just as he got there. He sat in the front, on the right-hand side. This meant he would be able to see the flyover drop as the bus passed. There would be a split second during which, as the bus turned left into North street and thence into the Nunhouse Road, if you knew where to look you could catch a glimpse of the inside of the central upright. It was unlikely anything would be there, for Mungo Cameron had gone away on holiday on Friday and would be away for two weeks, but there was a rare possibility a message might be left for him by Basilisk or Unicorn.

As it happened the bus went rather fast and took the turn fast but Charles was on the look-out and saw enough to make sure there was nothing taped inside the pillar. He could just remember when the route the bus took was a country road, nine or ten years ago it must have been, but that was all changed now. It was built up with housing estates and shopping malls all the way to Nunhouse. The bus pulled up by the old village green which still remained and Charles got off, looking for Fen Street. He made inquiries of an old lady who called him dear and he feared was going to pat him.

Number twenty-two was an old house, a cottage really and rather tumbledown. The front garden reminded him of the garden at the back of the safe house, though the nettles weren't quite so tall. On a patch of relatively bare ground, scattered with gravel, stood a dusty Citroën Diane. Charles looked through a pane of glass in the shack which must serve as garage or wood shed but could see inside no evidence of the occupancy of some near-contemporary of his own. Still, not all teenagers had bicycles or toboggans or footballs or even wellington boots. There was nothing in the shack but a couple of oil drums. Charles went up to the front door, saw there was no bell and tapped on the door knocker. He knew he was being over-bold but he couldn't think of any other way of entering the place and getting the information he wanted.

A woman came to the door, dressed as if to go out in a blue leather jacket. She looked at him. She didn't speak.

Charles said, 'Have you any jobs you want doing?'

She came out on to the doorstep, looked at the car, the weeds, the front gate from which one of the hinges was missing. 'Hundreds. What can you do and'—she hesitated—'how much would you want?'

Charles wasn't anxious to over-exert himself. 'I could clean the car,' he said. 'Two pounds to clean the car.'

'That seems quite reasonable. My—er, there's someone here who'll pay you. I have to go to work. I'm late already.' She retreated into the house, called out, 'Peter!

211

I'm off. There's a boy here who's going to clean the car. Two pounds—OK?'

Charles couldn't hear what reply was made. But she had told him what he wanted to know, that someone called Peter lived in the house. Her son presumably, a future Rossingham man, part of the new Lower Fourth intake. She came out, carrying a handbag this time, told him to find a bucket inside, in the kitchen, and went off hurrying down Fen Street.

The house was better inside. There was no one about, no teenage boy or father of teenage boy. Charles found the kitchen and a bucket with a wrung-out cloth folded over it. He looked out of the window into the back garden, a similar wilderness. If he could find the boy and have a preliminary word with him he wouldn't have to clean the car, an activity of which he had no experience apart from seeing it done by the car wash at the works.

Stairs led up out of a living-dining room. Carrying a bucketful of water, Charles stood at the foot of these stairs looking up and listening. He could hear someone moving about up there. At least he wasn't alone. Sooner or later this Peter Moran would appear. He set about cleaning the car in a half-hearted sort of way, his thoughts elsewhere, concentrated in fact on magic, or what others called conjuring tricks. It was time he progressed from such simple sleights of hand as producing strings of beads or coloured paper from people's sleeves. Learning to do card tricks was a good discipline, he had heard. He began swilling water about on the bodywork of the car. The sun had come out and the water dried rapidly in dusty streaks and patches. He thought he heard a window opened upstairs in the house but when he looked up there was nobody there.

The water in the bucket was dirty now and he emptied it away down a drain. He returned to the house with the empty bucket and met a man coming out from the living room. The man was tallish and fair with lank yellow hair, a fringe of which fell across his forehead, a bony face and dark-framed glasses. His skin had a white unhealthy look. They contemplated each other for a moment and then the man said:

'Is it you she said was cleaning the car?'

Charles nodded, smiling slightly.

'Have you come in for more water?'

Another nod and Charles was going to walk past him towards the kitchen when the man took the bucket from him. 'Here, let me.'

It was an opportunity Charles thought he had better take and he said carefully, 'Is your son about?'

'My what?' The man stared at him over his shoulder and the water frm the running tap flowed over the top of the bucket into the sink.

'She—the lady—called out Peter. I thought that must be your son.'

'That was me,' he said.

He carried the bucket outside, leaving a trail of drips. Charles followed. He realized that he had made a mistake, though he couldn't understand how. In assuming that Peter Moran belonged in the same category as Martin Hillman and Trevor Allan, was in other words a thirteen-year-old future Rossingham pupil, he had been in error. Aware that Mungo was testing him, his loyalty to the West, he wondered if this were part of the trial process. Further instructions would perhaps appear. In the meantime, he had better finish the job on this car, for he might as well get something out of it, if only the two quid.

The man called Peter Moran had gone away again but now he reappeared to ask Charles if he would like a cup of coffee. Charles said OK in his economical way. Peter Moran looked at the car and said it was fine, it hadn't been so clean for years. This gave Charles, following him into the house, something to think about. It was glaringly obvious that the car was not very clean, was streaky and blotchy and the glass parts filmed with scum. Peter Moran began fumbling around in some very untidy drawers in a sort of sideboard. He handed Charles three, not two, pound coins and a good deal of loose change.

'Go on, you may as well have it. You've done a good job.'

He smiled. Charles, who was able to assess people in a detached way, decided that the smile was ingratiating, even inviting, but not at all friendly. The man's eyes, pebble-like and still, were not involved in the smile. And then Charles did one of his feats of intuition or character-reading or whatever you called it, and knew in an instant what kind of a man Peter Moran was, a man who liked or fancied male persons of his age. The eyes moved now, flickering from Charles's face down his body, the smile cooling to ice. An intense expression replaced it.

Charles didn't feel afraid, for the front door which led straight into this room stood wide open. It was more an interest that he felt and a measure of admiration for his own sensitivity, his own discernment. How had he known what this man was while at the same time not really knowing, except in a blurred vague way, the kind of things he would like to do to him?

He was in no doubt as to the nature of the payment that was being made to him. But he took it just the same, being rather short at the moment, having already made big inroads into his August allowance. He took the mug of coffee too. The money is to make me like him, he thought, no more than that. Yet. Peter Moran indicated a chair at the table and when Charles didn't take up the offer, pulled it out for him. Charles sat down, looking at Peter Moran across the table. What did Mungo require of this man? What was supposed to come of their meeting? Beyond Peter Moran, as part of the back of the ancient sideboard, was a mirror in which Charles could see his head and shoulders reflected. If he had ever been ignorant of his own 'prettiness', choirboy or cherub-like graces, his mother would soon have put him wise to them. She positively fostered them. Behind

Peter Moran's intent rapt face he saw his own angel face, the clear and innocent blue eyes, the golden albeit very short, hair, and felt a cold thrill along his spine as if a key had been dropped down his back. Peter Moran said:

'What made you think a boy lived here?'

'Mr Robinson told me.' This was an answer Charles had long ago formulated for any questions of this kind put to him by adults.

'I don't know any Mr Robinson.'

Charles was ready for that one too. 'He knows you.'

This had a better effect on Peter Moran than Charles could have hoped for, had indeed intended. He could hardly have grown paler but his face seemed to blank. His eyes shifted and he pushed his chair back.

'Are you a scout or something?'

'Because I cleaned your car? No. I have to go now. Thanks for the coffee.'

A hesitation, a pause, as if some inner argument were going on behind those glasses, that broad pale forehead. Then carefully:

'I might have another job for you in a day or two. Not here though. We could meet. We could have a coffee in town somewhere.'

Charles smiled. He could afford to. He was out on the doorstep and two women with shopping bags had appeared, gossiping on the pavement.

'You haven't told me your name.'

'It's Cameron, Ian Cameron,' said Charles. 'Church Bar. It's in the phone book.'

THE HOTEL WAS NOT A BUILDING BUT A COLLECTION of little circular huts with grass-thatched roofs, very fancy inside and incorporating bedroom, bathroom and sun terrace. Mungo and Graham O'Neill shared one of these. After dinner with the family at a seafood restaurant in the village they came back here and wrote a postcard for Mr Lindsay, putting Corcyra instead of Corfu at the top next to the date. A sop to Cerberus, was the way Graham put it. So they wrote that as well, thinking it would please the frustrated classicist.

'Cerberus would do as an agent's name,' said Mungo. 'I don't know why we never thought of that one.'

'You can confer it on Martin Hillman,' said Graham, lighting a cigarette.

'Do you have to smoke? If Dad comes by he'll go bananas worrying about your lungs.'

'OK, I'm going to give it up but you can't expect me to give it up on holiday. A man must have some pleasures. You're such a bloody Calvinist. I suppose it's the Scot in you.'

'If you don't mind,' said Mungo, 'Calvin was *French*.'

Graham fell asleep first. He usually did. Mungo sometimes thought it was the smell of cigarette smoke that kept him awake. The glass doors to the terrace stood open and the moon was very bright. Mungo lay in bed watching a lizard on the stucco wall just beyond the open door. The moonlight gave it an elongated very black shadow with flaring crest. If he half-closed his eyes and squinted a bit the lizard appeared to grow very large, assuming dragon-like proportions. This reminded him of Charles Mabledene and thence of the Moscow Centre code. Somehow he didn't have much faith in the possibility of Dragon finding the key to that code. Not unless, that is, Rosie Whittaker had decided to abandon it for a new one.

He turned his head to look at Graham's digital clock on the bedside table between them. There was something of his father's nature in Mungo and he worried quite badly if he thought he was missing out on sleep. A digital clock wasn't the best sort for someone of that temperament because you could actually see the minutes clicking away. But it wasn't light enough in here to depend on watches. The clock told him it was eleven-forty-three and in that moment, in a flash of illumination, Mungo understood what the numbers at the end of Moscow Centre's messages were.

Not house numbers or phone numbers but the time. It was as simple as that. They were times, nine-thirty-one, three minutes past ten, twelve-fifty-eight. He considered waking up Graham to tell him but he didn't do this. Instead he got up and lay on the airbed on the terrace, looking at the lizard which had become a dragon walking with slow relentless deliberation across a vast empty plain.

10

THE POLICE DIDN'T COME BACK. JOHN RACKED HIM-self all weekend, trying to decide what to do. He thought of going to see Mark Simms and telling him of the interview with Inspector Fordwych, and he did get as far as picking up the phone and dialling. But there was no answer from Mark, though he made repeated attempts. News of Rodney Maitland's court appearance was in the papers, the *Free Press* as well as the nationals, and on television too. But he had been charged with only one murder, that of the Bristol girl whose death had taken place in June. Unless things changed and they charged him with Cherry's murder, John decided he need take no action.

One effect the police visit did have on him was to send him back to cats' green to try to put things right here. We ought to learn from our experiences, John thought, and there had been a lesson in the fear he had felt when Fordwych and the girl called Aubrey arrived. Better take action to exonerate himself now than risk the consequences of a real involvement. The difficulty was that he didn't know the code for August. He looked at the note he had of the last message. 'October men to take over from Sunday.' He remembered that he hadn't understood it at the time. Now he studied it.

It was the last message which had appeared at the drop during July and according to what seemed to be the rule should have contained in the old code an announcement of the new one. As far as he had understood it at all when he read it on the previous Thursday, he had taken October men to be a group of the gang, some recruits perhaps due to start in October. Yet it said they would begin operations on Monday and Monday had been 1 August, the first of the month when a new code would begin. Could *October Men* be the title of a book?

John called in at the library in Lucerne Road on his way home from work and asked the librarian if a book existed called *October Men*. It did. A novel of espionage by Anthony Price. They had a copy but it was out and an inquiry of the computer established that the central library copy and the Ruxeter Road copy were also out. Probably all borrowed by gang members, John thought.

Next morning he did something he had never done before, scarcely knew you could do. But you didn't know what you could do till you tried. This seemed to him a profound philosophical reflection and of particular application to himself. It cheered him up too. He phoned Hatchard's and asked them if they had a copy of *October Men*. Several, they said. John went out at once to buy the paperback, missing his lunch to do so but thinking it worth while.

It rained heavily all afternoon and Trowbridge's had few customers. The one woman who did come in after four left without buying anything after Gavin had upset her. John heard her ask for orange blossom or was its proper name syringa? In a superior tone Gavin told her it was neither, these were names wrongly used by the ignorant. It was philadelphus. She said she was sure it wasn't, she didn't know what to do now, and left saying she would try the Tesco garden centre. Gavin returned to feeding the mynah pine nuts which he called pignolias. In the houseplant house John sat on a high stool with *October Men* on the bench in front of him and worked out the August code based on its first lines: 'The General sat quietly in his car at the airport terminal waiting for his mother and his mistress...'

Gavin put his head inside the door.

'OK if I take Grackle home for the night?'

He had got into the habit of doing this most nights. Where he got the money from John didn't know but he had acquired a Metro and he said the mynah enjoyed a ride in the car.

'As far as I'm concerned,' John said.

On a piece of paper torn from his notebook he wrote in *October Men*: 'Leviathan to Dragon: Discontinue Peter Moran inquiry. Do not tail, do not observe.' He put it inside one of the small plastic bags they used for snowdrop and crocus bulbs. The rain still rattled down on the glass roof. It had been too wet that morning to come in on the Honda. He ran to the bus stop but by the time he got there the rain had stopped, the clouds spread out to the horizon and the sun started to blaze down. The long white wet road glittered in the sunlight, too bright to look at.

At cats' green he looked up into the inside of the central pillar. There was nothing. From the roll of sticky tape he had been carrying about with him in his jacket pocket for weeks now he broke two lengths and taped his message to the metal surface.

FOR THE FIRST TIME THIS EVENING HE WAS AWARE OF the passing of the year. By eight it was growing dark. Only three months now and it would be a year since Jennifer left him. He sat eating his meal of French bread, cheese and pickled onions—what the landlord of the Gander called a ploughperson's lunch—and read *October Men*. At nine he put on the television for the BBC's evening news. The first item was about the arrest of a man for the murder of a child in Lancashire. The little girl, missing for two weeks, had been found in a wood after being sexually assaulted and then strangled. John irresistibly thought of Peter Moran. These men probably didn't intend to murder their child victims. They killed them from panic, out of a fear of discovery, or to silence the crying and the pleas for help. It made John shudder. Suppose Peter Moran were to kill one of his victims? Of course it might be that he no longer had victims, that his court appearance and sentence, mild though that had been, had frightened him into controlling his impulses. But somehow John didn't believe this could be so. These propensities weren't so easily subdued. It was all very well for Jennifer to say he wouldn't hurt a child. How could she know?

It was almost at the end of the news, after all the stuff about Northern Ireland and South Africa and the Common Market and the Queen Mother, after all that, that the newscaster, almost idly it seemed, mentioned that Rodney Maitland, arrested last week for the Bristol murder, had today been charged with murdering Marion Ann Burton in Cardiff in 1970 and Cherry Winifred Creevey in 1971.

Once more John tried to phone Mark Simms. The phone rang and rang. It looked as if Mark might be away on holiday. John thought there was something astounding, unreal, about being able to do ordinary normal things, about being able to enjoy yourself, go away on holiday, that sort of thing, after you had done what Mark had done. Surely now Mark would confess to the police? Surely he wouldn't let an innocent man—or innocent at any rate of that charge—take punishment for his own crime? He tried the phone again at ten and when there was again no answer he phoned Gavin. The mynah didn't exactly answer the phone but it could be heard gabbling away very near the mouthpiece.

'Ha ha ha, damn!' it said. 'I'm a basket case, I'm an empty nester.'

'I'll be late in in the morning, Gavin. I won't be in till around eleven.'

Gavin didn't seem interested. 'Yeah. Right,' he said. 'No problem. Listen, can you hear him?'

'Grackle rules OK,' shouted the mynah.

The police station he went to was the one in Feverton. Fordwych had said he could be found there. John walked all the way. He knew he had to go but he wanted to postpone getting there. His route took him past the remains of city wall at the feet of which the council had made lawns and planted coleus and this summer's favourite, love-lies-bleeding. The tables outside the wine bar were all crowded. John knew he would never be able to pass it without thinking of Jennifer and remembering how she had cried.

In the police station he asked for Detective Inspector Fordwych and was told to wait. It was as bad as being in a hospital out-patients' department. He waited and waited. The police station had windows which when you were outside looked as if the glass was painted white on the inside, it looked opaque, but when you were inside you could see out all right. You could see people who walked by and stole glances at their own reflections. At last he was told Fordwych would see him now and to come this way. It was Constable Aubrey who came to fetch him. She took him into a small impersonal office with maps and charts on the wall. Fordwych got up from behind the desk, came over and rather surprisingly shook hands with him.

'I don't want to have to tell you about this,' John began, 'but I don't think I have any choice. I can't just leave things as they are.'

'This has some connection with the death of your sister, Mr Creevey?'

Now he was actually there and facing Fordwych, John felt that he was about to commit an unforgivable betrayal. But he couldn't think what other course to take. He was there now, he must do it. What loyalty did he owe Mark Simms? The truth was that he should have gone to the police weeks ago, as soon as he knew. He could hardly recall now why it was he hadn't gone. A glimpse of something else, something deeper came to him as he sat there silent, looking at Fordwych. Knowing what Mark had done, what an ordinary man like himself had done and got away with, had somehow corrupted him, had helped to make him feel it was permissible to do things outside the law if the provocation were great enough, it was all right setting hit men on to Peter Moran...

He began to speak. Quite baldly and lucidly he told Fordwych of Mark Simms's confession. He told how, after weeks of prevarication, Mark had at last broken down and kneeling in front of him confessed to the murder of Cherry. Fordwych listened. He didn't say anything and his eyes didn't meet John's. With his elbows on the desk and his fingertips meeting at a right angle, he kept his face averted as if the view outside the window—the CitWest tower flicking over, nine-forty-two, nine-forty-three, nine-forty-four, eighteen degrees, eighteen degrees, eighteen degrees—were absorbingly fascinating to him.

When John had finished and found himself inwardly trembling from the effort of it, though outwardly calm, Fordwych, who had previously not uttered so much as a 'go on,' said in a measured detached way:

'You were quite right to come and tell us.'

John nodded. He didn't know what other sign to make.

'Why didn't you come before?'

'I thought it was too late. I didn't think it mattered to anyone now if he was punished or not.'

'Justice isn't important?'

John heard the girl behind him draw in her breath. He found a plain honest reply and uttered it. 'It's because of justice that I've come now.'

Fordwych got up. He began to walk about. He stood by the window and then he stood by the desk in front of John, looking at him.

'What would you say if I said that what you've told me couldn't be true? That it bears no relation to the truth from beginning to end?'

John felt the blood come up into his face. 'I haven't been lying to you. I've told you the exact truth.'

He couldn't remain sitting there. He got to his feet and held on to the back of the chair so tightly his knuckles went white. The girl was looking at him with a strange expression. He thought it was pity.

'I've told you what he told me. He confessed to me that he'd murdered my sister. He even gave me details, the time, the place, everything.'

'Sit down, Mr Creevey. Don't blow your top. Let me tell you something. We've got it all on record and of course we've been taking a good look at our records since Maitland was arrested. You may never have been told any of this, you and your parents I mean. It was probably thought too distressing. But your sister clawed at the man who strangled her and she must have made deep scratches. Her fingernails were full of blood and tissue. Don't you suppose Mr Simms was the first to come under suspicion? Of course he was. His movements were checked and double-checked and everything he said sifted and examined. We're not complete fools, you know Mr Creevey. We do even sometimes know what we're doing. In the light of what we found under your sister's fingernails, he was the first man to be given a blood test, and he couldn't have been more finally exonerated. Mr Simms's blood is Group B negative. The blood under your sister's fingernails was Group O positive, which incidentally is the same as that of Rodney Maitland.'

11

EVERYONE WAS AWAY ON HOLIDAY. EVEN THE TRAFFIC in the city had got lighter. Leviathan and Chimera and Medusa, in other words Mungo and Angus Cameron and Graham O'Neill, were in Corfu. Scylla, or Keith O'Neill, was in Sweden. Unicorn or Nicholas Ralston and Basilisk or Patrick Crashaw had gone off somewhere or other with their families. Charybdis and the rest of the Hobhouse family had moved out to their cottage at Rossingham St Mary for a month. Only the Mabledenes, for some reason to do with Charles's mother's and father's respective businesses, would not be off until the last week of August.

Charles, therefore, expected to find no messages at the flyover drop. He was busy enough without that. It was proving surprisingly difficult to find out when the work of gutting and redesigning the interior of the safe house at 53 Ruxeter Road was due to begin. Nor had he got very far with his overtures to Martin Hillman, the apparently more enterprising of the London Central two possible recruits. An appointment had been made to meet Hillman at a café halfway between the Shot Tower and the Beckgate but when he got there, the only customers were Rosie Whittaker and Guy Parker. Rosie had put green dye on her spiky hair and was wearing black glasses with wire rims like Graham O'Neill's. Both were dressed from head to foot in fashionable dusty black. They addressed him cordially and Rosie actually asked him if he would like a Coke. Charles refused and went off in a thoughtful frame of mind. He wouldn't touch Martin Hillman now with a two-metre-long pole and he would give Mungo similar advice.

His new digital watch told him it was six-twenty-four. His father would be leaving for home at seven which gave him nice time to get to the garage by bus. Charles decided he might as well call it a day. The bus wasn't the same one as he had taken out to Nunhouse three days before but it followed the same route as far as Rostock Bridge. Sitting in the seat he always picked if it was vacant, the right-hand side up front, Charles reflected on the Peter Moran affair.

You couldn't say he had had a lucky escape, of course, because he had never been in danger. The front door of the cottage had been open all the time and besides that, he had himself almost from the first been aware that a definite threat existed. And this was always half the battle. Indeed, Charles felt rather proud of himself on that score, mentally patting himself on the back for his undoubted sophistication. But he couldn't help thinking how horrified and really frightened for him his parents would have been had they known about it.

Only a couple of years back his sister Sarah and a couple of girlfriends of hers had got talking with some man they met and had allowed him to treat them to the cinema. Sarah had been unwise enough to tell her parents about this. Nothing had happened, the man had merely been friendly and enjoyed their company, but Charles had thought his father was going to have a stroke or something. And as for his mother...! At the time Sarah started on all this his mother had been showing his father some new dress or suit or whatever she had bought that day. If he had been told anything would distract his mother from a thing like that he wouldn't have believed it, but this had. She had burst out screaming and crying and made Sarah solemnly swear never to speak to any man again as long as she lived. Well, almost. There had been an awful fuss. Charles could see that just as bad a fuss might be made over his encounter with Peter Moran. Not that he had the slightest intention of telling his parents about it. It was over anyway and no harm done.

From force of habit he glanced to the right as the bus swung left at the flyover. There was a message in the central upright. Well, it was unexpected but not impossible. No doubt it came from Charybdis, who had perhaps come in for the day from Rossingham. After all, he was always coming in from Fenbridge, the distance was much the same. Charles jumped off at the next request stop. It was still only six-forty, he could run the rest of the way across Rostock Bridge and his father would certainly wait for him.

October Men the code was. He had a note of it in his pocket. He wouldn't have dreamt of going out without that. Charybdis had put the package in very high up. Charles wouldn't have thought he could have reached that high, he could scarcely reach it himself. He had to jump and tug to pull it down. Stuffing the plastic into his pocket and unfolding the message quickly, Charles looked at it in some astonishment. Of course he couldn't read it just like that, most of it was incomprehensible, but the first word contained nine letters and he was pretty sure from his acquaintance with the *October Men* key that it was Leviathan. He was almost certain the first three words read: 'Leviathan to Dragon'. How could that be when the message was a new one, put into the upright in the past three days, while Mungo had been in Corfu for six?

'What have you been doing with yourself all day?' his father asked genially as they got into the Volvo.

Charles thought this expressed his intelligence activities, conducted solitarily, rather well.

'This and that,' he said and opened his notebook at the *October Men* key.

He began a rapid deciphering. Usually on these trips his father and he maintained a placid silence. When he was with his mother in her car she talked incessantly. Charles could have done with silence this evening but it seemed his father was determined to talk. There was something coincidental about the subject he had chosen: the danger to people of Charles's age, particularly those who were not large for their age, from molestation by those he called 'sick' adults. He also called them paederasts, mispronouncing the word, as Charles noticed rather sadly. It was the arrest of some man for assaulting and murdering a child up in the north which had led to this. The man had been mobbed and threatened by the crowd as he was hustled out of court by police. It had all been on television.

'I thought it would be a good idea to have a chat about this when your mother and sister aren't around.'

Charles reflected that they had been chatting, if that was the word, about it all his and Sarah's lives. But he only said OK and nodded. It would be rude to continue to look at his notebook. Besides, he had already deciphered the message: 'Discontinue Peter Moran inquiry. Do not observe, do not tail.' His father's tone grew embarrassed as he tried to describe the kind of overtures such a man might make. Charles had a terrible urge, which he knew he must resist, to magic around with his father's Silk Cut so that when he reached for a cigarette he would pull out ten metres of purple ribbon instead.

Their route took them along the river. Nunhouse

could be seen on the other side and Charles thought he could locate Fen Street and what was probably the roof of Peter Moran's cottage. He was aware of a nasty little chill of fear. One of Charles's strengths was his willingness to admit to himself that he was frightened but to conceal it from everyone else behind a face of inscrutability. Having more or less switched off his hearing, he made mechanical replies to his father. The decoded message was in his head and he repeated it over to himself with increasing disquiet.

Apart from the fact that Mungo couldn't have written and sent the message, the language was wrong. Mungo wouldn't have used 'discontinue' and 'inquiry' but would have said: 'Abandon Peter Moran project'. Therefore the message didn't come from the Director General of London Central but from someone else, Moscow Centre presumably. The *October Men* code had been broken—a simple matter with a mole in the department—and this message concocted by an agent who didn't know Mungo was away. Possibly even by Rosie Whittaker herself. After all, when Charles had seen her she had been no more than a quarter of a mile from the flyover drop.

All this would scarcely have been important, a matter merely for congratulating himself on seeing through the deception so early on. But it wasn't so simple. If Moscow Centre had countermanded Mungo's instructions they must have some good reason for doing so, they must be afraid of the outcome of the successful observation of Peter Moran. It was they, not Mungo, who wanted Peter Moran left alone.

'I think I've made it clear enough,' Charles switched on to hear his father say, 'that you don't in any circumstances whatever let anyone, even someone young and friendly, get himself alone with you. The people you get to know you meet at home or at school. It just isn't worth it, Charles. The risk is too great. In a nutshell, to use the old cliché, you don't talk to strange men.'

ʄʄʄʄʄʄʄʄʄʄʄʄʄʄʄʄ **12** ʄʄʄʄʄ

WITHOUT ACTUALLY BEING RUDE OR OFFENSIVE, Fordwych had indicated to John that he suspected him of stirring things. He suspected him of trying to make things look bad for Mark Simms, out of some kind of undefined malice, presumably. John didn't understand any of it. Well, he understood that Mark Simms was innocent of Cherry's murder and that for some reason he had lied. Was it possible he had lied about her manner of living as well?

He had gone to work eventually but he couldn't concentrate. This didn't much matter as they got less custom in August than perhaps during any other month. Walking about the rose gardens, nipping the dead heads off pink Wendy Cussons and vermilion Troikas, he was aware of an unexpected feeling. It was relief. His sky was lightening. His hands full of petals, he looked up at the overcast heavens and felt easier, less tense and stressed. The past had been wiped a little, if not washed clean. The immediate past too seemed less agonizing and less incomprehensible. And he hadn't committed the unforgivable able crime, the crime he could hardly now imagine he had contemplated, of perpetrating some act of violence, perhaps worse than that, against Jennifer's lover.

Gavin was putting the mynah through his paces for the benefit of an elderly couple and their grandchild

John remembered seeing at Trowbridge's two or three times before. The mynah uttered all its newly learned phrases obediently. Gavin rewarded it with offcuts of Mars bar. It was Thursday and they closed at one, Gavin and the bird he called Grackle going off inevitably together. John began thinking on the way home how Jennifer had said she hated him and would never forgive him for what he had told her about Peter Moran. Had he been wrong to tell her? Perhaps he had because he had told her from the wrong motive. Probably it was all in his own head, the idea of Peter Moran killing anyone or even of returning to his old tastes. It derived from all this stuff on television about the Lancashire child-killer and rapist. As soon as he got home, without even bothering about lunch, John sat down and wrote to Jennifer. He began the letter 'Dearest Jennifer', thinking that no matter what became of them, however distantly they might be parted and whatever other partners she might find, he would always write to her like that.

Dearest Jennifer,
If you still want a divorce after we have not been together for two years I will agree. I will do anything you want. I can't bear you to hate me and I tell you honestly that I am saying this so that you won't hate me. A kind of bribe to make you like me, if you want to put it that way!
I am not going to say anything more about Peter. People do change. You changed me, as I expect you know, so perhaps you have changed him too. I want to say though that I love you. Nothing has changed that. If you change your mind about a divorce, come back to me. I will always want you back.

There were too many repetitions of 'change' and 'changed' but never mind, it was what he felt. Tears had come into his eyes and he felt them slowly run down his face. They were tears of self-pity, he thought, and he rubbed them furiously away. Remembering their love-making didn't help, the tenderness, the gradual mutual learning of joy. He wanted to write pleading words, to ask her for reassurance, just to tell him it hadn't all been pretence on her part, that she had for a while felt love and desire for him. But he was afraid that if he asked she would never answer that part of the letter, so he wrote only: 'always your loving John' and ended it.

Colin and his mother were supposed to be coming at about four, calling in during one of their drives. They had been away for a week's holiday in the Lake District where it had rained all the time. John got himself another ploughperson's lunch and then went out to post his letter. Most of the afternoon he spent looking at Colin's holiday snapshots. There were also a lot of slides which had to be put into a contraption Colin had brought with him and peered at with one eye shut. They were all views of green mountains and grey skies, not a living creature in sight. Constance Goodman, immediately on arrival, had asked him oddly:

'Any news?'

'Leave it, Mother,' said Colin.

It took John a while to realize—and by then they were looking at photographs—that they had expected to find Jennifer there, that Jennifer had returned to him as a result of the information they had given him. This was an attitude that now seemed naïve, though he too had had faith in it once. The Goodmans had read about the arrest of the man for Cherry's murder. Would John have to give evidence? Would Mark Simms? Constance wanted to know if the police had been in touch with him.

'He doesn't want to talk about it, Mother. You can see that.'

'Not everyone is as inhibited as you are, chickie.'

'If someone is inhibited the parents are presumably to blame, notably the mother, I should think.'

They bickered for a while. John gave them tea, took them round the garden, showing off his fuchsias and the pink lavender. The greenhouse was admired, though Constance said what a shame he had to keep the Honda in there, and they left with a basketful of tomatoes and capsicum. It was a daunting thought that for the rest of his life the majority of his evenings would necessarily be spent alone. This was the first time he had faced it. In the fiction he read single men were always in demand by hostesses, but John had never found that this applied to him. No doubt, he didn't move in those circles. He couldn't recall that he had ever been invited to one of the drinks parties given by neighbours in Geneva Road. A murdered sister, a departed wife, set a man apart; people were wary of him, not knowing quite what approach to make, what subjects to avoid.

He watered the greenhouse, removed the yellowing lower leaves from the tomato plants. The aubergines were very susceptible to greenfly and though it went rather against the grain he sprayed them, choking at the noxious fumes. When the door bell rang he hoped it might be Jennifer. Was he going to feel like that for years every time the phone or the bell rang? You had no control over your initial reactions, he thought as he went to the door. All your resolutions, determined cheerfulness, 'pulling yourself together', were of no avail in preventing the leap of the heart, the spring of hope, the rushing into mind of the beloved name...

The woman who stood there wasn't Jennifer but Detective Constable Aubrey.

She said, 'Good evening, Mr Creevey. May I come in for a moment?'

He nodded. He knew he must look mystified.

'There's nothing to worry about. This isn't an official call.'

She followed him into the living room. The Goodmans had left their photographs behind and views of

Skiddaw and Ullswater lay scattered all over the coffee table.

'Have you been away?'

'No, I'm afraid not. They belong to some people I know.' Why hadn't he said friends? Why not 'friends of mine'? He began gathering up the pictures, replacing them in their yellow envelopes. She said:

'May I sit down?'

He flushed. 'I'm sorry. Yes, of course.'

She was wearing jeans, a striped shirt and a zipper jacket, masculine clothes, a man might have worn them without looking odd, but she remained powerfully feminine. He had seen that face in a picture somewhere, a reproduction in a book perhaps, those delicate features and that rosy translucent skin, the barely defined eyebrows, the red-gold hair. It was a pleasure to look at her, though academic only while Jennifer existed and came between his eyes and all other pretty faces.

She said in her pleasant gentle way, 'I came to talk about your sister Cherry, Mr Creevey.'

He nodded, wary now.

'Your visit on Monday, your talk with Mr Fordwych, it seemed to leave so much unanswered. What I really want to say is if you're upset or worried about what Mr Simms said to you, could you try not to be? Making false confessions is so common, it happens all the time.'

'But why?' he said. 'Why would anyone say he'd—done murder, when he hadn't? I thought you didn't believe me,' he added.

'Oh, we believed you. Let's just say we rather wondered that you ever believed him. It occurred to me that you might have been in a particularly receptive state for that sort of thing. Forgive me if I seem to probe. Had you been very depressed or nervous or anything?'

He looked at her, beginning to understand many things. 'I think I was on the edge of a nervous breakdown for months but I never quite tumbled in.' He said quickly, 'I still don't see why he'd make something like that up.'

'There are quite a few possible reasons,' she said thoughtfully. 'He might have resented something about you. I mean, perhaps he thought you weren't really interested in him, didn't listen while he talked? Is that possible? That he was lonely and wanted your attention and felt he didn't really get it because you—well, you had problems of your own?'

'It's more than possible,' John said. 'Miss Aubrey— Detective Constable—I'm sorry, but what do I call you?'

'Call me Susan.'

Somehow he didn't feel he could quite do that. He was sorry she had suggested it. It was too intimate. He framed his question again. 'Are you saying he was prepared to do anything to get my attention?'

'Something like that. People do suffer intolerable feelings of rejection, solitariness, sensations of being in glass walls, belljars, you know. And then he might also feel guilty about your sister. I'm not saying there's any possibility he killed her, there isn't, but he might feel guilty in other ways. Perhaps, for instance, for not calling for her that evening when he said he would but nearly an hour later. You didn't know that? It's all in his statement he made sixteen years ago. He had been going to break with her. He was going to tell her so, but he got there late and she had already left—with the man who is charged with murdering her, as we now know.'

John stared at her. 'So he did feel responsible for her death?'

'In a way. How much do you know about your sister, Mr—er, John?'

So it was true. Mark hadn't lied about that. 'Everything, I think.'

'Mark Simms had found out she had other lovers. Often he felt he would have liked to kill her. Do you begin to understand now?'

'Are you a psychologist?' John asked.

'I used to be. I did psychology at university.'

He offered her coffee and she said thank you, yes,

she would like that. While she drank it he talked a bit about Cherry, not speaking of her multifarious inexplicable love affairs or of her and Mark, but asking why she had been killed. Had she—and he tried to put it delicately—behaved in such a way to Rodney Maitland as to bring about her own death? Susan Aubrey said she didn't think so, Cherry knew him, after all, had probably gone innocently with him when he offered her his escort to her bus stop. Maitland, who lived in London, had only come home to his native city that afternoon, had left again immediately after the killing. That was why he had never been investigated, never suspected, while hundreds of local men were fingerprinted and their blood groups examined. He was, it appeared, one of those men who derived sexual satisfaction simply from killing a woman, from surprising her by sudden attack and strangling her before she could utter. Cherry had fought him, she had put up more fight than the others, she had not submitted to her fate...

Susan Aubrey's sympathetic manner tempted John to begin confiding in her about Jennifer, to tell her what had brought about his near-breakdown, but he resisted doing so. He had an idea that people who were trained psychologists kept a scientific attitude towards an opening of the heart, listening to confidences with a clinical detachment. It was only after she had gone, thanking him for the coffee, calling him John, that he thought how, if he had told her of his mental state, he must also have told her of his therapy, the mini-Mafia and its codes he had penetrated. Perhaps he should have told her. The novel idea came to him that it was his duty as a citizen to tell the police about this gang's activities and such instructions as that of 'remove and eliminate', for example. Now he had extricated himself from it with no harm done, he ought at least to inform the police of the drop at cats' green. He would do so on the following day. During lunchtime he would do it, he resolved, setting off for work on Friday morning. It wouldn't do to take any more time off.

Within an hour of his reaching Trowbridge's something happened to put everything else out of his head.

13

IT WAS THE FIRST DAY OF THE SALE. ALL THOSE plants that no one was going to pay the full price for at this season, overblown geraniums, herbs that had flowered and grown straggly, bushy begonias, were to be displayed on trestle tables at thirty pee each. It should have been set up by the time the garden centre opened but at ten-thirty Gavin was still selecting the plants and trundling them out of the greenhouses. That was when the elderly couple and their granddaughter or whatever she was turned up. They made as usual for the mynah's cage.

'Those two, they treat this place like a zoo,' Sharon said to John, 'always bringing that kid to see the mynah. They've never even bought a packet of seeds.'

'They don't do any harm,' John said.

Les had come up to them.

'They want to buy the mynah.'

'There you are, Sharon,' John said. 'That's better than a packet of seeds.'

He went over to the man, explained that the price of the mynah was eighty-five pounds.

'It's not in the sale then?'

'No, it's not in the sale,' John said, smiling.

'It's a lot of money but we reckon it's worth it, don't we, Mother? We've taken a long time to make up our minds, it's not a snap decision, we've really thought about the responsibilities involved.' The serious tone and earnest look suggested it might be the fostering of a child he was embarking on. 'We've read up on the subject, we've had books from the library.'

John was tempted to say something to the effect that he knew he could safely entrust the mynah to their keeping but of course he didn't. It was at this point though that he first thought of Gavin. He felt glad Gavin was out in the back, busily occupied, for although at that time he had no real notion of how strongly Gavin felt about the mynah he suspected that if he had been in the shop he would have attempted to discourage the sale. Started talking about Newcastle's Disease or *Gracula religiosa* being dangerous to children. In fact the little girl was poking her fingers into the cage, feeding the mynah from a packet of assorted fruits and nuts, and it was taking her offerings quite gently. The man meant to pay cash for it. Four twenty-pound notes and a five-pound were carefully unrolled. They had evidently called at the bank on their way here.

'Do we get his cage as well?' said the little girl.

'Yes, how much is that?' A look of near-dismay made it plain he had made no provision for this in his budgeting.

'The cage comes with the bird,' said John. 'Part of the package.'

They went off, carrying the mynah, towards the car park. John was watching them place the cage, with absurdly tender care, on the back seat of an aged Morris Minor, when Gavin came into the shop from the back. He started telling John that two of the shubunkins had fungus. Then he saw the empty space where the cage had been.

'Who's moved him?'

'That old couple bought your Dracula.' Sharon's tone was very slightly malicious. 'They've just this minute gone. Never even gave him a chance to say goodbye.'

Gavin rushed out of the front door. The Morris Minor had already gone, would by now probably be turning out on to the main road, but he was off in pursuit of it, pounding up the long gravel drive.

'He was very keen on that bird,' Les said.

After a minute or two Gavin came back, not flushed but white-faced in spite of his exertions. His eyes had a wild look. He said hoarsely:

'We've got to get him back. I'll buy him off them. I was going to buy him anyway, I've been saving up. I'd nearly got enough.'

'Why didn't you say?' John said. He was beginning to understand. 'You could have had him at a discount or on hire purchase or something.'

'It doesn't matter. We'll get him back. I'll go and see them, I'll go now. I'll tell them there's been a mistake. I'll tell them he's mine.'

John was appalled. He felt guilty, he felt he had betrayed Gavin by his thoughtlessness. 'Gavin, I don't know their name or where they live. They paid cash.'

'You don't know their name?'

'Look, I'm sorry, Gavin, but you know I can't refuse to sell customers something that's on sale.'

Until then the shop had been empty but now the swing doors opened and there was a sudden influx of customers. A woman picked up one of the wire baskets and came up to John with an inquiry. What it was he never found out, for Gavin, his face working and his eyes wild, turned and delivered at the table on which the mynah's cage had stood a powerful kick. It was a long table that also held terrariums and gardens in bowls and troughs. The kick dislodged a pyramid of glass vessels which juddered and crashed to the floor, sweeping the grass cloth with it, causing a cascade of stone urns and copper pots, flying earth and broken leaf. The noise it made was loud and reverberating and the woman who had come up to John gave a shriek. The other customers stopped where they were and stared at Gavin.

The attention he got seemed to fuel him. He drew back his arm and made a backhanded sweep along a shelf of bowls and vases. Some of these were of plastic but most were pottery. They shattered and the pieces flew. Gavin went mad then. He began grabbing at everything in sight and hurling it to the floor, plants in pots, vases, jars, wire baskets, tools. An elaborate barbecue device of metal and wood and glass he wrenched into its component parts and cast them to right and left, overturning a stone nymph and breaking a window. One of the women started to scream.

'Can't you stop him?' a man shouted. 'Can't someone stop him?'

Gavin was trampling on the broken bits of glass and pottery like a wounded elephant. His arms flailed among the bamboo mirrors. Upraised hands tugged at two hanging bowls from which ivy trailed. His voice had been silenced while his body made mayhem but now he began shouting and a stream of obscenities poured from him like the soil from the broken bowl. Les had got behind him and one of the men customers looked as if prepared to help. Paralysed for a while by the horror of it, John now came from behind the counter and began moving towards Gavin. Seeing him advance, Gavin leapt for the drum that bristled with a variety of garden tools like umbrellas in a stand. He grabbed a long-handled fork, its head small but with four sharp stainless steel prongs, and holding it like a javelin, made a lunge at John.

It was all ridiculous, grotesque. It was also frightening. John had sidestepped behind a stand hung with bulbs in packets but the lot came crashing down as Gavin rushed it. And this time his efforts succeeded. He let out a triumphant yell like some primitive warrior, jabbed at John with the fork, catching him a glancing blow on the shoulder. The pain was intense, savage. Gavin would have followed up his stroke with further stabbings, would perhaps have gone on till John was severely wounded or even dead, but as he aimed a second lunge Les and the customer grabbed him from behind, trying to pin his arms behind his back. Gavin fought them tigerishly, snarling and squealing and grunting, throwing back his head, twisting his neck and trying to bite Les's hand. Holding on to his shoulder from which blood was welling through his clothes, through the thick canvas coat, John was aware that Sharon was phoning the police.

It took the three of them, one of the women holding the door open, to get Gavin into the office. The blood was now actually flowing from John's wound. They shoved Gavin into the desk chair and Les was all for tying him up, trapping and immobilizing him inside one of the fruit cage nets. But John wouldn't have that.

Gavin was still holding on to his pike but he let John take it away from him. His hands were as limp as dying leaves. He hung down his head and sobbed.

ʕʕʕʕʕ **PART FOUR** ʕʕʕʕʕ

ϝϝϝϝϝϝϝϝϝϝϝϝϝϝϝϝϝϝϝϝϝ **1** ϝϝϝϝϝϝ

MUNGO WOULD BE HOME ON FRIDAY OR SATURDAY, Charles couldn't remember which. But that was a week ahead. Of course he could do absolutely nothing about Peter Moran until Mungo came back. He could simply do nothing and await further instructions. Charles could see that this really wasn't on. For one thing, this was obviously the test Mungo had said he would set him, this was the test of his loyalty, to follow and observe the behaviour of Peter Moran. Secondly, if he could ever be in doubt of the value of this exercise, the command to abandon it from Rosie Whittaker or Michael Stern or whoever confirmed its importance.

He did nothing on Saturday or Sunday. On Sunday anyway he couldn't do anything as neither of his parents went into town. Most of the day he practised card tricks. One of the things he practised was doing a waterfall, holding half the cards in each hand and letting them trickle from his palms in such a way that they interwove, one from the left, one from the right, feathering into a single pack of fifty-two. He hoped to be good enough at this to give a casual, apparently unrehearsed, demonstration to Sarah and his parents after tea, but he wasn't satisfied with his performance. If you are a perfectionist you are a perfectionist and there isn't much you can do about it.

It was said that Mungo was afraid of growing any taller, that he hoped desperately he had stopped growing. Charles was still only just over five feet. He knew he would get taller eventually, for his parents were of average height, but he would have liked some of that growth now. Looking at himself in the mirror, he considered dispassionately that if these things went on appearance alone what a marvellous child actor he would make. The male Shirley Temple of the eighties. His angel face gazed back at him and he recognized in it that other-worldly expression, as if the eyes were fixed on some distant beatific vision, which painters of the past gave to their cherubs and their infant saints. It was in the eyes of course, but in the delicate mouth too and faintly pearly translucent skin. Even his hair had achieved some unwanted growth in the past week,shaping itself into little curly tendrils. Bloody hell, thought Charles. Oh, shit...

Did Mungo know the kind of man Peter Moran was? Was this part of the test, the terrible part you either survived, thus proving your allegiance, or else perished in the attempt? Charles thought of what he had read somewhere about novice druids, in order to attain promotion, having to lie all night composing epic poetry in tanks full of icy water. Such an ordeal might almost be preferable to what lay before him. Picking up the cards again, splitting the pack into two, he felt a grudging admiration for Mungo, for his nerve, his ruthlessness. In the past he had often felt London Central was simply not tough enough. Mungo, and apparently Angus before him, had been stern about no actual lawbreaking, no theft, forgery, violence against the person; so much so that Charles had certain changes in mind when he succeeded Mungo as he meant to do. There would be no place in his organization for all this squeamishness.

In view of that he ought to be glad Mungo was coming out of the scruples closet. If only he hadn't been the object of this departure. Fear ran down his spine in as precise a trickle as the falling cards. It was hot again but his hands had felt cold all day. At any rate, he had perfected the trick, he would never do it wrong now, it was there, mastered, controlled, for ever. He went downstairs to show it off—well, to pick his moment when he could do it in full view of all of them as casually as anyone else might pick up and open a book.

'Good God,' said his father. 'Amazing. Do that again.'

Charles smiled the closed-lips smile they had all learned from Guy Parker, it seemed very long ago. He thought again and inescapably of how different his father's reaction would be, of his anger and fear, if he knew his son contemplated establishing a rapport with a paederast.

But he had decided to postpone a second confrontation. Going into town with his mother rather late in the morning, sitting beside her in the Escort, Charles had no plans to make the trip out to Nunhouse that day. Another one of those cold shivers erected the hairs on the back of his neck when he thought of Peter Moran phoning the empty Cameron house. Today, though, he would put all that out of his head, no point in worrying about it at this stage. He was on his way to the building firm of Albright-Craven, whose tender, he had at last discovered, had secured the contract for the conversion of Pentecost Villas. How exactly he was going to penetrate the place and make his inquiries he hadn't yet decided. Smallness of stature and juvenile looks were again a grave disadvantage.

As it turned out he never did get inside the building that day, for quite by chance he encountered Peter Moran again. By then it was late lunchtime. Somebody had parked on Charles's mother's ratepayer's parking space in Hillbury Place and they had to put the Escort a long way off in the underground car park in Alexandra Bridge Street. Then Gloria wanted to buy Charles a track suit she saw in Debenham's window, which

Charles didn't want and wouldn't have worn. Nor would he let her buy him lunch at Debenham's roof-garden restaurant. He was afraid Albright-Craven might close for lunch. It would take him half an hour on foot to get there anyway.

It was gone one by the time he reached Feverton Square that lay just outside the old city walls. He had seen the CitWest clock indicating twelve-fifty-seven and twenty-five degrees and a moment or two later as he passed through the Fevergate he heard the cathedral clock strike one. It was always a fraction fast. Because it was a hot sunny day the square was full of people sitting on benches or lying about on the grass or eating sandwich lunches. The strange thing was that though Peter Moran wasn't far from his thoughts, couldn't be in the nature of things, but so to speak lurking just behind the threshold of his consciousness, he didn't see him sitting there on the top of a low pillar at the foot of the Albright-Craven steps. He was about as observant as you could get, was Charles, but still he didn't see him until he was himself no more than a yard or two away. Peter Moran was sitting there with his back to the pavement, looking up the steps to the big ornate silver and black swing doors. He was wearing a very old white tee-shirt with short sleeves that showed pale hairy arms. His head was bent back a bit so that his rather long, greasy fair hair touched the neck of his tee-shirt.

As is so often the case with fear (though bearing this in mind never seems much use for next time, as Charles reflected) it went away immediately in the actual presence of what caused it. He could probably have got up those steps, or nearly all the way up them, before Peter Moran saw him but he dared not miss this opportunity. And there were people about everywhere. He was quite safe.

'Hallo,' he said.

Peter Moran turned round. Charles had anticipated a

delighted wonder would be registered but in fact he didn't look altogether pleased to see him.

'Oh, hallo. Hi.' A glance up the steps and then the pale pebble eyes returned to Charles's face, the expression growing friendlier. 'What brings you here then?'

'This and that,' said Charles. His courage had almost resumed its total proportions, which were considerable. 'Sorry if I was out when you phoned.'

'I did phone, since you ask. I didn't get any reply.'

He was only a man, a fellow human being, of average IQ, no doubt. Not all that bright. Charles was in the habit of assessing people quite coldly like this. He was also not a very large man, slight of build, a bit unhealthy looking, no more than—what? Five feet nine or ten? That voracious look that seemed suddenly to distort his features, maybe that was only because he was hungry. For food, that is, thought Charles.

'You said something about having a coffee.'

The glance went back up the steps. 'Not now. I couldn't now.'

It was said repressively as if not he but Charles had made the initial overtures, as if he were having second thoughts. And Charles was going to move off, either go into the building or return later, was going to think again about observing and tailing this man, perhaps observing and tailing were all he needed to do, when Peter Moran whispered—or it would be nearer to say hissed—getting to his feet and starting up the steps:

'This time Wednesday. Fevergate Café. Where they have the tables outside.'

Charles didn't say yes or no. A party of people strolling along the pavement, several of them his own age, engulfed him. Some would call it a piece of luck, for it removed the possibility of his being recognized by the woman Peter Moran had gone up to meet, the woman who had answered the door to him at the cottage in Nunhouse. They were coming down the steps together, not looking at one another, not holding hands or anything, but undeniably together. Charles drifted on with his new companions, foreign visitors they were, tourists with maps in their hands. Peter Moran's coolness was explained. You could understand he wouldn't want other people—sister? housekeeper? surely not a wife?—to know what he was up to. At the thought of what he might be up to Charles felt another cold tremor.

He didn't have to go to the Fevergate Café on Wednesday. He hadn't committed himself. Even if he had committed himself he wouldn't have to go.

ƒƒƒƒƒƒƒƒƒƒƒƒƒƒƒƒƒƒ **2** ƒƒƒƒƒ

ALMOST THE FIRST THING THEY DID AT THE HOSPITAL was to give John an anti-tetanus injection. After his wound had been cleaned and stitched up he thought they might let him go home but they said they would like him to stay in for a couple of days. He had lost a lot of blood.

The hospital was on top of one of the high suburb-clad hills and from where he lay he could look across the valley. On the other side of Hartlands Gardens he could see Fonthill Court where Mark Simms lived. The sun shone on the big picture windows, turning them all to golden mirrors. Next day he phoned Colin to tell him where he was and Colin came in to see him, promising to go back to Geneva Road and see the greenhouse got watered. But Colin was his only visitor. He wished he could rid himself of the absurd hope that Jennifer would come. Useless to tell himself that Jennifer didn't know, that there was no reason to suppose Colin would have told her, that even if she did know she wouldn't come. When visiting time came and the wives and girlfriends and mothers arrived, bursting in like a herd of hungry animals admitted at last to where the corn was, he found he was holding his breath, eyeing them, searching for her. Then he lay back on his pillows with an inner sigh of resignation.

Fortunately there were only two such occasions. On Sunday they had let him go home with instructions to keep off work for a few days. It was the first time he had been away from the house overnight since his honeymoon. It felt as if it had been shut up for years, the unmade bed, *October Men* lying face down on the coffee table, a tea mug and bread and butter plate in the sink, *Marie-Celeste*-like evidence of some long distant moonlight flit. There was no reply from Jennifer to his letter. He saw what he had done quite clearly, poisoned her mind against Peter Moran without at all advancing his own cause. She would stick to Moran because on his account she had been through fire and water, but she had no enthusiasm left at the prospect of a new marriage or the dissolution of the old.

Colin had flooded the greenhouse plants and the tomatoes, their leaves yellowing, stood in pools of water. John poured away the surplus water and stood there in the stuffy little lean-to that was full of buzzing insects, thinking about Gavin and about love, objects of love. Somehow he had always thought Gavin must have some wild sex life, a succession of glamorous girlfriends, a happy family, devoted mother and sisters too. Perhaps he had but it was a mynah bird he had loved. How astounded those people with the grandchild would be if they knew what their purchase of the mynah had led to!

Next day it was made clear to him that they would come to know. The police arrived to tell him Gavin was to be charged with something or other, unlawful wounding it seemed to be. It was in vain that John protested. Apparently, it wasn't up to him to decide. When he asked where Gavin was now they said—sheepishly, he thought—that he had been taken to Summerdale. This was the psychiatric hospital that in John's parents' time had always been known as Copplesfield after the district where it was, and called in those days a lunatic asylum. He would have liked to ask questions and he would have done if Susan Aubrey had been there but it was two policemen he had never seen before, wooden-faced, officious, talking as if tapes of requisite cop-speak played out of their mouths.

No sooner had they gone than the phone rang. John had given up trying to cure himself of thinking it was going to be Jennifer. He even elaborated on this. He even started thinking, it's looking after people she likes, it's people in need of care, dependent people, when she knows what happened to me... The voice of Mark Simms, not at all diffident or wary, said:

'Hallo, John. How are you then?'

He had no reason to replace the receiver now—or had he perhaps more reason?

'OK,' he said. He knew of old how pointless it would be to tell Mark anything about his encounter with Gavin, anything about his injury or being in hospital. Mark was probably going to apologize. John said, going carefully, to show Mark the way, give him a chance, 'I suppose you've seen they've got someone for the—for Cherry's murder.'

There wasn't even a pause. 'That's what I was ringing up about, as a matter of fact. Well, partly that. I wasn't sure if the police had been to you. They've actually kept me quite thoroughly informed, which was a bit unexpected to say the least.'

'They've been to me too.'

'Oh, good. I mean quite right too, but you never know with them. Well, all that's cleared up then, John, the questions answered, the mysteries solved. Old Maitland's son—would you credit it? I knew him by sight. Well, that door's closed for ever. Time to start afresh with a clean slate. And talking of starting afresh, who do you think I'm seeing tonight? Three guesses.'

'I don't know any of your friends, Mark,' John said.

'You know these. Scarcely friends yet though, but who knows? Jennifer and Peter, how about that? I'm invited round for a meal. They said to bring someone, they meant a woman of course, but I don't know any women. You know what a hermit I am. Much like yourself really. You're about the only person I could take and that wouldn't exactly do, would it?'

John said it wouldn't do. He put the phone down, having managed to resist promising to go out for a drink some time. It was a strange feeling this, being talked to by someone whose behaviour seemed to defy all the laws of normal human interchange. Weeping and cowering, exposing himself to blows, Mark had cringed at his feet and confessed to a murder he hadn't done and couldn't have done. Whatever his motive—loneliness, guilt, a desire for attention, drunkenness—he had forgotten all about it now, John was sure of that, he had even forgotten it had happened. Drink would do that too probably, wipe away everything except perhaps a vague memory that he had made a fool of himself.

And how did he know Jennifer? How did he know Peter Moran? The Fevergate Café, of course, when Jennifer had cried and Mark had got a taxi for her, had done more than that, it seemed, had taken her home in that taxi. After a bottle of wine or two he would maybe fall at Jennifer's feet and make some other false confession—that he had murdered his wife, for instance, or (shades of Colin's hints) had a homosexual affair with him, John. Anything was possible with Mark Simms.

ℱℱℱℱℱℱℱℱℱℱℱℱℱℱℱℱℱℱ **3** ℱℱℱℱℱℱ

Nothing much could happen in a restaurant. Charles knew now that he was going to have to keep that appointment, he had done well and he couldn't stop now. And nothing would happen. There would be some talk and possibly some suggestions made that he would find unpleasant and even frightening, but nothing he couldn't handle in that cool laid-back style he had cultivated and which was now second nature. The odd thing was that notwithstanding all this, he was still afraid.

Inescapably in his mind throughout all this was a kind of shocked wondering feeling. It was amazing and shocking that he should be contemplating this in the climate currently prevailing, a climate of universal or at any rate national terror of paederasty, assaults on kids, child-rape, child murder and all the rest of it. Adult reaction would be to label him innocent, ignorant even, naïvely unaware of what might happen to him. Charles, however, was not in the least unaware. Whatever state of ignorance he might have been in a week before, he had remedied this since and now knew more about sexual abuse of juveniles than his parents did. The library and then, when that failed, Hatchard's shelves, had afforded him all he could wish to know and more. He was going into it with his eyes open.

He watched the television news with his parents and Sarah. There was something on it about the schools' sex education controversy. Should this be left to teachers or to parents? Boys, apparently, seldom if ever discussed these matters at home. Charles, amused in spite of himself, reflected that it might be left to the kids themselves who could do it all in libraries and bookshops. Then a new child's face flashed up on the screen, a newly missing boy. Twelve years old this time. Younger than he was but, according to the description, taller. It was happening all the time, as many boys as girls. This one came from Nottingham. Charles was acutely conscious of himself as they sat there, of his sex and his size and yes, of his golden hair and angel face. He felt his parents' eyes glance fearfully at him and away. The missing boy's mother came on the screen, weeping, wringing her hands, crying when asked if she had anything to say, whoever's taken Roy, please, please, send him back...

'It isn't right, exploiting people like that,' said his father.

'She doesn't have to do it.'

'I'd rather die,' said Gloria. 'If something like that happened to one of my children I should die, I know that.'

His poor mother. Charles thought quite dispassionately how ridiculous it would be if the police came to break the news to her that her son was dead and there she was in turquoise blue tights and a skirt above her knees. He wondered what had happened to Roy—one of the nasty things described in his books, he supposed. The papers were full of child-abuse cases. Charles, who had picked up the *Free Press*, laid it aside. Probably there were no more of these cases than usual, it was his heightened awareness that drew his attention to them, like when he got his music centre for his thirteenth birthday and every paper was full of pieces about the newest albums and every other shop sold record players.

He went in with his father in the morning. There was no talk of paederasty. Charles did the cigarette packet trick with the purple ribbon and this was appreciated with guffaws and compliments, especially as the full Silk Cut pack was quickly produced. It was getting on for ten-thirty when they got into town but Charles still had a lot of morning to kill. A mist lay on the surface of the river and a haze, golden with sun, hung in the alleys between buildings on the eastern side. Someone was fishing from the embankment at the foot of the Beckgate Steps. Charles walked across Rostock Bridge and up to the green where the flyover drop was. If Moscow Centre didn't know Mungo was away they might have put another of their messages there, a message which by the very falseness of its commands might be of help to him. But there was nothing inside the central upright.

Charles made cat noises. These were not the usual mewing sounds humans make when they want to sound like cats but carefully studied long-practised soft yowls. The effect was immediate and then Charles wished he hadn't mewed so persuasively, for he had nothing to give the six or seven cats who came rubbing themselves against him and pushing whiskery faces against his jeans. It was too far to walk to Feverton even in the interests of using up time, so he went to the bus stop, trying to think positively about the meeting ahead. I have to know what it is Mungo wants, he thought, I have to know the purpose of this contact. It can't just be a test, can it? And if it is just a test, how will I know whether I have passed it or failed it? What I really need is a sign.

The Albright-Craven exercise proved in the end one of the easiest Charles had ever undertaken. It just went to show how pointless worry was, how wasteful of time and energy was all this speculation. He tried to make a resolution to stop worrying, to cease speculating. For he had no sooner entered the building by those flashy black and silver doors, had not even approached the lift or been accosted by the porter from the window of his cubbyhole, when he saw the pyramid-shaped stand in the middle of the foyer that proclaimed the Albright-Craven Pentecost Project.

On one of the triangular panels was an artist's impression of what the five houses in Ruxeter Road would look like when Albright-Craven had put new windows in and plastered their outsides and put up new balconies, and on another their renewed insides with arches and split levels and kitchens and bathrooms. On the third panel were all the details, specifications and costs and—more to Charles's interest—the projected dates when work on the building would commence and when be finished. 'Starting October,' it said, 'for completion by early summer.' But prospective buyers should secure units now as the demand was expected to be enormous.

The porter came over. 'Was there something you wanted, son?'

'I was looking for Mr Robinson,' said Charles.

'There's no Mr Robinson here.'

Charles went out into the sunshine. There was plenty of time still, time enough to put a message for Mungo about the fate of the safe house into the flyover drop. On the other hand perhaps not. Moscow Centre had the *October Men* code. Angus Cameron knew about the flyover, Angus had passed it on to his brother, Charles had heard. Suppose—was it possible?—Angus Cameron or Chimera, the former head of London Central, was the mole in the department?

It was dismaying even to think of it. Charles walked slowly riverwards. The mist had lifted, the water lay a perfectly flat clear silvery-blue, and a herd of swans came up out of the deep shadow under Randolph Bridge. It was all gardens and walks along the river here. Charles bought himself a Cornetto, chocolate mint, from the mobile ice-cream vendor parked in the open space a one-time Labour council had named Rio Plaza. On the river wall, throwing gravel chips into the water, sat Graham O'Neill's brother Keith, code name Scylla. They didn't know each other well, Charles and he, and their greeting was the bare acknowledgement of a lifted arm.

I could go up to Hillbury Place instead, he thought, and get Mummy to buy me lunch, Chinese maybe. With embarrassment he realized he had used in his inner reflections the name for his mother he had cast off two years before. Mummy indeed! Whatever next? Like a child... Up the steep street he went and through the Fevergate. There was a plaque here claiming the walls of the city to be of Roman origin. Charles stood reading the plaque which had been familiar to him since he could first read. It was still only twenty to one but he didn't want to get to the restaurant before Peter Moran did. He wanted to see Peter Moran arrive.

From here he could see the Fevergate Café with its awning and the tables spread with pink cloths set out underneath it. Peter Moran would also be able to see him. He moved along the wall into one of its embrasures, at this time of the year a mass of pendulous dusty plants. Charles squatted down on his haunches, licked the last of the ice cream out of his Cornetto and offered the wafer tip to a flock of sparrows.

He couldn't see the CitWest tower from here and he wasn't wearing his watch but it seemed to him that Peter Moran arrived rather early. He had made sure of arriving before his guest. He swung up the open space between the tables and into the comparative darkness of the restaurant. Charles got to his feet. He was queasily imagining being in a dark corner in there with Peter Moran when the man came out again and took his seat at one of the tables under the awning. It was a relief. Charles waited until he heard a single brazen stroke from St. Stephen's clock and then he sauntered across the wide paved walking area where no cars were permitted to go.

Peter Moran looked up and smiled. It made him think that there were some people, otherwise quite ugly, whose faces became nice when they smiled. He was wearing an open-necked shirt that looked quite clean and this somehow comforted Charles, though the fact that a silver chain hung against the pale hairs on his chest equally unaccountably did not.

'Hallo, Ian.'

For a moment Charles couldn't think what he meant and then he remembered he had given his name as Ian Cameron while they were in the cottage at Nunhouse. He sat down, saying nothing but doing his Guy Parker face, the enigmatic smile Guy was said to have achieved as a result of studying a reproduction of the Mona Lisa. Then something dreadful happened, or it seemed dreadful at first. Charles's skin and flesh shrank against his bones. Peter Moran leaned forward, put out his hand and touched Charles's face, one finger touched it anyway, at the corner of his mouth.

'You'd got ice cream on your chin.' The lifted finger showed a brown and green trace.

Charles nodded, dumb.

'What would you like to eat, Ian? I mean I suppose that ice cream isn't going to last you long. There's a menu up on that blackboard.'

The simple coffee idea had been forgotten then.

'Only don't have the specialities de la maison, so called, do you mind? I'm a poor man, your majesty. Frankly, I'm usually on the breadline. You don't mind my being honest, do you?'

Charles shook his head. He knew he had better say something and now.

'What do I call you?'

'Peter. We will be Peter and Ian. Do you know, it never crossed my mind to call you Mr. Cameron?'

Nothing can happen out here with all these people about, thought Charles. The funny thing was that while he was waiting in the embrasure of the wall he had actually wondered if he could have been wrong about Peter Moran and he wasn't a paederast, he was just a lonely person or someone who missed not having children of his own. The finger touch on his chin had put paid to any wishful thinking of that kind. He did another Guy Parker Mona Lisa, forced himself to read the blackboard and told Peter Moran he would have spaghetti bolognaise and chips.

This didn't seem to be too expensive and Peter Moran had it too. He also had wine, cheap wine perhaps because it arrived in a glass jug, but a good deal of it, maybe a whole litre. For Charles there was a can of Coke. Peter Moran began talking about food, Italian food mostly, telling Charles about pasta in Italy, coffee-flavoured tortellini filled with cream and blocks of chocolate, coloured orange or bright green, and cakes of marzipan made in the shape of heads of maize or pods of peas. He evidently thought Charles had a sweet tooth, evinced by the ice cream perhaps. It all brought back from infancy days tales of men who lured children with bags of sweets.

'Enough of this nonsense,' Peter Moran said suddenly. 'Now tell me about yourself. Tell me about Ian Cameron.'

Make up as little as possible, thought Charles, who understood the science of lying. He lived in Church Bar, he said, with his parents and his brothers. Although it went against the grain, it was almost painful to have to do it, he lowered his age by two years. Peter Moran seemed to have no difficulty in believing he was only twelve.

'Where do you go to school?'

'Rossingham,' said Charles. 'I'll be starting at Rossingham next term.'

The spaghetti came. Charles didn't feel hungry but he knew he would have to force himself to eat it. Peter Moran poured himself a third glass of wine. He said:

'I was at Rossingham.'

Charles looked at him. A year at the school had impressed on him its code of neatness and cleanliness. It wasn't unusual to take two showers in one day, commonplace to wear two clean shirts. This had already been Charles's way but some newcomers found it almost bizarre. Yet they conformed, they learned the habit. Peter Moran looked, if not dirty, scruffy. On each occasion Charles had seen him his hair needed a wash. So you could lapse post-Rossingham apparently, you could backslide. The accent was right, Charles suddenly realized, the accent which curiously had puzzled him by its familiarity. It was the Rossingham voice that Peter Moran had, that he too would have some day if he didn't already...

The subject had been changed while he was considering and now Peter Moran was talking about interests, hobbies. What did Charles like to do? Was he good at games? Did he collect things? How about the theatre? The cinema? Charles reluctantly admitted to a liking for films. His plate clean, he took the pack of cards out of his jeans pocket and did a waterfall, only a passable one though, not the tour de force with which he had entertained his parents and sister. Peter Moran was impressed. He asked for a repeat performance. As the cards fell for the second time, interweaving, feathering from the left and from the right and from the left, Charles thought how he must get the conversation back to Rossingham. He was aware of an uneasy chilly feeling, in spite of the warmth of the day.

'We might go to a movie together,' Peter Moran was saying.

Charles nodded, his smile small and tight. He put the pack away.

'Are you busy on Friday?'

'Friday evening?' said Charles.

'Well, maybe the five-thirty show if you want to get home late.' The thick glasses had a way of deadening his eyes according to how his face turned against the light. Sometimes they were just thick glasses, magnifying the pale eyes behind them to preternatural size, sometimes mirrors reflecting Charles's own desperate angel face, and sometimes opaque planes like roundels of dull metal, pewter perhaps or lead. There was quite a lot of sweat on his skin and it reminded Charles of the drops of moisture that are exuded from stale cheese. He hazarded a suggestion. A try-on it was. If Peter Moran agreed he didn't quite know what he would do. But he was sure he wouldn't agree.

'Do you want to call for me at my house?'

The glasses turned to lead as Peter Moran's head gave one of its sharp turns. 'I don't think that would be a very good idea, do you?'

That was coming out into the open, Charles thought. That was what he had once heard his father say wasn't calling a spade a spade but a bloody shovel. Peter Moran named a film. It was something Japanese and obscure and showing at the Fontaine in Ruxeter Road. They could meet outside, he said. He gave a broad smile that somehow this time didn't make him look attractive or nice but—Charles sought for a word and came up with an unwelcome one—wolfish.

He didn't have to go to the cinema, he didn't have to go near the place. Hadn't he done enough, far over and above the call of duty?

'When were you at Rossingham?' he asked quite abruptly.

'Oh, dear. That would be telling. You'll be asking me my age next. I always give the same answer. Somewhere between thirty and death.' He poured the last of his wine, turned and flicked his fingers at the waitress. 'Now it has to be paid for, Ian. Like everything you get in life, whether it's love or farinaceous strings in tomato sauce. I went to Rossingham in the year of grace nineteen sixty-five. You'll see my name on the list of past pupils in the chapel, hardly a roll of honour. I was in Pitt House and in my last year the incoming housemaster was a dusty eunuch of a Latinist called Lindsay.'

Charles stared at him, feeling the beginnings of an understanding of Mungo's purposes.

'Don't you believe me? The chapel will prove it to you. And if you need more, if you actually have to put your

hand in my side and feel the mouth of the wound...?'
The grin was wide and humourless again, not flecked
with foam of course, but somehow looking as if it should
be. 'When you get to Rossingham have a look in study
seven in Pitt House, in the old part, not the extension,
and under the lower bunk you'll see something—not so
much to your advantage as proof positive.'

It was the sign, thought Charles. It was what he had
been waiting for. Did he need further evidence that
Peter Moran had something or knew something Mungo
wanted? Wasn't study seven the very study Mungo
shared with Graham O'Neill and two others? He
watched the man, the ex-Rossingham man, wine-
drinker, and paederast, paying the bill with a dribble of
coins, feeling into the depths of pockets for the last necessary ten pee, and it took all the strength he had not to
run away.

ƒƒƒƒƒƒƒƒƒƒƒƒƒƒƒƒƒƒ **4** ƒƒƒƒƒ

LADY ARABELLA'S GARDEN WAS STILL WHITE, STILL
fresh and blooming in August. The cupolas and trellises
were hung now with the creamy fronds of the Russian
vine, and still flowering between the flagstones and in
the borders amongst ox-eye daisies and bleached to-
baccos were the white violas lasting summer through.
John sat on a stone seat looking at the flowers, a seat
that was carved with maidens and lions and swags of
leaves and which grew damp with green mould in
spring and autumn but was dry as dust now. His
shoulder pained him with a dull rheumatic ache. He
had come here to try to heal himself of various bruis-

ings, physical and mental. From encounters with the police at Feverton it was the obvious place to visit for such a purpose. One set of the gates to Hartlands Gardens faced the opaque deceitful one-way windows of the police station.

The two people who talked to him, a man and a woman, were not that man and woman he had seen before. They didn't want much from him, only that he should look through the statement he had made sixteen years before, reconfirm it, add to it if he had anything to add. Reading Cherry's name hurt and now caused a curious embarrassment as well. But it was all over and done with in fifteen minutes and the whole empty Thursday afternoon, and a hot sunny one, stretched before him. He sat and looked at the flowers in the sunshine and marvelled again how only white butterflies seemed to come in here, as if they knew.

That morning, from the central depot in Bristol, they had sent him a replacement for the mynah bird just as last Monday a replacement had arrived for Gavin, a lively red-cheeked young woman who had been one of a team of gardeners at some open-to-the-public showplace. Trees were really her field, she told John, which struck him as amusing. The mynah bird's successor was a snow-white and silent cockatoo. John rested his head back against the stone loins of a lion and thought how he had lost his sister for ever. He would never now be able to speak of her to others as he once had with reverence and sorrow. There would always be her excesses to remember and get in the way of grief, and Mark Simms's absurd false confession that he had swallowed so gullibly. These things would now be inseparable from memories of Cherry in life and death.

He understood now that those memories, unspoilt as they then were, had been something for him to hold on to after Jennifer had gone. They were lost as his code-makers, that other consolation, were lost. What was left to him now? Library books, thrillers and

Victorian novels. Colin and his mother. Trowbridge's. Tired of this list of questionable assets, he got up and moved away, his arm heavy in its sling, his shoulder stiff. The prospect of the evening ahead began to frighten him, for he could think of absolutely nothing to do with it, nowhere to go, no one to visit or phone, nothing he wished to read. And he realized that in all his unhappiness he had never quite felt this. He had never felt panic at the idea of a future, only sadness and—hope.

From the white garden he had achieved what he expected, a soothing of wounds. But nothingness, negation, vacancy, can be worse than wounds and all that shimmering scented pallor, those fluttering white wings, had in some strange way shown him a vision of emptiness. Thinking like this, struggling against a rising fear, he walked along the terrace where in the spring, before there was a leaf on these trees that were now foliaged past their prime, he had looked down and seen Jennifer sitting at one of the tables below. Then he had fancied himself unhappy but he had been full of hope, hope which had taken a lot of quenching, and his state in retrospect seemed to him enviable. He was looking down there now—inevitably —but he wrenched his eyes away, looked ahead of him and saw Susan Aubrey approaching along the terrace path.

Since his last sight of her, in Geneva Road when she had come on what was almost an errand of mercy, he had been glancing through the photographs in a library book, an art book about the pictures in the Frick Collection in New York, and had seen the face hers had reminded him of. It was that of a pale blond young girl with translucent skin and red-gold hair in a painting by Greuze called *The Wool Winder*. Remembering this somehow intimate thing made the blood come up into his cheeks now they were face to face again.

She didn't greet him. She said instead in a voice of

consternation, 'What happened to your arm?'

Incongruous that he should suddenly think of Peter Moran. He suspected, without real knowledge, that Peter Moran was a person who could make that kind of thing funny, tell it wittily. A madman who was in love with a talking bird duffed me up with a pitchfork, he would say. Something like that. John wasn't able to do it himself and never would be able to. Perhaps that was what Jennifer liked about the one of them she did like. Never mind all that stuff about people depending on her and needing her. He told Susan Aubrey the history of his injured shoulder in quite a straightforward way and then they were walking down the steps towards the tables and the cafeteria. It was she, not he, who happened to choose the very table he and Jennifer had sat at and she had told him she wanted a divorce.

When he had fetched their tea on a tray and two match-box-sized pieces of fruit cake wrapped in cellophane, he told her about it. He thought, what the hell, why not, and he told her. It had something to do with the empty feeling and nothing much mattering any more. He would have told her about Peter Moran being convicted for sexual abuse of a child only his inhibition on naming things like that in front of a woman, even a policewoman, held him back.

'You've had a bad time,' she said. 'A sea of troubles. I'd say the tide's bound to turn now.'

'I hope you're right. My father used to say, "Cheer up, things might be worse, so I cheered up and they got worse."'

She laughed and he felt that perhaps being a wit was possible even now. He was glad he hadn't added that his father never said that or anything like that after Cherry died. And then, as she finished her cake and brushed crumbs off her dark blue skirt, flicked with a fingernail a sugar granule from the Greuze chin, he thought, why don't I ask her to have dinner with me? Tonight—well, this evening, supper really, or a meal at that Indian place I went to with Mark, the Hill Station?

For two reasons, he thought. They had got up and were moving out of the circle of tables, about to separate, she to continue northwards across the gardens, he to seek the Feverton entrance. Two reasons—I would keep thinking of Jennifer, I would wish she was Jennifer, I might even make a fool of myself and call her Jennifer. And then I am afraid. I am afraid she would say no.

Perhaps that's really why I haven't asked, I can't ask, he thought as they parted and she turned back once and waved, I haven't the nerve or the resources to face rejection...

ffffffffffffffffffff **5** fffff

ON THE CROWN OF A HILL, AT A VIEWING PLACE, A telescope was sited for a better appreciation of the panorama of rocks, cypresses, olive groves, broken columns and gushing water below. A certain amount of drachmae had to be put into its slot in order to see more than a blur but the telescope no longer functioned and even its coin slot was blocked with dust. Mungo leant over the low wall, inhaling—so deep was his pleasure—rather than merely smelling the scent of the hillside herbs, the thyme and oregano and bay. It wasn't hard to imagine gods come to earth here, larger-than-life animated statues he saw them as, in robes like fluted cloud.

Down the slope Ian and Gail were chasing butterflies, not to catch them but to get a closer look at wing spans and colours unknown at home. The heat was intense but somehow light and dry.

'Seems funny to think this place once belonged to us,' said Graham.

'What do you mean, to us?'

'Well, it was a British Protectorate after the Napoleonic Wars. We had a governor here for about fifty years.'

Graham was marvellous on history, he was going to do history at university. While Angus asked him about it, about how the British ever managed to get a foot in the Ionian Sea, Mungo turned to examine the telescope. It was stupid having it here if it didn't work, its ineffectual presence an affront to nature. Then, as he touched the blackened brass band on the cylinder, a fuse of memory was lit and the solution he had been seeking for months exploded.

'Ang,' he said, 'Graham.'

'What?' Angus had already started down the slope. He turned round under the bay trees.

'I've broken Moscow Centre's code,' Mungo said. 'It just came to me in a flash of enlightenment. God, it was like one of those experiences mystics have. Everything was explained and made clear.'

'Saint Bean,' said Angus.

'You can mock but it was like that.' Mungo had his code-book out and was turning to his lists of Stern's messages, all with their ultimate numbers. 'Listen. We knew the numbers at the end were the time. I realized that last week—I told Graham, didn't I?—I realized those numbers were times, not nine hundred and forty-two but nine-forty-two, not one thousand and three but three minutes past ten. And I knew they were on a digital clock because Graham's got his with him in our room, but what I see now is that it's a particular digital clock. It's the one on the CitWest tower.'

'How did you see that on a hill in Corfu?' Graham said, grinning.

'Not because I'm a visionary. It was the telescope.'

Graham's eyebrows went up. He was wearing the tee-shirt he had bought in Corcyra with a genuine jelly-fish printed on it.

'Charles Mabledene took that photograph of Perch's room when he got into Utting. You remember that, don't you? It's in the departmental archives. The photograph didn't show much but it did show he keeps a telescope on the windowsill. That was the clue to the code only we never saw it. You couldn't see the clock on the CitWest tower from as far away as Utting but you could through a telescope. You couldn't see the tower from Rosie Whit-taker's—not at ground level you couldn't. But you would be able to from the top floor of their house. The rest of Moscow Centre's agents would all be able to see the tower with the naked eye, or if not, with telescopes or binoculars.'

Angus gave an angry twitch of his head. 'So what? When are you going to get over all this, Bean? I mean, isn't the joke wearing a bit thin?' He who never lost his temper roared suddenly, 'You have to live, do you know that? You have to be a normal human being. When are you going to have a life instead of a game?' And he plunged down the slope towards his father and mother unpacking picnic things.

'Take no notice,' Graham said kindly. 'It's just that he's pissed off over Diana not coming.'

Mungo wasn't concerned. 'What they do is, start with the date the person getting the message is to act on. That's what the first number is. Then they write the message in the code they directed yesterday or whenever and at the end they put the time in digits. It's the time on the prearranged date at which who-ever gets the message is to look at the digital clock on the CitWest tower and note the temperature. Say, for example, the message begins with nine and ends with nine two three. That means the recipient has to look at the CitWest clock at twenty-three minutes past nine on the ninth and if the temperature is twelve degrees, start making a code alphabet from the twelfth letter of the alphabet,' Mungo was writing now, dashing off numbers and letters in his book rested on the old stone wall. Graham came and looked over his shoulder. 'It does work. It's working out beautifully. You see, here's the last message we picked out of Lysander Douglas's hand. If you work from the message previous to that it directs with the numbers two seven then one zero one five. That means Perch, say, had to look at the CitWest clock on the twenty-seventh at ten-fifteen, record the temperature and work the code from whatever number in the alphabet the temperature was.'

'But we can't. We don't know what the temperature was.'

'No, but we can make guesses. Somewhere between twelve and twenty degrees, wouldn't you think? On the twenty-seventh of July at ten-fifteen in the morning? Or, that is to say, starting the code alphabet somewhere between L and T.'

'You couldn't do it with Fahrenheit,' Graham said. 'You could only do it with Celsius and in a climate where the temperature hardly ever goes above twenty-six.'

'If it does I expect they start again from the beginning, twenty-seven being one and twenty-eight two and so on. We'll try it later, we'll start by assuming it was fifteen degrees. That's Dad yelling for us. He worries some of us will get lost and carried off by brigands.'

Graham nodded, grinning. He held out his hand in a funny grown-up old-fashioned gesture. 'Congratulations.'

They shook hands. Mungo got embarrassed suddenly and vaulted over the wall and went running down to the picnic.

'SOMEONE WAS ASKING FOR A MONKEY PUZZLE,' said the girl called Flora, the new assistant manager. Flora in a garden centre among the flowers, it was absurd. '*Araucaria araucana*, the Chile pine.' She was as bad as Gavin with her Latin names, John thought.

'I suppose we might get her one.'

'I told her they'd gone out of fashion. You never see them.'

'There's one of them trees in John's road,' said Sharon, protruding sea-anemone lips into her handbag mirror, starting to outline them with red pencil. 'Geneva, is it, John, or Lucerne?'

'Geneva,' he said, having no idea how she knew about the monkey puzzle, not much caring. She could walk along there much as anyone else was free to do. He made an effort. Everything had become an effort, every utterance, even the 'Can I help you?' to customers. 'It's a fine specimen, I daresay a hundred years old, from when they were fashionable.'

'I'll come down and look at it one of these fine days. I'm partial to the old *Araucaria*.' The top flowerpot from the stack Flora was holding toppled and fell to the ground with a crash. That was the fourth thing she had smashed since she came less than a week before. John thought her the most accident-prone

269

giddy creature he had come across. 'Oh, sorry. Still, it's only a pot.'

John didn't say anything but went into the chrysanthemum house, into the warm damp and the bitter scent. It was Friday, a Friday coming to its end, and another weekend waited over the brink of it. You could easily reach a point in this world when you didn't know anyone, when you had no acquaintances, still less had friends. You could reach a point when all days were exactly the same, limbo-days, neither happy nor sad. And there could come time—for him he thought it might already have come—when all your memories were too painful to revive and although they were all you had, there was nothing for it but strive to crush them into oblivion.

People would call it self-pity but that implied being sorry for oneself and he didn't feel pity for anyone much, least of all himself. It was rather as if he had withdrawn from all involvement. With Jennifer only was there something left, a fear for her really, as to what would become of her in her chosen role of guardian and protector to Peter Moran. He walked along the aisle, testing the dampness of the soil in the pots with his forefinger. Someone had slightly over-watered them. Flora, probably. John didn't want to go home, he would have liked the afternoon to go on and on, five-thirty never coming, the shoppers continuing to trickle in, take their trolleys or baskets, choose their little pots of alpines or cacti or herbs, lingering outside in the hot perpetually five o'clock sunshine, for ever.

Les had gone out as he always did about this time for the evening paper and four Marathon bars. Trowbridge's sold only healthy snacks, tropical mix fruit and nuts, sunflower seeds, harvest crunch. It hadn't been a busy afternoon and the place was empty now. Sharon, reading the paper, said to Flora:

'They found that missing boy, the Nottingham one.'

'Alive, d'you mean?'

'Are you kidding? They never are alive.'

Half a dozen people came in through the swing doors. John went to help a man who said rather hectoringly that it was roses he was interested in, only roses. As he passed Flora on his way to the rose-garden exit he saw that, facing the shelves, her back turned, she was quietly weeping and he knew, with a kind of hopeless wonder, that it was for a child she didn't know in a place she had very likely never been to.

ƒƒƒƒƒƒƒƒƒƒƒƒƒƒƒƒƒƒƒ **7** ƒƒƒƒƒƒ

A CUSTOMER WAS COMING IN TO VIEW AND TEST-drive one of the big Volvos. This was the reason Charles's father had made an exception to his rule of not coming in on Fridays. He brought Charles in with him at three and to his son's consternation, started showing some interest in why he wanted to come in at all. Charles said truthfully that he was going to the cinema but untruthfully that it was to see *Aliens* at the Odeon.

'How are you going to get home?'

'The last bus, I expect.' Getting home seemed an unreal concept. Or as if he were getting to the end of a journey and the limousine that awaited him was standing in sight, but between him and it was a deep gulf probably too wide to jump. 'The last Fenbridge bus goes from the station at nine.'

'You weren't thinking of hitching, I hope.'

Truthful again, Charles said he hadn't been. His father started on another of his lectures about not speaking to strangers. Then he said Charles must get a taxi, not a bus, at the station and he gave him the money for the fare. Charles thought it was like deliberately spending a night in a leper hospital after you'd been told to mind and not catch a cold. He hung about the garage for a while. In the shop where you paid for petrol they sold chocolate bars and knick-knacks and weird things like cut flowers and plastic toys. Charles helped himself to a couple of Yorkies and, almost as an afterthought, to one of the penknives stuck on a coloured card that hung up among the ballpoints and key rings. He took it off its card and opened the blades. If they were each five centimetres long that was all they were and just remotely capable of injuring someone if handled, say, by a really experienced surgeon who knew exactly the site of the hyoid or the medulla or one of those things. Charles grinned ruefully to himself but he put the penknife into his pocket.

Just before four-thirty he went to get the bus. He intended to be early. This would be the first time he had ever been to this cinema, the Fontaine, which for as long as he could remember had shown foreign or controversial or less than generally popular films. There was no sign of Peter Moran. Charles started walking round a bit, though the area was familiar to him, harbouring as it did the safe house.

It hadn't occurred to him that Peter Moran might come by car, though he knew he had a car, having of course cleaned it at their first meeting. He recognized it at once, parked on a meter in Collingbourne Road. It was clear to him that while he had been walking round the other way, via Lomas Road and Fontaine Road, Peter Moran had parked here and gone to wait outside the cinema. Charles decided to try to avoid getting in that car if he could help it. He was wearing his watch today and saw that it was five to five. The heat had been intense all day, thirty degrees he had noticed when he saw the CitWest clock from the top of his bus. It made him wonder how high that digital recorder could go. Forty degrees? Forty-five? Perhaps they made different ones for different climates. The heat had somehow thickened during the afternoon and the sky grown overcast without much diminishing the sun's glare. He was aware of a powerful smell compounded of petrol and diesel fumes, gas and drains, something which he had noticed in the past was strongest just before a storm. He noticed something else different too. The corrugated metal was gone from the fronts of the houses in Pentecost Villas and their shabby front doors were exposed. Builders or architects or someone had been in.

Peter Moran was standing outside the Fontaine, apparently studying the poster of Samurai swordsmen. He had his white tee-shirt on. From the back he looked very thin and fleshless, his elbows, knobby, his legs like sticks. As Charles approached he turned round.

'Hi, Ian.'

'Hallo,' said Charles.

'I have to warn you I never make comments on the weather, however extreme.'

Charles smiled, saying nothing. He hoped the cinema would be crowded. They were directed into what was no more than a large room, carpet-lined, air-conditioned, claustrophobic—and empty. It was Charles's first moment of real fear. He had the sensation that he wouldn't have been able to get out if he had wanted to, of the doors having been locked behind them, though this of course must be nonsense. Their tickets were not numbered and Peter Moran chose to sit four rows from the front and in the centre. That at any rate was better than being at the side up against the wall. A curtain of black velvet with a gold pattern on it hung in front of the screen. It was silent when they entered but as soon as they sat down music of the popular classical kind began playing and Charles couldn't escape the rather uneasy conclusion that it had only started on account of their presence.

It wasn't the sort of cinema where they sold ice cream and soft drinks. Peter Moran had brought a bag of wrapped chocolates with him and these he passed to Charles while he talked about Rossingham. He talked about starting at Rossingham and the people he knew there and Pitt House and the man who was housemaster there before Mr Lindsay. Charles knew that this was what it was all about, it must be. This had to be the object of the exercise. Sooner or later Peter Moran was going to tell him some vital fact and he sensed too that he would know it immediately he heard it. But he couldn't help noticing Peter Moran's smell. He smelt very clean, of soap and possibly even some sort of cologne. And he had washed his hair which stood out soft and yellow with ragged split ends —with a mother like Charles's you observed that kind of thing—and which also smelt scented.

Just before the lights dimmed three more people came in. Being English, they sat as far away from each other and from Charles and Peter Moran as was possible. The curtain was swept aside and the ads and previews, followed by a cartoon, began. Charles felt better having the other people there. The lights came up again and Peter Moran excused himself to go to the men's. Charles hoped the other people would note his appearance and Peter Moran's just in case anything happened and he went missing and they needed witnesses. He stared into the faces of the two behind him, trying to give them a good view. Peter Moran came back and at last the Japanese picture started, almost an hour after they had come in.

It seemed darker in the cinema than during the cartoon. The film was not dubbed but sub-titled and there was not even much of that, for on the whole the characters, of whom there were dozens, didn't talk. It was beautiful to look at, Charles could see that, and there was some elaborate stylized dancing but just the same it was incomprehensible. Peter Moran seemed fascinated by it. Not so absorbed though as to keep from putting his arm lightly round Charles's shoulders. The arm was only on the back of his seat at first.

When he felt the hand touch him, though he was expecting it, he couldn't help a sort of leaping flinch. But he controlled himself, he made himself relax. And then he could almost feel the gratitude in the hand, the fingers pressing with relief at not being flung furiously away.

In this small auditorium it was quite cold. The air-conditioning created the temperature of an autumn day. Charles was rather glad of the cold, of feeling he wasn't wearing quite enough clothes, for it distracted him from his revulsion and his gradually increasing fear. Soon, he thought, he would start shivering. The film was fairly noisy, with drum beats and strange music and the clash of weapons if not with talk, but Charles could hear an occasional heavy rumbling as well. If this had been about the Second World War or Vietnam or something like that he would have thought it gunfire. Then there came a crash like a bomb and Charles knew it was thunder, outside and not in the film, that he was hearing.

The film seemed interminable. In a lighter sequence, the screen lit with Japanese sunshine, Charles looked at his watch and saw that it was already past eight. By the time they got out of here it would be getting dark. The thought horrified him. But then, before another five minutes had gone by, without any apparent warning in the story, it was all over and the lights were coming on. Peter Moran's arm had been quickly withdrawn.

'Strange stuff,' he said, 'or was it all crystal clear to you?'

'I couldn't follow it at all.'

'I'm sorry about that. My mistake. *Mea culpa*, as housemaster Lindsay might say. Should I have taken you to *A Hundred and One Dalmatians*?'

They were leaving the Fontaine and a brilliant lightning flash, followed by a clap of thunder sounding like wooden planks tossed on to a concrete floor, cut off

Charles's answer. True to his claim never to speak of the weather, Peter Moran said:

'I expect you're hungry. I've got something to eat in the car. I mean I brought it with me. As I may have told you, I'm an impecunious beggar, erratically supported by my woman who sometimes lets a few crumbs fall in my direction.'

Charles had eaten nothing since his lunch but the two Yorkies washed down with a cup of tea someone had given him at the garage and two of Peter Moran's chocolates. He wasn't in the least hungry though, he felt very slightly sick, his throat gagging. As they crossed the road, passing the front of Pentecost Villas, the first drops of rain began to fall, making big black circular splashes on the pavement. Once he got into that car, he thought, he would have no control at all over his movements. Peter Moran could drive them anywhere, out into the country perhaps, to some remote place of heath or woodland. And by then it would be dark.

The car was now in sight and Charles had a premonition Peter Moran would suggest they run for it before the rain came on harder. He thought of the safe house, empty, supplied with candles, well known to him and not known at all to Peter Moran. A truly 'safe' house in that it contained rooms into which one could if necessary lock oneself.

'I used to live there,' he said. 'My family used to live there. We moved out because they're going to turn it into flats. The middle one was our house.'

Peter Moran had a parking ticket stuck under one of the windscreen wipers. He tore it off, cursing. He hadn't put enough money in to last from five till six-thirty when metering ended. Opening the car door and feeling inside, he said:

'Who lives there now?'

'Nobody lives there now. I've got a key.'

'Have you now?' Peter Moran looked at him. It was a strange look, Charles couldn't have said what it ex-

pressed, but he didn't like it. He didn't like the tight-
ening of the facial muscles and the moistening of
those pale lips with a curiously pale tongue. 'Are you
saying we could go in there and eat our grub? Shelter
from the rain?' He began to smile. 'Better than a car,
maybe?'

'We have to go in the back way,' said Charles.

Peter Moran removed from the back of the car a half-
full carrier bag from which the neck of a wine bottle
protruded.

'Tuck,' he said. 'You'll have to see if they still call it
Tuck at Rossingham. I get the impression you rather
like hearing me talk about Rossingham, don't you?'

'Very much.'

The rain began in earnest as they turned the corner
into Fontaine Road. As the thunder receded to grumble
softly in the distance, the heavens seemed to open.

'Can we run for it?'

'Sure,' said Charles.

He opened the gate into that wilderness of a garden.
The back of the house reared up like a cliff. Lightning
flared and showed them a rampart with blank or broken
windows, a peeling facade hung with dying creeper.
Charles went ahead knowing he must get there first so
that Peter Moran wouldn't see he didn't actually have a
key. Some deft deceiving finger movements were made
and the door pushed open.

Down here it was pitch dark but there were candles
in the table drawer and matches beside them. Charles lit
the candles and pocketed the matches. He felt the knife
there, the small useless penknife.

'You come here often, I can see that,' said Peter
Moran.

'We'll go upstairs. It's nicer upstairs.'

Charles led the way. It grew lighter as they climbed.
He held two candles and Peter Moran one. The rain
roared on the windows, throbbing through the house.
Charles was quite wet, his shirt sticking to him and
water dripping from his hair. The first thing he looked

277

for on the threshold of the big room where the furniture was, was the key. He looked on the inside of the door and the outside but the key wasn't there.

'Nice place you have here,' Peter Moran said, holding his candle aloft and looking round. 'I particularly like the day bed.'

The long windows shimmered and looking out of them was like looking into an aquarium, flowing water only, streams of water, and distantly beyond it, dark blueness and a goldfish speck of light. A stuffy dusty warmth made Charles feel he was steaming. The food and drink was tumbled out on to the metal garden seat, a couple of wrapped pies, biscuits, a can of Coke. Peter Moran felt the wine bottle and pronounced it warm.

'But I don't suppose you have a fridge?'

Charles shook his head. The place was subtly different. It was changed, things had gone, two of the chairs, for instance. The long ragged pink curtains and as far as he could see most of the cobwebs had gone. And the keys had gone. Unless they were inside the doors, and London Central had never kept them inside, all the keys on this floor were gone.

'You're soaking wet,' Peter Moran said.

'So are you.'

'I could dry you on my jacket. I've got a jacket in here.'

In the bottom of the carrier, a woolly thing. Charles closed his eyes and felt a sinking of the heart, of more than that, as if all the organs of his body dropped, at his folly in coming in here, in coming up here. The cataracts flowing down the glass seemed to close them in more firmly than mere bricks and windows. He could see beyond the waterfall something green and distant winking on and off. The woolly folds of Peter Moran's sweater, sheep-smelling as soon as it absorbed the water, enveloped his head. Hands began a gentle rubbing. The two candles on the arms of the metal seat burnt with elongated steady flames. Their shadows were cast long and black, a Frankenstein monster, thin and stretched, Peter Moran looked like, grasping in its paws some hydrocephalic creature, strangling it perhaps or punching its wobbly head.

Charles broke free but not in a panicky way. He pushed his fingers through his damp hair, smoothing it. Peter Moran was very close to him, looking at him without actually touching him. He said:

'Come and sit down. We can have the food.'

He sat on the rotting silk cover of the chaise longue, patted the seat beside him. Charles felt himself creep to it, feeling his way as if he were blind.

'Come here.'

No power on earth, no act of will or need could have made Charles move nearer. The rain had become even more violent and the crashing it made against the facade and windows of the house gave Charles the illusion it was in his own head, his blood roaring. Peter Moran shifted up close to him, said in a bashful nervous monotone:

'When I was about your age and starting at Rossingham I was very lonely, I felt alone and abandoned. I was very happy at home and I didn't want to go away to school. I couldn't settle in at Rossingham, no one seemed to like me and I didn't like anyone.'

Charles was thinking about upstairs, about getting out on to the roof. It was quite possible, Mungo and probably Graham too had done it. You went up through the trap into the loft, pulling the ladder up behind you, and out of the loft on to the slates through a sort of hatch...

'There was this gardener at Rossingham, a groundsman I suppose you'd call him. Just an ordinary working man, young you know, about twenty. He was kind to me, he was loving to me—do you know what I mean?' Peter Moran's voice was breathy and excited. 'I'm talking about physically loving. I made him happy and after a bit I was happy too, I wasn't lonely any more.'

'I'm not lonely,' Charles said, his voice coming out as a squeak, babyish, terrified.

He was curiously hypnotized, unable to take his eyes off Peter Moran's pale windowed unblinking eyes. A paralysis held him still, listening to the sounds that might be the noises of storm or his own blood beating. Yet there was still a cold intellectual core somewhere a very long way inside him, a mind that said, is this it? Is this what I am supposed to discover? Peter Moran put out his hand and laid it on Charles's thigh. It burned through his jeans like a hot iron and he jumped up, grabbed one of the candles and ran to the door. The flame streamed and the shadows flew like a flock of monstrous birds. Peter Moran shouted:

'Ian, come back!'

Charles was out of the door and running up the last flight. Hot wax poured down the candle and the flame guttered. Peter Moran came out of the room holding the other candle. At the top of the steep stairs Charles leapt across the landing to the open door, the keyless door, and his candle went out. He turned, dreadfully at bay, the rooms, the doors, useless to him. Peter Moran stood two stairs from the top, lit by the flame he held, his own features and his glasses casting shadows on his face, and a great black shadow of the whole of him stark on the wall behind.

'You little devil. What the hell do you think you're doing?'

Charles's hand crushed the matchbox in his pocket. His thumb flicked out one of the small blunt blades of the penknife. In the light from the single candle he could see wound round the cleat the rope that held the heavy double ladder close up to the ceiling. The worn bit on the rope showed, no one had replaced it. Charles pulled the knife out of his pocket. He dropped the candle and the saucer broke. Peter Moran was looking at the knife and somehow Charles could see he thought he was going to throw it. He came up one stair. He said:

'Give me that.'

Charles shook his head. He couldn't speak, he had no voice, but his fear was going just the same. His fear was being sucked out of him and replaced by a springing hard energy, like pain. He put out the hand that held the knife, holding it steady, his thumb pressed hard down on the handle. He held it as if for an overarm stab. One stair more Peter Moran came up, made a lunge for the knife, and as he did so Charles raised it and brought it down hard on the frayed rope.

Afterwards he thought, he hadn't meant that, he only wanted the ladder. He only wanted even then to escape by the roof. It was the quickest way to undo the rope. But it wasn't really true any of that, he had meant it, he knew what he was doing, he knew in his adrenalin high what the outcome would be, what would happen.

It happened horrifyingly fast. There was no creaking hesitation, no pause or tremor before the cumbersome mass of wood and metal fell. It swept down in an avenging arc, missing Charles by inches but enough inches, and as if poised for this accurate strike, smashed into the man's jaw. He had tried to duck, he was aware enough for that, and he did duck, but it struck his jaw just the same with a sickening crunch of bone, and sweeping on, cast him backwards down the stairs. The extinction of the candle and Peter Moran's scream, a howling cry of pain, happened simultaneously. The ladder swung wide over the head of the stairs, back towards Charles who leapt aside, and shuddered to a stop.

Charles was left up there in the doorway in the darkness. He had fallen on to his hands and knees and he was screaming too, involuntarily, short sharp screams like a very young child.

PART FIVE

1

THERE WAS SILENCE. THE RAIN HAD CEASED. Charles stopped making those childish sounds. He got to his feet and stood still, forcing himself to take deep breaths, feeling the trembling in his legs gradually grow less. After a moment or two he bent down and grubbing about in the dark, picked up the candle Peter Moran had dropped and the saucer it was in which had not broken. He re-lit the candle and carrying it, crept across to the head of the stairs.

The storm, which he had thought past, reasserted itself in a last violent flare, a huge lightning flash irradiating all of this top floor, the stairwell, the angled slopes of the ceiling, the open doors and hollow empty rooms, the ladder, that engine of destruction. Thunder, as loud and sharp as the ladder striking the floor, followed in a split instant. In the flood of light Charles saw Peter Moran lying broken and twisted at the foot of the steep narrow stairs. He put his hand across his mouth to stop himself crying out again. The darkness came back, walls of it outside the leaping circle of candlelight. Charles began going downstairs.

With head averted, he passed the man who lay half on the bottom stair, half on the landing floor, and went into the room that had furniture in it. Peter Moran's woolly garment, the thing he had dried Charles's head with, lay on the chaise longue. Sprawled across the floor, where Peter Moran had perhaps kicked them over in his pursuit of Charles, lay a packet of sandwiches, crumpled paper napkins, the tissue wrappings of the wine bottle. The windows, washed clean, showed a clear brilliant darkness shot with jewel-like bright-coloured lights, the winking green clock: nine-sixteen and fourteen degrees. The temperature had fallen sixteen degrees since they went into the cinema. So much had happened since they went into the cinema!

Charles was still shaking. It was something he couldn't handle. Deep breathing failed to control it. He was shaking so much he was afraid of actually dropping the candle and he set it down in its saucer on the edge of the metal garden seat. Now he knew he must look at Peter Moran, he must make himself go over there and bend down and look at him. Charles took the matches out of his pocket. He lit a match to help him out of the room, leaving the candle behind him, lighting up the room, the metal seat casting a shadow of ribs and arcs like some strange, non-human skeleton. The door swung behind him, cutting off the light. His match burnt down, he lit another. He opened his eyes, which he had closed without meaning to, and made himself look at Peter Moran. Gradually he dropped into a squatting position.

Another match was needed. The initial bright flare of it showed Charles the dreadful purple contusion on the side of his jaw where the ladder had struck his face. The cheek was cut, lacerated by some metal protrusion probably, and had been bleeding but it wasn't bleeding now. Charles thought, I can't touch him. At once he knew he had to touch him, he had to know. The match burnt out, burnt his fingers. He was in darkness alone with Peter Moran, alone, still and silent. Curiously, the shaking had stopped.

Peter Moran must have struck the back of his head on the skirting board which stuck out at the foot of the stairs in a sharp-angled wedge. He had fallen backwards very hard and struck his head. Still in the dark—it was somehow better in the dark—Charles put out his hand, his hand crept to Peter Moran's face and felt the skin, felt the forehead. It wasn't cold but it was cool. It wasn't warm as his own forehead was warm. Charles was holding his breath and he expelled it now. He put his hand on his own chest and found his heart. It was beating away like anything, a strong young healthy heart that drove highly oxygenated blood round the body to cope with fear. Charles found the same spot on Peter Moran's chest and laid his hand there. For a moment he felt a terror that Peter Moran would suddenly sit up, clasp him in his arms. But nothing like that happened, nothing happened, there was a slack heavy stillness under his hand.

Charles drew in his breath with a harsh rattling gasp. He pulled away his hand as if something had bitten it. And yet he had known all along really, he had known from the moment the ladder struck, that Peter Moran was dead.

Another match dropped to the floor. He lit the last he was to light there. He touched Peter Moran again, feeling the skin again, feeling it colder surely, dislodging the head somehow so that it slipped and lolled on to the other side, the mouth falling open and showing a bloodiness inside. Charles shouted out in shock, it was too much for him, it was the pits of horror. He dropped the match-box and made for the stairs, running down in the dark past the grey streaming window, holding on to the banister. At the foot there was grey light, about as dark as light could be, coming in from open doors. He stumbled across to that kitchen they sometimes used for meetings, to the back door he and Peter Moran had come in by, pushed it open and stood on the back step in cold fresh air. The air felt as if it were new, or like pure oxygen. And at his feet Charles saw water, more than puddles, less than a flood. A great still pool of water lay covering the remains of a path. Avoiding it, he slopped through the wet long grass, under the dripping trees, up to the gate in the wall.

He didn't look back until he was out in Fontaine Road. Then he wished he hadn't looked back, up to the window set high in the wall of the stairwell between the first floor and the attics. For there was a light on in there, a light of a pale orange colour that moved and leapt behind the glass. He wasn't dead, Charles thought. How would I know if anyone was dead or not? He wasn't dead but he had got up and lit the candle and was coming down the stairs holding the candle aloft...

Charles started to run. He ran past the parked Diane, through the puddles, the sheets of water, across the road and down Ruxeter Road, putting the house and Peter Moran and the moving light far behind him.

ffffffffffffffffffff **2** ffffff

HIS ARM WAS OUT OF THE SLING AND ONLY A SMALL dressing was on the wound but perhaps it was a mistake to go out on the motorbike again so soon. His shoulder ached.

It was a mistake too calling on people without forewarning them. John realized that he hadn't phoned Colin because he was afraid of not being wanted, of being put off. But that was an unwise way to go on. And yet the worst he had thought could happen was that Colin and his mother would be out and he would have had a fruitless journey. All the way out there the idea was with him that he could talk to these two, especially to Constance, tell her of his new inability even to think about Cherry, use Constance as a kind of psychotherapist.

Colin came to the door. His face fell when he saw John, he looked almost laughably like Harpo Marx when he has done something wrong and is in trouble for it. Constance was out, he said, she was out as she always was on Fridays at some over-sixties whist club she belonged to. John hadn't known that, hadn't known about this Fridays club, or had forgotten. Of course Colin had to ask him in, but it was a near thing. John went into the living room and sitting there on the sofa was a woman, a youngish quite pretty woman with lipstick spread over her chin but none on her mouth.

Awkward introductions were made. John stayed no more than ten minutes, refusing the drink that was offered him. Was this what Colin did every Friday evening when his mother was out? John had never dreamt of it. It had shocked him rather and—yes, this must be confessed—made him envious.

Returning home on the Honda, he heard fire-engine sirens behind him as he came into town. He was in Ruxeter still, coming into Ruxeter Road, and he pulled in to let the fire engines pass him, travelling at high speed, their sirens howling. Ahead of him he could see a dense pall of brown smoke with a red glow in the heart of it. An inch of rain must have fallen just before he left home and in places the gutters were still full of water from overflowing drains. The wheels of the Honda were deep in gutter water. John pulled back on to the crown of the road. A few hundred yards along, diversion signs had been put up, directing the traffic round to the right.

The diversion led westwards nearly as far as the station. The slow heavy stream of traffic wasn't directed out again until Nevin Square was reached. There a policeman was directing traffic, letting more fire engines through, an ambulance. John wondered if some building back up there had been struck by lightning. It took him a further half-hour to get home and he had scarcely put the Honda away when the phone started to ring. John, who had believed he would never hear the phone again without expecting it to be Jennifer, didn't now even consider Jennifer as a possibility. It was very late for anyone to phone—or late by his standards. Perhaps, though, it was Colin, feeling the need to offer an explanation.

John sighed. He picked up the receiver, said hallo. Jennifer's voice, anxious, rather sharp, seemed to penetrate his body and run through his bones, to find the wound and pluck at it.

'John, is Peter with you?'

'Peter? With me?' He heard himself stammering. It was such a shock, it was so unexpected. 'Why would Peter be with me?' And he added, 'The last place surely...'

'I don't know. He might have come to you, I did suggest he ought to talk to you himself. About the divorce and the house and everything. I'm phoning everyone we know, everywhere he might be.'

Being lumped with 'everyone we know' hurt very much. 'He isn't here.'

'He was going to the cinema,' she said, 'with some friend of his, someone he was at school with. But it was the early showing. He said he'd be back by nine at the latest.'

He has left her again, John thought. He has left you, he wanted to say but he didn't say it. 'A bit premature, aren't you?' he said. 'It's only half-past ten.' His voice softened, he couldn't help that. 'Don't worry,' he said, and then, 'I'm here if you need me. Phone me again if you need me.'

After he had put the receiver down he thought, why didn't I say I would come to her? Why didn't I say I'd come and take charge? He lifted the phone to call her back but the line was engaged. He has left her, he has left her, he repeated over and over, silently first and then aloud to the empty house. Hope began once more to revive. When he has left her for the second time she will come back to me...

3

FROM THIS PART OF TOWN THERE WAS NO BUS DIrect to the main line station in South Hartland. Charles knew that no taxi driver he stopped in the street would be prepared to take him fifteen miles out into the country at this time of night. He had to get to the station, walk it in fact. He was finding that walking is not easy when you are in a state of shock. His legs trembled and, behaving like a paraplegic's, did not obey his brain's commands. They simply would not move quickly. What he probably needed, he thought, was brandy. Not that he had ever tasted brandy, and if what people said was true, it was the last thing one ought to have on an empty stomach. Charles's stomach was very empty, having received nothing but the Yorkies and half a dozen of Peter Moran's chocolates since lunch.

Whatever that light might have been it was not Peter Moran pursuing him. He knew that now. Most likely it was the candle he now remembered he had left burning in the room with the furniture. Perhaps the door to that room had blown open and revealed the light. Something like that. Ruxeter Road was quite crowded and with a lot of traffic. It was a busy part of

town with pubs and cinemas and restaurants and this
was Friday night. Charles crossed the street and
trudged on northwards, his pace steadying and quick-
ening after a while as control returned. The evening
behind him he had expelled from his mind or perhaps
his own consciousness had blanked it off, but now it
gradually came back. He supposed he had murdered
Peter Moran. Killed him anyway, killed him in self-
defence. How odd. How peculiar that he should have
done such a thing. He didn't feel any different and he
supposed he didn't look any different. It was quite
something to have actually killed someone when you
were only just fourteen, something that probably
hardly ever happened.

At first he didn't take much notice of the sirens. You
couldn't tell anyway if they were on police cars or ambu-
lances or fire engines. Charles did think for a split second that they could be police cars in pursuit of him, but
this he dismissed immediately. It was impossible. Then
he saw a fire engine, coming westwards from the fire
station at Feverton, its siren blasting away, the cars pulling in to let it pass. He hadn't far to go now, he had
already turned into the long King's Avenue that would
become Station Road.

King's Avenue went uphill and then down again to
where the station and the marshalling yards were. The
hill was the highest point in the city after Fonthill
Heights. Another fire engine came over the top and
Charles turned to watch it charge down the other side.
He could see the fire now, about a mile to the south.
Neither then nor at any time until he saw the local television news on the following morning did it occur to him
that the fire might have been in Pentecost Villas, in the
safe house. That the candle, precariously balanced on
the edge of the garden seat, might have fallen and ig-
nited all that paper never crossed his mind. Only the
idea of the fire itself interested him. He wished he were

nearer to it or it to him so that he might see what happened.

There were no taxis on the rank when he walked into the station approach. That meant a train must have just come in and the taxi drivers swooped on the passengers. He might have to wait as much as twenty minutes. The station sweet stall was shut, all the local eating places were shut except the pubs which he wasn't allowed into and which would soon shut anyway. Charles walked slowly up to the station entrance and then saw his father's car parked by the car park exit. His father was sitting at the wheel, reading the evening paper. Or pretending to read the evening paper. Clairvoyant intuitive Charles could sense his anxiety, his pretended casualness, from here. His father would probably spin him some tale about having to bring someone to the station or forgetting to do something at the office and on the way back thought he might as well...

He sauntered up to the car. His father lowered the paper and relief poured into his face, making it go red and soft-looking. He said:

'Oh, there you are. I had a package to put on the London train for a client so I thought I might as well look out for you.'

It could never happen to six-feet-four-tall Mungo. But then none of it could have happened to Mungo, thought Charles, getting into the car beside his father. Momentarily a wave of horror broke over him. It was something that was to happen a few times in the next eight or nine hours. Through the years to come it would happen occasionally. The horror broke and he thought, I killed a man. They drove south-westwards, crossing Ruxeter Road some half-mile north of the fire. The sirens were silent now but you could smell smoke everywhere. I killed a man, Charles thought, and he felt the penknife in his pocket with a little bit of fibre from the rope caught under its blade.

IT WAS AN EXTRAORDINARY EXPERIENCE FOR THE TWO of them, going to the safe house for the meeting there with Basilisk and Scylla, prearranged before Corfu, to find it razed to the ground.

'Like Carthage, old Lindsay would say,' said Graham. 'Only the Romans ploughed over the site of that. Probably stirred salt in too, I shouldn't be surprised.'

It was Sunday afternoon. They had seen no papers, heard no radio, watched no television. The whole household in Church Bar had only just got up. Mungo and Graham stood on the opposite side of Ruxeter Road, part of a small crowd gaping at the blackened space, the few remaining struts and timbers, the whole ruin now surrounded by a temporary wire fence. Mungo had the wild idea that Moscow Centre had done it: it had been only a matter of time before the location of the safe house became known to Rosie Whittaker. She was said to be ruthless and intrepid. She might even have done it herself, or some agent of hers... No, it was impossible, he mustn't let his imagination run away with him, it was far more likely to have been builders with a blow torch.

Graham lit a cigarette. He was wearing his sunglasses, though the day was overcast and rather dark and grey for mid-August. Mungo thought he only needed one of those soft slouch hats to look like a spy in a film of the thirties.

'There's not much to be done about that,' he said.

'We shall have to find another safe house,' said Graham. 'My brother says there's a house scheduled for demolition in Hartlands.'

Graham's brother Keith, or Scylla, should have been at the meeting. Of course he hadn't turned up because he must have known about the fire from the newspapers or TV. Mungo heard a man standing behind them say:

'There was someone in there. They found a body. They haven't identified it yet.'

'Yes, they have.' This from someone who had perhaps read a more recent paper or seen a more recent programme. 'It was a man. They found his car outside.'

Mungo and Graham began to walk off. They discussed going to the cinema, to the Fontaine, where a fairly appropriate old film, *The Mask of Dimitrios*, had succeeded the Japanese picture, but Graham said he might go to his aunt's instead, he might go and have a talk with Keith. Mungo went home, making a detour round Nevin Square to see if there was anything held in the statue drop but the hand of Lysander Douglas was empty. He had been anticipating with some excitement deciphering the next message, expecting it to begin, very likely, with seventeen for the date and end with something around ten-fifteen for the time. The empty hand was a bit disappointing.

ƒƒƒƒƒƒƒƒƒƒƒƒƒƒƒƒƒƒ **5** ƒƒƒƒƒƒ

PENTECOST VILLAS HAD BEEN STRUCK BY LIGHTning. That was one theory put forward in the newspapers. Another was that it had been arson and that Peter Moran was the arsonist who had fallen downstairs and stunned himself before he could escape. He was identified by the presence of his car outside, by the remains of his glasses and his watch and the bridgework in his mouth. Not much else of him remained. Charles read about it in the *Free Press*. Peter Moran was dead so they could say more or less what they liked about him. They quoted the police as saying that he had been convicted four years before of assault on a child under the age of thirteen. A patron of the Fontaine then told the *Free Press* that on the evening of the fire he had seen Peter Moran in the cinema with a boy of about ten. An inquest was opened and adjourned. Charles understood that as far as he was concerned it was all over and he had to swallow his indignation at being described as about ten. But he put a message in *October Men* into the flyover drop, asking for a meeting with Leviathan as soon as would be convenient.

Mungo also read about it in the paper. The only thing of much interest to him was that when he first moved into the study he had last year he had been groping about on the floor underneath his bunk and looking up, read the name Peter Moran carved on the woodwork of its underside. There was a date there too: 1965 and a dash. It wasn't necessarily the same person. He retrieved the message from Dragon next day. The difficulty was that they no longer had a safe house. Presumably Dragon would have to come along to Church Bar. There would have to be a showdown anyway, for according to Graham, Charles Mabledene had not passed the test set for him. What could you do with a traitor? No more than expel him, Mungo thought.

He sat down on one of the boxes someone had provided as cat shelters and concocted his reply: 'Leviathan to Dragon...' It was rush hour and the traffic going south rumbled overhead. Mungo put his message into Dragon's plastic zip-up bag and taped it back inside the central upright, remembering not to put it

oo high up out of Charles Mabledene's reach. Dragon
is traitor was probably capable of setting fire to the
afe house. Mungo wondered if that was what had in
act happened. The new king cat, a bull-shouldered
tringy-bodied yellow tom, rubbed himself in hopeful
ashion against his legs, and Mungo bent down to
troke him. There was a strong civet smell, a nice per-
umey sort of smell until you knew what it was.

Still thinking about Charles Mabledene, wondering
what he wanted, Mungo went down Bread Lane and
he Beckgate Steps to the river. A barge was coming
ip under Rostock with a dog standing in its bows,
arking at the fishermen. The sun shone white and
oft behind mist. For a moment he couldn't see the
op of the Shot Tower and then the mist moved like a
carf unwinding. This was Medusa's drop in the base
f the tower, but it was empty. The cathedral floated
ut of the haze and the sun painted it with a pale
vash, so that the hundred saints on its east front
eemed to step forward out of their niches to feel the
ight. The deep-throated bell on the clock began tolling
he hour, ten o'clock, as Mungo walked westwards
ver Alexandra Bridge. He was nearly across when the
nist uncurled and melted from the crown of the Cit-
West tower, or as it seemed to be, the tower like the
athedral saints stepped out of the whiteness into the
un where it showed in twinkling green: ten-O-one
nd seventeen degrees.

Mungo had been going straight home but it wasn't
ar out of his way into Nevin Square. He thought he
aw the Stern brothers in the doorway of Marks and
Spencer's diagonally opposite but when he looked
gain they were gone. There were people sitting on
he wall round the plinth on which Lysander Douglas
tood and they turned to stare when Mungo stepped
ver it to take the folded paper out of the bronze hand.
His habit was to copy it down there and then but not
under those curious eyes. He took it to one of the
eats on the paved walks among the flowerbeds.

Mungo, who knew practically nothing about horticul‐
ture, wondered why the council planted those crimson
flowers that trailed bleeding plumes like offal, like
butcher's discard.

Before he attempted a deciphering, as soon as he
looked at the paper, he knew something was wrong.
There was no number to open the message, no number
to close it. Moscow Centre had changed the code. In the
week since he had found the key to the code they had
changed it. That could only mean they knew the old
code was broken. He seemed to hear distant triumphant
laughter but he was imagining it, there was no one
there to laugh. Slowly he crossed the square and re‐
placed the message in the statue's hand. But he had told
no one that he had broken the code, or no one who
could possibly... Certainly he had said nothing to
Charles Mabledene, had had no opportunity to say any‐
thing. Had he been wrong then about Charles Mable‐
dene?

Perhaps he had. But it was not true that he had told
no one.

6

IT MUST HAVE BEEN LIKE WHEN CHERRY DIED AND
the police came to tell them. The police were with
Jennifer for a long time, questioning her about Peter
Moran. A man and a woman, Jennifer said, and from
her description John knew the woman must have been
Susan Aubrey. John hadn't seen Jennifer but had spo‐
ken several times to her on the phone. She told him
dully that she wanted to feel grief, she would have

wanted to be stricken with grief, for she had once thought of Peter Moran as the great love of her life, but all she felt was resignation and pity. The implication—though she didn't say this—was that John had been responsible for her indifference. John's telling her the truth about Peter Moran had spoiled her feeling for him. But John thought, if I hadn't told her when I did, she would know now. She would know from the papers—or the police. It wouldn't have made her hate them, so why should she hate me?

He phoned her every day. She wouldn't see him but she had stopped saying she never wanted to see him again. She had forgotten once saying she would never speak to him again. In the middle of the week after Peter Moran died he phoned her and a man answered. The police probably, John thought, a policeman who was with her at that interminable questioning. There was something about the voice he thought he recognized, so perhaps it was Fordwych, the detective inspector. The voice, though very familiar, was unidentifiable.

Thursday afternoon he spent in Hartlands Gardens. It was the day of the inquest. John thought that today perhaps he wouldn't phone but would go to her, would go straight to Nunhouse without returning home first. Old feelings of hope had reasserted themselves powerfully. He had left the Honda in the car park just inside the main gate. Emerging on to the road that wound up to Fonthill Heights, he sat waiting for the ascending stream of traffic to pass. It progressed slowly with frequent stops and John turned to look into each driver's face, hoping for the nod and the raised hand that would indicate he was to be let through. The third driver he looked at, sitting at the wheel of his red Escort, was Mark Simms. Beside him in the passenger seat was Jennifer.

Mark Simms lifted up his hand. It might have been the motorist's courtesy wave or something more, a sign that he recognized John behind the goggles and under the crash helmet. Or it might not. His headlights briefly flashed on, perhaps only because John hadn't moved but remained poised there, taking in what he saw, understanding the import of what he saw. Jennifer was looking at Mark Simms, she was talking to him, and she didn't turn her head. As far as John could see they weren't actually touching, only sitting side by side. He moved out quickly in front of the Escort, turning right, coming up behind a stream of traffic descending the hill. It seemed to him that superimposed over the back of the car in front of him was that picture his eyes had indelibly registered, that little scene of Jennifer in Mark Simms's car.

He understood. That voice answering the phone, that had been Mark Simms. She had rejected his, John's, offer of help in favour of Mark Simms. Anyone's company, anyone's sympathy, was preferable to his, this finally proved it, this was the end. If it hadn't been Mark Simms it would have been someone else, it would always be someone else. In that moment he understood how strong his hope had been, how he had hoped on and on in the face of all odds, even after she had asked for a divorce, even after she had rounded on him for telling her the truth about Peter Moran. And since Peter Moran's death, hope had positively burgeoned, he had believed her return inevitable.

The homeward route he hardly seemed aware of. The horse knows the way, though, the Honda knew the way. Usually he was very careful to switch off the engine before putting the motorbike away. He was afraid of causing damage to the plants with carbon monoxide. It wasn't the most convenient place to keep the Honda and sometimes he thought of getting a shed specially for it, he could get one at a discount from Trowbridge's. He sat on the saddle, pointlessly twisting the handlebar grips, lightly revving the engine. The greenhouse door and its windows were wide open, for it had been a very warm day, was still warm. Without switching off the ignition, John went into the greenhouse and shut the windows. He took off his crash helmet and goggles and gloves and laid them on one of the slatted shelves in front of the pots of capsicum. His mind had become blank and he seemed aware of only one thing, his intense isolation in this city of indifferent thousands, this world of uncaring millions. Beyond the gingko tree, beyond the garden wall, hung with a multi-flowering dark blue clematis, the sky was orange with sunset. The Honda purred evenly, animal-like, a useful beast of burden, friendly but ridiculous as might be an elderly fat donkey. Instead of turning the key and letting the engine die preparatory to humping it into the greenhouse where he would jack it up for the night, John got back into the saddle and coasted the motorbike in through the doorway.

He pulled the door behind him and closed it. The greenhouse was now quite tightly sealed up. He got off the saddle, still holding the handlebars, lightly twisting the grips. Already the fumes were strong. Gingerly he leaned the bike against the shelf, keeping the engine running, moving his hands rhythmically on the grips, staring out at the fading orange of the sky. He stared hypnotically at the sky, his hands rolled the grips automatically, he breathed in the choking chemical vapour. A dizziness began.

It was then that he heard the footsteps.

He didn't take his hands from the handlebars. He didn't even wonder who it might be, he knew who it couldn't be. Slowly he turned his head and saw coming out of the side way, walking towards him, Flora the tree girl. An immediate onset of panic must have made his face appear aghast, he was aware of his eyes becoming wide and staring. She flung open the greenhouse door as he snatched his hands off the grips and the engine stalled.

'What on earth were you doing? This place is a gas chamber. You could have gassed yourself.'

He muttered something about only putting the bike away.

'Are you sure?' She was looking penetratingly at him. 'You weren't trying to...? You weren't, were you, John?'

The very fact that he knew what she meant implied the truth of it. 'Oh, no,' he said. 'No, of course not.' And he hadn't been, had he? He hadn't really meant to kill himself. When the fumes got too strong he would have got out, wouldn't he? He had only perhaps killed the capsicum. 'I haven't done the plants much good.'

He was outside now, breathing clean evening air. Had she saved his life, this bright-faced curly-haired tree expert, or only provided him with an evening's company?

'Did you come to see the monkey puzzle?'

She sounded shocked, dazed. 'I was out looking at flats—well, bedsits really, somewhere to live. Then I remembered about Geneva Road and *Araucaria* and I came down this way. I haven't seen the tree.' Her eyes went to his face, then up at Cherry's bedroom window. 'Do you live all alone here?'

He nodded, still thinking, did I really? Might I be dead now? Shall I be glad one day that she came in the nick of time or shall I convince myself...? 'I've got two spare rooms,' he found himself saying, and then, 'Come on, I'll show you the monkey puzzle.'

7

HAVING SLEPT ON IT, MUNGO KNEW WHAT HE MUST do. First though he went to the flyover drop to pick up the message from Dragon, his agreement to a meeting later that day. Somehow and without making a drama out of it, he knew he would never come here again, never pick his way among the copse of metal posts or attach a message to the inside of the central upright. Angus would say it had happened, what he predicted. Mungo didn't much care what Angus said.

There was a new Yves Yugall coming out in September. Actual copies hadn't appeared yet but a poster advertising it was up in Hatchard's window: *Lion Loot*, 'his scintillating new bestseller.' Mungo thought it was a rotten title or was it perhaps just that he was fed up for the moment with that kind of fiction? He crossed Nevin Square, not bothering to see if Lysander Douglas was holding anything, into Hill Street, into Church Bar. Graham had said he was going to the new pool out at Ruxeter with Ian and Gail, they were all swimming mad, but he would be back by lunch. His father's car was half-in half-out of the garage, he had finished his morning calls early and had no surgery on a Friday afternoon.

Mungo let himself in by the side door and went downstairs to the kitchen. Fergus was seated at the table, reading *The Times* and drinking a cup of his famous cocoa. He offered to make Mungo a cup but Mungo, as always, as they all did, said no thanks.

'I didn't know Graham smoked,' Fergus said, his forehead all creased up.

'Didn't you?'

'He must have been very secretive about it, not to say deceitful. I had no idea. It's disturbed me very much.'

Mungo had a dreadful desire to burst out laughing, though it wasn't funny, none of it was funny. The irony . . . !

'He thought I was out, I daresay. There he was, down here smoking a cigarette. The great majority of smokers begin as teenagers. It's in adolescence that addiction starts. Did you know that, Mungo?'

'I did as a matter of fact.'

'Do you ever smoke Graham's cigarettes?'

'No,' said Mungo, and because the simple negative wasn't enough, 'I don't smoke any cigarettes. I don't like the smell.' Fergus was looking searchingly at him. 'Excuse me, Dad, there's something I have to see to.'

He only knew the music drifting down was Albinoni because Angus had often told him so. A respected Venetian composer of over forty operas admired by Bach, Angus said. Mounting the stairs, Mungo thought of Angus's old friendship with Guy Parker, a friendship he had vaguely heard about, dimly remembered. Had Angus betrayed Guy Parker, reneged on him? Or was it nothing like that? Was it the other way about? He would never know. The door, as usual, was wide open. The allegro stopped and Angus was changing sides to the adagio, a book held in his left hand.

'The death of a mouse from cancer is the whole sack of Rome by the Goths,' said Angus. 'You don't happen to know who said that, do you?'

'Me? No, I don't know. Why would I?'

'What d'you fancy for lunch? I told Mum I'd go out for takeaway. She phoned, she's got an emergency. How about Greek?'

Mungo, who hardly ever swore, said violently, 'Not bloody Greek, anything but that,' and he saw, quite plainly, one of what Ian would call his visions. He was standing on the hillside, on the viewing point, about to expound his solution to the code, but Angus hadn't stayed to hear, he had turned and said something about living life instead of playing games, said it angrily, and before Mungo spoke again was crashing down the slope among the scented herbs, between the olives and the cypress trees. Mungo looked at his brother, at his puzzled kindly face, and the vision melted like mist from the Shot Tower. 'Sorry,' he said. 'You know me, it's always Indonesian for me.'

Up the stairs went Mungo towards his own room. He stationed himself at the little round window under the roof. I shall have to take up collecting something. Take up fencing again maybe. Or just read a different sort of book. Graham and Ian and Gail were coming along from the Hill Street end. The others had their swimming things in a Sainsbury's carrier but Graham held his rolled up under his arm. He extinguished his half-smoked cigarette just before they vanished from Mungo's sight between the pavement and the side gate. Presumably that was what his father meant by deceitful.

Mungo came out of his room and went slowly down the top flight. Ian and Gail wouldn't come up, they would go down to the kitchen and make themselves the coffee they everlastingly drank. Mungo stood on the landing outside Graham's door, noticing that Angus had gone out. That was the only time Angus's door was shut —when he wasn't inside.

His hair still damp, plastered down like black paint over the crown of his head, Graham came up the stairs two at a time. He had the old tee-shirt on, the one with the octopus motif. Mungo said:

'Can we talk?'

He saw all the light and all the enthusiasm die out of Graham's face. Graham pushed open his bedroom door and let it slam softly behind them. They stood facing each other.

'You're the mole, aren't you?' Mungo said. 'I know you are, so don't try and deny it.'

'I wasn't going to deny it.'

'I ought to have known that time I made a mistake about the number of the *Armadillo Army* story, but I didn't. I was stupid. It was a genuine mistake. I told you "eight" when I meant "seven". That was why Moscow Centre couldn't break that code.' He felt a fool talking about Moscow Centre, as if it were real, as if it weren't all pretence. 'I wonder why you never told them where the safe house was. Or maybe you did and they didn't care. I never cottoned on. I trusted you.'

Graham lit a cigarette. 'It's only a game, isn't it?'

'What difference does that make?'

He didn't expect an answer and he didn't get one. 'Why?' he said. 'Why? If it was only a game'—he spoke carefully—'and after all we're young, we're still at school—I mean, you can't have been offered anything. Not money, not a bribe. Unless—' An idea came to Mungo. 'You weren't blackmailed, were you?'

Graham shook his head. He was tall but he still had to look up to Mungo. 'What would anyone blackmail me about, Bean?'

'Don't call me that. Only my brothers call me that.'

The scorn made Graham go red. 'It was for—the hell of it. Oh, God—it was for fun.'

'You betrayed me for fun?'

There was silence. A long way downstairs a door slammed. Mungo thought he knew what that thing Angus had said to him meant, about the death of a mouse being the whole sack of whatever it was. He went to the door of his room and opened it, for he had heard voices on one of the lower flights. Behind him Graham said:

'I'd better tell you. I was waiting for an opportunity to tell you. I'm leaving Rossingham, I'm starting at Utting next term.'

Angus's head appeared above the top of the stairs.

'Charles Mabledene is here, Bean. He says he's supposed to see you at one.'

Once Mungo would have said with some pomp: Show him up. 'OK,' he said. He had forgotten all about the appointment with Dragon. 'He can come up here if he wants.'

Who had made the appointment, Charles Mabledene or he? Mungo couldn't remember, still less why it had been made. He stood aside, holding the door open, leaning against it, to let Graham pass through. He kept his head averted, not daring to look at Graham because he was afraid of these unknown untried emotions that might make him do something he would later be ashamed of. The room stank of cigarette smoke. Charles Mabledene came in sniffing, turning his head and sniffing like some small fastidious animal.

'Hallo.'

Mungo nodded, silent.

'I've got some things to ask you.' The voice was still a treble, though a breaking one. He looked impossibly neat and clean as if bathed and polished up at that hairdresser's his mother had. 'Some questions.' Charles Mabledene hesitated before going on. Mungo didn't let him go on.

'I'm resigning,' he said. 'I'm giving up as head of London Central.'

A small pink tongue came out and moistened Charles's lips. 'Ah,' he said, and then, 'I suppose Medusa will be taking over from you?'

Mungo uttered a violent 'No!'

They looked at each other. Fergus's voice called from downstairs that lunch would be on the table in five minutes. Mungo said:

'I thought you might care to...?'

'Yes,' said Charles. 'Yes, I would.'

'That's settled then.'

'You're going to have your meal, so I'll go now. I can see myself out.'

He had suddenly started talking like someone of forty.

But he had always been a bit like that. After he had gone Mungo just stood there in the middle of the room. He had a curious feeling he might as well stand there for ever—well, for hours—empty, rather cold, pretty depressed really, for there seemed nothing else to do and as if there never would be. But presently he moved, screwed up his eyes, shook himself and soldiering on, went down to have his Indonesian lunch.

ℱℱℱℱℱℱℱℱℱℱℱℱℱℱℱℱℱℱℱℱ **8** ℱℱℱℱℱℱ

IT HAD BEEN A NEAR THING. CHARLES REMEMBERED just in time that he couldn't really ask Mungo those questions as to why he had been tested in that way, why he had been sent as decoy or prey to Peter Moran. He was a murderer, after all, and subject to the law. It was not something he was ever going to be able to talk about to anyone or even hint at.

He didn't mind. He could live with it. Probably he was going to go on dreaming of Peter Moran falling backwards down those stairs, hearing the sickening crunch, seeing that bloody jaw flop backwards—and waking up with a yell. His mother or father came rushing in, concerned. They said it was the onset of puberty. He could live with it, anyway. He could live with anything now he had got what he wanted: Charles Mabledene, alias Dragon, Director General of London Central.

They would see some changes now. Mungo-style scruple—relaxed inexplicably only in the matter of Peter Moran—would have no place in the new regime. When you considered what could be accomplished with scruples, all that planning information, the Ralston car affair, the retrieval of property, the rearranged invitations, how much more was possible when scruples were discarded? That code nonsense should go. It had always been artificial. What was the phone for? The ban on what Mungo rather naïvely called 'dishonesty'—that must be the first to go. A kind of Mafia, Charles decided he had in mind, but run by the cream of a rising generation, the country's best brains, a youthful public school elite, headed by one who had already killed his man...

A beautiful day: three minutes past one and twenty-four degrees. Charles crossed Hillbury Place towards the salon where his mother would be about to take her lunch break. About to entertain her son to lunch, he corrected himself. He pushed open the door and as she turned around from her conversation with a client, he smilingly drew from one of the overhead driers a clutch of painted eggs and a fluffy blue rabbit. He would have liked to produce a flock of doves but he hadn't learned how to do that yet.

ABOUT THE AUTHOR

Author of nearly thirty acclaimed mysteries, Ruth Rendell has won three Edgars, *Current Crime*'s Silver Cup, and the Crime Writers' Association's Golden Dagger Award. Two of her novels, AN UNKINDNESS OF RAVENS and THE TREE OF HANDS, were nominated for the Edgar Award for the best mystery of 1985. She lives in England.

The Queen of Suspense...

RUTH RENDELL